Carol Ericson is a bestselling, award-winning author of more than forty books. She has an eerie fascination for true-crime stories, a love of film noir and a weakness for reality TV, all of which fuel her imagination to create her own tales of murder, mayhem and mystery. To find out more about Carol and her current projects, please visit her website at www.carolericson.com, "where romance flirts with danger."

USA TODAY bestselling author **Barb Han** lives in north Texas with her very own hero-worthy husband, three beautiful children, a spunky golden retriever/standard poodle mix and too many books in her to-read pile. In her downtime, she plays video games and spends much of her time on or around a basketball court. She loves interacting with readers and is grateful for their support. You can reach her at barbhan.com

Also by Carol Ericson

Enemy Infiltration
Undercover Accomplice
Code Conspiracy
Delta Force Defender
Delta Force Daddy
Delta Force Die Hard
Locked, Loaded and SEALed
Alpha Bravo SEAL
Bullseye: SEAL
Point Blank SEAL

Also by Barb Han

Cornered at Christmas
Ransom at Christmas
Ambushed at Christmas
What She Did
What She Knew
Sudden Setup
Endangered Heiress
Texas Grit
Kidnapped at Christmas
Murder and Mistletoe

Discover more at millsandboon.co.uk

EVASIVE ACTION

CAROL ERICSON

WHAT SHE SAW

BARB HAN

MILLS & BOON

First Published in Great Britain 2020
by Mills & Boon, an imprint of HarperCollins*Publishers*
1 London Bridge Street, London, SE1 9GF

Evasive Action © 2020 Carol Ericson
What She Saw © 2020 Barb Han

ISBN: 978-0-263-28034-0

0620

MIX
Paper from
responsible sources
FSC C007454

This book is produced from independently certified FSC™
paper to ensure responsible forest management.

For more information visit: www.harpercollins.co.uk/green

Printed and bound in Spain
by CPI, Barcelona

EVASIVE ACTION

CAROL ERICSON

Chapter One

The snowy-white tulle of April's veil rustled as she climbed out the window. Her satin shoes landed in the moist dirt with a squishy sound. She yanked the frothy concoction from her head and stashed it behind a bush.

She took a deep breath and peered around the corner of the house, her curls falling over one shoulder. The stretch limo gleamed in the morning sun of New Mexico, and she shivered. The car looked more like a hearse now—her hearse. Who said New Mexico was the land of enchantment?

Narrowing her eyes, she chewed the strawberry-flavored gloss off her bottom lip. If she fled in the limo, it could be tracked, but at least it would solve her immediate problem of no funds. She considered creeping back through the house to retrieve her purse, but she valued her life too much—at least someone did.

How far could she get barreling down the highway in a stretch limo? Way too conspicuous—sort of like this wedding dress.

She patted the lace bodice of one side of her dress to make sure she still had the strange wooden disc she'd found in Jimmy's desk, and then drew out her cell phone from the other side. She tapped the icon for the car app loaded on her phone and smiled at the little dots on the map—her saviors.

She called up a car, and then strolled to the front gate, although her feet itched to break into a run. This couldn't be a clean getaway, not with Jimmy's security at his beck and call, but nobody suspected a thing at this point. She could play the blushing bride for another ten minutes. Hell, she'd played at being in love with Jimmy for the past six months.

Oscar, the guy working security at the front gate to Jimmy's estate, jumped to his feet. "Getting cold feet, April?"

"Just jonesing for a smoke. I know how much Jimmy hates cigarettes and I'm trying to squeeze in a few before I quit for good." She pinched the low neckline of her gown between her fingers and adjusted it. "You have one I can bum?"

Oscar's gaze followed the movement, his eyes widening for a second. "I—I do."

"That's what I'll be saying in an hour. I'd really appreciate it…and I'll step outside the grounds so Jimmy won't know a thing." She put a finger to her pouting lips. "You know I'm good at keeping secrets, don't you, Oscar?"

Oscar's face reddened, obviously remembering the time she caught him rummaging through Jimmy's desk, and he scrambled for a cigarette in his front pocket. "I know that, April, and I appreciate it."

He shook a cigarette free from a crumpled pack and held it out toward her.

Sliding it from the pack between her index and middle fingers, she said, "Thanks. Got a light?"

He flicked his lighter, and she leaned in to touch the end of the cigarette to the flame.

She waved the cigarette at the gate. "I'll just slip outside to enjoy it, and if Jimmy happens to smell it on me... I didn't get it from you."

"Of course not, thanks." He lunged for the gate, probably happy to get her out of his sight before she could get anything else on him to report to his boss.

Holding the cigarette in one hand and the skirt of her dress in the other, she stepped outside the gates of Jimmy's compound. She traipsed down the drive to the street, her breath coming in short spurts. Her gaze shifted from side to side. She'd better not bump into any guests arriving early for the nuptials—Jimmy's guests.

Once she turned a corner and got clear of Oscar's sight, she dropped the cigarette and crushed it under the toe of her shoe. Then she pulled out her phone again and texted Adam. The wedding is off. Don't come near the estate. Don't go near Jimmy.

The phone buzzed in her hand, and she answered the call from the app car on its way. "Hello?"

"I'm about a block away in a blue Honda. Big houses here. Can I get in the gate?"

"I'm outside the gate. I'll be waiting on the sidewalk. Hurry."

"Uh, okay."

Two minutes later, a Honda pulled up to the curb. April checked the license plate, compared the driver to the picture on her phone and jumped in the back seat. "Go!"

The driver's bugged-out eyes met hers in the rearview mirror. "Where am I going?"

"The nearest bus stop. Wait." Her fingers creased her satin skirt into folds. How could she buy a bus ticket? She had no money. No wallet. No credit cards. She'd be a sitting duck at any bus stop for Jimmy and his so-called business associates. Now she understood why he always had an entourage. *Idiot.*

"Keep driving." She pounded the back of the driver's headrest. "I'm thinking."

"Are you running away from your own wedding or something?" The driver adjusted his glasses and punched the accelerator.

"Yes." She reached into the front seat and grabbed his arm, turning his laugh into a snort. "What's your name?"

"Jesse."

"Jesse, I have a deal for you." April tugged at the diamond ring on her left hand. "I'll trade you this ring for your car."

Turning his head, he squinted at the ring cupped in her palm. "Nice rock, but I can't do it. I need my ride to make money. This is the only job I have."

She slumped back in her seat. She could pawn the ring for cash, but that meant she'd be wandering around Albuquerque in this damned dress.

"My friend Ryan might be down, though."

"Really?" She shot forward again. "Where's Ryan?"

"He lives about ten miles from here. He's trying to sell his car, and he might take that piece for it instead of cash."

"Perfect."

She waited until Jesse hit the highway. Then she buzzed down the window and chucked her phone outside. She wouldn't be able to contact Adam anymore, but Jimmy couldn't trace her whereabouts.

Thirty minutes later, the trade with Ryan went smoother than she expected, and he even threw in a hundred bucks, cash, to seal the deal.

She rolled up the money and wedged it into her

new car's cup holder. She scooped the wooden token pressed against her breast from the bodice of the dress and dropped it in the other cup holder. Running her hand across the dashboard, she yelled out the window. "No GPS?"

"Does that car look like it has a GPS?" Ryan shoved his hands in his pockets. "No refunds."

"I'm not looking for a refund." She cranked on the engine of her new vehicle. "Just point me in the right direction for the 25 south."

Jesse strolled to the car. "You going to Mexico?"

"Maybe." She leveled a finger at him. "You remember the rest of our deal, right?"

"Yeah." Jesse's Adam's apple bobbed in his skinny, razor-burned neck. "If anyone asks, I picked you up and dropped you off at a bus depot in the city."

"That's right. The 25?"

Jesse gave her directions and she sped off, leaving the two young men gaping in her rearview. After her first burst of speed, she eased off the gas pedal. She didn't have her driver's license with her, and Ryan's name was on the car registration. She didn't need any trouble. Her impulsiveness had gotten her into enough trouble.

The car had enough gas to get her out of Albuquerque and almost down to Hatch Valley, just over the halfway point to Juarez. She could lose herself in Mexico, do a little investigating, too, even though it sure seemed as if Jimmy had contacts south of the border.

She wouldn't be the first of her family to disappear in Mexico.

After about three hours on the road, April pulled into a gas station just out of Hatch and dashed into the convenience store. She grabbed a diet soda and smacked thirty bucks on the counter.

"As much gas as this will get me on pump number five, less the cost of the drink."

The female clerk nodded, eyeing her from the top of her poofy hairstyle to the tips of her satin shoes, peeking out from the hem of her wedding dress. "Are you going to the wedding or coming from it?"

"On my way. It's a beautiful day to get married, isn't it?"

"Uh-huh." The clerk popped her gum and rang up the purchase with her long, violet fingernails.

April pumped the gas, waved to a little girl giggling in the car next to hers and plopped onto the driver's seat, gathering yards of billowing material inside after her.

She continued south, heading for Las Cruces. Just another ninety minutes or so, and she'd be across the border. She didn't have any ID with her, but that never stopped people in the know from slipping into Mexico undetected. Her gaze shifted to the side, taking in the signs for the 10 west and Tucson. One hour to Mexico. Four hours to Tucson.

"Ah, hell." She veered toward the ramp that would take her to Arizona.

She had enough gas. The weather couldn't be beat. She didn't know anyone in Mexico. And when could she ever resist Clay Archer?

CLAY ARCHER SWATTED at the fly buzzing around his face and gritted his teeth as the sound of the young Border Patrol agent's retching finally subsided. He'd been there, done that. No shame.

The agent, Rob Valdez, straightened up, wiping his

arm across his nose and mouth. "D-do you think the head's in the tunnel?"

Clay spit onto the desert floor. "We'll find out soon enough. You wanna go back to the truck and get some water?"

"No." Valdez squared his shoulders. "I gotta see what's in the tunnel."

"You might not like what you see." Clay squinted through his sunglasses at the mound of sand and dirt that marked the end of an underground tunnel between Arizona and Mexico.

"I gotta get used to it. You're used to it." Valdez rubbed his eyes and replaced his sunglasses and hat, flicking the stiff brim with his finger.

Clay took a step closer to the headless woman at his feet, one arm flung to her side, the other crossed over her body, the fingers of her hand curled. His nostrils flared as he crouched beside her, avoiding the blood-soaked dirt with the tips of his boots.

He reached for the woman's hand, cold and stiff across her lifeless body, and pried open her fingers. Between his own thumb and forefinger, he pinched the object clutched in her hand and pulled it free.

"What is it?" Valdez hovered over him, the smell of vomit, sweat and fear coming off his body in waves.

"Do not upchuck on the body."

"I'm done with that." Valdez took a few steps back, as if not sure of his own statement.

"It's a calling card." Clay held up the housefly carved from wood, almost as realistic as the ones swarming the dead body. He waved it in the air.

"Las Moscas." Valdez glanced over his shoulder as if expecting members of one of the most murderous drug cartels in Mexico to come riding up on ATVs.

"Why would they do this to one of their own mules? And a woman?"

The pile of dirt at the tunnel's exit shifted and one hand clawed its way out of earth like a scene from a horror movie. They didn't need movies—they had their own, real-life horror.

Clay stepped around the young woman with care as if she were sunbathing in the desert instead of missing her head. By the time he reached the tunnel, it had already spit out half of Nash Dillon's body.

Dillon scrabbled out the rest of the way, empty-handed. He yanked the mask from his face and coughed. "Nothing. No head. No drugs."

Valdez let out a noisy sigh. "Agent Archer found something in the dead woman's hand."

Dillon raised his brows as he brushed the dirt and debris from his green uniform.

Clay cupped the wooden carving in his palm and held it out to Dillon. "This is the work of Las Moscas."

"Not surprised." Dillon tipped his head toward the woman. "Only a few reasons why I can think of that the cartel would kill one of its own mules—she double-crossed them, screwed up somehow or started working for us."

"She's not one of ours." Clay held up his hands, the wooden token held between two of his fingers. "As far as I know, we've never used a woman."

"Don't lie, Clay." Dillon clapped his hat back on his head and wiped his designer sunglasses on the hem of his shirt. "The DEA uses wives and girlfriends when they can get them on board—or when they've been wronged by their drug-dealing spouses or tire of the lifestyle."

"That's DEA, not Border Patrol." Clay squinted into the harsh desert light. "We've got company."

The two other agents swiveled their heads in unison toward a caravan of trucks and SUVs accompanied by a cloud of sand and dust.

"Hope there's a coroner's van among those trucks." Dillon stamped the dust from his boots, jerking his thumb toward the body. "They need to get this young woman out of here. Give her a little dignity, regardless of the mess she made of her life."

The trucks and law enforcement personnel brought a flurry of activity with them. The local PD in Paradiso wouldn't conduct the homicide investigation, as it was too small to have a homicide division—not that the department didn't see its share of murders along this stretch of the border.

The Pima County Sheriff's Department would take over the thankless job of investigating the murder, but as usual with drug crimes, there would be no evidence, no witnesses and a bunch of nameless, faceless suspects.

Clay studied the men and women going about the business of investigating a headless corpse in the desert, and he took a swig of water from his bottle.

"Crazy business."

"What's that, Archer?" Espinoza, a homicide detective for the sheriff's department, looked up from his phone and squinted at Clay.

"Nothing. Just thinking about the insanity that goes on in this town."

Espinoza spread his arms wide. "Paradise, right?"

"Yeah, some clueless gringo even got that wrong, didn't he? *Paradiso* doesn't even mean *Paradise* in Spanish."

"Wrong name—" Espinoza kicked at a pile of sand "—and wrong description."

Clay and the other Border Patrol agents packed it in,

and left the scene to the coroner and the homicide detective. On the way back to his truck, Clay poked Dillon in the back. "You taking some time off?"

"Heading to a rodeo in Wyoming. Can you hold down the fort?" Dillon swept his hat from his head and tossed it onto the passenger seat of his truck.

Jerking his thumb over his shoulder, Clay said, "Unless we find the head or the drugs, especially the drugs, there's not much for me to do on this one."

"The drugs will be on the street by the time I come back." Dillon nodded toward the new agent, hanging back, the green around his gills matching his uniform. "You think he'll work out?"

"He'll be okay." Clay leveled a finger at Dillon. "I remember your first dead body. You didn't do much better."

Dillon scooped his hair back from his forehead and flashed his white teeth. "I guess you're right."

"Don't break that pretty face riding one of those bulls." Clay turned and strode to his truck with Valdez waiting by the passenger side.

"You getting in or staying out here?"

Valdez's eyes bulged briefly. "Just didn't want to sit in the truck without the AC. Is that it for the day?"

"That's it for my day. You're gonna go back to the office and write up this report. Make sure you check in with the sheriff's department to see if you can add anything before you send it to the Tucson Sector."

They both climbed in the truck, and Clay cranked on the air. They'd gone several miles before Valdez turned to him, clasping his hat in his lap.

"Do you think they'll find the head? What do you think Las Moscas did with it?"

Clay raised his stiff shoulders. "I don't know. Don't think about it too much, kid. It'll make you..."

Clay drilled the desert horizon with narrowed eyes. He didn't finish his warning to Valdez because he didn't know what it made you. What had it made him? Bitter? Hard?

He blew out a breath. The work hadn't done that.

A half hour later, Clay pulled his truck into the parking lot of the Paradiso Border Patrol Office—one of several offices in the Tucson Sector.

For the most part, the residents of Paradiso chose to remain blissfully ignorant about the dangers at the border. The violence of the drug trade didn't affect them directly, so they were able to carry on with their daily lives—despite people meeting bloody ends several miles down south.

Livestock, lettuce and pecans had been kind to the folks of Paradiso. Its close proximity to the tourist trap of Tombstone hadn't hurt, either. They lived in a bubble. There hadn't been a murder within the city limits since... Courtney Hart.

Clay left Valdez in the office and swung by Rosita's to pick up a burrito on his way home.

As he slapped his cash onto the counter, Rosita put her hand on his. "We heard news of a body at the border."

Once the Paradiso PD was involved, news traveled fast. He couldn't blame them. The residents had a right to know—whether they cared or not.

"Unfortunately, that's true."

"Drugs?" Rosita's dark eyes shimmered with tears, and a knife twisted in Clay's gut.

Rosita's youngest son had gotten hooked on meth—it hadn't ended well.

"Yeah, probably a mule."

"A girl?" She clasped her hands to her chest. "We heard it was a girl this time."

"A young woman, yes. Ended up on someone's bad side." He shoved the money across the counter. "Keep the change, Rosita."

"Is there a good side when it comes to drugs?" Rosita swept up the bills. "Thanks, Mr. Clay."

He waved and reached for the door, stepping aside for a couple of customers coming in for dinner. He tossed his bag of food on the passenger seat and took off for home.

His house lay outside the collection of the newer developments that had sprung up in response to the pecan-processing plant. He preferred a little space between him and the next guy.

As he turned down the road that led to his house, he loosened his grip on the steering wheel and flexed his fingers. He swung into the entrance to his long driveway and slammed on the brakes to stop behind an old, white compact sporting New Mexico plates.

His muscles tense, he reached for his weapon wedged in the console and waited in his idling truck. The individual Border Patrol sectors were small enough that the bad guys could discover the identities of the agents if they had a mind to. He held his breath as the driver's side door of the car swung open, and a...bride stepped out.

Clay whipped the sunglasses from his face and hunched over the steering wheel. Damn, that was no bride. That was bridezilla—April Hart in the flesh.

Leaving his weapon in the truck, he shoved open his door and placed one booted foot on the dirt and gravel of his driveway. He unfolded to his full height, straightening his spine and pinning April in a stare.

She tossed a mangled mane of blond hair over one shoulder and offered up a smile and a half-raised hand. "Clay, it's good to see you."

Did she expect him to rush to her and sweep her into his arms? He folded those arms across his chest in case they got some crazy notion to do just that on their own. He dipped his chin to his chest. "April."

She dropped her hand and tugged on the top part of the dress that clung to her slender waist and rose to encase the swell of her breasts. "I suppose you're wondering what I'm doing here…in this dress."

"You took a detour on the way to our wedding two years ago and you just found your way back?" His lips twisted into a smile while a knife twisted into his heart.

"N-no." She clasped her hands in front of her, interlacing her fingers. "It's a long story. Can we talk inside?"

"Do you ever have any other kind of story?" Before she could answer his rhetorical question, he dipped back into his truck and swept his bag of food from the passenger seat and holstered his weapon.

He slammed the door of the truck and stalked up his driveway, brushing past April in her wedding finery.

The gravel crunched behind him as she followed his footsteps. "Someone left you a present. It was here when I drove up."

A round, pink-striped box sat on the corner of his porch. Clay tilted his head to the side, his pulse ratcheting up a notch. Nobody left him presents—especially the kind in pink boxes.

"You have your hands full. I'll grab it for you." April

barreled past him, the crinkly material of her gown skimming against his hand.

A spike of adrenaline caused him to make a grab for her dress, but she slipped through his fingers. The story of his life.

"April, wait."

"That's okay. I got this." She reached the porch and grabbed the ribbon on the top of the box. "This is heavy."

She lifted the box a few feet in the air. Then the lid came off and the bottom of the box hit the porch with a thud.

April's scream reverberated in his ears as the severed head bounced once, splattering her white dress with blood, and rolled off the porch.

Chapter Two

April opened her mouth to scream again, but the sound died in her throat, which seemed to be closing. She gurgled instead, falling back against the wooden railing of the porch, her hand still clutching the pink ribbon, the lid of the hatbox swinging wildly and flinging droplets of blood throughout the air.

"Oh my God. It's the head." Clay pointed to the soggy hatbox tipped on its side. "Don't touch that."

Her gaze darted to his face. Was he out of his mind? Why would she touch that box again?

She dropped the lid and swallowed. "It—it's a severed head."

"I'm sorry you had to see that." He pulled a cell phone from the front pocket of his green uniform shirt. "I'll get someone to pick it up."

"I would hope so." Her hands clutched at the skirt of her dress, until she noticed the streaks of blood marring the white billows. She dropped the material and folded her arms over her midsection. "You don't seem surprised. You called it *the* head. You know that head?"

"I do, although I didn't expect it to show up on my porch. I didn't expect *you* to show up on my porch, either." He started talking on his cell phone and held up his key chain, jingling it in the air.

She nodded and he tossed the keys at her. She caught them in one hand and opened the door to his house—a house and home that could've been hers.

She set the keys on a table by the front door. Closing her eyes, she took a deep breath and let it out slowly. Nothing with Clay could ever be uncomplicated. There had to be a head in a pink hatbox sitting on his porch the very day she decided to drop in for a visit.

Her eyelids flew open. Was that what she was doing?

Her gaze traveled around the room. He hadn't much modified his manly space…or his habits. Everything had a place. Even the pillows on the couch sat erectly and in order.

April sauntered to the couch and flipped one of the pillows on its face. She scanned the framed pictures on his bookshelf, looking for her face in vain.

She jumped as a siren wailed on its way to Clay's house. A few minutes later, what sounded like a hundred vehicles pulled up outside. She peeked through the blinds at the uniformed officers swarming Clay's driveway. The head obviously had something to do with Clay's work as a Border Patrol agent. He'd been almost more surprised to see her on his doorstep than the head in the box.

She crossed her arms, cupping her elbows, as a shiver zigzagged up her spine. Clay played a dangerous game down here at the border. Although part of the Tucson Sector, the Paradiso Border Patrol Office was small and everyone—including the drug dealers—knew the agents. Had someone left that head as a warning to Clay?

Good luck. Clay would always do his duty.

The door burst open, and her heart slammed against her chest.

Clay stuck his head into the room. "Detective Espinoza wants to talk to you for a minute."

April smoothed the skirt of the dress with shaky hands. "Is the head still on the driveway?"

"It is, but they're going to bag it soon. I'll ask the detective to come in here, if you want."

"I'll be all right as long as I stay on the porch."

He pushed the door wide, and she swept past him, the dress crinkling between them.

April stepped onto the porch, lifting her skirts to avoid the cone that had been placed next to the stain of blood where the box had sat.

A gray-haired Latino in a suit and a cowboy hat stuck out his hand, his eyes widening as they dropped to her dress. "Ms. Hart, I'm Detective Espinoza. Agent Archer told me you're the one who picked up the box and it had been here when you arrived."

"That's right." She took in his rugged features and frame from the top of his black hat to the tips of his silver-toed boots. He hadn't been one of the cops in Paradiso or one of the Pima County detectives during her family troubles.

"What time did you arrive at Agent Archer's house?"

She glanced at Clay from the corner of her eye. "About five o'clock."

"The box was already on the porch?"

"It was."

"Did you see anyone around the house when you got here?" His gaze flicked again to the wedding gown and then back to her face.

"Nobody." She snapped her fingers. "The dog. Clay, where's Denali? Do you still have him?"

"Of course I still have him." He lifted one eyebrow. "He's staying overnight at the vet."

"Is he okay?"

Espinoza cleared his throat. "So, you didn't see or hear anything unusual when you drove up to the house. Did you get out of the car?"

"I didn't get out of the car. I was tired from my drive and put the seat back to take a nap. Clay got here about an hour after I did, waking me up when his truck pulled in behind me."

"Why did you pick up the box?"

"Clay had his hands full." She shrugged. "Does it matter?"

Espinoza narrowed his eyes. "Hart. You're the daughter of C. J. Hart?"

April's pulse skittered and jumped. "I am. Does *that* matter?"

"Just asking." He waved his pencil up and down the dress. "Why the wedding gown?"

"I just came from a wedding." Her jaw tightened as Clay shifted beside her.

"We're going to want to test that blood on the dress. Did it come from the head?"

"I picked up the box by the ribbon on the top, thinking it went all the way around the box. It didn't. When I picked up the box, the lid came off in my hand and the box fell. The…head bounced out and splattered the dress, and then I dropped the lid."

Espinoza clicked his tongue. "That's a shame."

"Not really." She tossed her wilting curls over one shoulder. "I can rip a piece of the fabric out right now, if you like."

"No hurry. Based on what Agent Archer told us, we're pretty sure we know what happened here."

Another truck squealed up to the scene and, in the glare of the spotlights, Nash Dillon jumped out of his vehicle and hovered over the authorities transferring the head into a bag.

When they finished the job, Nash strode to the porch. "I guess we found her head, but damn, left on your porch? They're thumbing their noses at us, bro."

Clay shook his head. "I need to get some cameras at my house. I didn't even have Denali here to sound the alarm."

"Oh, hey, April." Nash raised his hand and continued his conversation with Clay, as if the appearance of Clay's ex-fiancée in a blood-spattered wedding dress made all the sense in the world. But then Nash Dillon had always been about Nash Dillon.

When the medical examiner's van pulled away, Detective Espinoza handed April a card. "You can drop off the dress anytime in the next few days."

"I'll do that." She snatched his card and spun around to the screen door, leaving Clay and Nash talking shop.

She paced the floor a few times, and then plopped down on the couch, grabbing one of Clay's perfectly placed pillows and hugging it to her chest. What was she doing here? That poor woman's severed head must be some kind of omen. She should've never shown up on Clay's doorstep. Should've never run to him for... what? Why did she come to Paradiso? Clay Archer had been the only bright spot for her here.

She couldn't recreate the magic they'd shared. She'd destroyed that, taken a sledgehammer to it.

The door opened and Clay stepped into the house, sweeping the hat from his head and unbuckling his equipment belt. His weapon clunked against the kitchen counter as he set down the belt.

"What a crazy day." He dragged a hand through his dark hair, which made it stick up in different directions. He held up the bag that contained his dinner and swung it from his fingertips. "I kinda lost my appetite. You want it?"

She stuck out her tongue. "No, thanks. Who was that woman?"

"Probably a drug mule who double-crossed Las Moscas. We found her body earlier, just outside a tunnel running across the border." He braced his hands against the counter and hunched forward. "Are you really interested in this?"

Her fingers dug into the pillow. Las Moscas? He had no idea how interested.

"How do you know it was that gang, Las Moscas?"

"Cartel. Drug cartel and we know because the people who murdered this woman left their calling card in her hand."

April swallowed. "A fly?"

Clay's eyebrows jumped to his hairline. "How'd you know that?"

Shrugging, she schooled her face. "Las Moscas. The flies. I mean, not like a real fly, right?"

"Well, there were plenty of those." He glanced up at her face, and his jaw tightened. "Sorry. They left a carved, wooden fly in her hand."

April jumped up from the couch and tripped over the wedding dress. She made a grab for the back of the couch to stay upright.

"Are you all right?" Clay had taken a couple of steps closer to her, his brow creased.

"I'm okay. Like you said, it's been a crazy day." Her words stopped him in midstride.

He blew out a breath and shoved his hands in the pockets of his green pants. "Do you want to tell me what this is all about, April? The wedding dress? Coming to Paradiso? Adam isn't here, is he? Is he in some kind of trouble?"

Oh, yeah, her brother was in all kinds of trouble, but he could get into trouble anywhere. It didn't have to be Paradiso—where all their trouble had started.

"Adam isn't here and I'll be happy to tell you all about this—" she plucked at the dress "—but I'd like to change first, if you don't mind. Detective Espinoza wants this dress, anyway, or at least pieces of it."

Clay's head swiveled as he took in the room. "Do you have a suitcase in your car?"

"No. I don't have a bag with me. I don't have anything with me." She linked her fingers in front of her, holding her breath. If Clay tossed her out on her rear, she wouldn't blame him.

Clay rolled his eyes. "All right. I have a pair of sweats you can probably use, and help yourself to a T-shirt. I'm gonna have a beer. You want one?"

"Sounds good." She pointed to the hallway that led to his bedroom. "I'll be right back."

She slipped into his room and closed the door behind her, leaning against it and closing her eyes. She didn't have to worry about a wife or a girlfriend. She'd kept tabs on Clay the past few years. She shouldn't be happy that he'd remained single, but he always would have her heart. Ridiculous to think she could blot out the memory of Clay with someone like Jimmy—no matter how much Jimmy had seemed like Clay...at first.

She hadn't known just how ridiculous until this morning—her wedding day.

She reached around and tugged at the zipper of the dress. She shrugged out of the straps, and the gown slipped from her body, pooling at her feet.

The shimmering white strapless bra and the lacy

panties had to stay. She stepped out of the satin pumps and over the heap of material resembling a small mountain of foam on the floor.

She rummaged through Clay's dresser and snagged a pair of army-green sweats with the Border Patrol insignia on the left thigh. She paired the sweats with a white T-shirt from a 10K in Tucson and tiptoed into the living room on bare feet.

Clay hadn't moved from the kitchen counter but now sat perched on a stool, hunched over his phone and a second bottle of beer.

"I'm going to have to do some catching up." She pinged his empty bottle with her powder-pink-tipped fingernail.

He shoved the other bottle toward her. "Haven't touched it."

"Are you sure you don't want it?"

"I probably need a clear head for what's coming." With his foot, he nudged the other stool in her direction.

Hitching up the legs of the sweats, she sat down and grabbed the beer. She raised the bottle. "Here's to catching the SOBs who murdered that woman and defiled her body."

"The particular SOBs? Probably not, but we're working night and day to bring down Las Moscas." Clay scratched at the damp label on the empty beer bottle. "That wedding dress?"

April took a long pull from her beer and squared her shoulders.

Clay's cell phone buzzed next to his hand and he held up one finger. "Hold that thought. I'd better get this."

How much should she tell Clay about Jimmy and the whole mess? She'd never even told him why she ran out on their *own* wedding—and she never would.

"You sure Adam's not here?" Clay held up his phone.

"Of course." She squinted at the call coming through and pressed a hand to her chest. "Why is Adam calling you?"

Clay lifted a shoulder and answered his phone. "Adam?"

He paused for a few seconds and then held out the phone to her. "He wants to talk to you."

"Me?" April's fingers curled into the soft cotton of the T-shirt. How did Adam know she was with Clay? She hadn't told him where she was going. Hell, she hadn't even known she'd wind up in Paradiso when she'd texted him.

She grabbed the phone from Clay's hand and hopped off the stool as he swept her beer from the counter and headed for the back rooms.

"Adam? How'd you know I'd be with Clay?"

"C'mon, April. Give me some credit. You're in one big mess. Where else would you go?"

Glancing over her shoulder, she said, "What do you know about my big mess?"

"I know a lot more than you indicated in your text. When you told me the wedding was off and to steer clear of Jimmy, I figured you'd found out."

April gritted her teeth but managed to grind out the question on her lips. "You knew about Jimmy?"

"I did." Adam had the decency to cough. "I'm sorry."

"Why? Why did you…?" April braced her hand against the front door. "Never mind. Don't tell me. I don't want to know."

"April, I know I don't have the right to ask you this, especially after what I just admitted, but do not tell Clay about Jimmy. You haven't told him anything, have you?"

"Not yet." She pounded the door with her fist. It was happening again. "Why shouldn't I tell him?"

"Because if you do, Jimmy will kill me…and then he's gonna kill you."

Chapter Three

"Everything okay?" Clay peered into the living room from the hallway.

April started and spun around, the phone clutched to her chest, her face as white as that wedding dress she'd stripped off. "Yeah."

"Or as okay as things can be with Adam." He cocked his head. "Is he still getting into trouble?"

"You could say that." She held out his phone. "Thanks."

He crossed the room and took the phone from her trembling hand. "Why'd he call for you on my phone? Where's yours?"

"I thought I told you. I took off with nothing—no phone, no money, no ID." She shrugged her stiff shoulders.

"Where'd you get that car?" He jerked his thumb toward the window.

"A—a friend. I got it from a friend."

"What's the story, April?" He held up the beer bottle, the label shredded to bits. "I finished your beer. Do you want another?"

"I'll take one." She smoothed her hands over her face and emerged with her lips stretched into a smile. "There's no real story."

She followed him into the kitchen and sat on the edge of a stool. "I ran out on another wedding. That shouldn't be a surprise to you, of all people."

He popped up from the fridge, beer in hand. He set the new bottle on the counter in front of her. "I never got the whole story on that wedding, either. I guess I can't expect to get the truth out of you when it comes to your wedding to someone else."

"I decided he wasn't the one for me." She pressed the sweating bottle against her pink cheek.

"You just figured that out on the morning of the blessed event?"

She nodded and took a sip of beer.

"What was the hurry? You took off in a borrowed car with nothing? Not even your purse? You didn't have the backbone to tell the poor sap?" He clicked his tongue. "April, April. You're getting worse and worse at ditching weddings and fiancés. At least you had the guts to tell me to my face."

April bit her bottom lip. "H-he's not a good guy, Clay."

"Did he hit you?" His fists curled at his sides, despite his resolve to steer clear of April and her problems.

"No. Nothing like that." She blinked her eyes. "But he has a bad temper, and I didn't want to deal with the fallout. Call me a coward."

"Will he come after you?" Like he never did.

She twisted a lock of blond hair around her finger, and Clay swallowed as he remembered the smell of that hair—all sunshine and foolish dreams.

"He doesn't know where I am. I was actually on my way to Mexico when I saw the highway for Tucson and thought…" She curled her hand around the bottle and took a swig of beer. "Oh, hell. I don't know what I thought. I just had a strong desire to see you again."

"Did you love this guy?" Clay held his breath. He couldn't stand the thought of April in love with someone else, wanting someone else the way she once wanted him.

She rounded her shoulders. "I don't think so."

"You have a bad habit of agreeing to marry men you don't love."

Her blue eyes flashed and her nostrils flared, but she pressed her lips into a thin line.

Had he been fishing? April *had* loved him. Nobody could fake emotion…and passion like that. But something had happened the week before their wedding. It was as if she turned off a switch. When she'd broken the news to him that she was backing out, it hadn't even surprised him.

"Why'd you get engaged…again?" He crossed his arms, digging his fingertips into his biceps. She'd already told him more about why she ended this engagement than why she'd ended their own. Maybe one thing would lead to another.

"I don't know. Maybe I was looking for some stability. Maybe I was tired of handling everything on my own."

"By everything, you mean Adam." He clenched his jaw. He could've handled Adam. He could've offered stability. He thought that's why she ran. She'd become addicted to drama and what he represented lacked excitement. Hell, he knew he worked too many hours, got too involved in his cases.

"Yes, Adam." Her eyes glittered a dangerous blue as she dragged a fingernail across the label on the bottle.

"Why did he call?"

"To make sure I'd landed here. To make sure I was safe."

Clay snorted. "When has Adam ever been concerned for your safety? Unless he's changed."

"He's had it rough, Clay." She sniffed and swiped the back of her hand across her nose. "He's the one who found Mom."

He passed on the opportunity to remind April that Adam had been a screwup before the murder of their mother. April would defend her brother come hell or high water.

He released a long breath as his stomach rumbled with hunger. "What now? Are you going to Mexico? How are you going to do that without ID?"

"C'mon, Clay." She tilted her head. "I'm a Paradiso girl. I know how to slip across the border with the best of 'em."

He jabbed a finger at the baggy T-shirt she'd picked from his closet. It had never looked so good. "Are you going to get some clothes? A bag? Toiletries? Or is Adam going to pick up your stuff for you?"

"Oh, no. He can't…he's not going to do that." She flipped her hair over her shoulder. "I don't want him to."

"You mean he couldn't be bothered." He held up his hand as she started her defense of her brother. "Save it. Do you have a friend who can get your stuff? Send it to you? Where is your stuff?"

"Albuquerque. Don't worry about it. It's just that—stuff. Anything I have of importance is right here in Paradiso."

Too bad she didn't mean him. "Your place looks good. Your cousin's taking good care of the house."

She twisted her mouth. "I suppose I should stay with Cousin Meg while I regroup here."

As he carefully picked up her empty bottle and turned toward the trash, he said, "Regroup in Paradiso?"

"I think I should at least try to get my wallet, ID, credit cards and all those other items that tie you to civilization." She clicked her nails against the tile counter. "People do disappear, though, don't they?"

"Your father did it. You thinking of following in his footsteps?"

She dropped her hands in her lap and slumped. "No."

Clay bit the inside of his cheek. Talking to April had become a minefield. He couldn't mention her brother, her mother, her father or her most recent fiancé.

He poked the paper bag containing his burrito, which must be a soggy mess by now. "Are you going to drive to the house? You can call Meg on my phone first to warn her."

She slid from the stool and stretched her arms to the ceiling, the loose T-shirt taking shape around her body. "Can I buy one more day at your place before facing the inquisition over there? I'll even drive into town and pick up some dinner for you. I can hear your stomach growling from over here."

"I'm good." He rubbed his empty belly. "I have some leftover pasta from last night. Do you want some?"

She covered her mouth. "Ugh, no. I can't get the squishing sound of that head hitting the porch out of my head. Makes me feel queasy every time I think about it."

"Do you mind if I eat in front of you?" He plucked up the bag from Rosita's with his fingertips. "This has been through the ringer tonight. Dropped on the ground, probably stepped on and who knows what got into the bag."

"I don't want to think about that, either." She crossed her hands over her chest. "Water?"

Clay retrieved the leftover pasta and a bottle of water from the fridge. He stuck the plastic bowl with the pasta in the microwave and poured the water into a glass with ice. As he placed it in front of April, he said, "You're serious about staying here tonight?"

"If you're serious about having me."

"I don't think I answered either way." The microwave buzzed, and he pivoted away from April as her lips parted. He picked up the bowl and dropped it on the counter as it burned his fingers.

She wrinkled her nose at the steam that rose from the pasta. "Better let me know one way or the other because I'll have to drive to the house, and I'd rather do it before it gets too late."

"Are you worried about who and what's out there?" He took the seat beside her and pointed his fork at the windows in the living room.

"Why did someone leave that head on your porch?" She pinned her hands between her knees, which bounced up and down. "You just found the woman's body today?"

"We found her this afternoon after an image came through from our drone we have out there. She was on our side of the border at the mouth of a tunnel. Nash crawled through the tunnel to see if she left anything behind."

"Like her head?"

"Drugs, money, cell phone." He twirled his fork in the pasta drenched with marinara. "Nothing. They left her with nothing."

"Except the carving of a fly in her cold, dead hand."

April jumped off the stool and took a turn around the room. "You didn't answer me."

"Sure, you can stay here for the night." Clay stuffed a forkful of spaghetti in his mouth. He could resist this woman for one night, couldn't he?

"Thanks, but that's not what I was talking about." She gathered the hem of the T-shirt in her hands, bunching it in her fists. "Why you? Why was that woman's head on your porch?"

He swiped a paper towel across his mouth. "I'm Border Patrol. I found the body. The other agent on the scene is a new guy and doesn't live in town, and Nash's property is too big and those pecan groves are monitored. I'm the default guy."

"It's dangerous that the drug dealers know you and know where you live."

"The cartel members from Mexico don't, neither do the runners coming through. It's just the guys who distribute locally. They're not going to make a move against the agents. That would be suicide for them." He planted his elbows on the counter. "I'm glad you didn't surprise them in the act. You didn't see anyone driving around when you arrived?"

"No, but I wasn't paying attention. I probably passed a couple of cars on the road before the turnoff to your place." She wagged a finger at him. "And before you ask, no, I didn't notice anything about the cars—make, model, color, license plate—nothing. I didn't realize we'd be finding a head on your porch. I would've told that detective if I'd noticed anything."

"What was it about Detective Espinoza that set you off? The man was just doing his job." Clay pushed away the bowl of pasta, losing his appetite all over again.

"Why was he asking about my dress?"

"You're kidding, right?"

"The dress had nothing to do with the head in the box."

"He's a detective. He's supposed to be curious." Clay rubbed his knuckles against the stubble on his jaw. He must look like hell and for once he cared. "What surprised me is that Nash *didn't* ask about the dress."

"Didn't surprise me a bit. That's Nash." A giggle escaped from her lips, and she clapped a hand over her mouth, her blue eyes wide and glassy above her fingers.

"Humor is allowed—even with a head on your porch, *especially* with a head on your porch. It's a coping device."

"Yeah, you're talking to the queen of coping devices." She tapped a fist over her heart.

"Your coping device is to take care of everyone around you and ignore your own pain." Except when she'd left him. He'd always told her to look out for herself, but he didn't think she'd take his advice at the expense of his happiness.

Be careful what you wish for, Archer.

She dipped her head and toyed with the ties at the waistband of his sweats, her hair creating a blond veil around her face. "I've kept you away from your routine tonight."

He glanced down at his dirt-smudged shirt and dusty boots. He *did* look like hell. "I think that pink box on my porch disrupted my routine…such as it is. But I'll take the hint and hit the shower."

Her head shot up. "I didn't mean that."

"I usually do take a shower as soon as I get off work, especially after a day like today." He snatched the bowl from the counter. "I won't be long. Help yourself to anything in the fridge, or if you're tired, I can make up the bed in the guest room."

"I can do that myself. Sheets?"

"There's bedding in the hall closet, top shelf. I just have a bedspread on that bed, but the sheets in the closet are clean."

Flicking her fingers in the air, she said, "You go ahead. I'll fix the bed."

Clay pushed open the door to his bedroom and tripped to a stop at the discarded dress on the floor. He gathered it in his arms, burying his face in the silky material to inhale the scent of April's perfume, mixed with her own undeniable smell of sweet and spice.

She'd had enough time to spritz on some perfume before the wedding. What really happened? He had a hard time believing April would put up with someone abusive, but she'd been through a lot in her life.

He tucked a trailing bit of lace into the pile in his arm and stepped out of the room. He'd probably never know the truth, just like he'd never know the real reason why she ran out on him.

When he tapped open the door to the guest room with his toe, April gasped and dropped the stack of folded sheets in her arms on the bed. Still jumpy.

"Sorry. I'm just going to leave this with you." He dumped the dress on a chair in the corner where it flowed over the sides. "You can figure out how you're going to get the sample to Detective Espinoza."

"I will." She nodded. "Pillows?"

"Not sure if I have extras. I'll check."

"Take your shower. I'll look in the closet."

He retreated to his bedroom, snapping the door shut. He peeled off his uniform and dropped it in the hamper in the bathroom.

The warm spray of the shower hit him midchest as he stepped under the water. Bracing his hands against the tile, he dropped his head. What was he doing? Inviting April Hart to stay at his place even one night meant trouble.

He'd never been able to get her out of his mind, out of his heart.

He scrubbed the grit and dust from his hair, digging into his scalp. Now, he'd have to not forget about her all over again.

He finished his shower and pulled on some gym shorts and a T-shirt. With any luck, April would be worn out from her drive and the terror of finding that head, and be fast asleep in his guest room.

He stepped out of the bedroom and peered around the corner at April, camped out on his couch cradling a hot drink, her feet on top of his coffee table. He pulled his bottom lip between his teeth. Luck had it in for him tonight.

"Did you find everything you needed for the bed?"

"All made up, except for the pillows. You don't have any extra, but that's okay. I'll do without." She tapped her feet together. "I made some tea. Hope you don't mind." Her gaze met his above the rim of her cup. "I didn't know you were a tea drinker."

"Those are left over from my mom's visit."

"How's she doing?" April's tight smile made it clear she didn't care how his mom was doing.

Mom had made it clear how she felt about April ditching her only son, practically at the altar.

"She's fine." His gaze darted to her bare feet propped up on his furniture and back to her face. "What time are you leaving tomorrow?"

She slid her feet from the table, curled one leg beneath her and then changed her mind, planting both of them on the floor. "In a hurry to get rid of me? Not that I blame you."

"Not at all." He waved his arms around the room in a grand gesture. "Stay as long as you want."

Her eyes widened for a second. "Be careful."

Pulling back his shoulders, he crossed his arms. He had to get a grip. One side of his mouth curled into a sneer. "Don't worry. Where you're concerned, I'm gonna be careful."

"Good call, Archer." She stretched her arms over her head and faked a yawn. "This show is boring, and I'm beat from that drive."

"I—I just asked about tomorrow because I have work in the morning."

"Whether you're here or not, I can make my way to my own house."

"Okay, I'll leave it to you. Help yourself to breakfast in the morning." His shoulders dropped as he walked to the kitchen to get some water. He'd go to work tomorrow, and she'd be gone by the time he returned—out of his life once again.

He walked into the living room clutching a glass of water and eyeing April, still ensconced on his couch. "Did you leave anything in the car that you need?"

"No, or just some cash in the cup holder."

"Not a great idea. Leaving things in plain sight in your car is what lures thieves to break in."

She tipped her head back against the couch cushion. "Hard to move. Must be the beer, or the six-hour drive."

"I'll get it for you." He pointed at the table to the side of the front door. "Keys to the car?"

"The only keys I have."

"Who does that?" He shook his head as he stalked toward the door and snatched the keys from the table.

Someone who ran out on two weddings, that's who.

He crossed the porch, the warm night air enveloping him as he trooped down the driveway, gravel and dirt crunching beneath each slap of his flip-flops. He pressed the remote, surprised this old beater even had one.

He yanked the door handle, and the dome light flickered. That would have to be replaced soon, but the car belonged to her friend, didn't it?

He shoved his hand in the cup holder, pinching the bills between his fingertips as he pulled them out. His fingers scrabbled in the bottom of the cup holder for any change, tracing the edge of a smooth disc. He grabbed it and pulled it out, cupping it in his palm.

He held his hand beneath the dome light, and his blood froze in his veins.

What the hell was April doing with a calling card from Las Moscas?

Chapter Four

April pushed up from the couch. Clay was sure taking his sweet time out there. He obviously wanted her to leave and probably wanted her in bed before he even came back into the house—just not his bed.

But the way he looked at her with that fire in his hazel eyes gave her the same old thrill. He couldn't hide his attraction to her because he hadn't been schooled in the art of deception, as she had. It had served her well. She probably could've even faked things with Jimmy after what she'd discovered about him—but she hadn't wanted to try.

Adam possessed the same skills as she did—learned from the same master. Adam had never given one hint that he knew what Jimmy did for a living. He'd introduced her to Jimmy and built him up to be this great guy...and she'd allowed Jimmy to sweep her off her feet at just the right time in her life.

Clay burst through the front door, his jaw tight, his face suffused with red rage.

April jerked back, digging her fingernails into the cushions of the couch. "What's wrong?"

"This." He thrust out his hand, and uncurled his fingers. "Why the hell is this in your car?"

She sagged against the couch. The token—she'd left

the token with the fly carved onto it in the cup holder. So, it wasn't a coincidence that the headless woman had something similar clutched in her hand.

"I found it."

Clay blinked, and his solid chest heaved. "You found it here? In my driveway?"

That would make the most sense to him. It would get her out of this particular predicament. She found it in his driveway when she drove up and dropped it in the cup holder, not thinking anything about it.

That would wipe the angry look from his face and allow her to squirm away from the truth. Sometimes a girl got tired of squirming.

She folded her hands across her midsection. "No, I didn't find it in your driveway."

"In town, then? On the street?" He spit out possibilities for her, his body stiff and coiled.

"I found it in my ex-fiancé's office."

The color flooded Clay's face again, and he squeezed his fist around the wooden disc. "You know what it is, don't you?"

"It's the calling card of Las Moscas."

"What does it mean, April? Who's your ex-fiancé? What have you gotten yourself into?"

She held up three unsteady fingers. "That's three questions."

"And you're going to answer all three of them." He strode past her so fast the ends of her hair stirred.

Clay dumped the token on the countertop where it clattered with a jarring, accusatory tone. "Start talking. Start telling the truth…for once."

"I didn't know about Jimmy's involvement with Las Moscas until today. I didn't even know about Las Moscas until you told me about the cartel." She hugged herself and sniffed.

"Jimmy what? What's his last name?"

"Verdugo, Jimmy Verdugo."

"You met him in Albuquerque?"

"Yes, when I went to visit Adam."

"Visit from where?"

She lodged the tip of her tongue in the corner of her mouth. It seemed as if Clay planned to use his interrogation to get to the bottom of a few other truths. "I was living in LA."

"That's where you went after…you left me?"

"I got a job in accounting. Lots of accounting jobs there."

"You hate accounting."

"Had to work."

He ran a hand across his face as if to readjust his questioning. "Let me guess. Adam knew what Jimmy was. He probably introduced you."

"I just found that out today, too. Adam knew Jimmy was a drug dealer, and he did introduce us." Her nose stung at the betrayal from her brother and she rubbed the tip.

"That son of a…" Clay slammed his hand against the counter and the disc skittered across the tile. "How did you find out?"

"Jimmy was busy this morning, before the wedding. Trying to close out some business for his—" she curled her fingers for air quotes "—import/export business. I took the opportunity to sneak into his office."

"You had to sneak into your fiancé's office?" He rubbed his palm on the thigh of his shorts.

"I know, right?" She pushed her hair from her face. "I had my suspicions about his business before today, but I thought maybe he was engaging in some shady practices. He never wanted me looking at his accounts, even though I'd offered my services for free."

"You're telling me you snuck into his office, saw his books and figured out he was running drugs?"

"You of all people know how these guys operate. Obviously not. While I was snooping in his office, I heard him coming down the hallway with his best man and business associate." She lifted her shoulders. "I hid."

"In that wedding dress?" He jerked his thumb over his shoulder toward the spare room.

"The sliding door to his balcony was open. I stepped outside. If he had pulled those blinds open, I would've been finished." She clenched her teeth against the chill snaking up her spine as she relived that moment of terror.

"You overheard his conversation with his associate?"

She dipped her chin to her chest once. "I did, and I got an earful. Did your mother ever tell you not to eavesdrop because you'd never hear anything good about yourself? Yeah, I'm sure *your* mother told you that."

"What did you hear?" Clay's hazel eyes darkened to deep green, making her pulse flutter.

"It—it's kind of unbelievable." She sank to the couch. "I still have a hard time believing I heard it."

"I'm all ears." He pulled the stool beneath him and straddled it.

"They talked about a drug deal, a shipment from Mexico, but it sounded like they were going to intercept it or something. From their conversation, there was no doubt in my mind that they planned to hijack this shipment for their own. Is that something Las Moscas would do?"

Clay scratched his chin. "No. That's something another organization would do to Las Moscas."

"He definitely had the calling card of Las Moscas in his desk. I stole that before I left."

"Maybe Jimmy's a member of the cartel, and he and his best man are planning a big double-cross."

She put a hand to her throat. "That doesn't sound like it's going to end well for Jimmy and Gilbert."

"Do you care?" He wedged his hands on his knees and hunched forward.

"About Jimmy? No." She drew her knees up to her chest, digging her heels into the cushion of the couch—and Clay didn't even object. "He was using me, Clay. The courtship, the engagement, the wedding—all a big farce. Jimmy never cared about me. He set me up, or Adam set me up."

"Set you up for what?" Clay cocked his head to one side. "What do you have to offer Jimmy Verdugo, a drug dealer? You didn't win the lottery after you left me, did you?"

She swallowed. Every time he said that she left him, the knife twisted deeper into her gut.

"Not money. Connections."

His eyebrows shot up to a lock of dark hair curling on his forehead. "What connections? Your drug-addled brother? Did he think Adam could provide him with a steady stream of clients?"

"Not my brother. My father."

"Your father?" The crease between his eyes deepened. "What the hell does your father have to do with any of this? He disappeared ten years ago after he murdered your mother."

She wrapped her arms around her legs and touched

her forehead to her knees. "The authorities never proved he killed her."

"I'm not going down that road with you again, April. What did Jimmy Verdugo want with your father?"

"You know how everyone said my father went to Mexico when he vanished?"

"Yeah, which is why most people around here believe he's guilty."

She balanced her chin on her knees. "Well, Jimmy and Gilbert believe he's some big-time drug lord down there."

"What?" Clay hopped from the stool and sat on the edge of the coffee table in front of her. "That's crazy."

"They mentioned a name, a nickname. You must know it. El Gringo Viejo."

The color ebbed from Clay's tawny complexion. "Jimmy thinks your father, C. J. Hart, is El Gringo Viejo?"

"So, you *do* know him."

"Every Border Patrol and every DEA agent knows of El Gringo Viejo."

"Given what you know about him, could he be my father?"

Clay raised his eyes to the ceiling as if running through facts and dates. "As far as we know, El Gringo Viejo started operating about eight years ago."

"That fits my father's timeline. He'd have been down there eight years ago."

"He moves around a lot. His people are loyal."

"Is he part of Las Moscas? From what Jimmy and Gilbert said, it didn't sound like it."

"He's not part of a cartel. He provides high-quality product to everyone, and lets them figure it out among themselves. He's a freelancer."

"Jimmy was convinced enough to date me and marry me."

"That Jimmy must've been some kind of smooth operator." A muscle flickered at the corner of Clay's mouth, and April wanted to press her lips against it.

She'd settled for Jimmy because he'd been a Clay clone. Adam didn't admit it on the phone, but he most likely trained Jimmy to push all of her buttons. She'd never love anyone the way she'd loved Clay—still loved him.

"I'm pretty sure right now that Adam coached Jimmy into my heart." She laced her fingers together, and her knuckles blanched.

"I'm sorry." Clay covered her hands with one of his own. "Adam needs an ass-kicking. He must believe this garbage about your father."

"We didn't have a chance to talk about it, but I'm sure he does. He may have even been the one to convince Jimmy of it."

"Why didn't you tell me any of this when you showed up here? Especially when I told you about the carving of the fly?"

"I was getting ready to tell you—most of it, anyway, even though it made me look like a fool."

"Join the club."

Her eye twitched. "But then Adam called."

"What did he say?"

"He told me if I told anyone about Jimmy and his business, Jimmy would kill Adam…and me."

Clay reached forward and wrapped his fingers around her ankle just below the elastic of the green sweats. "Did this guy ever threaten you before?"

"Never."

"But he raised your suspicions somehow. That's why you had to sneak into his office and eavesdrop on him."

"It was just the finances. He was always so vague about his business. Being an accountant—which you're right, I hate—I was curious about his numbers. He brought in a lot of money, lived a lavish lifestyle."

"Is that how he seduced you?" His fingers tightened around her ankle briefly before he released her.

"Are you calling me a gold digger?" She narrowed her eyes and curled her toes into the cushion of the couch.

"I don't blame you for wanting someone to take care of you. What Jimmy offered must've been attractive after what you've been through."

"I admit, the money made his life seem easy—people to handle the pesky details, private trainers, personal chefs, private jet. I was living in some kind of fairy tale until I woke up in that office and realized how fake everything was—including my feelings for Jimmy."

"I'm assuming Jimmy knows you ditched the wedding because you found out about him and his motives. Can Adam spin it? You got cold feet? Hell, it *is* kind of a pattern for you." Clay smacked his palm against his chest. "In fact, this is what I recommend you do. Call Jimmy and apologize for running out. Tell him you're not ready. Tell him you went back to your ex."

April's heart skipped a beat. *If only.*

"How long did you know him before the wedding?"

"Six months." She pulled her hair back from her face. "This could work."

"Perfect. You were too hasty." Clay pushed off the table and stepped over it on his way to the kitchen. "Do you think that moron brother of yours kept his mouth shut about you? He needs to convince Jimmy you don't know anything about his dirty business."

"I don't think he told Jimmy I eavesdropped on the conversation with Gilbert." She twisted her fingers. "I did take that carving, though. He probably missed it."

"Where was it?"

"It was one of several in his desk."

"Maybe he won't miss it. What would it mean to you, anyway?" Clay turned around, his phone in his hand. "You didn't tell Jimmy I was Border Patrol, did you?"

"I didn't tell Jimmy anything about you, other than I had been engaged before and ended things right before the wedding." April folded her hands and pinned them between her knees. She hadn't wanted to tell Jimmy anything about Clay—never even told him his name.

"That's good." He held up the phone. "Do you think it's too late to call Adam and warn him to stay quiet?"

"I can't believe Adam even kept your number in his phone."

"Probably insurance. Figured I could get him out of a jam if he ever needed the help."

"That sounds about right." She snapped her fingers. "I'll call Adam and find out. And if he told Jimmy that I know he's a drug dealer?"

"You'll have to convince Jimmy you won't tell any-one."

Clay placed the phone in her outstretched hand, and she went to his recent calls and tapped Adam's number. At the first ring, she leaned forward. At the second, she glanced at Clay. Adam's cell rang for a third time, and April licked her lips.

When the phone tripped over to Adam's voice mail, she put Clay's phone on speaker. "What now?"

"Don't leave a message." Clay lunged for the phone and ended the call. "Just in case."

"Just in case—" April pressed her fingers against her throbbing temple "—Jimmy has Adam's phone?"

"Or he gets to his voice mail. You don't want anything on record."

"Should I call Jimmy now?"

"Not from my phone." He held up his cell and then returned it to its charger on the counter. "You can pick up a burner phone tomorrow and call him from that. Maybe Adam will see the missed call from me and get back to you."

"I wonder why he didn't pick up." April rubbed her arms. "It's a little early for him to be in bed."

"Maybe he's with Jimmy and doesn't want to answer any calls, which would be the smart move." Clay lifted an eyebrow. "Is Adam still using?"

"Says he's not." She hunched her shoulders.

"But you don't believe him."

"You may think I'm overly protective where Adam is concerned, but that doesn't mean I don't see him for what he is."

"He's your brother. I understand." Clay grabbed his water glass and set it in the sink. "You can stay here if you want to watch TV. The spare room doesn't have one. I'm going to hit the sack. Unlike Adam, it's not too early for me, especially after the day I had."

"You must be exhausted." She pointed the remote at the TV screen where she'd paused her movie. "I guess I'll stay here and try to unwind a little."

"I'll toss one of my pillows onto your bed." He lifted his hand and disappeared into the hallway.

April let out a long breath she hadn't even realized she'd been holding. Being in the same room as Clay hadn't been as easy as she'd expected—even after coming clean about Jimmy.

Could she really call Jimmy tomorrow and act normal? Act as if she didn't know he was a drug-dealing scumbag who wanted to marry her to get to her father?

She restarted the movie and adjusted a throw pillow behind her neck. Sure she could. She'd been lying to Clay Archer for years.

Chapter Five

Clay woke with a start, his heart thrumming in his chest. *April.* She'd come back into his life, dragging her drama along with her.

He threw back the covers, fully awake, and planted his bare feet on the cool tile floor. His clock radio sounded the alarm with the news at six and he reached over and smacked it off.

He crept from his room and grabbed the doorjamb when he saw the door to the spare room ajar. The hinges creaked as he pushed it open.

Clay's jaw tightened as he scanned the neatly made-up bed. At least she hadn't left a mess when she sneaked out of here.

Grabbing the back of his neck, he dug his fingers into his knotted muscles. He'd told her what to do to alleviate Jimmy's suspicions. It was up to her to follow through.

He padded on bare feet into the darkened living room and flicked on the light in the kitchen. As he measured ground coffee in the filter, a soft moan floated on the air and he dropped the filter on the counter.

He charged into the living room, his fists clenched at his sides. A lump on the couch elongated, and a swath of blond hair rippled over the edge of the cushion.

He crept closer and peered down at April's face,

smooth in sleep except for a tiny crease between her eyebrows. She never could sleep soundly. What sinister dreams clouded her mind, creating that little line?

Her lips parted and she emitted a sigh that stirred the strands of shiny hair crisscrossing her cheek.

His fingers twitched to smooth the hair away from her face, but he didn't want to disturb her sleep. God knows, she needed it. What had possessed her to marry a man she hardly knew? Stability? He could've offered her that and more. Protection for Adam? That he'd never offer.

He turned away from her, cleaned up the coffee mess in the kitchen, set up another cup to brew and retreated to his bedroom. For those few minutes, he'd almost come to terms with having April out of his life again.

He took a quick shower and dressed in his uniform. Maybe they'd find out the identity of the dead drug mule today. If she had fingerprints on file somewhere, they'd ID her soon enough. It would take longer to match the DNA from the head to the body, but how many bodies without heads could there be in one day?

He pulled on his boots and returned to the kitchen where his coffee awaited him, the smell of the rich brew giving him a jolt. As he screwed on the lid to his commuter mug, April coughed from the other room.

She called out, "Are you still here?"

"Sorry if I woke you up." He'd had just the lights beneath the counters on, and he turned on the overhead lights. "Do you want some coffee? I have just a single-brew machine, but I can put some on for you now."

She sat up and yawned. "I think I'll have more of your mother's tea, if that's okay. I know your mom would probably mind, but she's not here."

"Did you sleep okay? Why didn't you use the bedroom? You don't even have a blanket or pillow out here."

She shrugged the afghan from her shoulders. "I found this on the chair. I fell asleep in front of the TV and just got too comfortable to move."

"I've spent a few nights on that couch in front of the TV myself." He put down his coffee mug and grabbed a tea bag from the shelf. "I'll leave the tea for you here, and you're welcome to cook breakfast before you head out to Meg's."

"Maybe I'll drive up to Tucson today and get some clothes...and that phone." She tousled her hair. "I suppose I have to make that call to Jimmy."

"I think that's your safest bet right now. How are your acting skills?"

She jerked up her head. "Pretty darned good."

"Then you shouldn't have any trouble convincing Jimmy you made a mistake, you're sorry, it's you not him. Blah, blah. You've done it before."

Clay snapped his mouth shut and sealed his lips. Reminding April what she'd done was not going to persuade her to open up to him and tell him the real reason why she left. He needed to give it a rest.

He buckled his equipment belt around his waist and holstered his gun. Grabbing his hat, he turned at the door. "When you get that phone, give me a call. I left my number on a sticky note that I slapped on a cabinet door."

He paused on the threshold. "Don't hang around here too long, April. There are some bad characters who know where I live. I'll have the Paradiso PD cruise by here a few times in the next hour."

"You just creeped me out." She pushed up from

the couch. "I can shower at Meg's and get breakfast there, too."

"Do you want me to wait until you're ready to go?" He glanced at the phone clutched in his hand. "I'm not going to be late, and I'm leaving early to pick up Denali."

"Is he okay?"

"He's fine." He tapped his cheekbone. "Just a minor eye irritation and I would've picked him up yesterday, but I got called out on that dead body. Drew offered to take him home for the night."

"Small-town vets." Her gaze shifted to the great outdoors behind him. "If you don't mind waiting, I'll hurry."

"Take your time." He patted the case slung over his shoulder. "I can check emails on my laptop."

By the time he'd powered up his computer and clicked on the first email, April had returned, the bedraggled wedding dress thrown over her shoulder like the pelt of some wild animal.

"That was fast. No shower?"

"Told you, I'll take one at the house." She plucked at the baggy sweats that couldn't conceal her shapely backside. "I didn't have anything to change into, anyway. I'll borrow some clothes from Meg."

"Do you want me to take this to the station for you?" He tugged on the hem of the wedding dress. "It's on my way."

"Could you?" She sloughed the dress from her shoulder as if shedding a layer of skin.

The dress landed in a heap between them. "That would really help me out because I wouldn't have to explain anything to Meg about the wedding."

"My lips are sealed, but plenty of people saw you last

night all decked out in your finest bridal attire." He left the dress on the floor and shut down his laptop. "You know how this town likes gossip."

"I know more than anyone." She brushed off the front of her T-shirt. "I'll deal with it when it happens. One thing at a time."

"You got it." He stuffed his computer in his bag and hitched it over his shoulder. Then he gathered the dress in his arms, resting his chin on the yards of fabric. Probably the closest he'd ever get to a wedding dress.

Tipping his head toward the door, he said, "Lead the way."

April scurried in front of him and held the door open as he squeezed past her. She grabbed the keys jingling from his outstretched hand and hit the remote for his truck.

"No ceremony needed. Just stuff it in the back seat." She opened the back door of his truck.

He shoved it inside, punching and squishing it into submission. It frothed over the headrest of the front seat. He yanked it down. "This thing is alive."

"Yeah, not really my taste. I'm just gonna claim temporary insanity."

He eyed her car over her shoulder. "You sure that thing runs?"

"It got me here, didn't it? I'll be fine." She tossed his key chain at him. "Thanks for sticking around."

"How long will you be in Paradiso?"

"Long enough to regroup and think about my next move."

"You're not really considering trying to track down your father in Mexico, are you?"

"I don't know. What if he really is El Gringo Viejo?"

"And your knowing that and tracking him down in

Mexico would benefit you, how?" His hand shot out, and he encircled her wrist with his fingers. "Let that go, April. Let it all go. Call Jimmy and let him know the engagement was a mistake and you're out of his life, and then get back to *your* life."

Her lashes swept over her eyes. "I just might do that."

She wobbled across his gravel driveway, a pair of pearly white pumps sticking out of the bottom of the sweats.

Shaking his head, he climbed into his truck. The wedding gown tickled the back of his neck, so he slapped at it and cranked on his engine. The truck idled behind April's car.

When her brake and reverse lights flashed, Clay backed out and rolled backward down the road to allow April to pull out ahead of him. He followed her to the fork, and she stuck her hand out the window as she peeled out, making a left turn.

He took a right and aimed the truck back toward town. Detective Espinoza worked for the county sheriff's department but he'd be camped out at the Paradiso PD station for the next week at least, to get a handle on this investigation.

When Clay reached the police department, he pulled into the small parking lot on the side for official vehicles. He swung open the back door and scowled at the dress. He should've offered April a pair of scissors to cut out the bloodstained material.

He wrestled the dress out of the car, and a male voice called out over the parking lot. "Is that your new girlfriend, Archer?"

Clay lifted his hand and flashed a one-finger salute at the cop and then gathered the dress to his chest, wrapping his arms around the voluminous material.

Ten of the dress April had planned to wear to their own wedding could fit inside this one flouncy mess. He'd seen the dress when he'd gone over to her house to pick up a few of his things when she left town. The picture in his mind of her in it had stayed with him longer than he cared to admit.

He staggered to the building, tripping on the dress more than once. He pushed into the lobby of the PD and peered around his delivery at Todd Barton, the officer at the front desk, wide-eyed and mouth gaping.

"This is for Espinoza. It has the blood from the head last night."

"Oh, right." Barton jumped from his chair and came out from behind the counter. "I'll take it into one of the rooms in the back and cut out the swaths of material we need and bag them for testing. Espinoza has already sent blood samples from the, uh…head to the state."

"She's all yours." Clay pressed the wedding dress against Barton's chest and brushed his hands together as if ridding himself of a dirty task.

Barton poked his head to the side of the white suds. "Are you going to take this back with you after I cut out the samples?"

"No way." Clay turned on his heel, almost bumping into Espinoza as he charged through the door.

"Just the man I'm looking for."

"I just dropped off the dress with the bloodstains from the severed head." Clay jerked his thumb over his shoulder at Barton, as if there was more than one blood-smeared wedding dress.

"Archer, we've got a problem." Espinoza rubbed the back of his neck.

Clay's pulse jumped. "What kind of problem?"

"That body you found yesterday and that head on your porch—they don't match."

APRIL CUPPED THE cell phone in her sweaty palm and dumped it on the table. She waved to the waitress balancing three plates in her hand. Once she delivered the food, the waitress scurried to her table.

"More iced tea?"

"Actually, I'm looking for an outlet." April dangled the charging cord from her fingers. "Just bought a new phone, and I need to charge it up."

"We can do that for you behind the counter." The server held out her hand, wiggling her fingers, and April pressed the phone and the charger into her palm.

"Thanks, and I'll have more iced tea when you get a chance."

The waitress smiled, but her eyes assessed April—hard.

April nodded and ducked her head to slurp some lukewarm tea through the straw. Had this young woman cut her teeth on crazy April Hart stories? Did she recognize her?

Meg had been suspicious of April's story about rushing out to help a friend—not that she expected her cousin to believe anything she said, but that fabrication sounded more worthy than the fact that she'd run out on a wedding—again.

Mom's side of the family always slept with one eye open around her and Adam, as if they'd inherited Dad's killer gene or something. Not that she was totally convinced her father murdered her mother. They'd had their problems and Dad was always a scammer, but he'd also loved Mom—or he'd been an incredible actor... or a sociopath.

If Dad were really this El Gringo Viejo character like Adam thought, maybe he did kill Mom because she found out something. Like *she'd* found out about Jimmy.

"Your phone is charging." The waitress hovered over the table with a plate of food in one hand and a pitcher of iced tea in the other. "And here's your sandwich."

She placed the plate on the table and filled up the iced tea glass. "Do you want a cup of ice for that?"

"Sure, thanks." April whipped her napkin into her lap and picked up one half of her turkey sandwich.

The front door of the café swung open and April nearly choked on her first bite as Clay charged through the door, his dark hair already askew.

"Glad I found you." He held up his hand to the waitress. "Can you bring me a cola, Larissa?"

Clay dragged the chair out across from her, scraping it across the tile floor, and sat down. "You're not gonna believe this."

Still chewing, April pointed to her mouth. She swallowed and took a sip of tea. "You almost made me choke on my food when you barged in here. I don't want a repeat. What is going on?"

Clay gripped the edge of the table as if to brace himself. "That head we found yesterday on my porch?"

"Yeah, I remember it." She nabbed a spot of spicy mustard from the corner of her mouth with the tip of her tongue.

"It does not belong to the headless body at the border."

The room tilted and April twisted the napkin in her lap. "What do you mean? There's another body without a head out there and another head missing its body?"

"Exactly." He rubbed his knuckles across his jaw. "That's crazy, even for Paradiso, even so close to the border."

April pushed away her plate, one perfect bite missing from her sandwich. "I don't understand. How did they discover that so quickly? You told me the DNA would take a while."

"Espinoza doesn't have the DNA test back yet, but the medical examiner has determined that the body belongs to a young Latina and the head is that of an older, Caucasian woman."

Goose bumps raced up and down her arms and she folded them across her chest. "How is this even possible? And why was the older woman's head left on your porch when you found the body of the younger woman?"

"They're obviously connected, from the same hit. Maybe both women came through the tunnel, Las Moscas killed the younger one there, leaving her body and taking her head, and then murdered the other woman elsewhere, dumped her body and left her head for me—just to mess with us."

"It's pure evil, isn't it?" April rubbed her arms. "Do they think this is some kind of joke?"

"This is business, and they're deadly serious." He glanced up at the waitress. "Thanks, Larissa." He sucked down half his soda before coming up for air.

"How'd you track me down here?" She poked at her sandwich. Coming to Paradiso had seriously done a number on her appetite.

"Happened to see your car out front as I was driving through town, and I remember this used to be one of your favorite places. I wasn't sure you'd be back from Tucson yet."

She leaned back and ran her finger around the neck of her new T-shirt. "Picked up some clothes and bought a phone."

"Did you make the call yet?" He picked up the untouched half of her sandwich. "Are you going to eat this, or did I just ruin your appetite?"

"You can have it and my new phone is charging behind the counter, so I haven't called Jimmy yet." She drummed her fingers on the table next to her plate. "What does Espinoza think about the two murders?"

"Same." He waved the sandwich in the air. "It's obvious they're connected."

"Really? 'Cause this morning you thought it was obvious that the head belonged to the body by the border."

"Good point." He scooted the plate back in front of her. "I'm feeling guilty. Eat your lunch."

She picked up the sandwich and nibbled on the crust. "How is Espinoza going to ID the body, fingerprints?"

"That's first, but if she never committed a crime and she's a Mexican national, we may not get a hit. Missing persons, maybe."

The waitress swung by again. "Clay, do you want to order something? I'm off in five."

"I just demolished half of my...friend's sandwich. I'm good, but I'll take a refill on my soda before you leave."

Friends? Is that what they were?

April cleared her throat. "And I'll take my phone and the check."

"Oh, your phone. I'll get that for you."

Larissa spun away, and April wrinkled her nose. "She looks familiar. The name is familiar, too."

"Her family has lived here for some time. She was into the drug scene for a while, but I think she's clean now."

April hunched forward. "Then she probably knows who I am?"

"That you're my ex-fiancée or that you're the daughter of C. J. Hart?"

"Both. Either."

He shrugged, a quick lift and drop of his shoulders. "Don't be paranoid, April."

"If you say so."

"How'd it go with Meg?"

"All right, except she kept watching me as if she expected me to steal the silver—and she doesn't even have any silver."

"There you go again." He nudged her small purse at the edge of the table. "She must've fronted you a little money to get you back on your feet."

"She did, but she is living in my house rent free."

"You're letting her live there without paying you anything? That's generous of you. There's a little housing shortage in Paradiso due to the new pecan-processing plant. You could get some bucks for that house."

"I don't know." She dragged her new purse in front of her and unzipped it. "I feel like I kind of owe it to her."

"You're not responsible for what your father did."

"Or didn't do."

His mouth tightened. "You don't owe your mother's family anything, April, no matter how guilty they make you feel."

Larissa set another glass in front of Clay. "Your drink, and your phone."

"Thanks." April studied the woman's dark brown eyes and shy smile. Then she snapped her fingers. "I know you. You dated my brother, Adam Hart, for a while, didn't you?"

Larissa's eyes widened. "Yeah, I did. I didn't think you'd remember me, but I remembered you."

"Well, it's good to see you again." April scooped up the phone and waited while Larissa put down the check and left the table. "Maybe I should try calling Adam again, too."

"First things first. Give Jimmy a call and clear the air." Clay half rose from his chair. "I'll give you some privacy."

"I don't need privacy to talk to Jimmy." She waved him back to his seat and tapped Jimmy's number into the phone.

She held her breath through the first ring and second ring, hoping for a voice mail.

"Who's this?"

Jimmy's voice, abrupt and gravelly, made her jump. He'd put on a totally different act when they'd met, but he couldn't keep it up forever, and even before she overheard his conversation with Gilbert, doubts had crept into her mind.

"Jimmy, this is April. I—I just wanted to explain what happened and to apologize."

"Are you coming back home, April?" His voice softened and a pleading tone had crept into it.

She lined up her spine against the back of her chair. "No. No, I'm not coming back, Jimmy."

"Then you'd better return what you stole, bitch, or I'm comin' for you."

Chapter Six

April clutched the phone so hard its edges dug into her palm. "The ring? You want the ring back?"

"I'm not talking about the ring—cubic zirconium, anyway."

Jimmy chuckled, which caused her fear to spike even more. Had he missed that wooden token?

"I don't know what you're talking about, Jimmy. The dress? The wedding. I'll pay you back for all of it."

Clay had shifted in his seat and curled his hands into fists where they rested on the table.

"Don't play with me, April. You took the flash drive from my laptop—and I want it back."

She let out a slow breath. She didn't take any flash drive, didn't even see one in the laptop on the desk. "I didn't take your flash drive. Why would I do that?"

Clay cocked his head, and she shrugged.

Jimmy paused. "You were in my office yesterday morning before you took off. I know you were. I found some beads or whatever from the wedding gown. So, you must've been dressed for the wedding and decided to snoop on me. Why?"

April swallowed. This had to be a good turn of events. He didn't seem sure that she knew about his business—and she wanted to keep it that way.

"I went into your office looking for you, to tell you I was having second thoughts. Who knows? If I had found you there, maybe you could've talked me off the ledge, but you weren't there and I left. That's it, Jimmy. I wasn't snooping on you. I didn't take any flash drive."

"Have you talked to Adam?"

"He called me yesterday just to make sure I was okay. We didn't talk long."

"How'd he reach you? I've been trying your phone ever since I realized you'd skipped out. You ditched it or it's not turned on."

"I'd rather not say, Jimmy. It's over and I'll be happy to pay you what I owe you for the wedding—even the cheap ring—but I didn't take anything from you and I'm not coming back. Why is this flash drive so important, anyway, and why would I want to take it?"

Clay kicked her under the table and she wagged a finger at him. She had to keep pretending she had no idea the nature of his business. She'd asked a normal question from an innocent person.

"Important information about my import/export business, and I know you were always asking questions about it."

"Just out of curiosity. I'm sorry someone took the flash drive but it seems like you're more upset about the missing flash drive than your missing bride, so it appears that I made the right decision. Goodbye, Jimmy."

Before he could answer, she ended the call and closed her eyes, the phone cradled between her hands.

"What the hell was that all about?"

She opened one eye and peered at Clay. "He doesn't know. He thinks I stole some flash drive because he knew I had been in his office, but he seemed to believe me when I told him I hadn't taken it."

"As far as he let on." He traced a bead of moisture on the outside of his glass. "I get that you didn't want to show your hand, but he didn't, either. He may still think you took the flash drive, but didn't want to get into a back-and-forth with you on the phone."

April plucked the straw from her iced tea glass and nibbled on the end. "I wonder what's on the flash drive."

"What did he say? You asked him."

"Business stuff." She tapped the straw against her tooth, flicking droplets of liquid on the table. "I'll bet it's business stuff. I wonder who took it. One of his so-called friends probably."

"You don't think Adam stole it, do you?"

A feather of apprehension brushed the back of her neck. That had crossed her mind as soon as Jimmy mentioned the theft, but she'd pushed it away as disloyalty.

"Why would Adam steal info about Jimmy's business?"

"C'mon, April. This is Adam we're talking about. If he could get rich quick, he'd do it and damn the torpedoes. What better way than to butt in on someone's drug trade."

Heat flared in her cheeks. "Adam wouldn't…"

She trailed off in the face of Clay's hard stare. He'd never had any patience for her coddling of Adam. He would always take her side over Adam's.

"You know he would, April. Didn't he set you up with Jimmy? Why'd he do that? Why'd he facilitate a relationship between you and a drug dealer?" Clay slammed his fist on the table. "If I ever get my hands on that boy, he's really gonna need the drugs."

Sighing, April buried her chin in the palm of her hand. "You don't understand him."

"I know he found your mom in a pool of blood,

stabbed to death." Clay traced his knuckle down her forearm to her elbow planted on the table. "He went through hell, but he didn't have to drag you along with him. You had your own hell to deal with."

"I'm not saying I forgive him for setting me up with Jimmy, but that doesn't mean he stole the flash drive. He'd have to know that Jimmy would think I did it."

"Yeah."

She fished some money from her purse, and Clay closed his hand around her fingers. "You'd better keep that until you pick up your debit and credit cards or get them replaced." He pulled out his own wallet and tossed some bills on the table. "Any chance that brother of yours can send your stuff to you? ID, cards, clothes?"

"I don't think that's going to happen. As long as Jimmy believes me, I'm safe enough. I can take a drive back up to Albuquerque and collect my stuff myself. I have a debt to pay back up that way, anyway."

"You're not really going to reimburse Jimmy for the wedding, the dress and the cheap ring, are you?"

"No, but I used that cheap ring to buy a car, and now the poor seller is out a car and the cash. I'm sure he got a rude surprise when he tried to hock the ring."

"You told me you borrowed that car from a friend." Clay's lips twisted into a half smile. "What other lies have you told me, April Hart?"

April kept her head down as she stuffed her cash back into the purse in her lap.

You have no idea, Clay Archer.

CLAY LEFT APRIL at her car with assurances from her that she wouldn't head back to New Mexico without him. He had to question his own sanity for getting involved with April again, but he couldn't just abandon her. She'd gotten mixed up with some dangerous folks and even if she were convinced Jimmy Verdugo had let her off the hook, he wasn't.

When he got back to the office, it was still buzzing with the news that the head and body didn't match. He didn't want to think about where that other head was going to turn up. Maybe on another agent's porch. And the other body? It could be anywhere in the desert.

He sat down behind his desk and two minutes later Valdez plopped down in a chair across from him.

"What do you make of it, Archer? There must've been two mules coming across the border."

"Looks like it." Clay kicked his feet up on the corner of his desk. "Two mules who were sent to intercept a shipment designated for Las Moscas. Two sacrifices. Whoever planned this had to know it was a death sentence for the mules."

"Canaries in a coal mine?" Valdez steepled his fingers and gazed over the tips like some kind of drug muse. "They send these two unsuspecting women to do the dirty work to see if they could get away with stealing from Las Moscas. Next time they'll try something else."

"You're probably right, Valdez." Clay dropped his feet to the floor and flipped up the lid of his laptop. "I'm gonna do some work. Did you finish the report from last night yet?"

Valdez reddened to the roots of his hair as he pushed up to his feet. "I did not. I just got the sheriff's report today. Do you want to check it over before I submit it?"

"Your last report was good. I trust you."

When Valdez had tripped off with a smile engulfing the bottom half of his face, Clay began tapping away on his keyboard.

Surely, April had done a cursory search for Jimmy Verdugo. She wouldn't date and then decide to marry some guy without doing a little research first. She didn't have the same resources he did, but she would've been able to search for a criminal record.

The woman had impulsive tendencies, but she had a healthy dose of skepticism. The only way she could've wound up so deep with Jimmy is if Adam engineered the whole thing.

April made the mistake of seeing her brother as a hapless druggie with PTSD. Adam might be a junkie with PTSD, but he was far from hapless. He used April with a cunning that she refused to acknowledge.

Clay had no doubt Adam had fed info to Jimmy about April—her likes, her dislikes, her wants, her needs. But why had April been so willing to marry someone…even if he were the perfect guy?

She'd twisted his heart and wrung it dry so thoroughly he didn't know if he could ever love another again. In fact, here he was, ready to do her bidding, ready to protect her. And in the end, she'd walk away from him.

Clay accessed the NCIC database and entered Jimmy Verdugo's name. He cocked his head at the display. None of these people could be a match for April's Jimmy. His mouth tightened. No, *not* April's Jimmy.

Even though his search of Jimmy had returned some James Verdugos, he entered James for the criteria this time.

He stared at the same results and sucked in his bottom lip. How did an associate of Las Moscas have a clean criminal record?

Maybe Jimmy hadn't been in this country long

enough to have a record here. April hadn't mentioned if he'd been born here or not.

Clay's fingers hovered over the keyboard. He didn't have any probable cause on the guy to request a report from Interpol on any activities in another country.

He shouldn't even be using NCIC for personal look-ups, but he could always justify his actions based on the carved fly April had found in Jimmy's office.

Taking a deep breath, he switched to a different database and did a search on El Gringo Viejo. Several releases popped up, but no pictures. Nobody had ever taken a photograph of El Gringo Viejo—at least not that they knew of.

Where had Adam gotten the crazy idea that his father was El Gringo Viejo? Clay squinted at the small print of the reports online. The dates did match up and C. J. Hart probably did cross the border after murdering his wife, but what else did Adam have?

If he could get his hands on April's brother, he'd interrogate him—after he got finished thrashing him.

The ringing of his office phone jarred his thoughts, and he picked it up after the first ring.

"Clay, this is Dr. Drew. Denali is more than ready to come home."

Clay's gaze darted to the time at the bottom corner of his screen. "Sorry, Dr. Drew. I didn't realize how late it was."

"No problem. I have him at the office with me and we'll be here for another few hours."

"I'll leave right now."

Clay hung up the phone and started to pack up his gear for the day. Denali would be overjoyed to see April. That dog loved her and would never forget her.

Clay snorted. Like master like dog.

APRIL SECURED HER purchases in the trunk of the car that really didn't belong to her. Poor Ryan. He'd probably gone to the pawn shop, found out the real worth of the ring and figured she'd double-crossed him.

On the way back to Albuquerque, she'd try to find Ryan and return the car—or buy it from him. Adam had been borrowing her car, and she'd left the fancy wheels Jimmy had bought her parked in his garage. Knowing what she knew now, Jimmy probably never bought her that car. It was either a lease or a purchase in his name.

How could she have been so stupid? She'd been manipulated by both Adam and Jimmy. This had to be the last straw with her brother. He'd done nothing but take from her, but she'd made it easy for him. She'd given up so much for him and had gotten nothing but betrayal in return.

Once she got back to New Mexico, she could make herself whole again—pick up her identity, literally— and start again.

And Clay? There had been no expiration date on that threat two years ago. Back in Paradiso, someone could be watching her right now.

She glanced over her shoulder as she got into her car.

Meg would still be at work at the pecan-processing plant, thank goodness. April didn't need her cousin's judgment right now—and Meg didn't even know about the ditched wedding.

April pulled up outside the neat, white picket fence surrounding a garden of succulents. The cacti had already shed their spring flowers, but their prickly stoicism always struck an answering chord in her heart. There they stood with their arms raised through the scorching desert heat, the dry winds and even the monsoons that swept through southern Arizona in the fall.

Tears welled in her eyes. This garden had been her mother's pride and joy. Her mother had been a transplant to the arid Sonoran Desert, deficient in rolling green lawns and neat concrete driveways and delicate dewy flowers, so Mom had created her own oasis, drawing from the beauty of the desert.

April sniffed and exited the car. She circled around the back to collect her packages, and then swung through the front gate.

She strode up the brick walkway, her step faltering as she caught sight of a brown box on the porch. She puffed out a breath. Meg told her she ordered a lot of items online to save trips into Tucson.

She wouldn't have even experienced that small frisson of fear that zipped through her veins if Clay hadn't found her in the coffee shop this afternoon and told her about the second body.

She rolled her shoulders back and continued to approach the porch. She took one step up, shook out the house key Meg had given her earlier and nudged the box with her toe. It didn't look like a delivery, as it had no address label.

She kicked the box. It jumped an inch. A trickle of blood seeped from the bottom.

Chapter Seven

Clay punched the accelerator of his truck and it lurched forward from the stop sign, causing Denali to slide off the seat.

"Sorry, boy." Clay patted the passenger seat and Denali scrambled back onto it.

What the hell was going on in this town? Why would someone leave that head on April's porch?

The perpetrators must still be in Paradiso. They'd connected April to him somehow, and decided to double down on their message. What was their message if not a threat?

His foot pressed on the gas pedal and his truck growled in response. Denali panted beside him, their reunion cut short when he got the call from Espinoza about April finding a head in a box on her porch. She must be regretting her visit to Paradiso even more now.

He rolled past her address and kept going, as emergency vehicles clogged the street in front of her house. The scene must remind her of the night Adam found their mother's body on the kitchen floor, and his heart ached for her all over again.

He parked the truck and slid out. He came around and opened the door for Denali. If he didn't let him out, the dog would be howling and eventually scratch through the door.

Denali kept up with Clay's long stride, undeterred by the lights and activity, nose in the air, ears pricked forward. Did he smell April already?

Clay spotted her talking to Detective Espinoza, her arms folded, her face a pale oval. Denali must've detected her at the same time because he tore away from Clay's side, making a beeline for April.

When she saw the dog running toward her, April dropped to her knees and wrapped her arms around his squirming body, burying her face in his gray-and-white fur.

When she looked up to meet Clay's eyes, tears streaked her face, but a wide smile claimed her lips. "He looks great."

To reward the compliment, Denali licked the tears from April's face.

Clay shifted his gaze to Espinoza. "Is it our girl from the border?"

"Without any scientific proof, I'd say it is. The head belongs to a young Latina. I paid attention this time, but maybe I shouldn't make any assumptions."

Clay swore. "Two heads, one body down, one body to go. What kind of game are they playing and why involve April?"

"They must've seen her with you, although why Las Moscas is targeting you is puzzling." Espinoza eyed him beneath the brim of his hat as if inspecting a bug.

"Hey, I have no clue." Clay held up his hands. "If you think I've been on their payroll or something, you're welcome to check me out. Do a full investigation. You won't find anything."

"Don't get your back up, but if you can think of any

reason why Las Moscas would be more interested in you than any other Border Patrol agent in the area, let me know."

"Maybe because I'm one of the few who lives in Paradiso. What surprises me is that someone is still lurking around depositing body parts in town. Usually, strangers are executing strangers at the border and leaving us to clean up after them."

April popped up beside them, brushing her hands together. "Has anyone notified my cousin yet? She should be home from work soon and she's going to be freaked out by all this. Do you think at least the head will be gone by the time she gets home?"

"April." Clay took her by the shoulders. "You don't need to worry about Meg right now. Are you all right?"

She swiped a hand beneath her red-tipped nose. "It was like déjà vu all over again—only the box wasn't as pretty this time. At least I knew enough not to pick it up, so the head didn't go bounding down the walkway."

The glassy blue of her eyes and the slight quiver to her bottom lip were the only contradictions to her flip words.

His fingers caressed her flesh beneath the light cotton of the blue T-shirt that matched her eyes. "I'm sorry you had to go through this again. It's my fault they left that for you."

"It's not your fault. It's your job." She addressed Espinoza. "Do you have the right head this time?"

"We think so, but we'll run the tests to make sure." Espinoza pointed down the street. "The Paradiso PD officers canvassed the neighborhood and, just like at your place, Archer, nobody saw a thing."

"If someone did, do you really think they'd step forward?" Clay scratched the top of Denali's head, still shaking with joy at his reunion with April. "People around here are familiar with Las Moscas. They're going to keep their heads down and not interfere with business. They don't want the violence at the border creeping up here."

A wail from the street had Denali stiffening and pointing his head, nostrils quivering a mile a minute.

"Oh, boy. Here comes Meg." April adjusted her position, pulling her shoulders back and widening her stance as if getting ready for a tackle.

Denali got ready, too, leaving Clay's side to take up his position in front of April.

Meg came bobbing and weaving up the walkway as if trying to gain purchase on the deck of a ship, a helpless Paradiso PD officer trailing in her wake, hand outstretched.

"A head? Did I hear that right? A head was on my porch?" Meg, all five feet of her, steamrolled up to Detective Espinoza. "Somebody out there told me a head was on my porch."

Espinoza, his face impassive, asked, "Are you the owner of the house, ma'am?"

"No, but I live here." Meg flung out an arm toward April. "She owns the house."

Meg stopped flapping her lips, froze and then turned toward April. "This is you, isn't it? You come back to Paradiso and heads start appearing on porches wherever you are."

Denali emitted a little growl. He'd never bitten anyone in his life, but he just might make an exception if Meg continued her verbal assault on April.

"Whoa, wait a minute, Meg." Clay took a step between her and April. "This is all me. It has something to do with a body of a mule we found at the border yesterday."

Meg's light-colored eyes flicked in his direction. "You *would* say that."

"It's the truth, Ms….?" Espinoza's question hung in the air unanswered. "These are two dead women, involved in the drug trade, murdered by a drug cartel. They're just trying to make some point with Agent Archer and probably saw him with Ms. Hart. I don't think you have anything to worry about."

Clay gave Espinoza a sharp glance. He wouldn't go that far. "Look, Meg. I'm going to get a security system installed at my house with cameras. I'll do the same for this house."

Her eyes bugged out. "Because you think this will happen again?"

"No, no, but it's not a bad idea, is it?" Clay turned to April and rolled his eyes.

Espinoza cleared his throat. "Ma'am, since you live here, can I ask you a few questions about any unusual activity you may have seen in the neighborhood starting yesterday?"

"Of course." Meg pointed a trembling finger at the box on her porch, roped off with yellow tape. "Is that it?"

"It is. We'll have it out of here shortly." Espinoza touched Meg's upper arm. "Can we talk over here?"

Meg followed Espinoza to his car.

"Well, that wasn't too bad." April scratched Denali behind one ear. "Were you ready to take her on, Denny?"

Denali's tongue lolled out of his mouth as his big eyes, one blue, one brown, looked adoringly at April. He clearly remembered her nickname for him, which Clay hadn't used since she left.

Clay coughed. "When everyone's out of here, I'm not comfortable leaving you and Meg on your own."

Hitching a thumb in the front pocket of her jeans, April said, "Does that mean you're going to assign Denali to guard duty?"

"That means I'm going to hang around for a while, if that's okay. I don't think you'll see any more trouble. I didn't, but a member of a drug cartel knows where you live and decided to put a severed head on your porch."

"I do still have my gun at the house." She tilted her head at him. "And I know how to use it because a hotshot Border Patrol agent taught me."

"It probably needs to be cleaned. Do you even have bullets for it?"

"He taught me how to do that, too, and I'll look for the bullets or buy them." She fondled Denali's ear. "But I wouldn't mind the watchdog."

Clay leveled a finger at her. "You're going to take the bodyguard along with the watchdog."

"Before, you asked me if it was okay if you stayed— now you're telling me?"

"I didn't think you'd reject my offer. I'll even pick up dinner for you two."

"You're going to make Meg very, very nervous."

April gazed past his shoulder, and he cranked his head around to watch Meg, body stiff, arms waving around as if casting a spell. She probably would cast a spell on April if she could.

"Let me handle Meg."

"Better you than me."

An hour later, the last official vehicle pulled away from the house, leaving behind the yellow police tape and some fingerprint powder on the gate and the porch.

Meg strolled down the two steps, making a wide

berth around the spot where April had found the box. "When are you getting those security systems, Clay?"

"Tomorrow. I'll install yours first and then mine. I'll get some advice, but I'm thinking cameras, motion-sensor lights, the works."

"Can you get one of those setups where I can tune in on my phone and watch what's going on?" Meg glanced at April.

"Don't look at me. I'm not going to be hanging around Paradiso much longer."

Her words pricked his heart.

"April's going to go back to Albuquerque to get the rest of her stuff, and I'm going with her."

Meg's eyes narrowed. "I thought you hightailed it out of there to help a friend in trouble. You're actually moving from Albuquerque?"

"Yes." April grabbed Clay's arm. "Clay has offered to buy us dinner tonight, Meg. I accepted on your behalf."

"I'm not going out. I'm exhausted." She jingled her keys. "I am going to move my car into the driveway, though."

"We're not going out, either. I'm getting takeout. Any preferences?"

Meg's gaze shifted from his face to April's, a crease forming between her eyes. "Because you're worried?"

"Let's just call it cautious." He held out his hand. "I'll move your car around, and then I'll get some Chinese."

"Chinese is fine. I'll eat anything, but I'm not liking this. I'll feel better when we get the cameras up and running." Meg poked April's arm. "Are you going with him, or are you going to stay here?"

"I'll stay here—me and Denali." April hunched forward and patted her thigh. "C'mon, boy. Let's go inside."

As Clay swung through the front gate, he made a half turn. "Kung pao chicken and orange peel beef for you?"

"Absolutely. You remembered."

The two women disappeared inside the house with Denali at their heels.

Clay let the gate slam behind him and murmured, "I remember everything."

Once inside the house, April rummaged through the bags she'd brought in earlier. "I did some shopping in Tucson and bought a few things."

"Seeing that head on the porch must've been horrible for you." Meg leaned her hip against the arm of the couch. "I'm sorry you found it."

April ducked her head inside one of her bags. "Would've been worse if you'd found it."

"Because I didn't see my mother murdered?" Meg clicked her tongue. "That doesn't make you immune to atrocities, April. I would think it would bring back memories and stress you out."

"Better to have all that stress going to one person instead of spreading it around." April popped up and shook out a blouse. "Pretty, isn't it?"

"Yeah, pretty." Meg shook her head. "How did the reunion with Clay go?"

April sat back on her heels, her lips twisting into a smile. "Not as well as the reunion with Denali."

The dog, hearing his name, thumped his tail but didn't move from his spot in front of the empty fireplace.

"Can you blame him?" Meg kicked off her shoes and

padded into the kitchen on bare feet. "I need a glass of wine after that horror show. You?"

"What goes with Chinese food?"

"All I drink is white, so I guess white." Meg pulled open the fridge and emerged with an open, corked bottle of wine. "Did you ever give the poor guy a reason why you ran out on the wedding? Did you *have* a reason?"

Nobody but Adam knew the real reason, and April didn't plan on revealing anything now—especially with these heads and bodies showing up.

April's hands convulsively clutched at the material of the blouse in her hands. This wave of violence couldn't have anything to do with that prior threat, could it? No, Clay had found that body by the border before she even arrived in Paradiso. Nobody had known she was going to show up here—except Adam. He'd figured it out.

"I had my reasons, Meg, and I don't want to talk about them." She plunged her hand into another bag and dangled a pair of stone-colored capris from her fingers. "Cute?"

"I'm sure they look cute on you." Meg took a swig of wine from her glass and set another on the end table for April. "Everything does."

"Aw, thanks, cuz." April gathered the bags and pushed to her feet. "I'm going to put these away, and then I'll join you for that wine."

She walked to her bedroom on knees that still trembled. As if sensing her shakiness, Denali popped up and trotted after her.

April put away the new clothes and washed her face and hands before joining Meg. Denali stayed by her side, determined to keep her in his sight. She'd missed the silly pooch almost as much as she'd missed Clay.

"Here you go." Meg thrust a glass at her as she returned to the living room.

April sat on one side of the couch, curling a leg beneath her, and cupped the wineglass with both hands.

"First, a toast." Meg raised her glass. "To no more drama."

April clinked her glass with her cousin's. "I'll drink to that."

"There's never a dull moment living down here, is there?"

"Or maybe it's just our family." April took a sip of the wine, lolling the citrusy flavor on her tongue before swallowing.

"Where are you headed once you collect your stuff from Albuquerque?"

"I'm not sure yet, maybe back to LA."

"You're not going to stick around and give Clay another chance?"

April snorted. "I'm sure Clay's finished with me."

Meg threw her head back and laughed at the ceiling. "Right. Not even Denali believes that."

The knock on the door made them both jump, and Denali scrambled to his feet.

"Must be Clay." April pointed at Denali's wagging tail. She nudged Denali aside and peered through the peephole. Swinging open the door, she said, "The man and the kung pao."

"That's me." Clay held up the bags and shuffled across the threshold, scooting Denali out of the way.

Meg turned off the TV and strolled into the kitchen. "Glass of wine?"

"Sure. I gotta tell you, word travels fast in this town."

"News of the second head out already?" April took

the bags from Clay and followed Meg. Was it too soon to ask for a second glass of wine?

"Yeah, there's some grim competition going on to find the other body."

"Ugh." April swung the bags onto the counter, once again feeling her appetite recede.

"Let's talk about something else." Meg thrust a wineglass at Clay, and the golden liquid sloshed over the rim.

Clay tipped his head. "Got it."

Sitting on the floor, gathered around Meg's coffee table, the three of them managed to avoid the subject of heads, headless bodies, drugs and the border for the entirety of their meal, finishing the last of it by cracking open fortune cookies and assigning absurd meanings to the fortunes within.

Meg wiped a tear from her eye and drained her third glass of wine. "Oh, wow, I needed that."

"The wine or the laughter?" Clay tapped her glass with his chopstick.

"Both." Meg yawned. "I'm going to fall into a deep sleep tonight."

"Otherwise known as passing out." April crawled on the floor toward Meg and took her arm, pulling her up. "You go to bed. Clay and I will clean up."

"You're welcome to stay the night, Clay. Both of the extra beds are made up, or you can stay in someone else's bed." Meg gave an exaggerated wink, distorting her mouth in the process.

April's cheeks warmed, and she tugged harder at Meg's arm. "You're tipsy, cuz. Off to bed with you."

Meg giggled as she staggered to her feet and weaved down the hallway.

"Lightweight." Clay held up Meg's empty glass to the light.

"She did drink more than both of us put together." April collected the rest of the glasses and dishes. "She needed it. She comes across as feisty but the head really spooked her."

"And you?"

Clay touched her arm, the pressure of his fingertips making her weak in the knees all over again—but in a good way.

"I'm okay. I didn't see anything this time except a little blood. No more images to add to my nightmares."

"Do you still have nightmares?" The touch on her arm turned to a featherlight brush.

"Not often."

"Do you want me to stay? In another room, of course."

"I think Meg would like that. If she mentioned it, she meant it." She stepped away from the warmth that emanated from his body and carried the dishes into the kitchen.

He followed her like she knew he would and leaned against the counter. "And you?"

"I think both Meg and I would feel safer with you and Denali here tonight." She dumped the dishes in the sink. "Do you want to help me with these?"

"You rinse, and I'll put them in the dishwasher."

They worked well together, just as they always had in the past, and it all felt so natural. She wanted this again. She wanted Clay. She'd been a fool to believe Jimmy could ever replace him.

She held out the last plate. "That's it. Do you want me to search through Meg's cupboards for a toothbrush?"

As he took the plate, he curled his fingers around hers. "I missed you."

Tears pricked the backs of her eyes and she blinked. She couldn't do this with him.

She slid her hands from the plate, grabbed a dish towel and flicked it at Denali's head. "I think he did, too."

Clay's jaw tightened as he hunched over the dishwasher to put away the plate. "Don't blame me if he jumps on your bed to sleep with you tonight."

"I'd like that." April spun away from Clay. "I'd like that a lot."

Too bad he meant the dog and not him.

THE FOLLOWING MORNING, April got up when she heard Meg banging around in the kitchen. She'd barely gotten any sleep the night before, anyway—between visions of headless bodies and the thought of Clay's very real body in the next room, she couldn't turn off her mind.

She crept up behind her cousin. "How are you feeling?"

Meg yelped and dropped a coffee cup, which hit the tile floor and cracked. "Oh my God. Why are you sneaking up on me?"

"I'm sorry." April crouched down and retrieved the broken pieces of the cup. "I figured you'd have a hangover. I was trying to be quiet."

"I do have a hangover, and I still have to go to work."

April patted Meg's back. "Sit down. I'll get your coffee."

"Did you and Clay kiss and make up last night?"

"Of course not." April threw a little pink packet of sweetener at Meg. "He was here to protect us."

"Yeah, okay." Meg's eyes widened. "Good morning, Clay. Did we wake you?"

"Sounded like you two were throwing glasses around

in here." He curled one arm behind his head and patted his flat belly as he yawned.

"Just an accident." April pointed to the pieces of glass on the counter. "How'd you sleep?"

"Great, without Denali crowding me. You?"

"Fine—with Denali crowding me."

Meg heaved a sigh. "Can you please pour that coffee into my commuter mug? I have to get out of here. When are you two going to Albuquerque?"

Clay answered, "Tomorrow morning. I have a few days off, but don't worry. I'll get your security system installed first."

"That would be great."

"Do you want me to leave Denali behind with you when we go to Albuquerque? He can serve as another layer of protection, and it would be easier for me and April to drive without him."

"About that." April set Meg's mug in front of her. "We'll have to take separate cars. I need to get that car back to its rightful owner."

Meg's hand jerked as she stirred the sweetener in her coffee. "Wait, you stole that car?"

"Not exactly."

Meg raised her hand. "That's enough. I'm off to work…and I'd be happy to take care of your dog."

When the front door slammed behind her, a heavy silence hung over the room.

April cleared her throat. "Do you want me to watch Denali while you're at work? We have some catching up to do."

"Are you going to stick around here all day, or do you want to stay at my place? Denali needs to eat."

"We can stay at your place, and I'll feed him." She held up her coffee mug. "Do you want some coffee?"

"No, thanks. I'll wait for you to get ready, and you can follow me over to my place. I'll shower and change there, and then leave you and Denali to your own devices."

She flicked her fingers. "You two can get a head start. I'll come over when I'm ready."

"Are you sure you're okay to stay here alone?" Clay spread his hands. "I didn't want to leave you alone."

"I won't be alone." She put her cup in the sink. "Leave Denali with me. I'm going to get my gun out, too. You can help me clean it and load it sometime today."

Someone knocked on the door and Denali growled.

"See how good he is?" April patted Denali's head on the way to answer the door, but Clay grabbed her arm. "Let me."

He leaned into the peephole and nodded. "Perfect timing. It's Charlie Santiago from Paradiso PD."

Clay opened the door. "Hey, Charlie."

"You here already, Clay? Doing some investigating?"

"No, I'm going back out to the site where we found the first body. You here to do some more canvassing?" Clay widened the door to include April in the conversation.

"Hello, Ms. Hart. I hope you and your cousin had an uneventful evening."

"It was. Clay's leaving and is nervous about my being here by myself. Can you let him know you can keep an eye on the house for the next thirty minutes or so?"

"No problem. I'll be in the neighborhood for about an hour." He adjusted his equipment belt, the leather creaking and handcuffs jingling. "I'll keep a lookout for anything suspicious."

"Problem solved." Clay winked at her. "Don't take too long."

With Clay gone, Charlie the cop patrolling the neighborhood and Denali parked outside the bathroom door, April showered, allowing the knot in her belly to loosen.

She grabbed her new purse and exited the house. She waved at Charlie in his patrol car as she patted the passenger seat of her ill-gotten vehicle and Denali jumped inside.

Before she started the engine, she tried calling Adam. Again, his phone rang without rolling over to voice mail. She tried a text and watched the display for the notification that it had been delivered. That notification never came through.

Why was he offline? Had Jimmy threatened him? Did Adam know who took Jimmy's flash drive?

Denali whined beside her and she touched his nose and said, "My brother's a mystery, Denali."

By the time she got to Clay's place, he'd already showered and changed into a fresh uniform. He'd always looked good in the Border Patrol greens that matched his hazel eyes. Hell, Clay Archer would look hot in a clown suit.

He shook a dog dish full of dry food. "I already got Denali's breakfast ready and changed his water outside. Just add a little warm water to his kibble when he's ready to eat."

"You're going to work and then to the hardware store to get the security systems?"

"Work, back here for lunch to check on you two and then to my friend's place. He installs the systems and I can get a couple from him. Will you be back here at noon?"

"I'll make sure of it. I'll even make us some lunch."

"What do you plan to do this morning?"

"I meant what I said. I'm going to get reacquainted with Denali—and try to reach my brother."

Clay raised his eyebrows. "No word from Adam?"

"Nope." She pushed her hair from her face. "Maybe he doesn't realize I called Jimmy and doesn't want to have any contact with me in case Jimmy finds out."

"You called Adam from your new phone, didn't you?"

"Yeah."

"Adam doesn't know that number. He wouldn't know to avoid it."

"I also texted him, letting him know it's me."

"Keep at it. I'm curious to find out what he knows about that flash drive."

"You'd better get going. Denali and I have things to do."

"Don't make him adore you more than he already does. You're gonna break his doggy heart when you leave again."

April swallowed hard. "Denali and I have an understanding."

"If you say so." Clay jerked his thumb over his shoulder. "I took out the supplies to clean your gun and left them on a workbench in the garage, if you're serious."

She patted the small backpack she borrowed from Meg. "Oh, I'm serious. I have my piece with me."

One corner of Clay's mouth turned up. "Okay, then you should probably clean your...piece."

"Go ahead and laugh. You know I'm a good shot."

"I know you are. Just be careful."

"With the gun...or everything else?"

"In general."

"I think the heads are just some kind of message to you. I don't think Meg and I have to worry."

"Probably not." He hitched his bag over his shoulder. "I don't like the idea that these people know you're connected to me somehow and followed you home. It means they're still here—watching."

She tightened her grip on the strap of the backpack. "I don't like it, either, but I'll be safe with Denali and my gun, once I get it ready."

"Then I'll see you at lunch." He waved on his way out the door.

April fed Denali, cleaned and loaded her gun, and then slipped into Clay's office where he had a tablet charging on his desk.

He didn't have a password on the computer, so she launched a browser and started a search for El Gringo Viejo. After scanning past a few results for Mexican restaurants, she zeroed in on a couple articles about the mysterious drug supplier in Mexico.

This guy didn't have the fame or notoriety of some of the other big-time drug lords—no fancy villas, no fancy girlfriends. In fact, nobody knew where he lived. Nobody knew what he looked like. Nobody knew much about how he operated.

Where would Adam get the idea that El Gringo Viejo was their father? Why would he tell Jimmy? None of it made any sense.

The articles didn't provide much information, certainly not enough to head down to Mexico on a fact-finding mission. Of course, if she went down there and let the word drop in a few circles that the daughter of El Gringo Viejo was searching for him, she might just get a hit. Or take a hit.

What did she hope to accomplish by finding her father? If he really were El Gringo Viejo, wouldn't that shoot her theory all to hell that he never murdered Mom? It would, in fact, confirm his guilt.

Sighing, she slumped in the chair. She'd just gotten out of a sticky situation with Jimmy. Clay was right. She should put this all behind her and move on—put Clay behind her, too. What was the shelf life for threats? She didn't want to find out.

Denali whined at her feet, and she kicked off a sandal and ran the bottom of her foot across the soft fur on his back. "Are you ready to go for a walk, boy?"

His ears cocked forward and his tail wagged in response.

She'd missed having a dog. Jimmy had claimed he was allergic. That should've been a sign right there.

She collected Denali's leash and stuffed a plastic bag in the pocket of her capris. She hooked him up and set out for the pecan groves about a half mile from Clay's house.

Nash Dillon's family owned this particular grove in addition to the one surrounding his house, had owned this land for years. Her sandals scuffed against the dirt, and she unclipped Denali's leash from his collar so he could roam a little bit.

April inhaled the slightly sour scent of the trees and soaked in the dry heat that seemed to permeate her skin and warm her bones. She could've been happy in Paradiso with Clay if her life hadn't taken a hard left turn her senior year of college.

If her father hadn't stabbed her mother to death in their kitchen. If her fragile little brother hadn't found the body. If she hadn't had to clean up everyone else's messes.

Denali's sharp bark pierced the air as he appeared

through the trees as if chasing a rabbit—or running from something.

He skidded to a stop in front of her, the fur on his back standing on end. He twirled around to face the grove that had just spit him out. His lip curled, one tooth hooked over his lip, but he remained silent, his entire body quivering.

His fear reached out to her, causing a chill to sweep across her flesh. "What is it, boy? Something coming after you?"

She tipped her sunglasses to the edge of her nose and peered through the trees. Maybe nothing was chasing him. Maybe he'd found something.

"Did you see something? Dig something up?" She shivered despite the heat beating on her shoulders.

Could there be another head? They seemed to be following her around in this town since she arrived. Maybe not another head, but there was definitely another body out there.

Crouching down, she attached Denali's leash to his collar and gave him a little yank. She had no intention of finding a woman's headless body out here on her own.

"C'mon, Denali."

He offered no resistance, scampering ahead of her, leading her from the grove.

She glanced over her shoulder once. "You and me both, Denali. Let's see what your dad has for lunch."

By the time she reached Clay's house, her heart rate had returned to normal. All kinds of things spooked dogs. It didn't have to be a dead body.

She filled Denali's water dish and gave him a quick brush before washing her hands and inspecting Clay's kitchen. For a bachelor, he had a halfway decent supply of regular food. Yeah, he had plenty of beer and a fair number of take-out containers with questionable contents, but he did have fresh vegetables and some eggs still within their date of expiration.

She whipped up a couple of omelets and mixed a salad of tomatoes, cucumbers and avocados. By the time Clay came through the door, she'd added a vase of flowers to the kitchen table and poured two glasses of iced tea.

He swept off his hat, his gaze bouncing from the table to her face. "You didn't have to go through all this trouble."

"No trouble. I can't believe how nicely those flowers are growing out back in this weather."

"You planted them." He swung his bag onto the kitchen table and the flowers wobbled on their stems. "I just keep watering them like you told me to."

"You do have a green thumb, Clay Archer."

Holding up his thumb, he inspected it. "I'm just good at following orders."

"Well, so am I." She ignored his eye roll. "I cleaned my gun with the stuff you left in the garage, took Denali out for a walk and managed to scrape some food together for lunch."

"Looks good." He unbuckled his equipment belt, which sagged on his hips. "I'm gonna wash my hands and dig in. Called my friend with the security business. He's going to help me outfit both houses."

"I'll pay for his services at my house."

He cranked his head over his shoulder as he scrubbed his hands beneath the kitchen faucet. "We'll take care of it. I feel like I owe Meg something for bringing that to her home…your home. What is that arrangement, anyway?"

"She'll stay there until I decide if I want to sell the

house or not." April pulled out a chair at the table, tucking the strap of Clay's bag beneath the satchel.

"You don't have to check with Adam?"

"Adam doesn't own the house. I do." She picked up a fork. "I—I mean I'll share the money with him if I sell it."

"Why should you?" Clay took a seat at the table and flicked the cloth napkin into his lap. "That's not what your mother intended, is it? That's why you got all her life insurance money, too. She didn't trust Adam with the money."

April nibbled on her bottom lip. "I was never able to reach him today. I want to check on him tomorrow when we go to Albuquerque."

"I sure hope Verdugo didn't find out that Adam took that flash drive."

"I don't think Adam would be that stupid to nab Jimmy's property—whatever it contains."

Clay snorted but refrained from commenting as he dug into his omelet. "Tell me about Denali's walk. Did you take him to the pecan grove?"

"Yes, but he saw something that spooked him. Ran back to me all in a tizzy, fur sticking up."

"Always happens." Clay plucked a glob of melted cheese from his plate and held it under the table for Denali.

"You spoil him."

"You should talk." Clay waved his fork over the table. "This is great, thanks."

"The least I could do." *Considering I ran out on our wedding.*

When Clay ignored Denali's demands for more table scraps, the dog scampered around the table in a big circle, sniffing the floor. On his second rotation, he crashed into the leg of the table and Clay's bag began to slip from the table.

April grabbed the strap, but Clay's heavy bag fell to the floor with a clump, anyway, a sheaf of papers sliding from the top.

"Hope he didn't break my laptop."

"It should be fine." She crouched on the floor as Clay scraped back his chair.

"I'll get that."

The papers fanned out in front of her on the floor, and she swept them into a pile and tapped them on the tile.

"I'll take those."

She glanced up at Clay's face, a little white around his pursed lips, and then shifted her gaze to the papers in her hand. She flipped the stack over, and a lump formed in her throat.

"Pictures of the head from yesterday."

"I'm sorry, yeah." Clay held out his hand. He repeated, "I'll take those."

She brought the printout of the photo close to her face and studied the gory details. Then she dropped the sheaf of papers and fell back onto the floor with a strangled cry.

"I know. I'm sorry, April. You shouldn't have looked. I told you not to look."

She brought a hand to her tight throat and her eyes met Clay's as she choked out, "I know her."

Chapter Nine

Clay snatched the printouts and crushed them to his chest where his heart thundered. "No, you just think you do. People in death don't look the same as they did in life—especially if they've been beheaded. She could be anyone."

April cranked her head back and forth, a blank stare in her blue eyes. "I know that woman. Her name is Elena."

Clay stuffed the sheaf of papers, now crinkled and creased, into his bag and took April by the hand to help her to her feet.

She rose and then immediately plopped down in her chair. If the chair hadn't been there, she would've wound up on the floor again.

She smoothed her palms over her thighs, over and over, ironing the wrinkles in her pants. "It's her. I know it's Elena."

"Here." Clay shoved the sweating iced tea glass under her nose. "Drink something."

"What does it mean? Why is she here?" April stopped the repetitive movement and grabbed his hand, her nails clawing at his flesh.

He curled his fingers around her wrist and squeezed. "Why do you think it's this woman Elena? The features are distorted, her skin discolored. Detective Espinoza was wondering at the office how we were going to put a sketch out. That's why the sheriff's department didn't realize right away that the woman's head from the day before yesterday didn't belong to the body we found at the border. Skin color, features, sagging, wrinkling… all change under those dire conditions."

"Look again." She poked at his bag with a trembling finger. "That woman has a nose piercing."

His pulse ratcheted up another few notches. "Lots of women have nose piercings."

"Look again, Clay." She folded her hands in her lap, twisting her fingers. "The piercing is a star, a small, gold star."

Clay's tongue stuck to the roof of his dry mouth. He didn't have to look. They'd already noted the star piercing on the woman's nose.

Lifting her chin, April placed a hand over her heart. "It's true, isn't it? You've seen the piercing."

"If you do know who this is—and I'm not conceding that you do—how do you know her? Who is Elena?"

Her fingers curled against the skin of her chest. "I met her at Jimmy's."

Clay closed his eyes as a stifling dread thrummed through his veins. When he'd believed that the cartel had left the head on April's porch because of him, it had angered him. If they'd left it there so Jimmy could send some kind of message to April, that scared the hell out of him.

His lids flew open. He couldn't let April know how much her words had struck terror into his heart.

He smoothed his palms over her arms, pulling her hands away from her throat where she'd scored it with red marks from her nails. He laced his fingers with hers.

"In what capacity? What was she doing at Jimmy's?"

"Sh-she is, was, Gilbert's girlfriend."

"Gilbert is the man you overheard talking with Jimmy in his office when you were out on the balcony?"

She nodded once, dropping her chin to her chest. "What does it mean? Did Jimmy kill her or have her killed?"

She jumped up from her chair so fast and with so much force she knocked him over and he braced a hand against the floor.

She buried her hands in her hair and screamed, the sound launching Denali to his feet. "I can't believe I was with that man. I can't believe Adam would set me up like that."

Clay grabbed the edge of the table and hoisted himself up. "I'm not defending Jimmy here or trying to tell you he's a great guy, but I don't believe he had Elena murdered."

"You think it's some great, cosmic joke that I met a woman at Jimmy's who winds up murdered and beheaded at the border and her head makes it to my front porch?" She stooped down automatically and patted Denali, frantically circling her.

"Can you sit down a minute? You're making Denali and me nervous." He grabbed the back of the kitchen chair. "Sit and drink some tea. I can get you something stronger if you want."

She wedged a hand against the nearest wall and her whole frame shuddered. "The tea will do."

She crossed the room and took a seat.

He pulled the other chair around to face hers and straddled it. "Let's slow down and think a minute. Jimmy belongs to Las Moscas, right? You saw the wooden tokens in his desk drawer. He wouldn't have those for any other reason than that he belongs to that cartel."

"That's right, and you told me Elena had one of those clutched in her cold, lifeless hand."

Clay huffed out a breath. April was going to get herself wound up again. "She did, but the other agents and I never believed that she was one of Las Moscas' mules. They killed her and left that token in her hand as a warning to others not to mess with Las Moscas."

"Mess with them? As in work against them?" She tucked the shimmering strands of her hair behind one ear as her eyes began to lose their glassiness.

"We interpreted the whole ugly scene as another gang moving into Las Moscas territory and Las Moscas reclaiming that territory in the most brutal way possible."

"You think Elena was working for a rival to Las Moscas and that Jimmy and Gilbert are those rivals?"

"I have a strong suspicion that's what happened."

"And why me?" She finally made a grab for the iced tea glass, almost knocking it over. She saved it and took a long gulp. "Why leave her head on my porch? I didn't even realize Jimmy knew about that house."

"You can be sure Adam told him all about you. Perhaps he even told him about me."

"That's bad, Clay. That's really bad news." She grabbed the back of his chair. "What if he thinks I'm over here giving you all kinds of information about him and his operation?"

That's exactly what he feared.

Shaking her head back and forth, her brow creasing, she said, "He was stupid to leave Elena's head on my porch, knowing I could identify her."

"That's just it. Jimmy wouldn't kill his own mules.

He didn't leave the head on your porch—Las Moscas did."

April blinked her wide eyes. "That's so much worse. It's terrifying enough to deal with an evil that you know, but Las Moscas? Do you think they tracked me down through Jimmy?"

"If Jimmy was part of the cartel, I'm guessing somebody in Las Moscas knows all about his relationships."

She clasped her hands, which had finally stopped trembling, between her knees. "What now?"

"Do you know Elena's last name?"

"I don't. Never heard it. I know Gilbert's, though. His is Stanley. Gilbert Stanley."

"He's not Latino?"

"He is." She jabbed a finger at his chest. "Half, like you."

"When you met Elena, was she in the company of an older, white woman?"

"She was not."

"Do you think the girlfriend story could've been a cover, or do you really believe she and Gilbert were a couple?"

"I don't have any idea. I didn't spend much time with them. She did go into Jimmy's office one time and I did wonder why she was in there when I had never been. They must've been giving her instructions then." She tapped her fingernails on the glass, rocking the slivers of ice left in the tea. "You're going to have to turn all this info over to Detective Espinoza, aren't you?"

"Of course. He needs to ID those heads."

"That means you're going to have to tell him how you know the name of the woman with the pierced nose. You're going to have to tell him that I know Jimmy Verdugo and was present in his house when he was plotting some kind of hijacking of Las Moscas."

He balanced his chin on the back of the chair. None of this would look good for April. "Maybe we can come up with a different story—just a different reason for your presence in that house."

"We can't do that, Clay. Once Espinoza talks to Gilbert…and Jimmy, they're going to tell him about me. And once he talks to them, Jimmy's going to know that I know about his business. It'll probably convince him that I stole that flash drive, too."

Massaging his throbbing temple, Clay said, "Then we don't tell Espinoza about your involvement at all."

"How are you going to explain that you happen to know the first name of a woman who wound up dead at the border?"

He shrugged, feigning a nonchalance he didn't feel. "I come in contact with a lot of mules, drug dealers, users, you name it. I'll say I came in contact with her before—remembered the nose piercing, remembered her name but nothing else."

"How is Espinoza going to tie Elena to Gilbert Stanley? He needs that connection to do a full investigation."

"I'll think of something. I don't want you involved any more than you are."

"Which is a lot, isn't it?" She stacked the plates on the table. "You need to get going on those security systems. Meg won't be happy if hers isn't in place before we leave for New Mexico."

"I'm going to tell Espinoza Elena's name first. The sooner he knows, the better. I'll do it on my way to Kyle's, my friend in security." He cocked his head. "Do you want to come with me? You'll have to keep quiet about Elena, though. Can you do that?"

As the words left his lips, he acknowledged their obviousness. April kept secrets better than anyone he knew.

Her eyebrows formed a V over her nose. "I don't want you to get into trouble covering for me."

"It's not like Espinoza isn't going to get the information we know. He is. The kind of trouble I'd be facing is nothing compared to the kind of trouble you'd be facing from Jimmy if he catches on that you know more than you're claiming to know. You're not out of the woods with that guy yet. This would put you firmly back in those woods—up a tree."

"Two years ago, you would've been happy to see me twist in the wind." Her bottom lip trembled, and he placed the pad of his thumb against the plump middle.

"Never. I never wanted anything but the best for you, April."

"Same. It's just that I knew the best for you wasn't me."

A spark ignited in his heart. Was that why she'd left him? Some stupid notion that because her father had been suspected of murdering her mother and her brother had gone off the rails after finding her body that she wasn't good enough for him?

"Did you…?"

She put up one hand. "Let's leave it. I'll clean up while you change into civilian clothes, and we'll break the news to Detective Espinoza together."

The spark he'd felt earlier died out, but he stoked it with hope that they could return to this conversation.

"Okay, just put the dishes in the dishwasher and leave the pan in the sink. I'll take care of it later." He pushed to his feet and strode to his bedroom to change out of his uniform.

An hour later, they pulled into the parking lot of the Paradiso PD and asked for Detective Espinoza inside.

Espinoza came bustling out of a back office, his cowboy boots clomping on the tile floor. "We ID'd the young Latina."

April grabbed on to Clay's belt loops in the back and tugged.

"That was fast. Who is she, and what's her story?" Clay crossed his arms over the folder with Elena's picture.

"Her name is Elena Delgado. We got a hit on her fingerprints for a couple of car thefts."

April's hold loosened. "So, she had a record?"

"Enough of one to have her prints on file, and those cases gave us an accomplice, too." Espinoza rubbed his hands together. "I'm guessing he's involved in this latest scheme that got his girlfriend killed."

"Elena has a boyfriend somewhere?" Clay shifted from one foot to the other.

"Jesus Camarena." Espinoza flicked open another file folder and jabbed his finger at the picture of a young Latino with a mustache. "Every crime that girl committed was in the presence of Camarena."

April seemed to freeze behind him. Even her breathing stopped.

Clay asked, "Where's Camarena now?"

"That's the big mystery. His name hasn't popped up in a while." Espinoza scratched his chin. "Last known address we have for him is in Phoenix."

April sighed, the air warm against the back of Clay's neck. "Maybe he got a new identity. Changed his name to start out with a clear record."

Clay jerked, and he reached back to tap April's leg.

They'd just been handed a present and she wanted to throw it back in Espinoza's face.

The detective hunched his shoulders. "Maybe, but we're gonna track him down one way or the other to find out his role in this mess. We have another person to ID."

"You're going to have to find the body to get her prints or wait for the DNA test results, but if she hasn't been arrested for a felony, her DNA isn't going to tell you much." Clay brushed the back of his hand across his forehead.

"The name Elena Delgado mean anything to you, Archer?" Espinoza narrowed his eyes, his gaze dropping to the folder in Clay's hand.

"Nope." Clay cranked his head back and forth. He held up the folder. "I was going to tell you she looked familiar to me from the photos of the head, but features in that condition are hard to distinguish."

"Just wondering why Las Moscas went to the trouble to leave one head on your porch and the other on your... Ms. Hart's."

"They want Border Patrol to back off." Clay smacked the folder against his hand. "They've sent us messages before—just not this extreme."

"Extreme times call for extreme measures." Espinoza wagged his finger between him and Clay. "I've been up front with you. You can be up front with me. Quid pro quo and all that. I've heard Las Moscas is stepping up its shipments across the border, financed more tunnels. They've monopolized some provider in Mexico."

"El Gringo Viejo." Clay's eye twitched.

"The old gringo—yeah, that's the name I heard. Any idea who that is?"

April sucked in a soft breath beside him, and he shrugged. "We don't know. Probably some old, white guy."

"Brilliant deduction, Archer." Espinoza clapped Clay on the back with a chuckle. "Why did you come in to see me?"

Clay waved the folder in front of him. "Just to tell you the woman looked familiar, but you beat me to the punch."

"We'll keep you posted on the drug angle if we get anything from this Camarena. That poor little lady didn't have a chance once she joined forces with that guy."

"And we'll keep you up to date on any activities at the border that might relate to this case." Clay made a half turn, putting his hand on the small of April's back. "I'll be out of town for the next few days. You have my contact info if something comes up."

"Agent Dillon's out of pocket, too. You're leaving me with that green kid, Valdez?"

"Put him through some paces. He'll be fine."

Once outside, April heaved a huge sigh, her shoulders slumping. "That was a piece of luck. We just had to lie by omission. We didn't have to flat out lie."

"There's a difference?" He raised one eyebrow. "Is this the world according to April?"

A pink blush rushed into her cheeks, and she turned away. "I'm glad they ID'd Elena Delgado. Do you think they'll track down Jesus, aka Gilbert?"

"So, that was him in the booking photo of Camarena that Espinoza showed us?"

"You couldn't tell by my reaction? I almost passed out."

"Yeah, I noticed." Clay grabbed the handle of the passenger door and paused. "Detective Espinoza could get an anonymous tip about a certain house in Albuquerque."

"It's totally possible that the cops would track down Gilbert after identifying Elena, right? Jimmy wouldn't necessarily suspect me of dropping a dime on them. Besides, Jimmy has no idea that Elena's head was left on my porch. Las Moscas isn't going to tell him anything."

"Jimmy has bigger problems than a runaway bride right now. He's probably sweating bullets wondering if his bosses in the cartel are going to tie him and Gilbert to the two mules trying to poach Las Moscas' shipment."

April leaned her hip against the car door. "They'll kill him, won't they?"

"If what they did to those two women is any indication of the wrath of Las Moscas, I wouldn't want to be in Jimmy's shoes right now." Not that he wasn't in Jimmy's shoes just two years ago when April had run out on their wedding. He popped open the door and held it open for her.

She started to slide in and then grabbed the doorjamb. "Are you wondering why I agreed to marry Jimmy so quickly?"

Clay clenched his jaw. "I think we established you were looking for some security and Adam had coached Jimmy into being the perfect man for you."

Clay had always believed he was the perfect man for April, and he couldn't imagine anyone less like him than a drug dealer.

"At the beginning...he was just like you." She dropped onto the seat and pulled the car door closed.

LATER THAT AFTERNOON, April stood on the walkway leading to her house, squinting at Clay and Kyle Lewis on ladders adjusting the cameras.

When Clay started his descent, she lunged forward and grabbed the ladder to steady it, enjoying the view of his backside as he made his way down.

She shifted to the side, and he jumped to the ground, his tool belt clanking around his waist.

"When Meg gets home, we'll have her test it out on her phone. I don't expect any more body parts to appear at your house, but I think this will make Meg feel a little better."

"One hundred percent." She darted toward the other ladder as Kyle made his way down.

"Are you ready for that beer now?"

"Absolutely. Let me clean up the site first."

April left Clay and Kyle to fold up the ladders, collect the packaging and put away their tools as she went into the house and got two bottles of beer and a can of diet soda from the fridge.

When Meg got home from work, Kyle showed her how to call up the security cam on her cell and they spent so much time with their heads together huddled over the phone April caught Clay's eye and jerked her head to the side.

Clay stood up and stretched. "April and I are going outside to check the sensors again. Let us know if something's not working."

Kyle glanced up, a surprised look on his face as if he'd forgotten their presence. "Yeah, sure."

Clay held the door open for her and they crowded on one side of the porch, away from where she'd discovered the head. He grabbed her hand. "Let's wander among the cacti."

She left her hand in his as they meandered along the brick pathway that wended through the garden of succulents. Small fairy lights cast a twinkling glow on their way.

The tears in April's eyes blurred the lights, turning them into a shimmering river. She sniffed and Clay squeezed her fingers.

"Your mother had a lot of imagination and charm. You must miss her."

"I do." She flung her arm out to the side. "Especially when I'm in this place she loved so much." She stopped and tapped the toe of her sandal against the wooden border that separated the path from the plants. "I wish I could talk to my father about what happened and why."

Clay swung around and grabbed her shoulders. "Don't get any crazy ideas about going south to find El Gringo Viejo. He's not your father, and if he were, what could he tell you? He murdered your mother because she found out about his involvement in the drug trade?"

"Why kill her if he were going to run away, anyway? Why not just run away to Mexico and disappear, like he did?"

"Maybe it was a crime of passion. Your mother confronted him, and he killed her." Clay's fingers dug into her flesh until she rolled her shoulders, and he dropped his hands. "Sorry."

"That's what I want to know."

"I can understand why you have questions, but it's not safe to track down your father—if you could. Law enforcement hasn't been able to find him. C. J. Hart was even featured on one of those most-wanted crime shows."

"The FBI received a lot of tips from that show."

"Lots of tips that led nowhere. Do you really think you can do better?"

"I'm his daughter. He'll want me to find him."

"Will he?"

April drew a circle in the dirt with her toe. Why would her father want to see her? If he weren't guilty, he would've contacted her by now to try to explain. All these years and not one word.

She blew out a breath. "You're right."

"Do you want me to spend the night again? We can get an early start for Albuquerque." He jerked his thumb over his shoulder.

"That's okay. We have our security system now, and I'll be up early." She tugged on his sleeve. "Denali's waiting for you."

"I would've brought him back with me, along with his food and toys, for Meg."

April's phone rang, and she held up a finger to Clay. "Hold that thought. Thank God, it's Adam."

She tapped the display. "Adam, where have you been? I've been calling you."

"April?"

The breathy female voice stirred the hair on the back of April's neck. "Kenzie?"

"Yeah, it's me. You haven't heard from Adam, either?"

"What are you doing with his phone? Where is he?" April pressed the phone against her chest and said to Clay, "It's Adam's girlfriend."

Kenzie choked out a sob. "I don't know where he is, April. I haven't heard from him since the day of the wedding. I finally decided to come over to your place to look for him. I didn't find him here, but I found his phone, turned off, and…blood. April, there's so much blood."

Chapter Ten

Clay glanced at April in the passenger seat of his truck and brushed his knuckle down her arm. "We'll find him."

"Will we? Jimmy must've taken him. Adam told me Jimmy was after him. I guess he got him." She clamped a hand down on her bouncing knee.

"Maybe he thinks Adam took that flash drive." Clay reached for his cup of coffee and took a sip, although the lukewarm liquid tasted more like vinegar than coffee. "Are you sure you don't want to call the Albuquerque police?"

"We can't do that, Clay. Kenzie didn't want to touch the drugs Adam left behind at my place, and I can't blame her. Can you imagine if the police showed up at the apartment to check out the scene and found all those drugs…at *my* apartment?"

"So, we go out there and get rid of the drugs first and *then* call the police? That's not gonna look good, either."

"It won't look good if they know about the drugs." She poked his thigh. "You're Border Patrol. You have contacts in the DEA. Tell them about the drugs if you want to dispose of them legally."

"What quantity of drugs are we talking about? Did Kenzie tell you what was lying around?"

"No. She was practically hysterical by the time she got off the phone with me when she realized I haven't talked to Adam since the day of the wedding, either. I didn't get much out of her."

"How'd she get into your place?"

"It was open. The front door was unlocked."

"Great." A muscle jumped at the corner of his mouth. "Adam brought his drugs to your place, and Jimmy scooped him up there—and not without a struggle. There's a reason why Jimmy left the drugs in your apartment instead of taking them."

"And it worked. He knew I wouldn't call the police—and I'm not." April drew lines on the thighs of her pants as she raked her fingernails up and down her legs. "I hope Adam doesn't have that flash drive. Jimmy will kill him—if he hasn't already."

"Depends on what's on the flash drive. If Jimmy gets it back from Adam, he might decide to use it against him. He just lost two mules."

April crossed her hands over her chest. "You think Jimmy will use Adam to intercept drugs from Las Moscas?"

"I don't know, April. It's one possibility." His hands clenched the steering wheel. "You shouldn't be rushing back into this mess. You don't owe your brother a thing after what he did to you—after what he's done to you."

Flicking her fingers in the air, she said, "I was coming here, anyway, although I wish I could've driven that car to return it to Ryan."

"With Adam missing and drugs and blood in your apartment, we didn't have time to make a detour to a location you may or may not remember." He made a grab for the cup again and knocked it from the cup holder."

"Nothing spilled." April plucked it off the floor and

squeezed his bicep. "Don't worry. I have you by my side, and I can't leave Adam hanging out to dry."

He kept his mouth shut and ground his teeth instead of talking. He'd said it all before about Adam, and April didn't want to hear it. She claimed he didn't understand because he was an only child. That could be it, but looking at her relationship with Adam made him glad he didn't have siblings.

They made a few stops on the way to Albuquerque and arrived at April's apartment by one o'clock in the afternoon. When they pulled into her empty parking space in the garage, April wedged her hands against the dashboard.

"My car's gone."

"We can add grand theft auto to the list of crimes we're gonna report." Clay withdrew his weapon as he got out of the car. "I doubt Jimmy's going to come back here if he's the one who took your brother, but the guy sounds desperate at this point. No telling what he might do."

April exited the car and stretched her arms over her head. "I'm not waiting down here. It's dark and Jimmy knows where my parking space is, even if I no longer have a car."

"Just don't go charging into your place. Did Kenzie lock up when she left?"

"She doesn't remember, but I hope not." She slammed her door and came around to his side. "I don't have the keys to my place."

Clay followed April upstairs to her apartment, and then squeezed past her when they reached her door. "Let me."

He placed his ear against the solid wood, curling his

fingers around the door handle. He twisted it and said over his shoulder, "It's still unlocked."

"At least I don't have to break into my own place."

"You don't have a manager on-site?"

"No, just a number to call for the management company." She tipped her head at the door. "Are we going in?"

"Me first." He eased open the door, his muscles tight, his finger on the trigger of his gun.

The door squeaked softly on its hinges. Clay tilted his head back and sniffed the air. Didn't smell like blood—or death.

He took a step into the living room, April clinging to the waistband of his jeans, her staccato breathing pulsing behind him. He swiveled his head back and forth, taking in the small room. "How many rooms?"

"This one, the kitchen, one bathroom and two bedrooms." She nudged his arm. "Down the hall that way."

Clay crept into the room, his gun at his side while April stayed behind. He poked his head into the kitchen and veered to the left and the short hallway. All three doors stood wide open, and he entered each room and checked the two closets.

He strode back into the living room, making a wide arc with one hand. "Where is all this blood Kenzie saw?"

"Not sure." From the living room behind the couch, April held her arms out to her sides, several plastic bags clutched in her hands. "But here are the drugs. Looks like crystal meth and weed."

Clay holstered his gun, shut and locked the front door. "You don't need anyone seeing you with that stuff."

April dropped the bags on the console table behind

the couch and put her hands on her hips. "I'm a little relieved. I expected the place to be turned over with blood soaking the carpet and packets of drugs."

Clay peered over the counter that separated the kitchen from the living room. "It's in here, April, the blood."

She appeared next to him in a flash, her face white, her eyes round. "It—it looks smeared. Do you think Kenzie tried to clean it up?"

"Looks like someone did." He patted her back. "Stay here."

He circled around the counter, avoiding the blood spots on the floor. More blood spatters decorated the inside of the sink and droplets had dried on the granite countertop.

"Someone washed up in the sink. Until we question Kenzie, we don't know if she tried to clean up or if this blood belongs to the assailant. Why did she assume this was Adam's blood?"

"His phone was here, turned off, and his drugs. Who else would have access to my apartment?"

Clay cleared his throat. "Uh, your fiancé."

"He never came here." Two splotches of red splashed her cheeks. "He doesn't have a key."

"Trash?" He nudged an elongated drawer with his toe. When she nodded, he pulled it open and tossed the garbage at the top with his fingers. "I don't see any paper towels or rags in here covered with blood. Do you have a laundry room?"

"Not in here. I can't imagine Kenzie cleaning up and then taking a bunch of bloody towels to the washing machines downstairs."

"You need to get her back on the phone and find out exactly what she saw when she came in here. This scene—" he waved his arms around the kitchen "—doesn't make much sense."

April took a wide stance in the middle of the room. "After I ran out on the wedding, Adam must've gone to Jimmy's, anyway. Maybe that's when Jimmy threatened him…and me. Adam picked up my purse with my keys and let himself into my place."

"That's your purse?" Clay pointed to a large bag on the coffee table that looked more like a small suitcase.

"That's the bag I brought with me to Jimmy's to get ready for the wedding." April swooped down to grab it and dug inside, a few of the contents falling to the floor in her haste. She twirled a key chain around her finger. "Keys."

"Car keys?"

"Yeah, but Adam has his own set of keys to my car."

"What did Adam do next, detective?" Clay crossed his arms and wedged a hip against the couch.

"He dropped off my stuff…"

"And brought his drugs."

She sucked in her bottom lip. "Maybe he just scored."

"Nice of him to bring them here." He held up his hands as she opened her mouth. "I don't know how we're going to locate Adam without the help of the police."

April snapped her fingers and pointed her finger at him. "Detective Espinoza should be contacting Gilbert…or Jesus. Maybe that will make Jimmy and his gang nervous enough that they'll release Adam."

"I wouldn't count on Jimmy getting spooked at this point by a few inquiries into Elena. Do you think Jimmy would take Adam to his house?"

"Maybe. What are you thinking?" April brushed her hands together as if to erase the drugs.

"You can't go out to Jimmy's place, but I can—just for a surveillance. I can check things out, and Jimmy won't even know I'm there."

"Except—" April skirted the couch, hitching her purse over her shoulder "—Jimmy has security cameras."

"As you found out, I happen to have a good friend in security and I know how to disable any system. I'm not going in with guns blazing. I'm just gonna see what I can see."

"I'm going with you." She sliced a hand in the air through his objections. "I'll stay out of sight, but first let's finish the cleanup."

"Do you have any cotton swabs and plastic bags? I want to take a sample of this blood in the kitchen and in the sink."

"I do."

They spent the next hour collecting blood samples and cleaning up. When they finished, Clay handed April's phone to her. "Try calling Kenzie again."

As Clay took out the trash, April called Kenzie on Adam's phone. She didn't remember Kenzie's own number. The call rolled over to voice mail, but April decided not to leave a message. She didn't trust that phone and didn't much trust Kenzie, either. That girl was flakier than a Paris pastry.

Clay returned to the apartment, rubbing his hands together. "I'm just going to wash up, and I'm going to flush those drugs down the toilet while I'm at it. You finish packing your stuff and we'll get something to eat. I want the cover of darkness on my side when we go out to Jimmy's place."

April packed the stuff she wanted to take back with her to Paradiso. She'd officially give notice and move out once everything was settled with Jimmy and she'd found Adam—dead or alive.

She said, "I know a good barbecue place where we can pass the time. It's not far from Jimmy's."

"He's not going to suddenly show up there, is he?"

"Too down-home for him. He prefers upscale steak houses and cocktail lounges."

They loaded her bags and suitcases in the truck, and she directed him to Benny's Big-Time BBQ.

An hour later, seated across from each other with a pile of ribs between them, April asked, "What's your plan?"

"I'll sneak onto the grounds, disable the security system, if I have to, and surveil the scene. See who's there, including Adam."

"You're not going to know who's who without me."

"Draw me some pictures." He aimed a rib bone at her. "If I get caught, I can make up some story. If you're with me, that story's gonna be a lot different."

"You know what Gilbert looks like, right? You remember the booking photo of Jesus that Espinoza showed us. That's pretty close, except Gilbert added a goatee to that moustache." She tore open a wet wipe package and dangled the wipe from her fingers. "Do you think Espinoza has already contacted Gilbert?"

"Probably not. If he wants to do any kind of search when he finds him, he'll have to secure a warrant. It's going to take him a few days before he can formally question Gilbert and search his possessions."

"Then Jimmy and his cohorts won't know anything."

"They'll know their mules didn't make it. I'm sure they had some sort of communication set up for when the women got across with the drugs. If he never heard from them, he'd know something went wrong."

"The heads were in the news. If he cared to check, he'd find that out." She swiped the last bit of barbecue sauce from her fingers and crumpled the wipe in her hand. "Did those news reports mention any names— like mine?"

"No, the location of the recovered heads was kept out of the news. Jimmy shouldn't know that you're involved in this at all. Even the identification of Elena can be explained by her fingerprints and her police record connecting her to Jesus." Clay dug his fork into his potato salad. "I suppose Jimmy knows you're from Paradiso if Adam already told him the story about your father."

"He knows that…but not much else—at least, not from me." She'd never told Jimmy about Clay. It had seemed almost sacrilegious to share any details of her and Clay's relationship with anyone else.

She couldn't imagine Adam would've told Jimmy that his fiancée had once been engaged to a Border Patrol agent. That wouldn't have meshed with Adam's plans of securing himself a drug-dealing brother-in-law.

Clay grabbed her hand with his sticky one. "Are you okay? Are you sure you want me to do this?"

"Yes. I'm just surprised you're willing to go to these lengths to find Adam. I know he's not your favorite person."

"He's not my favorite person because I don't like how he twists you all up. Look, I'm sorry the kid found his mother like that, but you don't owe him a lifetime of chances because of it. He needs to get off drugs and start seeing a good therapist." Clay disentangled his fingers from hers and handed her another wet wipe. "Sorry."

"I've told Adam that a million times. He tried therapy

once or twice, but it didn't work for him." She shrugged. Adam was the only immediate family she had left. She couldn't sit by and watch him self-destruct, but she'd never get pulled into one of his schemes again, and she should've recognized the setup with Jimmy as a scheme. She hadn't been thinking clearly at the time. She hadn't been thinking clearly since the day she left Clay.

"You're familiar with rock bottom, right?" Clay shoved his plate to the center of the table and planted his elbows on the linoleum.

"Yes, of course." She'd even hit it herself maybe once or twice.

"Adam hasn't hit yet because you won't allow him to. That's why he can't hear the therapist. That's why he can't get clean. You're not doing him any favors, April."

"And yet here you are ready to rush into danger to save him."

"I'm not doing this for him." Clay's eyes glowed with an intensity that made her stomach flip-flop.

She wrenched her gaze away from his and tapped the window. "Is it dark enough for you?"

"It will be once I take a bath with these wet wipes and pay the bill." He ripped open another little packet and scrubbed his hands. "You direct me to Jimmy's and a place to park where we won't stand out. I'll go in on foot and do some reconnaissance. I'll keep my phone on vibrate, so you can serve as an early warning system in case someone comes."

"What if someone's already there? What if a lot of someones are there? What if they have Adam?"

"That's a lot of what-ifs." He raised one finger in the air at the waiter. "We'll play it by ear. I told you, I'm not going to charge in there like a superagent. If

Adam's there and it looks like he's in danger, we'll call the cops."

"All right. I'll let you call the shots, but you need to listen to me. I know these people."

"Don't remind me." He plucked the check from the waiter's hand.

"While you're paying up, I'm going to wash my hands. I feel like I have barbecue sauce under my fingernails."

Clay squinted at his nails. "You probably do."

Back in the truck, April took a deep breath. "I hope this crazy plan of yours yields some results."

"You're accusing me of crazy plans? The woman who ran out on two weddings?"

She placed a hand on her belly. "If I hadn't run out on that second one, where would I be now? Probably scrabbling through some tunnel beneath the border with Las Moscas in my future."

"Where would you have been if you hadn't run out on the first one?" Clay didn't wait for an answer to his rhetorical question, instead cranking on the engine to his truck and peeling away from the curb.

April guided him to Jimmy's compound. When he turned on the actual street of houses set back from the curb, gates and long driveways protected the residents from curious eyes and casual passersby.

With her hands stuffed beneath her thighs, she tipped her head forward. "I'm going to slump down in my seat. Drive to the end of the cul-de-sac so you can get an idea of the layout and a sense of the house and grounds."

"How long is the street from this point to the end of the cul-de-sac?"

"Less than a quarter of a mile." She loosened her seat

belt and scooted down. "The houses are not cheek and jowl. There's some space between them."

"Is that how Jimmy was able to operate in relative privacy?"

"Uh-huh." The car veered to the right and her head bumped the glass. "After this bend in the road, Jimmy's place is on the left. He has a tall white gate around his property, and you can't see the house from the road."

"Got it in my sights."

"Is it all lit up?"

"Nope." Clay twisted his head to the side. "Some lights on the gate and softer lights down the driveway. Does he have sensor lights?"

"Not that I recall."

Clay swung the car around. "What's out there past the end of the cul-de-sac?"

"Nothing. Fields."

"I'll keep that in mind." He didn't slow down again on his way past the house. "Plenty of pickup trucks, so mine isn't going to stick out. Do you think it's okay to park at the top of the road? You'll have a view of who's coming in and out."

"You should be fine. Leave the keys in case I have to make a quick getaway." She pinched his thigh. "Not that I plan to leave you in the lurch or anything."

"By all means, leave me in the lurch. Like I said, I can always come up with some story." He hunched forward in his seat and pulled his wallet free from his pocket and tossed it in the console. "I'm not going to be caught with my badge and ID, either."

"But you're keeping your weapon."

"Have to. It might just get me out of trouble." He pulled into a dark space on the curb between two big, gated houses.

"Or get you into trouble."

"Don't worry, April. I know what I'm doing."

"I'm glad someone does because this is feeling more and more like a wild-goose chase."

"Have some faith in me." He threw the car into Park and left the keys swinging from the ignition. "You never did."

"Never did what?" She glanced across at him, her chin pinned to her chest.

"Had faith in me. You never had faith in me, April." He slipped from the car and pushed the door shut.

She popped up in her seat and tried to catch his silhouette in the rearview mirror, but he'd disappeared in the night, melding with the darkness.

She waited several more minutes and exited the car on silent feet. She had no intention of letting Clay creep into the lion's den on his own. Her brother, her problem.

Hunching forward, she kept to the hedges along the dirt that functioned as a sidewalk.

When she reached Jimmy's house, she squeezed through the end of the gate and some bushes, the needling branches scratching her arms. She stumbled to a stop in the sudden darkness.

Either Clay had gotten to work already, or Jimmy had sensed company and killed the lights outside. But why would he do that? Wouldn't he turn on the floodlights to expose the intruder?

Her gaze turned to the corners of the house where she figured Jimmy's security had stationed the cameras. Had Clay disabled them?

She dropped to her hands and knees near the porch and peered into the cloak of darkness that enveloped the house. The strangeness of the scene caused pinpricks of fear to assault the back of her neck.

Even when Jimmy went out of town, he didn't leave the house in complete darkness. Clay wouldn't have been foolish enough to cut off the power to the whole house. That would alert Jimmy and his goons, and if they had Adam, they wouldn't fall for the trick and fan out to find the perpetrator. They'd be on high alert.

She rose to a crouch and circled around the side of the house to the big windows on the great room that commanded a view of the valley. Nobody stopped her. Nothing tripped her up. She had a wide-open path.

Her heart thundered in her chest, causing a muted pounding in her ears. She dropped to the ground again when she got close to the window and a yellow glow of light from a lamp in the room.

She army-crawled on her belly across the wooden deck until her nose almost touched the cool glass of the window. Jimmy had fled. The guards, the henchmen, the security system...all demobilized.

Maybe Clay had been wrong. Perhaps Espinoza had paid a visit to Jimmy's compound looking for the man she knew as Gilbert and spooked them all into hiding. Of course, they'd fear Las Moscas finding out they were behind the double-cross more than they'd fear the law.

She hoisted herself up, curling her legs beneath her. As her eyes adjusted to the low light in the great room, she detected movement.

She held her breath, freezing in place, every muscle clenched into stillness. Then her breath hitched in her throat and her eyes widened to take in the sight of Clay bending over the dead body of Jimmy.

Chapter Eleven

April gasped, throwing out her hand to keep her balance and hitting the door, her ring scraping the glass.

Clay's head jerked up. He leveled his gun at her.

She staggered to her feet, waving her arms above her head. With her heart beating a mile a minute, she grabbed the handle of the slider.

Clay made a wide berth around Jimmy on the floor and yanked open the door. He reached through the space and dragged her inside. "What the hell are you doing here?"

"What the hell are *you* doing here? You killed Jimmy?" She shook off his hand and covered her mouth. "This is bad. This is so bad."

"Just stop." He pressed a finger against her lips. "I didn't kill Jimmy. He was dead when I got here."

Her relief caused the blood to rush to her head, and she pressed her fingertips against her temple. "Oh my God. H-how did he die?"

"Someone stabbed him to death."

She poked her head around Clay's frame and took in the saturation of blood on the Persian carpet, giving Jimmy a halo in death that he certainly never had in life.

"Is there anyone else here? Dead or alive?" She hoped there were no live ones…dead ones, either.

"There's no one here. I could see in an instant the house was deserted, so I slipped inside. As soon as I entered this room, I could smell the blood." Clay's nostrils flared.

April sniffed the air and then wished she hadn't. Once you smelled that odor of liquid metal, you couldn't get it out of your head—or your mouth.

She ran her tongue over her teeth. "Is there any sign of a struggle throughout the house? Any sign of Adam?"

"No Adam. Struggle?" He cranked his head from side to side. "I don't see it."

"Las Moscas." She clasped her hands in front of her, twisting her fingers. "They must've found out Jimmy was the one who sent those mules and then took care of business, but where are the others? Jimmy always had an entourage."

"Maybe Las Moscas took care of them, too, and their bodies are elsewhere. Maybe some of them convinced Las Moscas they didn't know about the betrayal, and the cartel took them back into the fold."

"Where's Adam, Clay?" She rubbed the goose bumps from her arms. "Now I'm more worried than ever. At least Adam had a relationship with Jimmy. If Adam did take that flash drive and gave it back to Jimmy, Jimmy might show some mercy. But Las Moscas? They don't show mercy, do they?"

"No." He holstered the gun that had been dangling at his side all this time. "We need to talk to Kenzie to get a clearer picture of what went down at your apartment. We'll leave this mess to the police. When Espinoza comes looking for Jesus or Gilbert or whatever he's calling himself, it's going to lead him to Jimmy Verdugo and it'll be up to the Albuquerque PD to process this crime scene."

She clutched the neckline of her shirt. "We need to get rid of our fingerprints."

"I've been doing that." He pointed at the sliding glass door. "Let's take care of those—yours and mine—on the door and be careful not to touch anything else, not that your prints won't be in this house."

"They will be, along with dozens of others. Jimmy had people coming in and out of this house all the time."

"But at least your prints don't have to be anywhere near the crime scene." Clay bunched up his black T-shirt in his hand and wiped down the handle of the sliding glass door, inside and out. "Did you touch the glass?"

"No." Her gaze darted to Jimmy on the floor, his head turned to the side, his handsome face in profile. "Clay, did you see a murder weapon?"

"Nothing." He slid the door closed and flicked the lock.

"There's so much blood on the floor. How do you know he was stabbed instead of shot?"

"He was like this when I came into the room—on his back. I didn't see any wounds, so I nudged him up and saw the carnage on his back and neck, slashing wounds that ripped his clothing. Also—" he aimed a toe at Jimmy's chest "—there's no exit wound. A bullet would've exited out his front."

She swallowed. "But no knife."

"Not that I can see. Las Moscas must've sent someone Jimmy knew for him to turn his back on the guy." He ran a hand up her arm. "I'm sorry. This must bring back memories of your mother and that other crime scene. Let's get out of here."

"Not yet." She scanned the familiar room where nothing seemed out of place except the owner's body on the floor. "I want to make sure Jimmy doesn't have any pictures of me around the house. The police may make the connection between me and Jimmy soon enough, but I don't have to make it easy for them, do I?"

"In my search of the house, I found it devoid of any personal touches. Who knows if he really owns it? Who knows if his name is really Jimmy Verdugo? I'm sure you already know, a search on that name doesn't return much."

"His entire life could've been a fake." She shivered and clenched her teeth against the chill washing over her flesh. "And I could've been a part of it all. What plans do you think he had for me?"

"If Adam was spreading lies about El Gringo Viejo being C. J. Hart, Jimmy probably wanted an introduction and a special deal for producing meth."

"For Adam to go that far, setting me up with Jimmy, he has to have some proof about our father."

Clay snorted. "Adam could've been playing Jimmy, too. Who knows? Maybe that's why Jimmy snatched him. He found out about all his lies. Do what you have to do here, and then let's bounce."

"Okay, I want to check his office. Did you go in there?"

"I did and thought about you hiding on the balcony in your wedding dress." He shook his head. "However irrational your actions, I'm glad you got out in the end."

"I am, too. I'll be right back." She jogged upstairs and used the light from her phone to look around Jimmy's office. If Adam were safe somewhere, she'd be able to put this entire ugly chapter of her life behind her—and move on to the next ugly chapter.

She opened the top drawer of his desk, using her blouse to cover her fingers. The tokens from Las Moscas were still there. The cartel didn't care if the police knew Jimmy had been one of theirs. Even better for them to warn others in their employ not to cross them.

Her gaze swept his desk. Looked like Jimmy had already disposed of the framed picture he'd kept of the two of them. Good. It had all been a fake, anyway. A fake relationship with a fake person, a person Adam had done his best to mold after Clay. Did Adam ever tell Jimmy why he wanted him to act a certain way, like certain things? He may have mentioned an ex-fiancé in her past, but Adam never would've told Jimmy that ex-fiancé was Border Patrol.

She blew out a sigh and turned on her heel. She didn't need a fake. She had the real thing now.

BACK IN APRIL'S APARTMENT, Clay studied his former fiancée's face. They'd returned to her place in hopes of being there for Adam. The danger to April in her apartment had disappeared with Jimmy's death. A lot of things had disappeared with Jimmy's death.

If only Adam would come traipsing back in here, a smile on his hapless face, another scheme cooking in his brain, April could be free. As long as her brother remained missing, she'd stay hooked into his drama.

She glanced up from her phone. "What?"

"No luck reaching Kenzie?"

She clicked the phone on the coffee table facedown. "I texted her."

"We could try the Albuquerque PD now. You could report your car as stolen. If Adam's in the car, he'll be found."

"And arrested for car theft."

Clay rolled his eyes. "You don't have to press charges."

"If Adam is safe and driving around in my car, he

would call me and tell me what happened unless he's still worried about Jimmy. He wouldn't know about Jimmy yet…unless he was there and Las Moscas has their hands on him now."

"April, you could come up with about a hundred different theories about Adam right now and still be wrong. There's no telling what your brother is up to. Leave it for the police. If he gets arrested for drugs, it could be the best thing for him."

"You're saying I should leave Albuquerque…or not, and forget about Adam?"

Clay's pulse picked up pace. "I think you should definitely leave Albuquerque. The place doesn't seem to agree with you."

"I wish Kenzie would call me back."

Clay wedged a foot against the coffee table. "You're not going to wait around here for Kenzie, are you?"

"You think we should leave?"

"Let's spend the night here like we'd planned and leave tomorrow." He toed off one shoe. "You don't have to be in Albuquerque to talk to Kenzie…or Adam."

April placed her hands together as if in prayer. "I hope he's okay."

He didn't feel like talking about Adam anymore or speculating about what happened to him. The guy had dragged his sister into a mess, all because of some hunch about El Gringo Viejo and dreams of riches. April's parents had made sure all their possessions would go to April because they couldn't trust Adam, even back then. Of course, April had done her damnedest to share her money with her brother. Nobody could ever talk her out of her support for Adam. She'd been loyal to a fault…to Adam.

Clay pinched the knotted muscles in the back of his neck. "Do you mind if I take a shower?"

"Go ahead." She hopped up from the couch. "I'll get you a clean towel and make up the other bed, while I'm at it."

Clay's jaw hardened. She was as controlled as the day she left him. If she could ignore the sexual tension that had been simmering between them from the minute she showed up in Paradiso, he'd have to follow suit.

He'd explored every inch of this woman's body intimately; it seemed absurd for them to camp out in different beds. But she probably had the right idea. What good would one night of passion do them if she planned on packing up and leaving him again?

His mouth watered as he followed behind her gently undulating hips to the hallway. That one night of passion could do him a helluva lot of good, come to think of it.

She swung open the door to the hall closet, almost bashing him in the face. "Sorry. I didn't realize you were right behind me."

He held up his hands. "I was daydreaming."

Her gaze shifted to his face as she reached for a towel. She pressed it against his chest. "Here you go. You brought toiletries in your bag, right?"

"Yeah, toothbrush, floss, the works." He shook out the towel and backed up to the small bathroom where he hung it over a rack on the outside of the shower door.

April seemed stuck in the bathroom's entrance, and he squeezed past her. "Do you need to use the bathroom before I hop in? I'm just gonna get my bag from the living room."

"I'm not even going to brush my teeth right now. I know I have a few beers in the fridge if Adam didn't drink them. Want one when you get out?"

"Absolutely."

She followed him to the living room where he snagged his overnight bag.

"I won't be long."

"Take your time." She waved a hand at him.

He didn't want to take his time in the shower alone. He wanted to hurry and spend all his time with April before they parted company again—maybe for good this time.

Seeing her again had only drilled home the point that he needed to get on with his life. She hadn't offered any explanations for running out on their wedding, even though the heat still burned between them.

Sometimes he caught a look of regret and sadness in her blue eyes, but whatever feelings lurked in her soul they weren't strong enough to overcome whatever objections she'd had to their marriage. He had to respect that.

He scrubbed his body hard with a washcloth as if trying to wash April Hart out of his pores. If only a little soap and elbow grease could do the trick.

He dried off and pulled on a pair of gym shorts and a white T-shirt—the more covered up, the better. Maybe he'd luck out and she'd be sound asleep after the events of today.

Did she really think he'd killed Jimmy when she saw him over his body? Not that the idea of April being engaged to a scumbag like that didn't cause rage to boil in his veins. Adam and Jimmy must've really done a number on her—or she'd been so lost she wasn't thinking straight.

Lost because of him? That's how he'd felt without her—lost, half a man.

He shook his head and draped the towel over the rack

to dry. He stepped out of the bathroom and dropped his bag inside the door of the spare bedroom, which she'd already neatly made up for him.

The TV hummed from the other room, and he poked his head around the corner. "Still awake?"

She twisted her head around while pausing the TV show. "I'm not tired. Are you? I think I still have adrenaline pumping through my body from finding Jimmy."

He strode toward her and dropped on the other end of the couch. "I'm sorry. You must've loved him once."

"Never." She tightened her lips. "It was all fake. All make-believe, and I think I knew it even before the wedding day and my eavesdropping."

"Why didn't you make a run for it before the big day?" He crossed his ankle over his bouncing knee. Would she shut him down?

She shrugged. "Didn't relish the idea of being a two-time loser."

"Yeah, much better to be married to a man you suspected of criminal activity." He rolled his eyes. "Do you have those beers?"

"Just waiting for you." She half rose, but he sprang to his feet.

"I'll get them."

Her refrigerator contained a few bottles of water, a few bottles of beer and an expired yogurt. Why would it be stocked? She'd left this place to get married. Had they planned a honeymoon? Probably Mexico for a surprise visit to the bride's father.

He twisted the caps off the beers and tossed them on the countertop with a clink. "Do you want a glass?"

"You know me better than that."

He knew her better than anyone—or he used to.

He walked back into the living room on bare feet and

handed her one bottle. She'd changed from the black leggings she'd worn earlier into short, pink pajama bottoms and a white top with spaghetti straps.

He pointed at the husky puppies on her bottoms. "Those look like Denali."

"Why do you think I bought them?" She dropped her lashes and rubbed a thumb across a white dog printed on the material. "It reminded me of Denali and…"

Her voice died away in a whisper, and a knife twisted in his gut, engulfing him in the same pain that came on every time he thought about April.

He dropped to his knees. "Why, April? Why'd you do it? Why'd you leave us?"

Her sparkling eyes flew to his face, color rushing into her cheeks.

Okay, that had been a cheap shot throwing Denali in there.

She folded her hands around the bottle. "Would you believe me if I told you I did it to protect you?"

Clay curled his hands around her calves. "This sounds like the old 'it's me, not you' excuse. In fact, that's the reason you gave me two years ago."

Leaning forward, she placed her hands on his shoulders. "Does it matter to you right now?"

Clay swallowed. Did it? To have this woman in his arms again, loving her, pleasing her, meant everything to him.

He closed his eyes. He'd just been telling himself to move on with his life. Making love with April was not a good step on that path.

She cupped his jaw with one hand. "I missed you so much, Clay."

His lids flew open, and he found himself almost

nose-to-nose with the one woman he'd loved more than life itself.

It didn't matter why she left. It didn't matter that she'd made terrible choices since then. It didn't matter that she intended to leave him again once she found her brother.

He scooped a hand through her hair. This mattered. Only this.

He brought her in inches closer and angled his mouth across hers. Her warm, soft lips opened, and she invited him inside. His tongue explored her mouth, and she sighed against his kisses.

She dropped her hand to the neck of his T-shirt and hooked her fingers over the neckline, rubbing her knuckles along his collarbone. Opening her legs, she hooked them around his torso, almost coming off the couch and knocking him backward.

He steadied himself and planted a trail of kisses along her inner thigh. The dogs on her pajama bottoms wiggled, and he smiled against her flesh.

He tucked his hands beneath her derriere and hoisted her back up on the couch, following her up and pressing his body against hers.

His erection, strong and sure, poked at her through the thin material of their clothing.

She wedged her hands against his chest. "You're squishing me. Let's trade places."

In a single movement, he wrapped his hands around her waist, turned and lifted her, taking her place on the couch.

She straddled his hips and pressed a kiss against his mouth. "Much better."

Tugging the undershirt over her head, he said, "Much, much better."

He cupped one pert breast with his palm and teased her nipple with the tip of his tongue.

She gasped and threw back her head. "That's wicked good."

"I don't want the other one to suffer." He dipped his head and swirled his tongue around the other nipple while pinching the one he'd already tantalized to a rosy peak.

She rocked in his lap, chafing against his erection, driving him crazy with desire and need.

He'd always needed April. It had gone beyond love. She'd percolated in his blood for years like some kind of addiction. He could almost pity the poor bastards dependent on drugs because April was his drug.

"Why are you still wearing this?" She clawed at his T-shirt, dragging it up his chest.

He yanked it over his head, and she immediately pressed her bare skin against his. "I love this feeling."

Her soft breasts brushed against the flat planes of muscle across his chest, and he soaked in the sensation. He traced one knuckle over the beads of her spine and slipped his hands into her shorts, splaying his hands against the curve of her buttocks.

He growled in her ear. "I love *this* feeling."

She wriggled against his erection, driving him crazy, and then dipped her head to his chest and grazed one of his nipples with her teeth.

Leaning against the cushions, he tipped his head back and concentrated on a little water stain in the corner. "You're going to take your time, aren't you? You're going to do all kinds of little things to my body to tease me."

"I have an ulterior motive." She shoved her hand down his shorts and grabbed the length of him. "I'm going to make you so hard you're gonna go all night. You're going to please me like only you know how."

He dug his fingers into the soft flesh of her derriere and flipped her on her back, stretching out beside her.

As she started to roll off the edge, he grabbed her. "I don't think this couch is big enough for what I want to do to you—all night long."

She pressed a finger against his lips. "Let's continue this romp in my boudoir."

"Romp." He scooped her up again and staggered to his feet. "I like the sound of that."

He ignored the alarm bells in his head, determined to get his fill of this woman once and for all—as if he could ever get enough of April Hart.

Clay took two steps away from the couch with April clinging to his body, and then nearly dropped her when he heard the handle of the front door rattle.

Her arms tightened around his neck, and he brushed her ear with his lips. "Shh."

The door handle twisted again, and April slid from his body, stumbling backward.

The lock clicked, and Clay lunged for his weapon on the kitchen counter. He shoved April behind him and said, "Get back. He's coming."

Chapter Twelve

April crouched to the floor and peered between his legs at the front door, now easing open.

Clay shouted, "Stop! I have a gun."

"Clay?" The door opened wider, and Adam stepped over the threshold, brushing his dishwater-blond hair from his eyes. "Don't shoot, man."

April blew out a breath and pulled her discarded camisole over her head before jumping to her feet and rushing her brother. She threw her arms around his neck, momentarily forgetting that he'd set her up to marry a drug dealer.

"Oh my God. I'm so glad to see you safe."

Adam patted her back. "I'm all right, but we need to get out of here."

"Why?" Clay shoved his weapon in the back of his waistband, his jaw a hard line.

April stepped back from Adam. Now Clay would really hate her brother. Adam had just interrupted their reunion sex.

Adam glanced at Clay and then shifted his blue eyes back to April. "What does he know?"

"He knows everything, of course, and I think we even know more than you do." April tugged on the hem of her camisole. Adam wouldn't even notice their state of undress, Clay in gym shorts with his shirt off and she in skimpy pj's. Adam didn't notice much if it didn't concern him.

"What are you talking about? What could you possibly know that I don't? Jimmy abducted me. He thinks I have something that belongs to him."

April opened her mouth, but Clay crossed the room and stepped between her and Adam. "If Jimmy snatched you, why are you here? How'd you get away from Jimmy?"

"He was distracted. The cops are looking for Gilbert and it led them to Jimmy." Adam hunched his thin shoulders. "Let's just say, Jimmy had other problems besides me."

"You can say that again." Clay crossed his arms over his bare chest. "Jimmy's dead."

Adam's eyes bugged out of his head. "That's impossible. The guy had me captive as late as this afternoon."

April said, "We saw him, Adam. Saw his dead body."

Adam smacked his hand against his forehead and jerked his head toward Clay. "Y-you didn't kill him, did you?"

"I did not kill him, and you're lucky I'm not gonna kill you, either." Clay leveled a finger at Adam. "You set up April with this lowlife, manipulated her into marrying him for your own selfish reasons, not giving a damn about her or her feelings."

April pressed a hand against her fluttering heart. Clay had always stood up for her, always would.

Adam backed up against the wall. "Jimmy wouldn't have hurt April. He just wanted an in with our father, one that I couldn't give him."

"Cut it, Adam." Clay sliced his hand through the air. "Your father is not El Gringo Viejo. Get that insane idea out of your head. And if you didn't think April was in danger being married to a man like that, you're as stupid as you've always been."

A mottled red suffused Adam's cheeks. "I didn't force her to marry him."

"I know how you operate. Don't try to pull anything over on me." Clay rolled his shoulders as if to gain control of his emotions. "Did you know Jimmy and his gang were double-crossing Las Moscas?"

Adam held out both hands. "Hey, I had no idea until he told me today. That's why Jimmy wanted that flash drive. It contains tunnel locations along the border for the cartel's drops. I'm telling you the same thing I told Jimmy. I don't have it. Do you think the cops killed Jimmy?"

April perched on the arm of the couch, wishing she and Clay were wrapped around each other again. "The cops are not going to kill a drug dealer and leave his body on the floor of his house…or anywhere else."

"That's where you found him?" Adam's skinny neck worked as he swallowed hard. "Las Moscas."

"That's what we're thinking." Clay strolled to the couch, the gun still tucked in the waistband of his shorts, and put his hand on April's shoulder. "It's over. Don't involve April in any of your crazy schemes again. Don't ask her to search for your father in Mexico or anywhere else. Or you're gonna have to answer to me. Got it?"

Adam's gaze darted between April and Clay. "Are you two back together?"

God, she wished.

Clay must've felt the stiffening of her body. He dropped his hand from her shoulder. "We don't have to be together for me to look out for April's interests."

"Okay, whatever, man. I'm done with this stuff. I just escaped with my life." He rubbed his arms and sauntered to the table behind the couch. "Did you happen to find my stash here?"

"Disposed of it." Clay widened his stance, as if Adam would dare to take on him and his muscles.

April gestured toward the kitchen. "What happened here, Adam? Kenzie called me in a panic and told me there was blood all over my place. We didn't exactly find blood all over, but we did find smears of it in the kitchen and droplets in the sink."

"Yeah, um, Jimmy attacked me here." Adam danced from foot to foot, already missing his fix. "Hit me on the head and hustled me out. He must've cleaned up my blood before he left."

Clay tapped the cheekbone beneath his eye. "Outside of that shiner you're gonna get, you look in remarkably good shape for just being abducted by an angry drug dealer."

"Yeah." Adam traced his fingertips around his eye socket. "He roughed me up. Blood must've come from my head wound."

"Where did he hold you?" Clay narrowed his eyes.

"I don't know, man. They put a hood over my head. Then they got some calls, had some discussions and then stuffed me in my car… I mean, your car, April, and dropped me off in the desert. They loosened my ties so that I could get out, but not before they took off. I knew there was trouble with the cops."

"You're lucky they didn't kill you." April tapped her head. "Do you need some ice or treatment for your head?"

Adam's hand darted to the back of his head and he shoved his fingers into his long hair. "No, it's okay."

Clay asked, his face still tight, "Did you ever convince them you didn't have that flash drive?"

"I don't think so. That's probably why they let me live. If they offed me, they'd lose that information. They figured they could always pick me up again if they wanted."

"I wonder why they didn't just tie you up and leave you while they dealt with the cops." Clay rubbed his knuckles along the edge of his jaw.

"How am I supposed to know? I didn't have a clue how that guy's mind operated."

"And yet you were willing to marry off your sister to him." Clay's hands curled into fists at his sides.

April hopped off the couch. "Did they say why the cops were looking for Gilbert?"

"I didn't get all of that." Adam tucked his hair behind one ear and made a wide berth around Clay on his way to the kitchen. "You got a beer?"

She shifted a glance to Clay and took a deep breath. "We *do* know."

Adam ducked his head in the fridge. "Why were the cops after Gil?"

Clay strode across the room and hunched over the counter. "The guy you set your sister up with sent two mules—women—into one of those Las Moscas tunnels, but they didn't make it. Las Moscas caught them, beheaded them and proceeded to leave their body parts around Paradiso."

"Damn." Adam took a long pull from his beer. "That's brutal."

"Do you remember Gilbert's girlfriend, Elena?" April came up behind Clay and put a hand on his back. His rage at Adam kept bubbling to the surface and she didn't want to clean up any more of her brother's blood from this kitchen.

"I remember." Adam held his hand about chest-high. "Cute little Latina chick with a tight little body."

"That cute little Latina chick doesn't have a head on her tight little body anymore." Clay smacked his hand on the counter.

Adam jumped, and the blood drained from his face. "Are you kidding? Gilbert sent his own girlfriend into the tunnel?"

April set him straight…in case he didn't already know. "His name isn't Gilbert. It's Jesus, and he and Elena have been quite the Bonnie and Clyde over the years. That's how the cops traced her to Gilbert."

"Unreal." Adam shook his shaggy head and gulped down some more beer.

Clay fell back on the stool at the counter, straddling it. "You wouldn't happen to know the older woman Elena was working with, do you? White, maybe in her forties."

Adam rolled his eyes toward the ceiling. "Doesn't ring a bell. Damn, can't believe they used women. Did they think Las Moscas wouldn't kill a female mule?"

Clay ground out, "They were wrong."

"Are you going to stay here, Adam?"

Clay kicked her foot.

"I'll leave you guys and stay at my place, now that I know it's safe."

"Why'd you come back here?" Clay stood up and grabbed his gun from the counter.

Adam's gaze tracked Clay's weapon into his hand. "Honestly, just to get my drugs. I didn't know you'd be here."

"I didn't mean this time. I meant why'd you come back here when you knew Jimmy was looking for you?"

"I knew it was empty. I figured he'd try my place first or Kenzie's, so I wasn't going to go back there. Just needed a quick place to crash."

"And get high." Clay jabbed his finger at Adam. "You need to get clean, get your act together. April's not going to be bailing you out anymore. She doesn't owe you a damned thing."

April pulled her bottom lip between her teeth. Of course she owed Adam. She owed him for being her parents' favorite. She owed him for inheriting all of their mother's assets. She owed him because he'd been the one to find Mom murdered on the kitchen floor while she'd been off at school enjoying herself.

"Kenzie's thinking about going into rehab. I might join her." Adam tossed his empty bottle in the trash. "This just might be rock bottom for me."

"Did you drive my car back? Where did you park that you didn't realize someone was here? Clay's truck is in my parking space."

"I didn't want to advertise my presence." Adam jerked a thumb over his shoulder. "I parked down the block. Can I take your car to Kenzie's? You can pick it up tomorrow morning, but I will need my allowance a little early."

"Allowance?" Clay's eyebrows snapped together.

April ran her hand along the corded muscles in Clay's forearm. "Take the car, and we'll pick it up tomorrow morning. Leave me Kenzie's address because I have no idea where she lives, and she hasn't been answering my calls to your phone."

"Good girl. She probably turned it off so Jimmy couldn't track me." Adam pulled open a kitchen drawer and grabbed a pen and a sticky note. "I'll write her address here, and I'll leave the car on the street in front of her apartment building. You can pick it up tomorrow morning."

"That'll work." She peeled the sticky paper from Adam's proffered finger. "And Clay's right. The two of you need to get clean. Stop associating with people like Jimmy."

Adam formed his fingers into a gun and pointed it at her. "Got it. Think allowance."

April cranked her head around the apartment. "Do you have anything else here?"

"No, unless you were kidding about those drugs." Adam raised his eyebrows at Clay, who scowled at him.

"I guess that's it, then." Adam skirted the counter and pulled April into a one-armed hug. "Take care. Let me know if you want me to pack up this place and get you moved out."

"You, too." April's nose stung. She couldn't help it. Adam would always be her little brother, a little lost and confused from the start.

He backed out of the apartment, jingling the car keys. "I'll leave these tucked in the visor in case we're not home."

April called after him, "Be careful. Jimmy might be dead, but we don't know anything about the others or the guys who killed him."

Adam waved a hand behind him before slamming the door.

Clay turned toward her stiffly. "Allowance?"

"Don't blame me." She patted her chest. "That was a condition of Mom's will. I got everything, but I pay out an allowance to Adam from the money. It's a cash stipend so he can't blow it all at once."

"He must love that you control the purse strings."

"He's used to it, but it's what fuels his get-rich-quick schemes or that's just genetic from Dad."

"Why are those schemes always illegal?"

"I don't know." She wrapped her arms around Clay's waist and rested her head against his broad chest. "I'm just glad he's safe—for now. And thanks for not ripping his head off."

"You could tell I wanted to?"

"And so could he." She caressed his face. "Let's go to bed."

Clay kissed the top of her head and then set her aside. He went to the front door and flicked the dead bolt at the top. "Too bad he didn't leave your keys."

"He'll need them if I have him empty out this place."

"If?" Clay slipped his hands behind his back and rested against the door.

"With Jimmy gone and his associates on the run, maybe I can settle in Albuquerque. It's not a bad place."

"Adam is here."

"For now."

"Do you think he's going to give up on his dreams of El Gringo Viejo?"

"Probably not."

Clay swore. "As long as he doesn't involve you, because if he goes traipsing down to Mexico asking the wrong questions of the wrong people, his encounter with Jimmy Verdugo is going to look like a picnic."

"I don't know." She plucked up the remote control and turned off the TV, which had been silently running in the background of their drama. "Maybe he learned his lesson."

Clay pushed off the door. "It didn't look like Jimmy taught him much of a lesson. Except for that redness around his eye, Adam didn't have any marks on his face for a guy who'd been beaten by a couple of thugs."

"He said Jimmy hit him on the head. That's probably where all the blood came from. Head wounds bleed a lot, right? That was enough to incapacitate Adam and allow Jimmy to take him away."

"Maybe." Clay covered his face with his hands and then dragged his fingers through his hair. "I'm sick of Adam and his problems. Promise me you won't fall prey to one of his scams again."

"Yeah, no, I'm on to him."

Clay drew close to her and brushed the pad of his thumb across the skin on her chest, right above her hammering heart. "You have a soft spot for Adam, and he knows it."

Standing on her tiptoes, she kissed Clay's irresistible lips. "I have a soft spot for you, Clay Archer."

He swept her up in his arms. "That's funny. I have something hard for you."

She halfheartedly pummeled his chest with her fists. "You have a one-track mind."

"Jimmy's dead. Adam's safe." He strode to her bedroom and kicked open the door. "What's stopping us now?"

THE FOLLOWING MORNING, April packed up again and went from room to room to make sure she wasn't leaving anything important behind.

As she cleared the bottles of water from the fridge, Clay entered the kitchen. "Are you going to leave those beers?"

"Might as well keep them here for Adam. It'll be his payment for closing up my apartment if I decide to leave Albuquerque." She shook out a plastic grocery bag and put a bottle of water inside. "Speaking of payments, I think I can find that guy's house again—the one with the car. Maybe I could even leave him my car as payment."

"I suppose you could do that if you're not attached to your car. The one you got from him is a junker."

"Mine is only slightly better, and I owe him for his trouble."

Clay touched her waist. "When are you going to stop feeling so guilty about everything? And when are you going to start spending some of the money from your mom? Why are you driving an old car when you can afford a new one?"

She balled up a fist and pressed it against her midsection. "Would you be freely spending life insurance money you got from your mom's murder?"

"Your mom had the policy and named you beneficiary. However she died, she wanted you to benefit from it. That's how life insurance works. Look at my mother. After my dad died, she didn't hesitate to use his life insurance money to enjoy her life. It's what he would've wanted."

"Your father wasn't murdered." She tossed another plastic bottle into the bag.

"A car accident isn't much prettier."

Rubbing Clay's back, she said, "Your dad was a great guy. I miss him."

"But not my mom."

"Your mom never liked me, so it was hard for me to warm up to her." She lifted the bag and swung it from her fingertips. "She must positively hate me now."

"She's on a cruise somewhere in the Caribbean. I don't think she hates anyone right now." He snatched the bag from her hand. "I'll put a couple of these in the front for the trip, or one...you can take the other in your car when we pick it up from Kenzie's place. You can follow me. I'll keep you in my rearview."

"You don't have to worry anymore, Clay."

"What are you going to say if Detective Espinoza finds out you were engaged to Jimmy and questions you?"

"Tell him the truth. I was engaged to Jimmy, didn't know his line of business, left him when I had my suspicions."

"And if he asks you about Gilbert? He showed us his picture when he was Jesus."

She shrugged. "I never saw Gilbert or Jesus or Elena or any of them."

"You'd be lying."

"Sometimes you have to tell lies that don't hurt anyone if those lies protect other people." She grabbed her purse and hitched it over her shoulder. "Let's get out of here."

As she locked the dead bolt from the outside, Clay clicked his tongue and said, "Keep telling yourself that, April."

When they reached Kenzie's block, April spotted her blue compact across the street from her apartment complex. "There's my car. At least he followed through with something."

"Does Adam have a car, or does he always use yours or Kenzie's?" Clay glanced over his shoulder as he parallel-parked his truck three cars down from hers.

"He has a motorcycle." She threw open the door of the truck and stepped onto the curb. "Now let's see if he followed through with the keys."

Clay slammed his door and locked the truck with a beep. "Are you gonna go up even if he did?"

"No. By leaving me the car keys, I think he made it clear he didn't need to see me before I left town."

April held her breath as she stalked up to the car. She pulled the door handle and released a sigh. "It's open."

She ducked into the car and flipped down the visor. Her key chain, with the big red *A* for the University of Arizona, slid down and she caught it.

Jingling the key chain at Clay, she said, "He actually followed through."

"Give the guy a medal." Clay smacked the top of the car. "Pop the trunk."

She straightened up and folded her arms on top of the open car door. "You don't need to put my bags in the trunk. I told you, I plan to leave this car with Ryan in exchange for the other one."

"I know that. Adam said Jimmy loaded him in the trunk of this car after holding him and dropped him off in the desert." He pounded a fist on the trunk. "Humor me."

Cocking her head to one side, April pressed the button on the remote to open the trunk. It clicked and sprang up a few inches.

Clay pushed it up and bent forward, shoving his sunglasses on top of his head.

April joined him, bumping his hip with hers. "Find what you're looking for?"

"I don't know what I'm looking for." He reached into the trunk and pulled out a hand towel, shaking it out.

April sucked in a breath and stepped away from the bloodstained towel. "Well, there you have it. Jimmy must've stuffed a bleeding Adam into the trunk. I even recognize the towel as one of Jimmy's."

Clay jerked the towel by one corner so that it danced in the air. "This is a towel from Jimmy's house?"

Wrinkling her nose, April pointed to the edge of the towel. "It's the same color as the towels in his guest bathroom downstairs and has the same raised pattern on the bottom."

"All right." Clay kept hold of the towel and shut the trunk.

"What are you going to do with it?"

"You can't leave a bloody towel in the trunk of a car you plan to give away."

"You have a point there." Avoiding the towel, she leaned in for a kiss.

They jumped apart as a voice called from above.

April twisted her head around and spied Adam waving from a second-story window. She lifted her hand. "I wonder if he wants us to come up."

Then Adam disappeared from the frame and closed the window.

"Guess not." Clay opened the car door for her. "I'll follow you over to this guy's place. Do you think it's safe?"

"They're a couple of young guys whose only violent tendencies probably come from the video games they play."

"Who got duped into trading a car for a worthless rock."

"I'm going to make good on that."

"You've never been the best judge of character, April." Clay shut the car door on her retort and strode back to his truck.

She bit her lip as she watched him in the rearview mirror. The only character she'd ever accurately judged was his.

The drop-off with Ryan went smoother than expected.

That might've had something to do with Clay's large and in-charge presence hanging over the negotiations.

She made things official by signing off on a transfer and then joined Clay in his truck.

They spent the hours-long ride back to Paradiso catching up, as before they'd been too busy discussing heads and headless bodies and Jimmy and Adam and mules. Jimmy's death had freed her, and she couldn't even feel sadness for the man he'd been when they first met—because he'd never been that man. That Jimmy had been Adam's creation—and she'd fallen so easily into his trap in her desire to push away the memories of Clay.

She turned her head to the side and drank in his strong profile. As if she could ever forget about Clay.

Maybe they had a chance now. Maybe the ugliness that had swirled around her after Dad murdered Mom and disappeared had taken a permanent hiatus, and she could start living the life she wanted.

Clay jerked his head to the side. "What?"

"Just contemplating my future." She stretched her arms in front of her, entwining her fingers.

"Our immediate future involves getting back to Meg's so that I can pick up Denali."

She adjusted her sunglasses as Clay headed west on the turnoff for Paradiso. "I wonder if Meg and Kyle have gone on a date yet. He's not married, is he?"

"No. You think they hit it off?"

"Duh." She cracked open her window, preferring fresh air to AC. "I'm surprised they hadn't met before. Paradiso is hardly a bustling metropolis."

"I've never played matchmaker before—except maybe between you and Denali. Now, that was love at first sight."

She whispered, "I missed...that dog."

"He missed you." Clay's knuckles turned white as he gripped the steering wheel. "And he'll miss you again."

April pressed her lips together as a pulse beat in her throat. She'd have to play this by ear. She had no right to spring random thoughts on Clay until she'd had a chance to examine all angles. Hell, maybe he didn't want her back, anyway.

Ten minutes later, they were rolling up to Meg's house. Clay parked his truck behind Meg's car in the driveway.

"Good, she's home."

"It *is* Saturday." April jerked her thumb over her shoulder. "What are you going to do with that bloody towel you found in my trunk?"

"I'm not sure yet, but don't tell anyone about it...including your brother."

Grabbing the door handle, she cocked her head. "I'm sure he already knows about it."

"Then there's no need to tell him we have it." Clay raised his eyebrows before jumping out of the car.

She didn't blame him for being suspicious of Adam, but did he think he faked his own abduction?

Halfway up the walkway, the front door burst open and Denali bounded down the porch steps. He shot past Clay and danced and circled around her legs.

April laughed. "Good boy. You know who's gonna give you the treats."

"Some welcome home." Clay crouched down, and Denali barreled into his chest, licking his face. "That's more like it."

"He heard your truck and started going crazy." Meg stood on the threshold, framed by the door, propping the screen door open with her foot. "Everything go okay in New Mexico?"

"Just fine." April waved her hand in the air. "Everything okay here? No more body parts showing up, I hope."

"N-no, nothing quite like that." Meg crossed her arms.

Clay's head shot up. "Did the other woman's body turn up?"

"No." Meg turned toward the house. "It's probably nothing. I'll show you."

April poked Clay in the back as she followed him up the porch steps. When he twisted his head over his shoulder, she rolled her eyes.

Once inside, Clay tripped to a stop and April plowed into his back.

"Hey, Kyle. You checking up on the security system?"

Kyle raised his beer. "Something like that."

April nudged Clay's upper arm and he rubbed it as if she'd punched him. "Why do you keep poking and prodding at me?"

She winked and then turned to Meg, hovering by the kitchen counter. "What did you have to show me?"

Meg slid an envelope off the counter with two fingers and held it up. "This was stuck under my windshield wiper today. It has your name on it."

April caught her breath but forced a smile to her lips. "Mysterious. You didn't see who left it?"

"No. I was at the grocery store. My car was in the parking lot and it was there when I came out."

Under Meg's watchful eye, April inserted her thumb beneath the flap and ripped it open. She withdrew a single sheet of paper, and her blood ran cold in her veins.

Chapter Thirteen

Clay nodded as he responded to Kyle's question, but his heightened senses were focused on April, a white sheet of paper in one hand and an envelope crushed in the other.

He held up one finger to Kyle. "Excuse me a minute. What's that all about, April?"

She held up the paper in front of her face and flipped her hair over one shoulder. "Just a note from a friend… Carly. She heard I was in town, but didn't know how to reach me."

Meg fanned herself. "Whew. I'm glad that's all it was. Why didn't Carly just come to the house and see me or leave the note in the mailbox?"

"Not sure." April squinted at the letter, which Clay would give anything to see. "She doesn't go into it here. Probably just saw your car in the parking lot and decided to leave a note."

April folded the paper, creasing it with her thumb, and shoved it into the wrinkled envelope. Clay followed the path of the folded envelope from hand to front pocket as a muscle twitched at the corner of his mouth.

Maybe it was another communication from Adam. Maybe another scheme. He knew damned well it wasn't a note from Carly. And now he knew April would never stop lying to him.

"We've gotta get going." Clay scratched the top of Denali's head. "I'll bring your bags in, April."

"Oh, April's staying here?" Meg raised her brows, but Clay caught the quick glance she threw Kyle's way.

"Of course I'm staying here." April flung her arms out to her sides. "But don't mind me. I'm exhausted from that quick turnaround trip to New Mexico. I'm going to grab a snack, a glass of wine and head to my bedroom to fall asleep in front of the TV."

All smiles, Meg responded, "That sounds like a plan."

Clay turned on his heel and April called after him, "I can come with you to get my bags."

"I've got it. Find yourself that snack and let me have my dog back." He whistled and Denali trotted after him, giving April one last longing look. Clay refused to emulate his dog.

The only reason he'd want to be alone with April was to tackle her and grab that note, but if she wanted to continue lying to him, who was he to stand in her way?

He yanked her bags from the back and eyed the bloody towel in the corner. Two could play these games and have secrets.

Clay dropped April's bags just inside the door and held up a hand. "Have a good night, everyone, and thanks for watching Denali, Meg."

He knew April wouldn't try to stop him from leaving. She wanted him out of here as fast as he wanted to be out.

Despite Jimmy's death, or maybe because of it, Clay heaved a sigh at the thought of Kyle spending the night with Meg. He couldn't shake the feeling that April's trials and tribulations weren't behind her. Maybe they never would be as long as she kept her brother in her life, but she'd made that choice. She'd made a lot of choices he didn't agree with.

He punched the accelerator and the truck leaped forward, leaving Denali scrabbling for purchase on the seat beside him.

"Sorry, boy." He rubbed the dog under the chin. "Looks like April is getting ready to bolt again."

Denali whined, rolling one ice-blue eye at him.

"Don't look at me like that. I tried, but at least this time I'm not letting her get away without knowing the full truth."

After he arrived home and unpacked, Clay scanned through his contacts for the phone number of Duncan Brady, a buddy of his in forensics for the Pima County Sheriff's Department.

He placed his phone on the kitchen counter and put it on speaker, getting ready to leave Duncan a message on this Saturday night.

When Duncan answered on the third ring, Clay snatched up the phone. "I didn't expect you to be home."

Duncan snorted. "Did you forget Olivia and I had a baby a few months ago? I'm pretty sure we got your gift."

"I guess your Saturday nights are booked up, huh?"

"Baby swings, diapers, trying to catch a few winks during those rare times the baby conks out, still rubbing Olivia's feet—although I'm beginning to think that one's a scam." Duncan snorted again. "Must sound like hell to a single guy like you."

Clay squeezed his eyes closed. "Yeah, sounds rough."

"In fact, probably the only reason you're not out raising hell on a Saturday night is because of that mess you have going on down there. Two heads and one body. Female mules. Makes me sick." Duncan sucked in a breath. "Is that why you're calling? Need some help with that?"

"Unofficial help if you're offering."

"I owe you a few. I can't remember which one of us is due now, but I'll hit you up later." Duncan took a sip of something, probably a cocktail, before continuing. "What do you need?"

"Need you to run a couple of DNA tests on some blood." Clay glanced at the two plastic bags on the counter—one with blood taken from April's kitchen and the other with the towel taken from the trunk of her car. "Under the radar."

"This is outside of Detective Espinoza's investigation?"

"Congruent with. I'm not doing a runaround on Espinoza, but you know how it is with multiagency investigations. Stuff that's important to you won't get a second look from the guy and agency in charge—and Espinoza is in charge."

"I can do it for you, Archer." A baby wailed in the background. "Duty calls. When can you bring me these samples?"

"You're still in Bisbee?"

"Same place. You wanna bring them by the house tomorrow?"

"If I'm not going to crash your baby party."

"Hey, it's a party every day around here. Best time for me is around noon. Can you make it?"

"I'll be there." Clay cleared his throat. "And congratulations, man."

Clay ended the call and spun his phone around on the counter. Duncan had been a hard partyer back in the day when Clay had been with April. Now Duncan was the family man, and Clay had no one.

Denali barked and pawed at his leg.

"Yeah, okay, I have you. But let's face it. Even you have more loyalty to April than you do to me." Leaning forward, he cuffed Denali's sharp ears with both hands and touched his nose to the dog's wet snout.

When his phone buzzed, Clay grabbed it. His heart bumped against his rib cage when he saw the call was from Meg.

"Everything okay?" He couldn't keep the edge out of his voice and Denali perked up his ears.

"I—I'm not sure, Clay." Meg's voice dropped to a whisper. "You know that note April got?"

"Yeah." Clay forced the word past his dry throat.

"I opened it."

"You stole it from April?" Great minds must've been thinking alike. "I hope you didn't have to tackle her."

"What? No. I opened it before I gave it to her, and then I resealed it. I'm sorry if that makes me nosy, but... it's April and she found two heads on two different days."

"So?" Clay licked his lips. "I'm guessing it wasn't from Carly. What did it say?"

"The note was weird, like in one of those kidnapping movies with the letters cut out of magazines."

The blood pulsed in his veins. "What did it say, Meg?"

"It said, 'Nothing has changed. Stay away from him.'"

As THE LIGHT of day edged into the room through the gaps in the blinds, April felt beneath her pillow for the hundredth time since she'd stashed the envelope there. Sleep had eluded her all night.

Her fingers curled around a corner of the envelope and she dragged it out. She stared at the white oblong in the semidarkness.

Who was watching her? Who was torturing her? Had this malevolent presence been waiting for her to show up in Paradiso again? And why?

She knew nothing. She had no information to give Clay about anything. She hadn't even known Jimmy when she and Clay had been engaged. It couldn't be him or his associates.

Her father. Was Adam right? Was their father some big-time drug dealer who didn't want his daughter married to a Border Patrol agent?

She buried her face in the pillow. It didn't make any sense. But she knew it was no hoax.

The first time she'd received the warning, the week before her wedding, her tormenter had tampered with the brakes on Clay's truck to show her he could get to Clay when and where he wanted. Then he'd kidnapped Denali.

Clay had no idea these events were connected or had any greater meaning than a patch of bad luck—but she knew. The person threatening her made sure of that.

She could've told Clay. He would've assured her that he could protect himself and her, just like he always had. But what if he couldn't? What if some day out on the lonely border, working on his own, Clay met with violence? It would look so natural—a Border Patrol agent running into a bad guy and winding up dead. It did happen.

But she would know. She'd know that she brought that danger to Clay, and she wouldn't have been able to live with herself. So much better to hurt him once, hard and fast, and leave him to find someone else, someone less complicated, someone less…cursed.

She rubbed her stinging nose. She'd been so close to staying here with Clay and making a life with him. She'd been trying to create that with Jimmy when Adam had given her a Clay substitute in Jimmy, but she'd known all along on some level that it was all a big lie. Nobody could ever replace Clay in her heart.

But this time, she planned to fight for him, fight for the life they deserved together, and if the puzzle started with her father, then she needed to go to the source.

By the time she dragged herself into the kitchen, the two new lovebirds were chirping at each other over breakfast.

Meg looked up from her omelet. "Kyle made me breakfast. Do you want some?"

Kyle held up his fork and circled it in the air. "I can whip up another omelet for you, April."

"Coffee's fine for me." She reached for a mug on the shelf and poured some coffee for herself. "How'd the security system work the past few days?"

"Perfect." Meg fluttered her lashes at Kyle. "I felt so safe."

"I don't think you'll be finding any more heads on your porch." Kyle entwined his fingers with Meg's.

"I certainly hope not." April smiled into her coffee cup as she took a sip. "Did Denali behave himself?"

"He's high energy. I took him to doggy daycare on Friday, so he could frolic while I was at work. I forgot to tell Clay, but I know he's used that place before." Meg traced a finger around the rim of her orange juice glass. "Have you heard from Clay this morning?"

"Why would I? After two days together, I'm sure he needs a break from me."

"Sure he does." Meg rolled her eyes. "What happened in New Mexico? Did you close up your apartment? See Adam?"

"Might be keeping my place there, and I did see Adam."

"Is he still a troublemaker?"

"He still has issues. Why wouldn't he?" April's cheeks warmed in Adam's defense.

"C'mon, April." Meg's gaze shifted to Kyle, busily scanning through his phone. "Adam was trouble before…it happened."

"I know that, but finding Mom didn't help matters." April tossed her coffee into the sink.

"Of course not. That's just unimaginable, but you survived it."

Did she? Did you ever survive a trauma like theirs? "Everyone deals differently."

Kyle held up his phone. "They found her."

"Who?" Meg reached across the table and dabbed a string of cheese from Kyle's chin.

April gripped the edge of the sink. "The second headless body?"

Kyle nodded. "In the pecan groves down from Clay's house."

April clenched her teeth. She'd been walking Denali out there the other day. Had the body been there then? Had Denali sensed it? Smelled it?

She eked out a breath between her teeth. "Hopefully, they can identify her and put both of these women to rest."

"They were mules, working for a cartel." Meg screwed

up one side of her mouth. "I wouldn't waste too much pity on them."

Folding her arms and grabbing her upper arms, April said, "They were exploited, probably told their mission didn't hold any risks beyond getting arrested by Border Patrol."

"Some women are easily duped." Meg collected the dishes on the table. "Kyle and I are going to Tucson today. Do you have any plans?"

"Just some errands. Have fun." April left the newly minted couple goggling at each other over the table and returned to her bedroom to shower and get dressed.

She knew she wouldn't be contacting Clay today. Whatever this was, this threat over their heads, she had no intention of bringing it down on Clay. He had enough threats in his life with Las Moscas littering the town with body parts. But this time, she planned to track down the threat. If that meant traveling to Mexico to find El Gringo Viejo, that's what she'd do—and she'd need Adam to do it.

When she got out of the shower, she glanced at her phone. Clay hadn't contacted her yet. He'd been suspicious about the note. Maybe his suspicions would steer him away from her for now.

She texted Adam to let him know she was ready to look for Dad—wherever that led them.

She hadn't been lying to Meg about errands. She had to get that car in her name, get some money, make some inquiries…avoid Clay.

By the time she left, Meg and Kyle were gone. April locked up the house and walked out to the car that almost officially belonged to her. She couldn't afford to run down to Mexico in a stolen car.

She took care of most of her business and decided to

get some lunch before the next round. She ducked into the air-conditioned confines of a small café at the end of the main street and ordered a sandwich.

While she waited, she cradled her phone in her hand. Nothing yet from Adam and nothing from Clay. She must've sent Clay the keep-away message last night loud and clear.

She flattened her hand against her chest, over her aching heart. She'd come back to Clay one day—free and unencumbered by the dark cloud that hung over her head.

When she heard her order number, she picked up her sandwich, refilling her soda on the way back to her table. She stumbled and her drink sloshed over the side of her cup when she saw a man sitting at her table, his large frame spilling over the sides of the chair.

She hadn't left her purse there, but she'd left some napkins and the lid to her cup.

She cleared her throat as she approached the table. "Excuse me, but I was sitting here."

The man spread his fleshy lips in what looked like an attempt at a smile. "I know that, April. That's why I'm sitting here."

She swallowed, her grip tightening on the paper cup in her hand. "Who are you?"

"Have a seat, and I'll tell you all about it." He pushed out the chair across from him with his foot, and it scraped across the floor, setting her teeth on edge.

She almost dropped her plate as she set it on the table. Sinking to the chair, she held on to her drink like a security blanket, all her nerve endings on high alert. "What do you want?"

He hunched forward, his double chin tripling. "I think you know what we want... Mrs. Jimmy Verdugo."

The drink in her hand jerked, spilling onto the table. "I'm not… I didn't…"

He held up his hand, his sausage-like fingers encircled with several glittering rings. "I know you ditched the wedding at the last minute—smart move. But we know you have Jimmy's flash drive, or your brother has it."

"I don't have it. I never saw it."

"If you don't have it, your brother does." He lifted the loose shirt he wore over his large frame to reveal a gun strapped to his body. "And you're gonna get it and him for us…or what happened to those two mules is gonna look like a garden party."

Chapter Fourteen

Clay's adrenaline spiked when he saw the big man who'd entered the café seconds before sit at the table April had been occupying. He dropped his binoculars on the seat beside him and charged out of the car. He burst into the restaurant and several people, including April and her tablemate, glanced up at him. He ate up the space between him and April in two long strides.

"Is this man bothering you?"

April shook her head, her pale face belying her response.

The man scooted back his chair and rose to his feet, patting his belly. "Just taking a load off. It's hard for a man my size to wait on his feet."

Clay's eyes narrowed. He didn't have any right to arrest this man or question him if April didn't open her mouth.

He put a hand on her shoulder. "Is that right, April?"

"H-he was just sitting for a minute." She'd pinned her gaze to the man's right hand, resting on his hip.

The man rapped his knuckles on the table. "You have a good day now, miss."

He walked out of the café with more grace than expected from a man carrying that extra weight.

When the door whooshed shut, Clay took the seat

across from April that the man had vacated. "What was that all about?"

April picked up her grilled cheese sandwich and nipped a bite off the corner. She dabbed some crumbs from her lips, and then took a sip of her soda. Then she dusted off her fingertips over her plate.

Finally, she raised her eyes to his. "He just threatened me over that flash drive."

Clay jumped from his chair, knocking it to the floor with a bang.

As he took a step toward the door, April grabbed his hand. "He's gone. I made sure of that before I told you, so you wouldn't get killed."

"Why are you telling me this now when it's too late?" He shook off her hand. "I could've arrested him."

"He would've killed you." She lifted her shoulders. "He had a gun. When you were at the table, his hand was hovering over his weapon. If you'd made a move, he would've shot you."

Clay righted the chair and waved at the guy manning the counter. When he sat down, he scooted in close, almost touching his nose to April's. "I'm a Border Patrol agent. It's not your job to protect me. It's your job to report crimes or threats and let the authorities, including me, take action."

"I couldn't have warned you about the gun. I have no doubt in my mind he would've drawn on you and shot you—and then probably abducted me in the process." She waved her arm around the room of regular people enjoying their lunches. "Do you think any one of these people would've done anything to stop him?"

"You don't have much faith in my abilities, do you?" He raised his brows and took a gulp from her cup.

"When it's a fair fight I do, but not when it's a sneak

attack or ambush. Anybody can get to anybody else if they really want to."

Clay smacked his hand against his forehead. "I'm not your brother, April. You don't have to look out for me."

"Speaking of my brother, he wanted Adam." She ripped the crust from her sandwich. "It's the flash drive again. He thinks Adam or I have it."

"Damn it." Clay pounded his fist on the table. "When is this going to end? Adam must have the flash drive, and I'm gonna get it from him."

"He said he didn't…"

Clay skewered her with a look and she trailed off, too embarrassed to continue.

"Exactly. We can't trust anything Adam says…about anything. He's probably had it all this time. Who knows if Jimmy and his guys would've been able to get it out of him, if they hadn't been distracted by their other troubles? I wish they had, and then when Las Moscas came to call on Jimmy, they would've gotten the flash drive from him and this would be over."

"And Adam would be dead."

"He's dead, anyway, April, unless he turns over that flash drive to Las Moscas. Do you think the fat man is fooling around? But now, Adam has dragged you into it—just like he always does."

"Maybe I can convince Adam to give it up. If it does contain a map of Las Moscas' border tunnels, Adam doesn't have the connections to make use of that information, anyway."

Clay spread his hands on the table, his thumbs touching. "Was this the note? Did this guy leave you a note to meet with him?"

April blinked several times in rapid succession. "Yes.

I thought he was going to give me some information about why the heads were left on our porches."

"Do you have the note on you? Can I see it?"

"I burned it." She picked up her ragged sandwich and took a big bite.

"I could've taken prints from it." He cocked his head. "How did he know Meg's car?"

"He was probably watching the house before." She dug her elbows into the table and rested her chin on her palm. "How'd you know I was in this café? How'd you know to come charging in here? You always seem to know exactly where I am."

"Paradiso's a small town. I was driving out this way and saw your car parked on the street—just like before. I was coming in to join you for lunch when I saw that goon at your table." He could lie with the best of them.

"So join me for lunch." She glanced over her shoulder. "In case he comes back."

"You told him you didn't have the flash drive?"

"Of course I did." She toyed with her straw, scattering drops of liquid across the table. "I don't know whether or not he believed me, but if I don't have it, he thinks Adam does."

"I'm with him there. Any way you can talk Adam into giving it up? To spare both of you?" He grabbed her drink before she sprinkled it all over the table, and chugged it back so fast the carbonation brought tears to his eyes. "Scratch that. He's the one who set you up with a dangerous man in the first place."

"I can try to talk to him. I may have a way to convince him." She lowered her lashes, which told him she had no intention of telling him what she could use to persuade her brother to give up the flash drive.

At this point, he didn't care as long as it didn't involve marrying another drug dealer—or marrying anyone at all. He drilled his fist into his other palm. "How about some good old-fashioned violence?"

She flattened her lips into a thin line. "You propose to beat Adam until he tells you where the flash drive is? Yeah, that's not going to work, and if you don't think Adam would press charges against you, you don't know Adam. He'd see that as an opportunity for a lawsuit and some easy money."

Clay curled his hand around his clenched fist.

"You're right. I don't know Adam that well. I'd always seen him as trouble, but more of a hapless, sweet screwup. But setting you up with Jimmy Verdugo?" He skimmed a hand across the top of his head, his short hair tickling his palm. "That's a low I didn't think he had in him."

"I didn't, either." April pushed away her plate. "I'm going to text him and tell him what happened here. I'm going to convince him to turn over the flash drive to you."

"Even if he does that, April, he's still in danger from Las Moscas. He may no longer have the info they don't want him to have, but turning it over to us isn't going to endear him to the cartel. They'll want their revenge. He's gotten into some real trouble—and dragged you with him."

"And I'm going to get us out of it." She held up a hand, palm facing outward. "Don't ask. Don't try to stop me. I know what I'm doing."

"When it comes to your brother, I doubt that." He placed his palm against hers and clasped her hand. "But you do what you have to do."

And he'd do what he had to do. He'd already dropped off the blood samples to Duncan. Two could play this game. Could he help it if she were so much better at it than he was?

APRIL HAD TWO different sandals on in front of the mirror as she turned this way and that.

Meg and Kyle had convinced her and Clay to come out to dinner, although neither one of them was in a festive mood.

After lunch this afternoon, Clay had shut down on her, and for the first time since she met him, she felt as if he had more secrets than she did.

The rotund cartel member who'd threatened her in The Melt hadn't left that note. Now she had danger coming at her from two different fronts.

Or were they different?

Had Las Moscas been behind the warning delivered to her two years ago about marrying Clay? Adam could've already been involved with Jimmy and Las Moscas at that time and maybe his new associates didn't want Adam to have a brother-in-law working for Border Patrol.

She covered her mouth, meeting her own eyes in the mirror as a little shiver rippled down her spine. Perhaps Adam had told Jimmy about his sister and his father, El Gringo Viejo, a long time ago and Jimmy had already determined the best way to get to the drug supplier down south was to marry his daughter, and to do that, she'd have to be single and available for his courtship.

She dropped to the edge of the bed and toed off the flat sandal in favor of the one with the low heel.

Adam had finally answered her text and agreed to fly out to Phoenix to meet her tomorrow. She planned to get to the bottom of this…and offer him her deal. All without Clay's knowledge, of course. He'd try to stop her and she couldn't allow that.

Meg tapped on her open door. "Oh, that's a pretty sundress. If you're wearing that for Clay, does that mean the two of you have patched things up?"

"Patched things up?" April rose and flicked the skirt of the dress. "We didn't have anything to patch up. We're fine…as friends."

"Some friend. He sure seemed like he couldn't get out of here fast enough last night. Picked up Denali and—" Meg whistled "—out of here."

"We were both tired, Meg."

"Blah, blah, blah." Meg squared her shoulders in the doorway. "What's the real reason you ran out on the wedding? What was the excuse you gave Clay? 'It's me, not you?' 'You're too good for me?'"

"Ugh." April covered her eyes. "I don't want to talk about it, please. Can we just have a pleasant dinner without bringing up body parts or weddings?"

"Yeah, because both of those are equally horrific." Meg rolled her eyes. "Kyle and I intend to have more than a pleasant dinner, despite you two."

"It's not too late to disinvite us." April yanked a light sweater from the bed in case of overactive AC in the restaurant.

"Oh, no. You're not getting out of it that easily."

April breezed past her cousin and tugged on one chocolate-brown lock of hair. "When you're in love, you want the whole world to be in love."

A half hour later, the four of them were seated on the outdoor patio of Sinbad's, a Mediterranean restaurant in the center of town.

If she were on edge, searching for the distinct outline of the man who'd threatened her today, Clay matched her in jumpiness.

She knew he had his weapon on his person. He always carried off-duty. Kyle was probably packing, as well. The big man would be a fool to make a move in a public place with two armed men at the table.

So, when would he make his move? Would he wait for her to come up with the flash drive...or else? And then what? Clay seemed to believe neither she nor Adam would be out of danger even if they no longer had the flash drive.

Of course, if her plan worked and Adam gave her the flash drive, the two of them would be long gone after she turned it over to Clay, anyway.

When they placed their orders, April swirled her wine in her glass and said, "Have the authorities identified the other body?"

Kyle groaned. "Are you really going there? Now?"

"You need more wine." Meg grabbed the bottle of chardonnay from the bucket and attempted to top off April's glass.

"I've barely had two sips of this." April placed her hand over her glass. "It was just a question. One question."

"Answer her." Meg tipped her glass toward Clay. "And then that's it. No more of this talk."

"The short answer is no."

Meg did a karate chop with her hand in the middle of the table. "Let's keep it to the short answer."

As Meg and Kyle relived their idyllic day in Tucson, April scooted her chair closer to Clay's and dipped her head. "What's the long answer?"

"They took her prints, but there's no match in the database. They'll start looking at some missing persons. She could be up from Mexico."

"But she wasn't Latina?"

"A lot of gringos live south of the border." Clay shrugged. "How are you doing after your encounter this afternoon?"

"I'm okay. Just wondering when the other shoe is going to drop. How long is this guy going to give me to convince Adam to turn over the flash drive before he takes action?"

"You should be far, far away from here when he decides it's time. Do your best with Adam and then go into hiding. Leave the country if you have to. You still have plenty of money." Clay encircled her wrist with his fingers. "Start spending it to protect yourself."

"I've been texting with Adam. I think he's close to at least admitting he has the flash drive."

"I didn't tell you, but Detective Espinoza didn't find Jesus, the man formerly known as Gilbert, in Albuquerque." He pinged his wineglass with his fingernail. "But he did find Jimmy's dead body."

"Imagine that. Does he concur that Las Moscas can take credit for that one?"

"He thought it strange, as did I, that Las Moscas would use a knife to kill a rival instead of a gun with a silencer to the back of the head." Clay put a finger to his lips as the waiter approached the table with their food.

Everyone got busy with their food, and Meg aimed her skewer from her kebab at April and Clay, waving it back and forth between the two of them. "I'm sure your conversation is not fit for polite society, but at least you're talking again."

"Meg—" April dragged a piece of pita bread through the hummus on her plate "—please mind your own business."

"I second that." Kyle pinched Meg's chin between his fingers and placed a kiss on her lips.

Meg and Kyle's infatuation for each other left April and Clay free to discuss their morbid topic. The more April picked Clay's brain about what he believed happened in New Mexico, the better prepared she'd be to do her own search. That search might go easier with Clay by her side, but he'd never agree to it and she'd already been warned about keeping away from him.

April's eyes darted around the patio strung with lights. Could her tormenter be watching them right now?

By the end of the meal, April and Clay had abandoned their speculations and joined Meg and Kyle in more pleasant conversation. Meg had a glow about her that twisted a knife in April's gut.

She couldn't be happier for her cousin, but she missed that giddy feeling of uncomplicated love. She and Clay had that once. Or had they? Had her life ever been uncomplicated since the murder of her mother and the accusations against her father?

Clay had been here at the time of the murder, a brand-new Border Patrol agent. She'd been away at school and they didn't start dating until she'd come back to Paradiso after the murder and after she'd graduated from college. The events swirling around her family had already tainted her by the time she met Clay, already changed her.

She'd been carefree, majoring in dance choreography, the world wide open. When she returned to school, she'd changed her major to accounting. She'd wanted stability, security, order. She'd been determined to take care of Adam, who'd gone into a treatment facility immediately after the murder.

Maybe that's why she fell for Clay. He'd represented stability and security to her.

And then Adam had stripped that away from her, bit by bit. Her brother's catastrophes had become hers.

Their dinner wrapped up with the two guys fighting over the bill until Meg plucked it from their dueling fingers and waved it and her card in the air for the waiter. "This was my party, and I'll pay for it."

Kyle bundled a tipsy Meg into his car and winked at April. "We'll leave you two the house. I'm going to take Meg back to my place."

As Kyle roared off, April raised her eyebrows at Clay. "Kinda pushy, isn't he?"

"Are you okay at the house by yourself with the security system in place?"

"Of course." April gave silent thanks to the dark desert night that hid her hot cheeks.

Clay was making it easy on her to stay away from him. She wouldn't have to convince him to drop her off tonight. She wanted an early start for Phoenix tomorrow morning before Clay could even realize she'd left.

"I have my gun, too. I'll be fine."

Clay opened the door of his truck for her. "Are you going to try to talk to Adam tomorrow?"

"Yes." She pulled the door from him and slammed it. Clay hadn't asked if that conversation was going to take place face-to-face—and she wasn't telling. She'd take that two-hour drive up to Phoenix and meet Adam's plane. Then she'd present him with her proposition.

Clay aimed his truck out of town, back toward her house. The wine and the meal had a somnolent effect on her, and her eyelids drooped as she leaned her head against the window.

Clay turned down the music on the country station playing on the radio and hummed off-key to the song.

April's lips curved into a smile. Clay had always been a lousy singer, but that never stopped him.

A loud noise reverberated in the truck, and April's head banged against the window as Clay jerked the steering wheel.

Another crack came out of the night. The back window shattered, raining glass down on her head. She squeezed her eyes closed and screamed.

The truck squealed and the back wheels fishtailed on the road.

"What happened? What did you hit?" She peeled one eye open and focused on Clay's profile.

His jaw tensed. "I didn't hit a damned thing. Someone's shooting at us…and he just got my tire."

Chapter Fifteen

Clay wrestled with the steering wheel. It took all the strength he had to keep the truck on the asphalt—and he *had* to keep the truck on the asphalt.

If he swerved onto the shoulder, the truck could flip or skid out to a stop. They couldn't stop. Whoever shot at them wanted to disable the vehicle. Wanted them to be stranded in the desert.

Through his teeth, he ground out, "Call 911 now. We just passed mile marker 11, just before the pecan grove."

He heard April scramble for her phone as the truck rattled down the road, lurching to one side as the air escaped from his tire.

She spoke breathlessly into the phone, giving the details of their location, vehicle and situation.

Clay shifted his gaze to the rearview mirror and swore.

April ended the 911 call and cupped the phone between her hands. "What? What now?"

"I see lights behind us. The bastards are coming after us and our crippled truck."

"Go faster, Clay." April's fingernails dug into his thigh through the denim of his jeans.

"I'm afraid to go too much faster on that bum tire.

We're riding on the rim now. The whole wheel could come off."

"If they catch up to us, they'll shoot out the other tire." She twisted around in her seat. "I can't see any lights, but then I think we went around a curve in the road."

"How fast will the highway patrol be here?"

"The 911 operator said they were on their way. Out here, who knows how fast that is?" She snapped her fingers. "Your weapon. Give me your weapon."

"You can't go shooting into the dark." He reached under his seat for his gun and pulled out the holster. "Be careful with that thing. It's a little heavier than yours."

The truck jumped and wobbled.

"The better to shoot someone with." April grabbed the gun with two hands. "Loaded?"

"What would be the point otherwise?" He pushed the barrel of the gun toward the windshield. "Only take a shot if the car comes up beside us."

"He may not have to come up beside us." She jerked her thumb over her shoulder. "If he comes up behind us and shoots out the other tire…or the driver, we're in trouble."

The truck bucked against his control and he smelled burning rubber. "C'mon, baby. Keep going."

"Only a few miles to your place, Clay." She smacked the dashboard. "We can make it."

"There has to be more than one person ambushing us. They gotta know I'll be armed, and they're prepared to take me on."

"Us. They're taking *us* on."

The truck protested, rattling and weaving the remaining miles to his house, but they made it and he hadn't seen a return of the headlights in the rearview. Of course, their attackers could've killed their lights and be rolling toward them right now under the cover of the velvety blackness of the desert.

He turned into his driveway in a hail of dust, grit and smoke. He held out his hand. "Give me the gun, gunslinger."

April turned the butt toward him. "Are we going to stay here and wait for them?"

"Are you nuts?" He snapped his door handle. "I'll come out first and cover you into the house. We lock the door, and wait for them behind it. Get down."

He slammed the door as April's head disappeared. Squinting down the road, he circled the car and opened the passenger door.

"Let's go." He took April's arm as she slid from the truck. He pushed her forward in a crouch and protected her body with his like a shell, curving over her, one arm extended behind him, his hand clutching his gun.

They stumbled up the porch, passing the spot where the pink hatbox had rested only a few days ago, and a hot rage thumped against Clay's temples. He'd kill any man who came for April.

When they reached the front door, red and blue lights bathed the house and a highway patrol car squealed into his driveway behind the lopsided truck.

Clay shoved his weapon into the back of his waistband and raised his hand, blinking into the lights.

An officer eased out of the driver's seat, his flashlight already playing across the truck's rim. "You the ones who called 911?"

"We are." Clay pressed his keys into April's hands. "Open the door and turn on the floodlights for the driveway."

April pushed through the front door and flicked on the lights.

With the scene lit up, Clay took a step down the porch. "Someone back there at mile marker 11 shot out my back window and my left rear tire. I kept the truck on the road and made it home."

"Did they come after you?" The officer shoved his flashlight into the equipment belt hanging low on his hips.

The other patrol officer crouched next to the back wheel and whistled. "Looks like you made it just in time. This rim is destroyed."

Clay took another step forward. "Officer, I'm Clay Archer, Border Patrol. I have a weapon in my waistband."

The officer studying the wheel popped up. "I know you. Female mule's head was left on your porch. This porch."

"That's right." Clay felt April behind him, breathing heavily. "You didn't see another car on the road?"

"We didn't, but it could've been hiding in the grove. We radioed for another car. They're doing a search now."

"Do you want to come inside to take a statement?" Clay tipped his head at the open door, April in the frame.

Denali had come to the door to investigate the commotion. He sniffed at the officers' heels when they came into the house and then sat beside April, who rested her hand on his head.

Apparently, the dog was a better protector than he was. He'd allowed them to get too close to April. Had they been hoping to take him out and kidnap her to force her deadbeat brother to turn over the flash drive?

Did they ever have the wrong guy. Clay had no doubt in his mind that Adam wouldn't turn over the drive to save his sister or anyone else—but they didn't know that.

Clay cleared his throat and answered the officers' questions, indicating that this latest incident had roots in the drug trade and the two dead mules.

He avoided talking about the flash drive because pointing the finger at Adam and getting the police involved wasn't going to help April.

He didn't give a damn about Adam at this point.

He and April took the authorities through the chain of events on the road and Clay allowed them in his truck to look for the bullet that had crashed through his back windshield.

They found it lodged in the dashboard, and the anger and stress gripped Clay by the back of the neck. That bullet could've found its way into April's head.

When the officers left and he and April stepped back into the house, Clay shut the door and wedged a hand against it. "I'm not letting you go home to stay there by yourself. You're going to stay here tonight."

"Gladly." She entwined her arms around his neck. "But I hope you have some beers in the fridge because I need something to take this edge off."

"I'm with you there." He made a detour to his laptop. "I'm going to check the security footage just to see if anyone's been creeping around my house."

"I'll get the beers." She disappeared into the kitchen and said, "There's one road to and from your house. They didn't even have to know where we were to wait for us."

"You're right, and everything looks quiet on the security cam."

She emerged from the kitchen, a bottle of beer in

each hand. She thrust one at him. "Here you go. I don't like to drink alone."

He clinked the neck of his bottle with hers. "Here's to surviving close calls."

She pressed the bottle against her lips and tilted her head back. "That was some driving you did. If I'd been at the wheel, I'm sure I would've flipped the truck."

"We should've been more careful. I should've predicted they'd try something."

"Why would you?" She tugged at his sleeve. "Let's sit."

"Why would I? Because that dude threatened you in broad daylight in public."

"That's just it. He approached me like we had a business meeting or something. Gave me a proposition to think over. If he'd wanted to abduct me, he could've come into that restaurant and stuck a gun in my ribs. I would've gone with him without hesitation."

He sank beside her on the couch and propped up one foot on the coffee table. "So what are you saying? This ambush wasn't initiated by the big guy with Las Moscas?"

"I don't know." Sighing, she placed her bottle on the table next to his foot. "Turn around. You're hunching your shoulders."

He twisted around, presenting his back to her. He couldn't deny that his shoulders ached with tension.

"You know what?" She snatched up her bottle and rose to her feet. "Bring your beer into the bedroom, and I'll give you a proper massage."

He jerked his eyebrows up and down. "I was hoping for an improper massage."

"That could be arranged." She batted her eyelashes. "Everything locked up?"

"Locked up, secured, surveilled, Denali on duty, cops patrolling and my weapon by my side."

She blew out a breath. "I might just be able to get a few hours of shut-eye."

"Not before my improper massage."

"Of course not."

He staggered to his feet and listed to the side. "Whoa. That beer hit me hard. Must be the contrast between the adrenaline rush and a depressant."

"Good. We both need to relax." She took his hand and led him into his bedroom.

He should resist the temptation of her invitation. She'd lied to him about that note from last night. He shouldn't get in any deeper with her until he got some straight answers from her.

She nudged him down to the bed and unbuttoned his shirt. She slipped it from his shoulders and pressed a kiss against the flesh of his upper arm.

She grabbed the beer he'd placed on the nightstand, and held it out to him. "Finish this and lie down on your stomach. I'll release those knots."

He downed the rest of the beer and stretched out on the bed, his lids so heavy he couldn't keep them open.

April kissed the back of his neck and trailed a hand along his spine. Then she dug her fingers into the bunched-up muscles at the base of his neck.

He reached around to stroke her thigh as she crouched beside him, but moving his arm took too much effort. His heavy limbs seemed to sink into the bed.

As he drifted off, he felt April's hair brush his face. Her lips caressed his ear as she whispered, "I love you."

A smile tugged at his lips, but he knew he was dreaming.

CLAY ROLLED OVER and ran his tongue around his dry mouth. He rubbed his eyes, and then flung out an arm to reach for April, his fingers skimming over her coarse hair.

Jerking his hand back, he shifted onto his side and peered at Denali next to him in the bed.

"You're not April."

Without even opening his eyes, Denali flicked his tail twice and burrowed farther into the covers.

Clay dragged himself up against the headboard and massaged his temples. What the hell happened last night? He'd been melting under April's soothing hands one minute and comatose the next. He didn't even remember her crawling into bed next to him—he was sure he'd remember that.

He called out. "April?"

Denali whimpered beside him, but the rest of the house remained silent.

Clay rolled up in bed, disappointed that he was still wearing his jeans. Maybe that was a good thing. He'd sure hate like hell to have made love to April and not remember. Impossible.

He called her name again, and as the fog began to clear from his brain, his senses amped up and his nostrils flared. Did someone sneak in here and snatch her?

The sudden thought had his limbs jerking and he kicked aside the covers as he stormed out of the bedroom, Denali at his heels. His head cranked back and forth looking for April's purse, signs of a break-in... blood.

Instead of all those things, a single sheet of paper on the kitchen counter beckoned to him. He crossed the room and snatched it up, his eyes skimming the note April had left him.

She'd left early, didn't want to disturb him, had a

lot to do today, blah, blah, blah. He crumpled the note in his fist.

She'd left to do something she didn't want him to know about. He slammed the balled-up paper on the counter and lunged for the beer bottle on the sink. He tipped the almost-full bottle back and forth and then emptied it into the sink.

He'd drained his own bottle. She'd made sure of that. He cranked on the faucet and slurped some water from his cupped hand. He swooshed it around his arid mouth and spit it into the sink.

He flung open a cupboard door and snatched a small bottle of sleep aid he used sometimes when the job got to be too much and he couldn't turn off the horror. He shook it, as if that could tell him if it were missing one or two tablets.

He didn't need to verify missing tablets to know what April had done. She'd had every intention of making her escape to God knows where with God knows who this morning, but had run into a detour last night with the shooting. So, she did the next best thing—slipped him a mickey so she could sneak out this morning without questions.

She knew there'd be no way he would allow her to go off on her own after the events of last night.

But what she hadn't counted on? He pulled his phone from the charger and brought up a GPS app. He could find out exactly where she was going—ever since he'd put that GPS tracking device on her car yesterday morning.

Chapter Sixteen

April glanced in her rearview mirror for the hundredth time since leaving Paradiso. With her gun resting on the seat beside her, she felt safe enough but she wanted to be ready in case someone came at her like last night. Because she didn't know who had ambushed her and Clay.

It could've been the big man from yesterday, making his move to kidnap her and force Adam to give up the flash drive. She snorted. As if that would ever happen.

Or it could've been her silent tormenter who'd seen her out with Clay and wanted to give her a little reminder of what would happen to Clay if she didn't stay away from him. Just like the reminder she'd gotten loud and clear two years ago when she'd called off the wedding to him.

Meeting Adam in Phoenix could kill two birds with one stone—she could get Las Moscas off her back by getting Adam to give them the flash drive and she could convince Adam to do that by helping him look for their father—and if he *were* this Gringo Viejo character, maybe she could get to the bottom of this plan to keep her away from Clay. It all had to be connected in some way.

She loosened her death grip on the steering wheel. She'd hated tricking Clay, drugging him, but he'd never have allowed her to leave on her own. He'd understand someday.

She'd make him understand. Her explanation would go a lot further if she could also hand Clay that flash drive with the locations of Las Moscas' tunnels.

She'd left Tucson behind her about forty minutes ago, and barring any traffic jams going into the Phoenix Sky Harbor Airport, she should be there with time to spare before Adam's plane landed.

If Adam believed El Gringo Viejo could set him up in business, he might be willing to give up that flash drive. He didn't have the personnel to take over business from Las Moscas, like Jimmy did, even with a map to all their tunnels. He had to understand the foolishness of that plan.

She wished she could make Adam see the foolishness in all of it—using drugs, dealing drugs, being hooked into that whole lifestyle—but she'd never been able to talk any sense to Adam. Her brother hadn't been a bad kid, but he never viewed the world through the same lens of right and wrong as everyone else did.

Sometimes she felt as if she were the only person standing between him and total destruction. If she let go, like Clay had wanted her to so many times, where would Adam be now? Prison? Dead?

She flexed her fingers. She couldn't allow that. He was the only family she had left. She owed him that. She'd tried to be the parent Adam had never had. For some reason, her parents never could seem to love Adam the same way they loved her. She never understood it, but when she tried to ask Mom about it, her mother had shut her down.

Forty-five minutes later, April rolled into the metropolitan Phoenix area, the shiny new buildings rising from the desert floor just like their city's namesake. Phoenix was Tucson's brasher, more modern cousin.

An hour early for Adam's flight from Albuquerque, April pulled into a short-term parking structure and swiped her debit card at the meter.

She located Adam's gate and took a seat with her strawberry-banana smoothie and a paperback snatched from the shelves at the souvenir shop—not that she needed to read a murder mystery at this point.

The book turned out to be the right choice, as delving into someone else's problems made hers seem almost tame in comparison. She jerked her head up from the book at the garbled announcement for Adam's flight. All she heard from the loudspeaker was Albuquerque, but that was good enough.

She shoved the book in her purse and pinned her gaze on the gate, now open for business.

She didn't realize she'd been holding her breath until she released it when Adam's shaggy blond head appeared among the disembarking passengers.

She raised her hand, but he'd already spotted her, a big grin splitting his face. At least someone found it easy to keep his spirits up.

She hugged him as his backpack slid down his arm and he patted her back. "Good to see you under better circumstances than last time."

"Are they better?" She cocked her head, taking in his new shiner. "I told you that goon from Las Moscas made contact with me in the middle of the day, and then someone was taking potshots at Clay's truck last night—almost killed us."

"But Clay saved the day." He hoisted his pack back onto his shoulders. "It's gonna be okay."

She touched the abrasion on his scruffy chin, which

she'd missed before. "Have you recovered from your injuries already?"

"Kenzie's a good nurse."

"Do you have any idea if the detective from Pima County Sheriff's found Gilbert, formerly known as Jesus? As of yesterday, they hadn't."

"I don't have a clue. Nobody ever contacted me—sheriffs or drug dealers. I did see a few articles online about Jimmy's death." He lifted his narrow shoulders. "They chalked it up to the drug trade. Imagine that."

"Let's get out of here." She prodded his arm. "Do you have anything to pick up at baggage claim?"

He punched the pack on his back. "I have everything I need right here."

"I came early. My car's in the parking structure."

He ducked his head and tugged on a lock of her hair. "You've changed your mind, haven't you? You're going to help me look for Dad down in Mexico."

She whipped her head back, her hair slipping from his fingers. "How'd you know that?"

"You're my sister, April. I know you better than I know anyone."

She murmured under her breath, "I wish I could say the same about you."

When they got to her car, Adam tripped to a stop, his eyes narrowing. "What's this car?"

"It's my new ride." She knocked on the hood with her knuckles. "My new, old ride."

"Where's your other car?" He twisted his head around as if expecting to see it in the lot.

"I kind of did an exchange." She threw open the door to the back seat. "What does it matter?"

"I was kind of attached to that other car."

"Yeah, since you drove it more than I did." She

grabbed the strap of his backpack and had a fleeting urge to take it and run off with it. If he had the flash drive in his pack, she could turn it over to Clay.

Adam wrenched the backpack out of her grasp and tossed it onto the seat. Then he slammed the door.

Oh, yeah, he had something in that backpack he didn't want her to see.

She noted the twenty minutes left on the meter—just enough time for her proposition.

With Adam in the passenger seat next to her, she rested her hands on top of the steering wheel. "I have a deal I want to make with you."

"I knew it wasn't going to be easy." He slumped in his seat. "What do you want?"

"I will go down to Mexico with you to search for Dad and El Gringo Viejo…but you need to give up that flash drive you stole from Jimmy." She crossed one finger over the other to form an X and held it in front of Adam's face. "Don't even try to tell me you don't have it. That's why Jimmy and his guys came after you. They know you have that flash drive—and now Las Moscas knows you have it. Give it to them, and you can start a new life with Dad, if you want. If he's who you say he is, he'll protect you."

After several seconds of quiet, April stole a look at Adam's sharp profile. He had his eyes closed and his hands in his lap.

Then he cranked his head to the side and his lips twisted into his boyish grin. "Sure, April. I'll give up the flash drive."

THE RED DOT on Clay's phone had stopped moving at the Sky Harbor Airport in Phoenix. His heart flip-flopped in his chest. If she'd gone there to take a flight some-where, he'd never find her.

His foot pressed down on the accelerator of Meg's car. April's cousin had gladly given up her vehicle to him when she found out April had disappeared...again. Meg even did some sleuthing in April's bedroom and reported to Clay that her cousin had taken her suitcase that had been parked in the corner since she got back from Albuquerque.

Where the hell could she be going? Was she foolish enough to fly to Mexico and search for her father? At least that would get her out of the clutches of Las Mos-cas—on this side of the border, anyway. He knew they had operations on the other side of the border, as well.

As he drove north on the 10, he kept one eye on his phone. When the red dot started moving, he pounded his fists on the steering wheel. "Yes!"

As he barreled toward Phoenix, he watched April's location move from the airport to Tempe, near the uni-versity. The pounding urgency in his head didn't stop until that red dot did. With any luck she'd stay put.

He had the tracking device on her car, not in her purse, which would've been a much riskier proposi-tion. If she parked her car and walked, he'd have to stake out the vehicle.

He was about thirty-five minutes out as long as April didn't move. Did she really think he'd allow her to dis-appear from his life again?

After a while, he sped through the traffic into the city and took the turnoff for Tempe. He turned up the sound on his phone so he could follow the directions to April's car. They led him to Mill Avenue, an area bus-tling with restaurants and shops.

As he cruised down the street, he had to hope that

he saw her before she saw him. Of course, Meg's silver compact was a lot less conspicuous than his white truck with the back windshield shot out.

The GPS directed him to make a right turn and he practically ran into April's car parked in the last spot at the curb. He crawled forward, looking for his own parking space. He made a U-turn and parked across and down the street from her car.

He drummed his thumbs on the steering wheel as he watched the pedestrians zigzag back and forth across the street. Should he get out and look for her in the many restaurants and coffeehouses or sit here and wait for her to return to her car?

She wouldn't be leaving her car in a place like this if she were taking off for somewhere else. She definitely planned to come back to the car—if she could.

What if this were the real meeting associated with that anonymous note? What if she were in danger right now?

The thought had him clutching at the door handle as a spike of adrenaline shot through him. He could at least try a little reconnaissance. He didn't want to put her in even more danger if her…associate? captor? tormentor?…saw him charging up to save the day.

He dragged his gun from under the passenger seat and shoved it into the holster beneath his loose-fitting shirt. The O.K. Corral was farther south in Tombstone, but if he had to engage in a shoot-out to save April, he'd be ready.

He slipped from the car and looked both ways before jogging across the street. From the sidewalk, he hunched forward and cupped his hand above his eyes to peer into the car.

His gaze tripped over a sweatshirt bunched up on the back seat and he said, "Damn it."

He recognized that sweatshirt as Adam's.

She'd rushed up here to pick up her brother at the airport and was probably buying him breakfast right now.

He banged the heel of his hand against the car window. Figured. He rubbed his hand against his thigh as he retreated to his car.

At least he didn't have to go rushing in to rescue her from Adam—he could wait until they got back to the car. Then he'd break up that little tête-à-tête, along with any harebrained and dangerous scheme Adam planned to drag April into.

He got back into the car and slumped in his seat, cradling his phone in his hand. He scanned through his messages and paused over the one from Duncan. He'd asked Duncan to put a rush on those samples, and he knew Duncan had contacts.

He tapped it. Duncan had gotten the results back on the blood samples and had some info for him in an email. Clay brought up his email and located the one from Duncan. He tapped it and downloaded the report Duncan had included.

He skimmed through it and enlarged the area that contained the results. His fingers froze and he brought the phone closer to his face.

The blood in April's kitchen didn't belong to Adam. That blood belonged to a Jaime Hidalgo-Verdugo, whose corpse was found two days ago. It didn't take a crack detective to figure out that Hidalgo-Verdugo was really Jimmy Verdugo.

Clay's heart pounded in his chest as he scrolled down to the next set of results. The blood on the towel in April's trunk? That belonged to Jimmy also.

Dread pounded against his temples. It had all been a big lie—a hoax. Adam didn't have enough wounds on his body to produce that much blood. There was only one way Jimmy's blood could've wound up in April's kitchen and on a towel in her trunk.

Jimmy hadn't assaulted Adam. Adam had murdered Jimmy. Sweet, hapless Adam was a killer.

What did that make him capable of now?

Chapter Seventeen

April dragged the tines of her fork through the salsa on her plate next to her half-eaten omelet. Adam had agreed to turn the flash drive over to Clay after Adam located El Gringo Viejo, but April didn't trust him.

"Just give it over now, Adam. It belongs with Clay. Can you imagine what the Border Patrol could do with a map to the tunnels of Las Moscas?"

"Yeah." Adam downed his second cup of coffee and put his finger in the air for a refill even though his leg was already bouncing uncontrollably beneath the table. "They could do some serious damage to the drug traffic into this country."

"Exactly."

"Exactly." His blue eyes met hers over the rim of his coffee cup. He smiled, but the emotion didn't reach his eyes. It never did.

She'd always put that down to the drug use. How could you really feel anything if drugs altered your emotional state? But if she looked at the past honestly, Adam always did have a flat affect, even as a child.

"Adam, you don't have the infrastructure in place, like Jimmy did, to take over for Las Moscas. What good is that information going to do you?" She dropped her fork where it clattered against her plate. "I told you. I'll come with you to Mexico to help you find Dad. If he is El Gringo Viejo, you can start a new life down there with him. You don't need the flash drive for that."

"I give you the flash drive now for Agent Clay, and you bail on me." He held up his mug to the approaching waitress and nodded his thanks as the steaming brown liquid filled his cup. "Besides, if you found Dad would you really let him slide? He killed our mother, after all. You'd let him get away with that?"

She dropped her hands to her lap, folding them, her fingers twisting around each other tightly. "He's in Mexico. If he is El Gringo Viejo and the authorities haven't been able to get to him yet, why would they be able to get to him just because I dimed him off?"

Adam shrugged. "They probably wouldn't. But can you imagine what I could do with knowledge of Las Moscas' tunnels *and* backing from El Gringo Viejo?"

"That's not our deal." She wrapped her fist around her fork and stabbed her eggs. "What you *could* do? I thought you just wanted money in exchange for that flash drive. I thought you just wanted some protection from Dad. What are you planning?"

"Dream big, April." He shook out a packet of sugar and dumped it into his coffee. He stirred it so that it created a whirlpool in the liquid. Then he placed the spoon on the table with a hand not altogether steady.

She glanced sharply at his eyes, dilated and darting around the room. "Are you on something now?"

"Not at all." He rubbed his hands together. "I'm high on life. Isn't that what you always told me to be, April?"

"I don't understand why you need me to find Dad."

"You know why." He blew on the surface of his coffee and then slurped it up. "You were always their favorite. You could do no wrong in their eyes. Dad never paid much attention to me. Why would he want to see me now? But you?"

"He hasn't tried to contact me once since he disappeared."

"Because he thinks you think he killed Mom, but we know better, don't we? If we could somehow get word to him to let him know we don't believe in the setup, he'd want to see you in a heartbeat. C'mon, you want to find him, too, or you wouldn't be here."

April clasped the back of her neck and dug her fingers into her flesh. "I meant what I said about the flash drive, Adam. I want to turn that over to Clay."

"Clay, Clay, Clay." Adam smacked the table three times with each utterance of Clay's name. "I thought you were over that guy."

"Over?" April sat up straight, lining up her back against the booth. "This doesn't have anything to do with my relationship with Clay. He's Border Patrol. Just when they think they have all the tunnels under surveillance, another one pops up. That flash drive could be tremendously helpful in their efforts to stop drug traffic across the border."

"What are you, a public service announcement?" Adam snorted and started picking potatoes off her plate.

"Adam, I had no idea you were looking to get into the drug trade yourself. I don't support that at all."

"But you support my working with Dad in the drug trade?"

She shoved her plate away. "You don't even know if Dad is El Gringo Viejo. This whole thing could be a wild-goose chase. Clay said…"

"Stop. Not interested in what Clay has to say." He tapped his knife against his plate. "Is that why you're agreeing to helping me find Dad? You don't believe we will find him or, if we do, he's not El Gringo Viejo and he'll take me off your hands. Then you'll be free of me, and you can spend all of Mom's money and sell her house and not give any to me."

April had heard this poor-me story many times before. This time it raised a flag of anger in her breast. If Adam had more self-control, Mom would've trusted him with money and a share of her home.

"My goal was never to help you become a drug dealer. You must know that or you wouldn't have had to trick me into marrying Jimmy."

"I didn't force you to marry him. You agreed to his proposal all by yourself."

"Because you modeled him into something and someone he wasn't. You took advantage of my vulnerable state. I can't believe you set me up, and I can't believe I fell for it."

She covered her eyes with one hand, but she didn't feel sad or broken. Anger had started percolating in her veins. Adam wouldn't even make this deal with her. She'd help him find Dad or maybe they wouldn't, but he'd never turn over the flash drive to her.

"Jimmy wasn't going to hurt you. He wanted access to El Gringo Viejo, just like I do. After you helped us, I'm sure Jimmy would've consented to a divorce or annulment." He slurped his coffee. "Probably would've paid you off, too."

"As if that's what I wanted." She dug some cash out of her purse. "But you must've decided to go it alone without Jimmy when you stole the flash drive. Why'd you do that?"

"Opportunity presented itself one day."

"Who thinks like that?" She smacked down her money for her half-eaten meal. "I'm done, Adam. If you won't give me the flash drive now, I'm not going to help you find Dad or El Gringo Viejo or any other gringo. I'll tell Clay that you have the flash drive with intel on Las Moscas, and the authorities will arrest you. Whether or not you can keep safe from Las Moscas in prison is going to be your concern. My concern will be staying alive, as you've seen fit to put my life in danger."

Throughout her tirade, Adam had shoved his hand into his backpack. Maybe she'd gotten through to him. Maybe he'd give her the flash drive now.

Instead, he dropped his hands into his lap, and his lips curled up into a smile. "You're not going to do any of that, April. You're going to help me, just like you always have to make up for our parents' treatment of me."

"I'm sorry for the way Mom and Dad treated you, but that's not my fault, either." She draped the strap of her purse across her body. "I'm going back to Paradiso."

"No, you're not. You're coming with me just like you promised. And if you don't? I'm going to shoot you with your own gun, which is pointing at you right now."

CLAY SHOT UP in his seat as April rounded the corner with Adam close by her side, holding her arm. Adam never displayed much affection, so April must've agreed to do his bidding. If so, he probably hadn't told her he was the one who'd killed Jimmy. Even April wouldn't condone that from Adam.

He gritted his teeth. He now had in his possession a surefire way to pry April away from her unhealthy codependence with her brother—and he planned to use it.

He threw open the car door and stepped into the street. Adam must've seen him immediately because his head jerked up and he moved behind April's car.

"Damn him." Clay jogged across the street, facing them down the sidewalk. As he moved rapidly toward them, April swiveled her head around and held out one hand.

Adam created some space between himself and April, and Clay lurched to a stop when he saw the gun jabbed into her side.

Clay's eyes darted to the pedestrians on the street behind Clay and April. Nobody could see a thing.

With his hand hovering over his holstered gun, Clay drew closer to the car. "Let her go, Adam. I know everything. I know you're the one who killed Jimmy. Jimmy's blood was all over, not yours."

April gasped and wrenched away from Adam.

Adam pinned her between his body and the passenger door of the car, the barrel of the gun still beneath her ribs. "Stay back, Archer, or I'll kill her, too."

"He means it, Clay. Let us go. I'll be okay."

Adam reached back and yanked April's hair. "You told him you were meeting me? You liar."

April opened her mouth, but Clay growled. "Of course she told me. She didn't trust you."

Adam snorted. "That's rich. She didn't trust you, either. That's why she never told you why she called off your wedding. Thing is, Archer, she was having a fling with Jimmy Verdugo while she was engaged to you."

"Clay." His name ended in a cry on April's lips as Adam yanked her hair again.

"We've got some business to attend to. So, back off or I'll shoot her right here, right now. You don't think I'd hurt family? Think again." Adam chuckled, and the hair on the back of Clay's neck quivered. "I did it before."

April sagged against the car, her mouth gaping open.

"Now, back off or I'll kill her and find my own way to my father. At least this way, once she helps me, I'll let her go. And don't send the cops after us because one hint of that and I'll off both of us."

Adam opened the door and forced April in ahead of him. He held the weapon on her as she crawled over the console into the driver's seat.

The only thing keeping Clay from charging Adam was that gun pointed at April…and the fact that he'd be able to track them wherever they went. Adam believed April had told Clay where she was going, and he wanted to make sure Adam was still under that impression. Did April realize he'd tracked her car through GPS?

He wanted to give her some sign, but he didn't want to reveal anything to her psycho brother—and he was a psycho. Had he really killed his own mother, as he'd implied?

Clay held his hands out to his sides. "If you harm one hair on her head, I'll come after you, Adam. I don't care if you're in Mexico or Morocco. I'll find you."

Adam slammed the door and waved a hand out the window as April made a U-turn and rolled up to the intersection.

As he charged back to Meg's car, Clay brought up the GPS app. He'd have to stay far enough behind them so that Adam wouldn't catch a glimpse of him, but close enough so that he could help April if she needed it.

She needed it.

He got behind the wheel and gripped the top with both hands, ready to take off now. He had to take several deep breaths to keep still and not make any rash moves.

What Adam told him about April and Jimmy was a lie. Whatever April was, she wasn't a cheat. Adam had wanted him to turn on April, abandon her. That would never happen.

He'd follow April to the ends of the earth. And when he got her back—he'd kill her brother.

Chapter Eighteen

As they barreled through the Sonoran Desert hell-bent for the border, April licked her dry lips and flicked a glance at Adam, still pointing the gun at her. They'd barely said two words to each other on the ride from Phoenix. Too many thoughts had been jumbling around her brain for her to give voice to any of them—until now with the border looming ahead of them.

"What did you mean back in Phoenix about killing another family member?" A sob escaped her lips despite her best efforts. "Did you kill Mom?"

"C'mon, April. You never suspected?" He tucked a long strand of dirty-blond hair behind his ear. "You always saw what you wanted to see when you looked at me—the little brother in need of rescue."

"When I should've seen what?" She dropped her voice to a raspy whisper. "What Mom and Dad always saw?"

"That's right." He turned his blue eyes on her, more vacant than usual. "They were afraid, ashamed, to admit that I might have issues. So, they just shut me out and tried to punish the disturbed kid who liked to set fires and kill birds."

"The pecan grove by the Dillons' house?"

"Yeah, that was my handiwork." He took a swig of water from the bottle in the cup holder. "Old news."

"It's not old news to me. Why'd you murder Mom?"

"Money, mostly." He rolled his shoulders. "Of course, you got the big bucks, but I always figured I could get more out of you than Mom."

"And Dad? Why did he run if he didn't do it?" Her gaze dropped to the gun leveled at her midsection. Maybe if she kept Adam talking, the gun would slip and she could get away from him.

She scanned the vast, empty desert that stretched before them. She wouldn't be able to get away from Adam unless she killed him. "I actually admired Dad's get-rich-quick schemes, but he did wander into illegal territory. I was tracking his activities. I knew exactly what he was involved in—and I hate to shatter your illusions, but he was dabbling in the drug trade."

"That doesn't explain why he ran, why he took the rap for Mom's murder. He must've known he was a suspect."

"He did. The drug dealers who killed Mom made sure of it."

"You killed Mom. Why did Dad think drug dealers got to her?"

Adam flicked his fingers in the air. "I made him think that. You may be the one with the college degree in the family, but I was always smarter than you, April. My IQ tested off the charts."

"Deviousness is not intelligence." She grabbed her throat. "The threats. The threats I got regarding Clay. That was you?"

"I couldn't have my own sister married to a Border Patrol agent. That would seriously put a crimp in my activities. I had to keep you on my side. I knew Archer could turn you against me."

"But you weren't in Paradiso the other day when I got that note."

"I still have friends in Paradiso, very loyal friends. This particular friend even followed you home from dinner and shot out Archer's tire." He chuckled with no humor. "Larissa always was a good shot."

"Larissa? The waitress at the Paradise Café?"

"I told her to keep an eye on you two and let me know if you were together. I knew it would be trouble if you ran to Archer—and I was right." Adam curled his leg and bashed his foot against the glove box. "He found evidence in the trunk of your car, didn't he? Evidence that he must've had tested to prove Jimmy was the one bleeding and in distress, not me."

"Clay was telling the truth? You murdered Jimmy?"

"Hey." He patted his chest with his open palm. "I thought you'd like that one. Jimmy never got physical with you, but he probably would have. He was a scumbag. I would've saved you from him even if you hadn't figured out his true identity."

"Why?" She held out her hand. "Never mind. You killed him over the flash drive, didn't you?"

"The minute I saw the information on that flash drive, I knew I had to have it. It's my big break, just like Jimmy knew it was his big break." He hunched his shoulders. "One of us had to go."

Adam directed her off the highway, down a utility road, and April's gut twisted. He was going to force her across the border—probably through one of the tunnels Las Moscas detailed on the map.

Would Clay be able to find them? She knew as soon as Clay told Adam that she'd texted him with their location that he must've put some sort of tracking device on her car or in her purse. That's how he'd found them in Phoenix. That's why he'd risked letting her get in the car with Adam—not that he could've done much in that situation. The minute he pulled his gun, Adam would've shot her. She had no doubt in her mind that her brother was a stone-cold sociopath. He had no feelings for her other than a need to use her.

If Clay had planted the GPS device on the car, once they left the car he'd no longer be able to find them. As her gaze tracked over the desert landscape, she knew they were going to leave the car.

"If Dad knows what you are, why do you think he'll help you now?"

"As El Gringo Viejo, Dad has moved up in the world. I didn't know he had it in him. He'll understand now how much I can bring to his organization." Adam patted her hand on the steering wheel. "You'll help me find him, April. You'll help me, just like you always have."

His touch made her flesh crawl, but she tried not to jerk away from him. "I will help you, Adam. We'll look for Dad together, and then you have to let me go. You can stay down here and work with El Gringo Viejo. I'll go back to LA and forget all about this."

Adam twisted a strand of hair around his finger. "No, you won't. You'll go back to Archer, just like you always do."

"I won't. I swear I won't. It's over between us. H-he'd never take me back, anyway." She curled her hands around the steering wheel so tightly the car wobbled.

"Right. That guy would take you back even if *you* were the one who committed murder." He drove a finger into his chest. "Even someone like me who doesn't understand love can see that Archer will never let you go—but he has to. Do you understand me, April?"

"I do. I do. I'll go to LA." She swallowed a lump in her throat. "I did it before. If Clay's life is in danger, I'll never see him again."

Adam swept his finger from pointing at himself to pointing at her. "Don't forget that. If you don't forget that, everything will be fine. You might even want to stay with me and Dad. You could do his books with some creative accounting. It could be a family business."

April managed a weak smile as she nodded. "Maybe."

But she knew in her heart that Adam would kill her. Once she'd served her last purpose for him—finding their father—he'd get rid of her.

Adam pulled a piece of paper from his pocket and consulted it. "We're almost there."

Five minutes later of hard driving over a sand-swept utility road, Adam knocked his knuckles on the window. "Here. Pull the car over by that rock."

April parked where Adam directed her. "Is someone going to pick us up here?"

"Why would I need that?" He shook out the paper in his hand. "I have a map to a tunnel that'll get us right across the border. We'll have to walk some on the other side, but I've made arrangements. It's amazing what doors are opened for the daughter of El Gringo Viejo."

"It's hot. Do you have water?"

"I've taken care of everything. I only pretended to be an idiot to get your help." He winked. "I'm not really an idiot, April."

You're something worse.

"Open your door and get my backpack and sweatshirt from the back seat. Then start walking toward that cactus on the right. I'll be right behind you."

With her fingers resting on the keys in the ignition, she said, "You don't have to wave that gun at me anymore, Adam. Where would I go?"

"You're not going anywhere without me." He slapped her hand away from the ignition and yanked the keys out. "But if I don't have the gun, you could get your hands on the gun."

"I—I'd never hurt you, Adam."

He cocked his head and a lock of hair fell over one eye, like it used to when he was a kid. "Out of the car. No sudden moves."

She followed his instructions and studied the sand beneath her feet. Could she leave footprints for Clay to track her to the tunnel? The sand in the desert never stayed smooth. Animals, reptiles, birds, the wind, the rain…all had an impact on the environment, leaving indentations and imprints on the desert floor. One step in the sand might look like a footprint, but the dry, shifting winds could just as easily cover it up.

Clay would know the direction of the border, but how long would it take him to find the entrance to the tunnel? It's not like they had neon welcome signs at the entrance. But Clay was Border Patrol. He'd found his way into many tunnels along the border.

Adam scrambled out of the car, still keeping her at gunpoint. "Let's get moving. The tunnel is just about a five-minute walk."

In desperation and with her back to Adam, April yanked the double strand of beads from her neck and curled both fists around the smooth, wooden pellets.

If Clay couldn't follow their footprints, she'd leave

another kind of bread-crumb trail. She'd been protecting him all this time from her brother. Now she needed
Clay's protection.

CLAY ZEROED IN on the stationary red dot on his phone's
display. Thank God, they'd stopped moving. They'd
stopped moving in the middle of the Sonoran Desert,
just north of the border. Adam planned to cross through
to Mexico from one of the cartel's tunnels.

Would he be able to discern Adam and April's direction once they left the car? And if Adam saw his
car roaring up? He didn't have a choice. He could leave
the car farther back, but he had to get close enough so
that he could reach them before they went too far into
Mexico.

As he rumbled along the access road, he noted just
enough undulation in the landscape that he could keep
the car out of sight.

He caught his breath when he saw April's car abandoned by a large rock. He pulled to the side of the road,
and then made his call to Border Patrol. By the time
the agents showed up, April wouldn't be under Adam's
threat anymore.

He'd make sure of it.

He left his own car and made the trek to April's.
When he got to the car, he gulped back some water and
wiped his mouth with the back of his hand.

Nobody on the horizon. They must've already entered the tunnel. He estimated the location of the border,
but the tunnel could be anywhere along there.

Trying to track footprints wouldn't do much good.
He dropped his head and scanned the ground, an un-
relenting sea of beige tones.

A darker pebble caught his attention and he strode

forward and crouched down. He reached for the object and sucked in a breath when he cupped the blue-and-yellow painted wooden bead in his hand. April had been wearing this necklace—and now she was using it to show him the way.

APRIL DRAGGED IN lungfuls of fresh air as she staggered from the tunnel, blinking in the waning daylight. When Adam had pushed her through the entrance to the tunnel on the other side of the border, she'd expected crawling the half mile on her belly, warding off scorpions and desert rodents. Instead, she'd walked upright through a large space fortified with wood and swept clean of debris.

She had two seconds to herself before Adam joined her outside, the gun still clutched in his hand as it had been through their entire journey.

"What now?" She rubbed her arms with hands now empty of all the beads she'd deposited at the mouth of the tunnel on the US side of the border.

"We walk to a meeting place about a mile ahead. I arranged transportation for us to Rocky Point. We went there with Mom and Dad when we were kids. Remember?"

She nodded, blinking back tears. She remembered Mom trying to create some family memories that didn't include trying to manage Adam.

Once they walked away from this tunnel and got into a car, Clay wouldn't be able to find them. He wouldn't be able to save her.

She scuffed through the sand, away from the tunnel, and perched on the edge of a rock, wrapping her arms around her legs. "I need to rest before we undertake a mile hike through the desert."

"It's almost night." Adam spread his arms wide. "The sun will set shortly. We'll be fine."

"I want to wait until it goes down a little more. I'm kind of claustrophobic. Walking through that tunnel drained me."

He leaned against the outcropping that masked the tunnel's entrance, taking refuge in the shade of the scrubby bush that protruded from the rock—just where she wanted him. "Don't try anything stupid, April. There's nowhere for you to run, and once my associates get here there's not going to be anyplace for you to hide, either. Let's just find Dad, and then we'll figure things out."

Figure out how to kill her and get rid of her body.

"What if Dad isn't El Gringo Viejo? What then?"

"If he isn't, which I highly doubt, I still have the flash drive with the tunnels. With that information, I'm sure I can gather a team to help me take over business from Las Moscas."

"They'll kill you."

"They haven't yet." He rubbed a hand across the dark blond stubble on his chin. "They've been easy to play."

"Play?" She rolled her eyes. "You've played Las Moscas? Like that big man who came to Paradiso to threaten my life—and yours?"

"Yes, play, as in directing their attention to Gilbert and the others in Jimmy's crew, while I took care of Jimmy."

"Gilbert and Jimmy's entourage are all dead?"

"Do you think I'm an amateur, April? Is that what you think? I've been playing these games for years—you just never wanted to see it. Your obtuseness came in handy, or—" he tapped his boot against the rock "—maybe it was a survival mechanism. Maybe you knew on some level you had a dangerous sibling, and you stayed on my good side to protect yourself."

A slight movement in her peripheral vision caught April's attention, but she kept her gaze focused on her brother, pretending to be fascinated by his words when in reality she'd grown tired of him and his confessions.

Maybe he was right. Maybe she'd always known what he was on some level. Now that his mask had completely slipped, he no longer bore any resemblance to the brother she'd tried to build up in her mind.

He'd murdered her mother. Set up her father. Tricked her into staying away from the man she loved.

While Adam opened his mouth to continue his bragging, his jaw dropped and his eyes bugged out of his skull.

The weapon in his hand wavered, and April dropped to the sand.

Clay had emerged from the tunnel like some avenging desert creature of the night, tackling Adam to the ground. Adam squeezed off a shot that pinged off the rock where she'd just been sitting.

The gun must've recoiled in his hand when he pulled the trigger because as Clay took him down, it flew from his grasp. The two men grappled on the ground, Clay clawing the sand to reach his own weapon that he'd placed just outside the cave to wrap his arms around Adam's legs and destabilize him.

Adam's wiry strength and manic energy made up for the weight and muscle difference between him and Clay. As Clay landed a punch on Adam's face, Adam squirmed out from beneath him and scrabbled for Clay's gun, shoved up against the rock.

An adrenaline rush surged through April's system

and she launched herself forward, snatching up the weapon that had flown out of Adam's hand. Her weapon.

Hitching up to her knees, she swung the gun toward the two men rolling closer to the other gun, Adam's fingers stretching out for the barrel.

"Stop!" She wrenched the word from her parched throat. "Stop, now. Leave the gun, Adam."

He smiled through bleeding lips. "You're not going to do it, April. I'm your little brother."

As both Adam and Clay made a final, desperate grab for the gun, April took aim and fired.

Epilogue

April buried her face in Denali's fur, the coarse tex-
ture tickling her nose. "How's the progress on those
tunnels going?"

Clay placed a glass of wine on the firepit, and the
flickering reds and oranges filtered through the shimmering liquid. "We've gotten to half of them already.
Some are crude, some are sophisticated, all were con-
duits for drugs and God knows what else for Las Moscas."

"It's a gold mine of information, isn't it?" April
stretched her hand to the fire and wiggled her fingers
before pinching the stem of the wineglass and taking a
sip of the cold chardonnay.

"Thanks to you."

She tipped her glass in Clay's direction. "Officially,
thanks to you."

"Less complicated for me to take credit for shooting and killing your brother than you." He swirled the
wine in his glass. "Unless you've changed your mind."

She shoved her hair behind her ear and sniffed. "I
don't want it to be known that I killed Adam—even
though he deserved it."

"Not only did he deserve it, you took the shot in

self-defense. He'd abducted you at gunpoint, and if he'd reached that gun before I did, he would've killed you."

"At that moment, I didn't even think about that." She ran her fingertip around the rim of her glass. "It was you I was worried about. Always you, Clay."

He pushed up to his feet and sat next to her on the other side of the firepit in his backyard. He set down his glass and draped his arm around her shoulders. "Misplaced worry. If you had just told me two years ago that someone was threatening you, threatening us, I probably could've nipped this entire thing in the bud."

"If we'd gone through with the wedding, Adam would've killed you. I'm sure of that." She grabbed his fingers brushing her arm, and entwined hers with them. "Why didn't my parents try to get him help?"

"Maybe they just didn't recognize what he was. You didn't."

"I was a child, and he was my younger brother."

"You didn't recognize him for what he was even when you were both adults. I guess he got better at hiding the fact that he didn't have any real emotions, no human feeling."

"He's right. I didn't want to see it. Especially after Mom…died and Dad disappeared." She bolted upright. "Dad should know. He should know he's no longer a suspect in Mom's murder."

Clay stroked his hand down her back. "Maybe someday, April. If he really is El Gringo Viejo, you don't want him back in your life, anyway."

"If?" She cranked her head to the side. "You were so sure he wasn't. What changed?"

"Adam believed it with all his heart—of course, that's not saying much. Did he convince you?"

"I'm not sure. He would never tell me what evidence he had."

"You know what's curious?"

"Lots of things. What?"

"The other female mule? They ID'd her. She was an ex-pat living in Mexico, may have had connections to El Gringo Viejo."

"Which means El Gringo Viejo may be working against Las Moscas?"

"Maybe. He's Mexico's problem right now. We'll have our hands full destroying those tunnels."

"Hey, you two." Meg stood at the patio door, music floating outside from behind her. "The party's in here… or maybe not."

April waved. "We'll be there in a minute."

When Meg closed the door, Clay scooted in closer and nuzzled her hair. "Or two, or three."

Cupping his jaw, she whispered, "Have I ever told you I love you?"

"Not for a few years, but your actions speak louder than those three words ever could." He kissed her throat. "Don't ever try to protect me again without telling me about it first. Besides, that's *my* job."

"That's *our* job, together. Isn't that what's in the wedding vows?"

"I'm not sure. I never got to say those vows."

"Me, either."

"When are we going to remedy that?"

"How close is Vegas?"

"Not close enough."

And as Clay wrapped his arms around her and pressed a kiss against her willing mouth, she whispered against his lips, "Not close enough."

* * * * *

WHAT SHE SAW

BARB HAN

All my love to Brandon, Jacob and Tori,
the three great loves of my life.

To Babe, my hero, for being my greatest love and
my place to call home.

And to book lovers like Amy McWilliams,
who I also get to call my friend.

Chapter One

Deputy Courtney Foster sat at the oblong wooden conference table in the sheriff's office, clicking a pen. The distraction helped her focus on work and not the sick feeling swirling in her stomach, building, threatening to send her racing to the trash can. She'd skipped her usual early-morning cup of coffee in favor of salted crackers.

"I just got a call from the Meyers," her boss, Zach McWilliams, said on a frustrated-sounding sigh. "They've decided it's not safe in Jacobstown anymore. Trip Meyer made a point of telling me that he's afraid for his daughters to come home from the university over spring break."

"I'm sorry," Courtney offered.

Deputy Lopez shuffled into the room with coffee in hand and took a seat next her.

"Morning," he practically grumbled.

"Does 5:00 a.m. count as morning? Or is it still the night before?" She tried to lighten the heavy mood.

"Technically, I think it's still the night before," Lopez agreed.

Everyone was up early and taking extra shifts in order to ensure the town's safety.

"Do we know the exact timeline for when the small-animal killings began?" she asked Zach. He'd been working on the case with a volunteer. Lone Star Lonnie was also a close family friend and foreman of KR, Kent Ranch, one of the largest and wealthiest ranches in the state of Texas.

"We've been able to reach back as far as a year ago with the help of a forensic team out of Fort Worth," Zach responded.

The twisted psycho who had been dubbed the Jacobstown Hacker had begun killing small animals a year ago? The man had moved onto a heifer, butchering its left hoof and then leaving the poor animal to bleed out and die near Rushing Creek on the Kent Ranch.

There'd been more heifer killings after that, spaced out over weeks. It appeared that the twisted jerk had begun on small animals like rabbits and squirrels before moving on to bigger game. All the animals he'd butchered had been females, which had been a warning sign to all the women in town. And he graduated to killing a person—Breanna Griswold.

An investigation revealed that the twenty-seven-year-old victim had been in and out of group homes in Austin for the seven years of her life leading up to her last. She'd grown up in Jacobstown but had moved away during high school. Courtney remembered her from years ago. Breanna had moved back to town a couple of months before her murder.

She was a loner, known to sleep in random places around town when she was on a bender. She was murdered with the same MO as the animals—a severed left foot.

With Breanna's recent murder and the fact the killer was still on the loose, everyone seemed on edge. Courtney started working the clicker on the pen in double time.

"Do you mind?" Deputy Lopez motioned toward the noisemaker in her hand. Lopez was average height, in his mid-thirties and had dark hair and eyes. He was medium build and had a pronounced nose.

"Sorry." Courtney released the pen, and it tumbled onto the desk. Her unsettled stomach made all kinds of embarrassing sounds. For the second time this morning, Courtney thought she might throw up on the deputy who was seated next to her.

She was pretty certain that Lopez would not be amused. She'd been on the job a few weeks now and was still getting her bearings in the small, tight-knit sheriff's office. Coming home to Jacobstown was supposed to be a safe haven from her stressful job working for Dallas Police Department as a beat cop...

An involuntarily shiver rocked her as she thought about the past, about what had happened in Dallas.

"We're no closer to finding answers. Breanna deserves better from us." Zach tapped his knuckles on the table. Everyone knew the victim and her circumstances. Her only family, a mother and a brother, had walked away from her and moved to Austin years ago. Breanna had tracked them down there, but rumor had it she became homeless shortly after.

Her mother had a reputation for drinking and using

physical violence on her children. Even so, every mother—even the bad ones—deserved justice for a murdered daughter. Breanna had been a grown woman who made her own mistakes, but people cared that she was gone. The horrific murder had rocked the bedroom community.

Another bout of nausea struck, and Courtney's breakfast threatened to make another appearance. She glanced up in time to see Zach staring at her.

"Everything okay?" he asked.

"I'll be fine." She could only hope this would pass soon. "I'm sure I ate something bad at the potluck yesterday. I should know better by now, but I can't resist beef and bean taco casserole."

"You're braver than I." Lopez cracked a smile, breaking the tension. Courtney glanced at the scar on his neck. He'd taken a bullet trying to protect a mother and daughter a few months ago, when the quiet town had experienced its first crime wave since the Hacker began his work.

"I stick to vegetables and dessert. No one ever got sick from eating raw carrots," Lopez touted.

"No one ever enjoyed them, either." Courtney smiled, but it was weaker than she wanted it to be. She couldn't force it right now through another wave. Acid burned her throat, and it was taking all her energy to keep from losing it.

"Tasted fine to me." Lopez shrugged.

"We're short on solid leads." Zach steered the meeting back on track, and the mood immediately shifted to all business. Zach had mentioned that she'd be a good addition to his team when he hired her. The Jacobstown Hacker was all anyone could think about, he'd said. The town needed someone with big-city experience. People were getting anxious. Everyone was willing to pitch in to help, which created a whole different kind of chaos. A volunteer room had been set up in the office down the hallway, where folks volunteered to man the tip line.

The fact that people cared about each other was one of the many reasons Courtney had moved back to Jacobstown. She'd missed that small-town feel when she lived in a big city. The sheer volume of cases in Dallas caused law enforcement to focus most of its energy on high-priority cases. Whereas here at home, even the marginalized were cared for. People looked out for each other as best they could, and that included every resident. Even the ones who seemed intent on harming themselves.

Courtney had friends here. She'd been good friends with Zach's younger sister, Amy. She'd also been close to Amy's cousin Amber Kent at one time. But Courtney didn't want to think about the Kents. Especially not Jordan, who'd been two years ahead of her in school when they were all kids. He'd also ignored her for most of her life and teased her as teenagers. And then there were those few days at the cabin six weeks ago.

That week, great as it had been, was over. He'd gone back to Idaho and the property his family owned there, and she'd moved on to start her new job as a deputy for his cousin.

"Is there no one besides Reggie Barstock on our suspect list?" Courtney asked.

Zach shook his head.

"There have to be others," she continued.

"No one as strong as Reggie," Deputy Lopez said.

"Because he has a criminal record?" She didn't see how burglaries catapulted him into the category of serial killer. "How old is Reggie now?"

"Thirty-three." Zach clasped his hands and rested them on the conference table.

"I didn't know him very well growing up. He was quite a few years older than me, but I'm picturing someone with a higher IQ here. Am I alone?" From everything she knew about serial killers, they were intelligent, lacked a conscience but could be incredibly charming when it served them. At least, the ones who got away with their crimes were. And this perpetrator had the presence of mind to ensure he left no DNA behind. That took some calculating on his part.

The first heifer had been found near Rushing Creek, and the other animals had eventually been found near there. Breanna had been discovered two miles up the creek on the Kent family property. Courtney would have to speak to family members as part of the investigation. She figured it wouldn't be too difficult to bypass Jordan, since he lived out of state. The last thing she wanted to do was run into him again while she still felt so vulnerable after their fling.

"Do you have any other ideas for suspects?" Lopez leaned toward her.

"No. But the Jacobstown Hacker is careful, calculating. He's methodical," she continued. "I'm not completely convinced that I'm seeing that in Reggie's file."

"I feel the same way about Gus Stanton." Lopez snapped his fingers. "He's been home on worker's comp after an accident a few years ago unloading his rig. He lives on the outskirts of town on a couple of acres. Keeps to himself mostly."

Having returned to town a month and a half ago, Courtney had to defer to Lopez and the sheriff for up-to-date information about residents. She hadn't heard of Gus Stanton growing up, so he must've moved to the area after she'd left.

"Why don't you go out and check on him? See if you can get a feel for his emotional state," Zach said. "If he has a bad left foot from the accident, I want to know about it."

"Does Gus have a family?" Courtney asked. The guy she was looking for was a loner.

"He's divorced with two kids. I believe his ex moved the kids to New Braunfels to be with her folks a couple of years back," Zach supplied.

"Sounds like we've doubled our list of suspects," Courtney said. There were half a dozen names that had been submitted and cleared almost immediately. The pair of suspects they had didn't exactly fit the loose profile they'd developed. It was impossible not to feel like they were letting the community down.

All the townsfolk were antsy, sitting on pins and needles in anticipation of another strike. People had taken to locking their doors and looking at their neighbors twice. Tips were coming in, but most people were on the wrong track. Every kid who'd ever thrown a rock in the wrong place at the wrong time had been named as a possible lead.

Zach leaned back in his chair and pinched the bridge of his nose as though to stem a headache. "Since Lopez is taking Gus, why don't you interview Reggie's former teachers, friends, neighbors. See what you can come up with about what kind of student he was. If he's smarter than we're giving him credit for, I want to know that, too."

"Will do, Zach." It was habit to call him by his first name after growing up friends with his sister, and yet it felt awkward after the formality of working in a big-city department.

Courtney picked up the pen and started clicking it again. She caught herself this time and set the pen down. She stretched her long, lean fingers over it.

"Go see what you can find out, and we'll meet again tomorrow." Zach glanced up at the whiteboard on the adjacent wall, where there were two names.

"Have there been any new Reggie sightings?" Courtney stood up, got hit with another wave and had to plant a hand on the table in order to steady herself.

"You sure you're okay to work?" Zach's brow creased with concern.

"I'm good," she responded a little too quickly. "No more potluck for me."

"To answer your question, yes. There's a new sighting almost every day. Nothing has panned out so far," Zach said.

Getting out of the stuffy office where she could grab some fresh air was her top priority. The department-issue SUV assigned to her was at the opposite end of the parking lot.

Taking in a lungful of crisp late-morning air, she was reminded how good it felt just to breathe. She'd taken a new job in a new city—not technically new, but she hadn't lived in Jacobstown in almost a decade—and this was supposed to be a fresh start after what had happened in Dallas when a protest turned into civil unrest. Eight officers had been killed that day, three of whom she'd been very close to. One of whom she'd been intimate with.

Courtney had barely escaped with her life. She'd gone back to the job after a three-month recovery and counseling stint after being shot. But living in the city, doing that job had lost its appeal. Since law enforcement was all she knew and at one time had been her passion, she'd called Zach and asked if she could come work for him.

The rest, as they said, was history. Courtney climbed up and slid behind the wheel of her SUV. Her white-knuckle grip did little to calm her churning stomach. She already knew a few teachers she wanted to speak to, and Zach had said he'd have his secretary, Ellen Haiden, send over their home addresses. School was still in session, and only one of Reggie's teachers had retired in the last decade.

But Courtney had something to do first.

The drive to the big-box store in Bexford took a solid forty-five minutes from the office. She could only pray she wouldn't recognize anyone once she got inside.

Courtney parked her vehicle off to the side of the

building and took the walk to the front door while fighting against the urge to vomit. She walked past the row of neatly stacked carts. She didn't need one but didn't exactly want to hold a pregnancy test out in the open, either. She picked up a handbasket instead, figuring she could load it with a few items.

Part of the reason she'd come to this store was the fact that it had self-checkout stands. That and the point that she didn't want the whole town of Jacobstown to know she thought she might be pregnant. If she was, then, yes, she would have to have an awkward conversation with the baby's father, but she'd rather not deal with the gossip if she turned out to be stressing over being late on her cycle for no reason.

Walking through the aisle caused her pulse to race. A man walked past. She froze, pretending to be interested in a feminine napkin package. She mentally chided herself for being ridiculous. But this felt so much bigger than she could handle. If word got out, there'd be questions, and there was no way she wanted this tidbit getting around.

Her heart played a steady beat, hammering her rib cage.

It was then she realized she should've bought the other items first so she could immediately cover what she came for.

Taking in another deep breath brought enough calm over her to pick up the pregnancy test and drop it into her basket. She moved over two aisles and randomly threw in any item that she might ever need. Allergy pills. Stomach acid reducer. Cotton balls.

It shouldn't be a big deal to get from where she stood in the middle of the store, and yet it felt like miles away.

She turned and out of the corner of her eye caught sight of a youngish man who favored his left leg when he walked. The hairs on the back of her neck pricked. She told herself that her reaction was most likely because of the conversation she'd had with Zach and Lopez a little while ago and not because the Jacobstown Hacker was in The Mart walking twenty feet in front of her.

His back was to her, but she could see that he was average height and build, maybe even a little wiry. She'd learned the hard way that wiry guys could be surprisingly strong. His hair was light brown in a short cut, commonly referred to as a buzz. He wore Carolina-blue basketball shorts and a dark hoodie.

There were all kinds of logical reasons that could account for his slight limp, Courtney reminded herself as she kept one eye trained on him. He turned at the end of the aisle toward the sporting goods section. This guy could be coming from the gym. He could have strained a muscle in a workout. Or he might play sports and could have tweaked his ankle during a game. It could've been a pickup game. How many of her colleagues in Dallas had done the same during last-minute lunch-hour basketball rounds?

She was being paranoid, but with no answers in Breanna's murder after weeks of investigating, everyone with a limp was worth checking out. The reality that the killer knew the area struck. He really could be any guy she'd just walked past in order to follow Blue Trunks. Ice-cold creepy-crawlies trailed up and down her spine when she really thought about it. A familiar shot of adrenaline jacked her heart rate up a few notches. She used to get a burst of excitement when that happened. Now, it felt a lot like dread as she reminded herself to control her breathing. Her stress response was out of whack after what had happened on her last job.

Courtney increased her speed as she rounded the aisle. She ran smack into a hard, male chest that felt more like a wall.

Before she could tell the man to watch where he was going, she blinked up. Jordan Kent.

"What are you doing here?" The words flew out, and her cheeks flamed with embarrassment. If he saw the pregnancy test in her basket…

No, he could not see that. She subtly shifted her elbow backward in order to use her body to block the contents in the basket. Her skin still sizzled from the weeklong fling they'd had a month and a half ago.

The tall, over-the-top handsome rancher took a step back. His dark curls were barely contained underneath a black Stetson. A slow grin spread across perfect lips and straight white teeth in one of those smiles that had been so good at seducing her. He had the sexiest dimple on his right cheek. He was one seriously irresistible, hot package. Another bout of nausea struck. She didn't want to be reminded of exactly how tempting he'd been.

Jordan quirked a dark brow. "Shopping. Why? Is it against the law now?"

COURTNEY STARED AT Jordan like he had two foreheads. He'd been used to teasing her when they were kids but running into her in the least likely place a month and a half ago, he'd seen her in a whole new light.

"Why aren't you still in Idaho?" She blinked at him like he might be a mirage or something.

"Family business. I was asked to come home." The last time he'd seen Courtney ten years ago, she'd been the cute but young friend of his little sister. Running into her after a decade of absence had caused him to see that she'd grown into an intelligent, strong and beautiful woman. An attraction like wildfire had spread through both of them, and they'd been consumed by the flames for a solid seven days and nights.

But their time together wasn't all incredible sex and lighthearted teasing. She woke in the middle of the night many times shaking and crying. He'd comforted her until she fell back asleep. When he'd tried to sit her down and talk about it on the seventh day, she'd made it clear that she had a job to begin and a new life that didn't involve him.

He'd thought about her more times than he cared to admit in the past thirty-seven days. Her quick wit. Her soft curves. Those pink lips.

Hell, he had no business appreciating those anymore. She'd been real clear on where they stood. It was most likely his bruised ego that had him thinking about her more than he knew better than to allow. Usually he was the one walking out, not the other way around.

"What's wrong?" he asked as she tried to look around his shoulder. Did she have a boyfriend? The only thing he'd known for certain about her during their fling was that she wasn't married. He should've asked about a relationship but assumed she wouldn't have spent the week in bed with him if she'd been dating someone else.

He'd also thought about that haunted look in her eyes when she first woke from a nightmare. That, he might never forget.

She was almost a foot shorter than his six feet three inches. She had to come in at five feet six, maybe seven. Her shiny auburn hair was pulled back in a low pony-tail. She had just enough curves to be a real woman, and his fingers itched to get lost on that silky skin of hers again.

"Sorry. I was just watching someone, and…" Her face twisted, and she took a step to the right in order to get a clear view of the person.

Jordan had never felt awkward with a woman be-fore. Normally, he spent time with people who didn't expect much in return. After a few rounds of hot sex and mutual enjoyment, they'd part ways. Neither side tried to drag out the fling or make a big deal out of walking away.

He told himself that he felt a pang of jealousy with a strong dose of heartache seeing her again because he knew Courtney, but that wasn't completely true. He couldn't put his finger on exactly why this felt different from the many others he'd spent time with. It just did.

"Well, I should get out of your way, deputy," he said to her. Her cheeks flushed, and her tongue darted across full pink lips. Jordan ignored the warning shot to his chest.

It didn't matter. Courtney seemed to have no interest

in him. But the week he'd spent with her had felt like a homecoming. Not since he'd lost his parents—and maybe even long before then—had Jordan felt like he belonged somewhere. Sure, he and his five siblings had taken over the family ranching business along with associated mineral rights. Their inheritance was spread across three states, with significant holdings in Texas.

No one in his family needed to work another day for a paycheck. They got up at 4:00 a.m. to face a long day of work because ranching was in their blood and they loved the land. Jordan was no different. But the ranch didn't feel like home to him anymore.

He stepped aside.

Courtney grabbed his arm and motioned for him to scoot back over.

Well, he really was confused now. "What's going on, Courtney?"

"I'm sorry. I was watching a possible suspect." She glanced at Jordan, and those eyes with cinnamon-colored flecks sent a bolt of lightning straight to his heart. He needed to develop a thicker skin when it came to her, because right then he wanted to haul her against his chest and welcome her back home properly. But that ship had sailed when she'd refused to speak to him again.

Damned if she wasn't distracted now. Sure, his ego took a hit. Most women made themselves a little too available for the youngest and only single Kent brother.

He told himself that was the reason he felt a sting in his chest and not because he had stronger feelings for Courtney.

"Don't let me stand in the way of your job." Hadn't those been the words he'd used when she'd told him that their time together had been special, but she needed to focus on her work at his cousin's office?

"I'm sorry, Jordan. It's a case I'm working on. It's getting inside my head a little bit," she said by way of apology. "I should go."

Courtney turned toward the front of the store. He should've walked away right then and there. It was his fool pride that had him standing his ground like it didn't matter. His bruised ego wanted to say otherwise, but that's all it was.

Jordan glanced down, and then he saw something in her basket that gave him pause.

Was this the reason she'd rejected him?

Evidence that she had been in another relationship stared back at him.

Chapter Two

Courtney issued another apology before ducking down the nearest aisle in order to put as much distance between her and Jordan as possible. She could only pray that he hadn't seen the contents of her basket.

Blue Trunks had disappeared. She searched aisle after aisle with no luck. Biting back her frustration and shock at seeing Jordan in Texas again, Courtney used the self-checkout machine and stalked toward her SUV. Her situation was bad enough without running into Jordan.

As she tossed the bag onto the passenger seat, she saw Blue Trunks moving through cars.

She closed the door to her SUV and hit the auto lock on her key ring. She stuffed the keys inside her pocket before resting her hand on the butt of her weapon. The sun was high in the sky, and it was cold enough to require a coat. She wore a deputy jacket, which essentially was like a billboard. She didn't mind as she doubled her stride so that she could get a look at Blue Trunks's face.

He stopped at his vehicle, an older-model pickup, which was not uncommon in these parts. He glanced around, and her blood chilled. She was still too far away to make out the details of his face.

"Excuse me, sir," she shouted, but his head dipped, disappearing before he acknowledged her.

She might not have been close enough to get a description of the color of his eyes, but he'd heard her. She'd bet money on the fact. Didn't that send another chill racing up her spine?

It meant he was guilty of something. The pickup jutted forward as she got closer, and then it disappeared before she could get a look at the plate. There were enough cars moving in and out of the busy lot to block her view.

Running to catch up to Blue Trunks caused her to be winded, which wasn't normally a problem for her. She'd been athletic growing up and had easily passed the department's physical fitness requirements, a stumbling block for many applicants. She woke every morning at 5:00 a.m. to run. It was a habit she'd picked up after playing high school sports.

Courtney's mother had disappeared with her baby brother when Courtney was ten years old. Her brother, Cord, had been supposed to start kindergarten that year. With a mother who could walk away from a ten-year-old child and a father who had no problem with lengthy punishments, what chance did Courtney have at being a decent parent? She'd asked her ob-gyn to shut off the possibility of parenthood permanently, but he'd said she was too young to make a lifelong commitment to that decision. Courtney had other ideas. A wave of panic washed over her, and she needed to talk herself down as she realized her hands were shaking.

A wave of panic slammed into Courtney at the thought of being pregnant. What if parenting skills were inherited?

There was a strong possibility that she wasn't, she reminded herself. As she turned to make the walk back to her vehicle, she chewed on a few facts. She and Jordan had used protection every single time. She would've been on the pill except that it had been a waste of money after the cop she'd been dating seriously enough to have sex with had been killed practically in front of her eyes. Since sex had been the last thing on her mind when thinking about returning to her childhood hometown, she hadn't bothered to get a new prescription. Plus, she would be changing doctors once she got settled.

A wave of nausea struck like a physical blow. She pushed through and kept walking.

Back at her vehicle, Courtney opened the passenger door and held on for dear life. She took in a few deep breaths, reminding herself to blow them out her nose slowly in order to calm her racing heart and churning stomach.

The overwhelming feeling of panic crushed her ribs.

"Are you all right?" She'd recognize Jordan's voice anywhere. It had that deep timbre that wrapped around her. That man could make reading the ingredients of a soup can sound sexy.

"Yeah. Got a hold of something at a potluck that isn't agreeing with me." She tried to wave him off.

"Can I get you some water?" There was genuine concern in his tone, and it caused her heart to squeeze.

As much as she didn't want to come off as a jerk, she

couldn't afford to let him stick around. Especially with the way her body reacted when he was close. Muscle memory had her wanting to feel his hands on her, rough from working outside. For having such rough hands, his touch had been surprisingly soft. And those were more things she couldn't afford to think about.

The pregnancy test should be safely tucked inside the bag, but she'd tossed that onto the passenger seat before she'd turned away. She didn't want Jordan seeing something he shouldn't or asking questions she didn't have answers to.

Courtney took in a deep, fortifying breath. "I'm okay. Thanks for offering, though."

A stomach cramp doubled her over. She turned away in time to empty the contents onto the parking lot. So much for being fine.

The next thing she knew, Jordan was next to her, comforting her. His hand on her back caused a whole different kind of reaction in her body. One that was totally out of place under the circumstances.

"That must've been some potluck," he commented.

She didn't respond.

"I saw the test in your basket, Courtney," he said flatly. "Are you pregnant?"

COURTNEY STOPPED THROWING UP. Jordan expected a response to his question. He waited. Because if she was pregnant, that meant she'd been in a relationship with someone else during their brief fling. Jordan might have the reputation of a playboy, but there were lines he never crossed and that was one of them. "Courtney—"

She stood up straight and stepped away from him.

"Take this." He handed her a bottle of water, which she took and then used to rinse out her mouth.

"Are you planning to answer me?" This whole scenario was off. He couldn't imagine she would use him to cheat on someone else. He didn't normally misread people or their intentions.

Courtney locked gazes with him. "If I knew the answer to your question, I wouldn't need the test, now would I?"

"Why didn't you say something about being in a relationship?" he pressed.

She issued a grunt and twisted up her face with a *how dare you* look. She was offended?

"Is that what you think? I could—" she made eyes at him "—with *you* while two-timing my real boyfriend?"

Jordan started to speak but was cut off.

"Because if that's the kind of person you think I am, this conversation is over."

What exactly was she saying?

Jordan had to stop a second to let her words sink in. The gears in his head started grinding. The realization struck him like lightning on a sunny day, fast and out of the blue. *He* was the father. *If she was pregnant*, a struggling little voice in the back of his mind called out.

"If you'll excuse me, I have a murder investigation to get back to." She walked past him, and her shoulder bumped him as she passed by on her way to the driver's side of her vehicle.

Ignoring the intentional snub and the rockets of electricity from contact, he turned and caught her by the elbow. "Hold on. You're not getting away that easy."

"Neither one of us is if the test comes back positive," she retorted.

"I didn't ask for the easy road, but I deserve to know the outcome as much as you do." He held his ground. He got it—Courtney was scared, and she didn't do weak. The brave front she put up could be equated to a bull in a china shop, but she seemed to be clinging to hope, so he didn't call her out on it. He could tell that she was forcing her strength by the way her chin jutted out. Knowing her since they were kids had its advantages—being able to read her was one of them. And even though she'd annoyed him in his teen years, he'd noticed quite a few of her little quirks. They'd been damn adorable then—a fact he hadn't wanted to acknowledge in high school—and had turned straight-up sexy as an adult.

He almost laughed out loud. Courtney Foster would balk at being described as adorable.

The tension in her shoulders released like a balloon letting out air. Now it made sense why she was out here shopping on the outskirts of town when there were plenty of stores in Jacobstown. She didn't want to take the chance that anyone would see her buying a pregnancy test. He got it. Everyone in town knew each other, and people talked. Having a baby would be a big story. The news that Courtney Foster had come home after living in Dallas for the past decade had just died down after a month of hitting the gossip rounds, according to his sister Amber. She'd said there'd been talk for weeks.

It was a main topic of conversation and had given the townsfolk a break from chewing on the other big news in Jacobstown—the Hacker and the possibility he would strike again soon.

"I have one stop to make, and then I'm on my lunch break. You can come if you want. It was never my intention to hide anything from you, Jordan. There might not even be anything to discuss." The hope in her voice at the end of her sentence made him realize this had taken her by surprise as much it had him.

"We were careful," he reassured. "It'll be fine."

"It was probably the potluck," she added, and the hopefulness in her voice struck him again.

"I'll bring my truck around to follow you." He didn't know where she lived. After their tryst, he'd gone back to Idaho. This was his first time back to Jacobstown since.

"What kind of family business brings you to town, anyway?" she asked.

"I already told you. Family business."

She used the contents of the water bottle to wash the concrete instead of pressing for a better answer.

A few minutes later, he was behind her on the road.

Jordan hadn't given much thought to becoming a father. His brothers and sister had all found happiness in the past few years with children and spouses. The Kent brood as a whole had grown exponentially, and that was good for them.

Fatherhood was not a job that Jordan had ever craved. If Courtney was pregnant, there was no doubt that he'd do the right thing by her, by his child. But that didn't mean he had to be in a relationship with Courtney to be there for his child.

They could start as friends, because they'd need common ground in order to co-parent.

And that's where Jordan stopped himself. Co-parenting and babies and entanglements weren't on the schedule for him. Besides, the two of them had been careful to use a condom every time. This was probably nothing more than a scare.

Half an hour later, Courtney pulled up in front of a small ranch-style house with crisscross wire fencing.

His eyebrow shot up as she approached his vehicle.

"Do you mind waiting for me at the gas station a block away?" she asked.

"No problem." He forced his gaze away from her sweet backside as she walked toward the home's front door. He pulled away thinking that he was probably seeing things, but he could've sworn she had a different look, a glow. And maybe a few more curves that looked damn good on her, but he reminded himself how easy it had been for her to shut down any budding feelings and force him out of her life.

That was the last kind of person he needed to be around. Damn, if she was pregnant, both of their lives were going to change. He thought about the baby boom happening at the ranch. The fact that he couldn't stick around too long in one place without going a little crazy. He loved his nieces and nephews. But he'd always been the outsider in the family. He'd always chosen the lone path of living far away from Jacobstown, out of Texas.

True to Courtney's word, she didn't take long. She

didn't circle back to talk this time as she pulled up beside him. She navigated onto the two-lane highway that led to Jacobstown. He could only assume they were heading to her house. Jordan had no idea where she lived. They'd stayed at her uncle's abandoned fishing cabin, and then he'd left town at the end of the week.

A baby? What in hell's name had they done to their lives?

Jordan pulled in behind her at a small bungalow-style house on Acorn Street. She parked and then motioned for him to follow her inside. The place sat on what looked to be a quarter of an acre, in his best estimation. The house was made of white siding and had wood shutters. There were decorative flower pots on a small porch. It looked like something out of one of those home-decorating shows. Jordan had been subject to a few episodes while dining at small eateries on the road back and forth from Texas to Idaho.

Reality was a gut punch as he caught sight of the bag in Courtney's hand.

In a few minutes, he'd learn if he was a father. He couldn't even contemplate the ways in which his life would change. He stopped her at the door before she opened it.

A question had been churning over and over in his mind on the ride over.

"Was there even a potluck?"

Chapter Three

"Technically, yes. But, no, I didn't eat anything," Courtney admitted. Ever since she'd gotten food poisoning her rookie year at her department's potluck, she'd skipped the line. She always brought her own food. She'd been so sick that she didn't even risk eating raw vegetables. That's how freaked out she was by them.

The best way to avoid eating the food without raising any eyebrows was to get a plate, excuse herself from line by saying she needed to take a call and then put her own food on the plate before returning to her table.

Later, she'd go along with saying Tony's meatballs were perfection and Angela's pasta melted in her mouth. She couldn't think about work without thinking about her old crew. The memory of her dead coworkers crashed down hard on her, squeezing air out of her lungs. The scene. The mob. The blood.

She looked up at Jordan, who'd gone sheet white. "Let's get this over with."

He nodded. His sunglasses hooded his eyes, and his expression was impossible for her to read. He'd been clear about never wanting kids even when they were young. She hoped that she wasn't about to cause his hopes and dreams to crash down around him.

"If it makes you feel any better, I'm totally freaked out by the remote possibility of having a baby," she said, pushing the door open. She didn't bother to check his reaction. He seemed pretty freaked out by how much his life might change. She'd just started a new job. Jacobstown was supposed to be a fresh start for her. A baby was nowhere in the plans. Besides, she wasn't in the right emotional place to bring a life into this world.

But if that's what she was dealing with, she needed to know now.

"Make yourself comfortable," she said to Jordan. He'd removed his hat and sunglasses, and he was pretty damn devastating-looking standing in her living room.

His white-knuckle grip on his hat belied his calm exterior.

He shot her a look that said her comment didn't make him feel any better. "What do you need to do?"

"I take this into the bathroom with me, do what I have to and then we wait." She held up the plastic bag in her hand.

"May as well put all this behind us," he said.

Courtney couldn't agree more. She peeled off her jacket and then disappeared down the hall. She returned a minute later holding the white stick that had the power to change both of their lives forever. She placed it on her coffee table on top of a magazine and stared at the little window. "Two lines will show up in there if I'm pregnant."

If Courtney hadn't already thrown up the contents of her stomach, she would be now.

Three minutes had never taken so long. Neither spoke. Then the stick test yielded a positive reading.

Jordan took a few steps toward the front window and stared out it. If he was waiting for her to speak, he'd be waiting one hell of a long time, because there were no words for what she was currently feeling.

She feared that he might be concocting a plan to ask her to marry him. "You don't have to do that, you know."

"What?" He finally found his voice after a few beats of silence.

"Propose." Her heart squeezed, which made it a total traitor. Courtney had no plans to get married. Especially not because she'd gotten pregnant. That hadn't worked out so well for her parents. Being in a loveless marriage had to be the worst sentence, and she understood why her mother had taken off when Courtney was barely ten years old. What she could never understand was why the woman took Courtney's baby brother but not her.

And she'd never know, because her mother and brother had died in a car crash on a Texas highway a month later. She'd never had the chance to ask why her own mother didn't love her enough to take her away from the father who'd abused all of them.

"I wasn't going to." Jordan raked his fingers through his hair. He turned around to face her, and his expression was granite. The sharp angles and hard planes made for one seriously gorgeous man. But he gave away nothing of what he was thinking.

He was a Kent, and that name meant something. Her family might've been a hot mess, but there was honor in being a Kent.

"This is a lot to take in all at once," she said, unable to read his thoughts.

"It's simple to me. I have every intention of stepping up to be a father, Courtney. You should know that off the bat," he started.

She tried to interrupt him, but he brought his hand up to shush her.

"Looks like both of us are thrown off by the news, but that doesn't change the fact that a baby is coming, and it deserves the best from both of us." She couldn't agree more about that part, and when she regained her bearings she figured that she would be saying the same thing. It was foreign to her to hear that from the opposite sex, but then, she'd never been in this situation with her boyfriend and fellow officer Bradley Decks. He'd had a nine-year-old son from a marriage that had ended badly, a boy he never saw. Decks had no plans to marry or have more children. That had most likely been the cause of her initial attraction to him when she really thought about it. He'd been safe.

"I never thought about becoming a mother," she admitted in a moment of weakness. "I mean, I never thought it was a job I'd ever want."

The expression Jordan wore told her that he felt the same way about fatherhood. "But here we are."

"Are you saying that you're not upset that having this baby is the only option for me?" she asked.

"Did I mention anything about that?" he asked, and

she saw the first crack in his calm facade. Good—that meant he wouldn't try to pressure her into doing something she couldn't. For a brief second, she thought about adoption. But she'd always worry if her child was being treated the way she'd been.

"No." She'd just put a down payment on a new car. The house was a rental, and she didn't exactly have stores of money in the bank after using her personal savings to set up a college fund for her former boyfriend's kid before her move to Jacobstown. It only seemed the right thing to do considering Becks had lost his life on the job. Babies cost money. This unexpected turn of events definitely threw a wrench in her future plans.

"Good. Because we got into this situation together, and I'll see it through with you." The out-of-the-blue news had clearly caught them both off guard. She had no idea what that meant, but the determination in his eyes had her reaching for her purse.

"I have to get back to work," she said.

"No, you don't. Not after dropping that bomb. You don't get to run away so fast this time."

JORDAN PACED IN Courtney's living room. The place was cozy and had just enough feminine touches to make it feel homey. The warm-toned twin sofas faced each other in the main living area. The fabric looked like the kind he could sink into. A glass coffee table with a stack of novels, a magazine that was now in the trash and a vase with fresh flowers anchored the seating area.

There was a table for two in the dining area. He couldn't see the kitchen from where he stood. His world had tipped on its axis, and he was noticing her furniture? Damn, Jordan was losing it.

Courtney excused herself and came back with a glass of water. "I'd ask if you want something to drink, but you won't be staying long enough."

"You should eat." He stared at the glass in her hand.

"I don't need someone looking over my shoulder, Jordan. Say what you need to get off your chest and then go."

"Are you really this hardheaded or just mean-spirited?" He regretted those words as soon as he heard them come out of his mouth. Chalk that up to his impulsive nature.

"You remember where the door is, don't you?" Fire shot from her gaze, and he could almost see her temper rising.

Maybe this wasn't the best time to try to sort this out, heat of the moment being what it was. The news was too fresh. The shock too great.

"I spoke before I thought," he offered by way of an apology. Jordan was no good at those. He was even worse at talking to someone who'd made it clear she had no use for him in her life, but that didn't stop him from digging his heels in anyway.

"Yeah?" was all she said.

"You made it clear a few weeks ago that you didn't want or need anyone in your life," he started.

"Well, it's too late for me to continue thinking that now." She touched her belly, and he wondered if she realized she did it.

"Like it or not, I'm going to be in your life, too." That

point needed to be made. He needed to be very clear. Surprise pregnancy or not, Jordan Kent didn't walk away from his flesh and blood.

She drew in a deep breath, making it very clear that she was tolerating him at this point. If they were going to be successful with a child, they needed to learn to work together.

"It's important that we establish some ground rules—"

"Is that right, Jordan? Do tell what you have in mind." Her nostrils flared.

"Settle down. I'm not trying to make this more difficult than it already is. If you haven't noticed, I'm attempting to do just the opposite." He used the same tone when he came across a spooked mare in the stable.

"You're right," she conceded. "It's a little difficult to start negotiating with you when I don't have the first idea of how I'm going to handle any of this." She still fumed, but he appreciated her honesty.

Normally, he'd push his point until he won. This was different. He didn't want to make Courtney more upset, especially in her condition. He was concerned about the nightmares she'd been having, too.

"Do you want to sit down and talk?" He never could get her to talk about herself, her past. Courtney's quick wit and their history made for long conversations. But he'd taken note of how she wormed her way out of any conversation that got too personal. It was just as well, considering neither one had wanted to be tethered by a serious relationship. Besides, they'd been together a week after not knowing each other for a decade. She'd changed. He'd changed. Life was much bigger than what happened in high school.

"Not really. I mean, I don't know what to say right now, and I have an ongoing murder investigation that needs my full—"

"Can you ask to be removed from the case?" Zach wouldn't keep her on it if he knew she was pregnant anyway. Speaking of family, he had a feeling that Amber was going to flip out when she heard the news.

"No." That sounded final. She offered no follow-up explanation.

"When do you plan to tell your boss about the baby?" Jordan asked. The minute Zach learned she was pregnant, he would put her on a desk for precaution. There was no way Zach would want her chasing down the Jacobstown Hacker with nausea threatening every few seconds. When she'd mentioned a murder investigation earlier, he'd known exactly which one.

"I haven't given it any thought, Jordan. Please don't tell anyone until we figure this out," she pleaded.

It wasn't a smart idea.

"Can you take a few days off? Call in sick?" he asked.

"I just started last month. How will that look?" She folded her arms, and he could see the wall coming up between them. He'd seen it before. They'd have a round of the best sex of his life—and, his ego hoped, hers— and then while still tangled in the sheets, they'd talk into the early morning hours. She'd settle into the crook of his arm, and he'd hold her. They'd laugh about the past, about how two years of age difference at fifteen and seventeen had seemed like so much but how little it mattered now in their late twenties and early thirties. Conversation would inevitably move to her past or family, and she'd put up that same wall. The one she'd erected now. The one that shut down any meaningful progress.

Since this conversation had taken a wrong turn down a bad path, he needed to step away.

"You know what?" His frustration made that question come out harsher than he'd intended.

She didn't answer, probably couldn't see over the wall. If she didn't want to try, why should he make her?

"I'm not doing this. You seem determined to figure this out on your own, so I'm done." Walking out that door made him feel like the biggest jerk in the world. All momentum stopped the minute he sat inside his vehicle and he was suddenly unable to drive away.

Courtney was struggling. He could see it on the concern lines of her forehead. She was standing in quicksand. Amber had mentioned recently while making small talk while waiting for the others to join them on a conference call what had happened to Courtney in Dallas. Jordan had looked up the massacre. The attack on officers had been brutal. The organizers of the peaceful protest had no connection, no idea what was about to happen. The bloodshed. The officers. The scene out of a horror show.

It explained the nightmares.

He'd heard gossip about an abusive father in town years ago. There'd been so much disdain in the voices as they recounted his acts of violence. The beatings became so bad the summer before Courtney's senior year that a neighbor had heard about them and finally stepped in. Amber and Amy had been distraught because they'd been friends with Courtney. She'd never let on about what was happening at home.

Courtney's father had been arrested. She'd been taken into the foster care system until she turned eighteen, which had been ten months later. And then, as far as Jordan knew, Mr. Foster had died a couple of years after that.

At the same time, Jordan had been in his own world, a sophomore at the University of Texas. He'd dropped out that summer and moved to Idaho, where he'd stayed all these years.

Coming home to Jacobstown when his mother had died and then not too long after his father followed in her footsteps had been foreign. But then, he'd always been the kind of person who needed to make his own way in life.

Jordan Kent relied on no one. And preferred it that way. So, why hadn't he started his engine and pulled away yet?

Jordan bit out a string of curses before pushing open the driver's side door and getting out of the cab of his pickup.

He stood there in the cold for a long time, staring at the bungalow.

And then the front door opened. Courtney stood there with her balled fist on her right hip.

"You stand out there on my lawn any longer and you'll freeze to death."

Chapter Four

"I'm sorry." Jordan hoped those two heartfelt words were enough.

"You want coffee?" Courtney opened the door a little wider and walked away.

"Is that a good idea for you?" He had no idea what the rules were for a pregnant woman, but coffee only upset his stomach when he was already nauseous.

"Probably not. It's not for me," she said. "I'm having water, and we'll see if I keep that down."

"Coffee sounds good." He closed the door behind him and took off his hat.

"Have a seat." She motioned toward the table.

Jordan took her up on the offer, figuring a little goodwill on his part would go a long way toward figuring out what their next steps were going to be.

A few minutes later, she joined him at the table and handed over a fresh cup of steaming brew. He thanked her and took the first sip, enjoying the burn on his throat.

"What family business has you back in town?" she asked.

"Everyone's concerned about the Hacker. I came so

we'd have extra eyes around the ranch." He denied the part of him that said he'd hoped to run into her again.

The reason for his timing seemed to dawn on her as she rocked her head. "Right. Breanna was found at Rushing Creek as were the heifers."

"There was no sign of struggle, and the jerk got past increased security, which doesn't sit well." Jordan took another sip as guilt took a shot at him. He felt the blow square in his chest. That old, familiar voice resurfaced. He should've stuck around when he was home a few weeks ago. He might've been the difference. Now, because of his absence, a woman had been killed on the family's property, land that was sacred to them.

"You guys own so much acreage. It would be impossible to cover every inch with a person—or a camera, for that matter. The creek itself is how long?" Some of her color was returning to her cheeks. With her hair pulled off her face she was even more beautiful than he remembered, and that realization caused a second shot to his chest.

"Twenty-seven miles," he supplied.

"I spent so many summers playing around that creek. I hate what happened there, and I can only imagine what Breanna's family has been through." The sympathy in her voice softened her intensity a few notches. "Zach wants all hands on deck to lock this jerk away for his lifetime."

Was that her explanation as to why she didn't want to tell Zach about the pregnancy yet? She didn't want to disappoint her boss?

"Hear me out on this, Jordan. Okay?" Her eyes pleaded.

He nodded.

"I'm serious. Don't give me that nod you do when you're only half listening," she warned.

His hands went up, palms out, in the surrender position.

"What if I don't work? What if I take leave? What if *I'm* the reason someone dies?" Her voice rose, along with her blood pressure, based on the heat crawling up her neck.

"What if something happens to you or the baby because of the case? Zach would never forgive himself." He may as well lay his cards on the table.

When she hesitated, he added, "This is Zach. You can ask him to keep the news under wraps. I'm not talking about taking an ad out in the paper or renting a billboard—"

"Yes, you are. No secret stays quiet for long in this town." She made a good point.

"There are a few people I trust. Zach is one of them. He wouldn't even tell me if you asked him not to," he countered. "He wouldn't like being put in the position, but he would honor your wishes."

"I see your argument. Here's mine. I know my body, and I'm used to exercising. I have no problem consulting an OB about what's right and what's not right to do during the pregnancy. But if my doctor gives a thumbs-up to working and maintaining physical activity, you should know I plan to take that advice. As long as there's no risk to the child, I'll keep working at full capacity until it creates an unhealthy environment for the baby or I can't anymore." Her hands fisted, and he figured she probably didn't even realize it.

It was easy to see that she'd dug her heels in. There was no denying she'd thought this through the minute she realized it was a possibility, and he couldn't blame her when he really thought about her argument. If the shoe were on the other foot and a doctor told him it was safe to continue work on the ranch until the baby was born, he'd take the same stance.

An argument could be made that her work inherently put her in danger, but it was early in the pregnancy. He made a note to ask one of his sisters-in-law how she would deal with the situation. Jordan almost laughed out loud. His brother Deacon had married a strong-willed Fort Worth detective. Leah Cordon wouldn't back off her job unless she'd been forced. The same was true of Courtney.

"For now, promise me you won't tell Zach or anyone else about the pregnancy. I hear it's bad luck to talk about it before the second trimester anyway." Her eyes pleaded, and Jordan was reminded how easy it had been for her to get her way.

"And you'll make the announcement if the doctor says to?" He needed that much from her.

"I'd say happily, but I don't want to lie." Her shoulders slumped forward. "I just never thought this would happen to me."

"An unplanned pregnancy?" he asked.

"*Any* pregnancy. I was never that girl who dreamed about her wedding day or clipped out pictures of flowing white dresses," she admitted.

"You aren't exactly a tomboy, either." He wasn't sure why he felt the need to point it out.

"True. I liked some girly stuff. But parenthood? Jordan, come on. Are you seriously telling me you're ready for that commitment?" It was a fair question.

"What does the answer matter? It's here. This is what we have to deal with. It won't do any good to wish the situation would go away and that wouldn't be fair to the kid anyway." His honest answer seemed to deflate her shoulders a little more. A stab of guilt niggled at him. He could've put it more delicately. Damn, he could be a bull in a china shop without even trying.

"Promise me we won't be like my parents."

Those words struck like a physical blow.

COURTNEY WAITED FOR a response from Jordan. She studied his expression, and it was unreadable. "I should probably get back to work."

"I will love and care for any child that belongs to me but I'm more concerned about you right now. Promise me you'll take it easy?"

"I ride around in an SUV most of my shift. My other responsibility is talking to people. How bad can it get?" Coming back to her hometown had been meant to shield her from the harsher crimes in Dallas. But then no one knew for certain the Jacobstown Hacker had remained in town. He could've easily moved on. A little voice reminded her the odds of that happening were slim to none. That same voice insisted Jordan looked even better than she remembered, but that was probably heightened hormones and the fact that he was the father of her child. It was biology at work and nothing more.

Jordan stood, and she walked him to the door. He reached out and touched her arm as he stood a foot away from her. Suddenly, heat rushed through her body, and her skin sizzled with electric impulse. She instantly recoiled. If this was what she had to look forward to for the next seven or eight months, she was in for a real treat.

A few seconds of silence passed between them before Jordan spoke. "Be careful out there."

"Of course." She realized that her hand had come up to touch her belly when his gaze stopped there.

Jordan turned and walked out the door. It was like the moon covering the sun, eclipsing her in total darkness.

COURTNEY HAD HAD a day for the record books. First off, it was cold outside. She didn't *do* cold. This was Texas, land of eternal sunshine, and her blood was too thin for temperatures hovering above freezing.

Winds howled and tree branches snapped as pea-size hail dinged the hood of her SUV. It was getting late, but she didn't care. She exited the vehicle and turned on her flashlight. A hunch had led her to Rushing Creek. She'd received permission to be on the Kent property and had checked in with Isaac at the guard shack.

It was the kind of eerie night that felt like early fall, around Halloween. Clouds covered the moon, making it almost pitch-black outside.

A branch snapped behind her. Courtney spun around,

weapon drawn and held along with her flashlight. What made the sound? An animal?

Courtney took a few steps toward the direction of the sound. The trees were thick in this part of the land, making it a perfect place to hide. Was someone tracking her? The hairs on the back of her neck pricked.

A blast of frigid wind sent a shiver racing up her arms and down her back. Icy tendrils wrapped their long, lean fingers around her spine. Another crack sound sent her whirling to the left. Thoughts of a wild animal stalking her crossed her mind. Part of the reason she'd left Jacobstown was to get away from the country. It struck her as odd that this was the place she'd wanted to come back to.

Her cell buzzed. She didn't have a free hand, so she ignored it. Her radio was close to her ear and it had gone quiet. This was a good time to get the hell out of the woods. She'd call for backup if she could identify a threat. But then, she already knew the closest deputy was at least twenty minutes away. Courtney had grown up on the Kent property, having been friends with Amber and Amy in their teenage years.

What did it say that she hadn't contacted either one since returning home? Courtney tried to lie to herself and say it was because they were busy with lives of their own, but there was so much more to it. She'd gone behind everyone's backs when she had a fling with Jordan. It had been a wild seven days, and she'd gone out of her way since to avoid seeing her old friends. Besides, they'd barely kept up on social media. High school friends were just that. And Courtney didn't feel like she belonged in Jacobstown any more than she felt like she belonged in Dallas. It was strange to want to be part of something but always feel like the outsider looking in. Had it been that way her whole life?

Courtney backtracked, taking one step at a time and keeping watch where she'd heard the last branch snap. If wildlife was out there, and she knew it was, it wasn't getting her today. Slowly and cautiously, she eased one foot at a time. Her boots were heavy, but they kept her toes from freezing.

Wind whipped her hair, causing her ponytail to swish around and slap her in the face. She wished she'd pulled on a hat, because her ears felt like they were frostbitten already. It would also keep the ends of her hair out of her eyes.

This wasn't the time for a bout of nausea, but it happened anyway. Her stomach churned, and she thought about the fish tacos she'd eaten for dinner—she'd known even then that eating them could come back to haunt her. She'd chalked her craving up to stress but questioned the reason now. Was it the pregnancy?

And then she heard a voice. She froze, not wanting to draw attention to herself. She turned off her flashlight. Thoughts that never would have plagued her before the ambush in Dallas surfaced. An image of Breanna flashed in Courtney's mind, too.

Blood pumping, Courtney took another step backward. Her backside hit something hard. She sucked in a burst of air as she felt around, half expecting a blow to the head to follow. When none came and she felt the rough bark of a tree, she released the breath she'd been holding. She tried by sheer force of will to stop her hands from shaking.

Leaning against the tree in order to stay upright on rubbery legs, Courtney held back the urge to vomit. Bile rose in her throat, burning a hot trail as she palmed her service weapon. The Glock's metal was cold against her ungloved hand. She stood frozen, perfectly still for what felt like an eternity, waiting for the next sound.

A voice came over the radio, breaking the silence. The image of the young guy in Carolina-blue basketball shorts came to mind. As did the picture of Reggie Barstock shared by Zach McWilliams.

Another wave of nausea struck, harder this time. Courtney couldn't stop herself from folding forward and emptying the contents of her stomach. The taste of burning tacos lit her throat on fire. She had a feeling this would be the last time she could stomach tacos, which was unfortunate, because she loved them.

This time, when she came up for air, she saw someone dart behind a tree.

Chapter Five

"What are you doing on the south side of the property alone?" Jordan's warm voice cut through the cold air as he moved into view from behind the tree.

"My job," Courtney retorted, but she couldn't deny that she was relieved to see him. In fact, her nerves settled below panic. She'd never questioned her ability to handle any situation that came with being an officer of the law until recently, until the tragedy that had taken too many lives too early.

"Your job has you coming out here without backup?" It was a valid question. One she planned to dodge answering.

"Why are you here?" She stood straight and holstered her Glock. Then she tucked her flashlight into her belt.

He stood there staring her down for a minute, and she knew why. The question was whether or not he'd let her get away with a non-answer.

"Protecting my family's land," he finally said.

She leaned against the tree, and his expression took a dive.

"You okay?" He was at her side in a heartbeat.

"You're freezing out here. Come back to the main house with me."

There was no use fighting it. She didn't want to be left alone, even though she'd eventually find her way back. She'd gotten herself turned around on the massive property. She'd been overconfident, and it had nearly cost her. She resolved not to make that mistake again.

"I'd like that," she admitted. "I just need a minute."

"Or I can give you a hand. My ATV isn't far from here." He froze. "Is it safe for you to ride one?"

"Should be fine," she reassured, and it warmed her heart more than she wanted to admit that he was concerned for her well-being.

Courtney let Jordan help her to the ATV.

"Take my gloves. Your hands are like icicles," he said.

She'd argue, but he was right. "What will you use?"

"I'll be fine until I get home. How long have you been out here?" He took off his gloves and handed the pair to her.

"An hour. Maybe more." She took the offerings and felt an immediate difference as soon as she slid them on her fingers. They were already warm from his hands, and it instantly felt like someone held her hands over a campfire. "Ah, thank you for these. I didn't realize a pair of gloves could feel so wonderful."

An emotion flickered behind his eyes that she couldn't quite pinpoint. His tough facade returned almost immediately as he said, "Hop on the back. It'll take about thirty minutes to reach home, so get comfortable."

Courtney did as he said and scooted back far enough

for him to throw his leg over and take the driver's position. He was true to his word. They arrived at the main house almost a half hour on the dot later. She briefly prayed no one else was home, but the thought of being alone with Jordan again didn't sit well, either. On balance, she figured it was best if they had company. From the last time she was there, she remembered Kents coming and going almost constantly. Good. She didn't trust herself not to say the wrong thing while the two of them were getting their footing in this new...*reality*, for lack of a better word.

The main house had a fire going in the fireplace in the kitchen. Courtney made her way to it quickly, taking off Jordan's gloves and placing them on the hearth next to her.

"Can I take your coat?" Jordan stood close enough for her to feel a different kind of heat.

She shrugged out of her jacket and handed it over to him.

"How about something warm to drink?" he asked.

"Any chance your sister keeps any chamomile in the pantry?" She rubbed her hands together in front of the flame.

"I wouldn't know. I can check." His intense eyes had a way of looking right through her, so she sidestepped his gaze and moved back to the fireplace, where she kept her back to him. She removed her belt and felt instant relief from not having to carry the extra weight around. Her shoulder holster came off next. She placed those items on a dining chair before she reclaimed her seat on the hearth. The warmth from the fire started immediately thawing out her frozen limbs. She flexed and released her hands, trying to expedite the return of feeling to her fingers.

Jordan went to work pouring himself a cup of coffee—the smell of which didn't do great things to her stomach—while a pot of water came to boil on the stove. "I don't know what to do besides pour the water into a cup over the tea bag."

"It's pretty much that simple." The smell of supper still lingered in the kitchen, and her stomach growled.

"Are you hungry?" he asked.

She'd be embarrassed by the fact her stomach had just announced that it was empty, but that ship had probably sailed, considering it hadn't been all that long ago that the two of them lay naked and tangled in the sheets of her uncle's fishing cabin. She could lie about the fact that she could eat an entire side of beef courtesy of pregnancy hormones or come clean and admit to being hungry again. At least she hoped this weird vomit-eat-nausea-eat-vomit-eat routine could be attributed to something that made sense. "Soup sounds good. And a toothbrush if you have a spare."

"You remember where that is?" It was more statement than question.

There were always extras in the guest bathroom. The Kent family was prepared for just about anything. Once, when the town lost power due to flooding after one of the wettest springs on record, the Kent family hosted a barbecue to feed as many folks as possible. Their generator allowed them to open their home to the elderly and mothers with small children until the power company could sort out the issue and restore electricity. The Kents had always been good people, and she was sorry to hear they'd passed away. She couldn't imagine seeing one without the other.

"Yes, down the hall." She mentally nudged herself out of the reverie. "I'll be right back."

The toothbrush and toothpaste felt like gifts from heaven as she splashed cold water on her face, rinsed her mouth and then brushed. Being here in the main house with Jordan after their fling and recent news should feel stranger than it did. She chalked it up to having been there before in her teenage years and tried to forget it. She sent an update to Zach via text, noting that she'd found nothing by the creek.

By the time she returned to the kitchen, there was a cup of tea sitting on the table. She took a seat near the fireplace and stared at the folded stack of clothes she recognized as belonging to her.

"You left those at the cabin. I had them cleaned." There was an edge to his voice that she recognized from their earlier conversation. Nothing about this day was going right. Sure, he'd been on her mind. And now it seemed everywhere she turned, he wasn't far. To be fair, she was on his ranch. It wasn't like he was stalking her.

Of course, she was grateful for bumping into him on the property tonight. For the first time in her career when she'd come upon a possibly sketchy situation, she'd frozen.

After her friends had been ambushed in the protest that had turned deadly last year, nothing was the same.

She couldn't rely on her body to cooperate when her stress levels skyrocketed.

"Thanks, but I should probably—"

"Hear me out before you finish." He put up a hand in protest.

She picked up her cup of tea and took a sip, already feeling more relaxed than she'd felt in longer than she could remember. Well, that wasn't entirely true, because she'd felt pretty darn comfortable in his arms during their fling. Jordan had a way of putting her at ease, and she knew better than to get comfortable in the feeling. She nodded, hoping her cheeks weren't flushing thinking about the amazing sex they'd had for seven days and nights that had gone by way too fast.

"We have everything you could possibly want or need right here." He didn't mention that he could keep an eye on her, but she figured that had to be part of the motivation.

"I have a home to go to, Jordan. What about that?"

"You don't have any pets to take care of, so you could always go home tomorrow morning." He made a good point.

"Why should I stay here? I have a perfectly good bed—"

"Because I'm asking you to." He held out his hands, palms up. "I'll admit that I got hit with what felt like a boulder earlier, and I doubt that I reacted the best way I could've. I'm sorry for that."

"There's no right way to find out you're going to be a dad unexpectedly," she offered. He was beating himself up for nothing. The news had caught them both off guard, and she hadn't exactly been dealing with it well, either.

"And then there's the murder investigation…"

"Breanna." It was difficult to say her name without getting choked up.

"Right. I know it's your job to investigate, and I respect that. But you'll go home to an empty house, and you shouldn't be alone right now. This news hit you, too. I remember what you said about not ever wanting to be a mother." The rim of his coffee cup suddenly became very interesting.

"You feel responsible for this?" Of course he did. Guilt was written across the worry lines on his forehead. "Wait. Don't answer that question. It's obvious that you do, so I just want to remind you that it takes two people to make a baby."

"That part I'm aware of." He smirked, and it was devastatingly handsome. She didn't want it to tug at her heart, but it did. "Like it or not, we're in this together."

"What's that supposed to mean?" she asked.

"I remember what happened when you tried to sleep—"

"People have bad dreams," she said, a little too quickly. She could feel tension in her shoulder blades, especially on the left side, which sent pain up her neck and threatened to give her a terrible stress headache.

"That's not how I'd describe what I saw you experience." Great, now he was an armchair psychologist?

"I'm okay." Her body belied her words, trembling just thinking about the nightmares.

JORDAN COULD SEE Courtney's body shaking. Hell, he wasn't trying to upset her. "I'm probably going about this all wrong. But I'd like you to stay the night so I can make sure you're okay. You're in the middle of a tough investigation, and you got hit with news I know you weren't expecting or wanting. You just started your job here at Zach's office, and now you're going to have to take time off at some point for maternity leave. It's more than most could handle, but this is you, Courtney. You're one of the strongest women I know—"

Courtney's face was turning redder and redder with every word he spoke. He seemed to be making a mess of things.

"I'm not here to make things worse. At least let me feed you before you run out of here," he said by way of compromise.

She nodded, and he wouldn't look a gift horse in the mouth. He finished heating dinner and set a bowl of soup on the table for her. She finished it within minutes.

"Thank you. It was amazing," she said. "I can't remember the last time I was this tired. I'll take you up on the offer to stay the night if it still stands. I'm too tired to get behind the wheel, and it has been a long day. Taking a shower and then dropping into bed sounds like heaven about now."

"You already know where the guest room is. Clothes are there." He motioned toward the stack. "You need anything else, just give a shout. Someone is always around."

"Will do. Can I help clean up in here first?" she asked.

"I got this." He shook his head for emphasis.

She picked up the folded stack and disappeared down the hallway. The freshly-made soup provided the first smile since Courtney arrived at KR. His chest puffed out with pride for giving her something to make her feel better.

Co-parenting would require that the parents actually get along. Making progress on their complicated relationship felt good. Jordan had had the benefit of growing up with parents who'd loved each other. Although their life together as a couple hadn't always been easy, his parents cared for their family and the community. Their reputation for generosity was one Jordan and his siblings intended to uphold. Being a Kent meant walking in big shoes, but Jordan had every intention of living up to his family name.

Of course, he wasn't exactly doing a stellar job of it so far. The pregnancy news had caught him off guard, tipped his world off its axis. Getting married because of a child was noble but not exactly the recipe for a happy relationship. He couldn't even imagine growing up in a household where the parents weren't head-over-heels in love with each other. Besides, Courtney seemed more opposed to the idea of marriage for a child's sake than he did.

Jordan had some work to do in order to gain Courtney's trust. But then, she didn't seem capable of trusting anyone after her upbringing and then what had happened in Dallas. He'd learned about what had happened to her and then read the story in the news following their brief fling. She'd been the lone survivor of a terrible tragedy, the kind of heartbreak that changed a person's view on life. The fact that she'd survived when several of her team didn't seemed to weigh heavy on her. He could imagine that came with the kind of guilt that could swallow a person whole.

Jordan finished with the dishes and drained his coffee mug. His thoughts bounced from Breanna and her family and back to Courtney. There was no way he'd get any shut-eye with all that was rattling around in his mind. Shutting down his brain would be next to impossible. He took a shower to help clear his thoughts and then changed into clean clothes.

There was no use fighting his urge to stay awake. He'd learned a long time ago that it was easier to go with the flow. So he settled down at the kitchen table with his laptop and a notebook. He tried to think back to who Breanna's friends had been. He was drawing a blank. For as long as he could remember, she'd been a loner. And then there was Reggie Barstock. He had a limp on his left side, a grudge, and seemed to slip in and out of town without being seen. Jordan's sister-in-law Chelsea was a distant relative and had inherited the Barstock family home and business. Trouble from Reggie had followed, but then Chelsea's ex-husband had come to town and tried to scare her into getting back together with him.

It was that incident that had brought Chelsea and Jordan's brother Nate together. Nate was a volunteer firefighter. The two had met and then fallen in love after Nate answered a call from dispatch not long after Chelsea moved to the area. Her craft pizza place had opened downtown last year after a fire nearly took her life. Everyone had suspected Reggie Barstock, but he'd been innocent. Her ex, Travis, had been responsible.

Barstock could stay on the suspect list. Courtney had mentioned someone who lived on the edge of town, a former truck driver. Jordan made a note to ask Zach about the guy.

Didn't Courtney mention something about following someone in blue shorts at The Mart? He'd ask her about that later. Although she might not speak to someone outside of law enforcement on an ongoing investigation. The fact that a murder had happened on Kent land made this personal. He figured he'd stick around this time in order to pitch in to find the murderer. He recapped the situation in his mind. A guy started out by killing small animals before moving onto larger ones, the heifers. And then he killed a woman.

Jordan wrote down, *has a problem with women.* He leaned over and picked up his laptop. He opened it and powered it up. Then, he looked up "characteristics of serial killers" before skimming the results. Working for the family ranch at the Idaho location gave him flexibility with his job.

Based on the search, he scribbled down a few key words and phrases that caught his attention. *Easily bored. Lacks empathy. Remorseless. Superficially charming. Grandiose. There weren't many but they impacted society most.*

Questions swirled, so he wrote those down, too. Could the person everyone was looking for be someone young? Someone in his early twenties? Or maybe someone who went away to school but came home for breaks? What was the tie to Jacobstown? Why did he cut off the left foot? Was he born deformed? Ridiculed? Was he injured at a young age? Teased?

There was no doubt these same questions had been asked by his cousin Zach. There was also no doubt that Zach was working toward answers. More questions struck, so he jotted those down, too. What was the killer's next move? Was this guy looking for some kind of a prize?

Damn. That one hit hard and fast. Since the killing happened on Kent property, Jordan had to assume the guy was somehow connected to the land or the family. The jerk was butchering livestock and then a woman under their noses. He couldn't even think about Breanna's murder without being slammed with anger. Even with increased security and strategically placed cameras, the guy had gotten away with murder.

Of course, the Kent ranch was sprawled out over thousands of acres and spread into three states: Texas, Idaho and Wyoming. As far as anyone knew, this guy had only struck in Texas. He'd hit other ranches in the area. So he must be tied to the community in Jacobstown. He also seemed to have an affinity for water, specifically the creek. Jordan jotted that down, too. It seemed a case like this could use as many eyes on it as possible.

He made a note to talk to every woman in the Kent family. It wasn't safe for any one of them to be out alone until this jerk was safely behind bars. A Kent would be considered a prize due to the family's status in the community. There was no way Jordan was willing to wait for something to happen to someone he loved in order to find out.

A question burned. Why start killing now? Didn't serial killers always have some kind of trigger? The event that sent this man spiraling might've happened on that date.

But then, the holidays played a number on a lot of people's emotions. It might be that simple. The date had more to do with leading up to Christmas.

These were all easy questions to ask and assumptions to make. Jordan was certain his cousin would've thought of everything written in the notebook. Maybe this case required more out-of-the-box thinking. Dates could represent an anniversary or could be some kind of twisted code. Then again, people got depressed around the holidays. Jordan had read somewhere that depression spiked this time of year. Which also made him think this could be the anniversary of the death of something.

The method of also killing had to have some type of meaning attached to it. The killer had used a weapon with a sharp, clean edge. A hatchet?

With half the town pitching in to take shifts on neighborhood watch groups or volunteer at Zach's office, there were more folks outside than usual. Zach had also said a few folks were getting out of Jacobstown for a while, saying they felt safer going to Colorado or New Mexico to ski rather than stick around town this year.

Jordan glanced at the time. It was half past two in the morning. Zach would most likely be sleeping, so disturbing him in order to discuss the case was out of the question. Courtney was in the guest room, hopefully asleep. It was most likely the pregnancy, but he'd never seen her look so tired. His heart stirred thinking about her, but he shut it down quickly. It wouldn't do any good remembering how soft her creamy skin was when she settled in the crook of his arm to sleep. Or how much he actually liked staying awake into ridiculous hours of the morning talking. Or how fiery hot the sex had been.

A cold glass of milk later, and he settled down at the table again.

A pad of paper stared back at him.

A bloodcurdling scream got him to his feet and moving down the hall faster than a thoroughbred at Lone Star Park.

Chapter Six

Courtney sat up and pulled the covers up to her neck. She felt disoriented and like her head might split in two. She tried to stop her body from shaking as the bedroom door burst open. A familiar face—Jordan's—was next to her bed barely a second later.

"Are you okay?" he asked.

"I'm good." But she was not all right. And part of her feared she never would be again. Beads of sweat trickled down her forehead, and she realized that she must've screamed for him to come running in like he did.

More sweat beaded, rolling down the side of her face, and she could feel that she'd soaked her shirt.

Slowly, her bearings started to come back. She was at Jordan Kent's family home. It was the middle of the night. She was sleeping in his guest room. The night terrors that had plagued her for the past year were relentless.

"You're safe now." Jordan said other words meant to soothe her as the mattress dipped under his weight. He sat next to her, and she instantly felt the air charge around her. Attraction replaced fear. She didn't debate her next actions. His arms opened to her, and she embraced the invitation, burying her face in his masculine chest.

Memories flooded her as she breathed in his all-male, uniquely Jordan scent. It was a mix of coffee and campfires, outdoorsy and spicy. She missed that smell. It would be so easy to get lost in it now and let Jordan be her strength. She was tired. Tired of being the strong one. Tired of standing alone. Tired of missing him.

There was a baby to think about now. A child who would have a better life than Courtney had had. She took in a breath meant to fortify her but only ushered in more of Jordan's scent. That was about as productive as trying to milk a beetle.

Pulling on all the strength she had left, she moved away from him and hugged her knees to her chest. "I'm sorry about that. I won't make it a habit."

"Promise me that anytime you need someone to lean on, you'll call me." There was so much honesty and purity in the words, she almost gave in. But that would mean so much more than the surface of being there for a friend. Trusting *anyone* wasn't her gig. Some people weren't made like that, and she was one of them. Growing up with an abusive father after her mother had abandoned her wasn't an excuse, but she figured it didn't help.

Those weren't the words he needed to hear based on his frown, and yet she couldn't lie to him, either. Instead of agreeing, she took a breath. "They're getting better. The nightmares. They're not as vivid anymore."

"That's good." The edge returned to his voice, and

she wondered if he felt the sting of rejection. She didn't mean it that way, but if the shoe were on the other foot, she'd probably take it the same.

"It's just something I have to handle. You know?" She hoped he could understand, because she really wasn't trying to be a jerk. Letting anyone else in was just hard…too hard.

He nodded by way of response, and she appreciated the fact that he was making the effort.

It didn't help that Jordan Kent had a reputation for sticking around for no one without the last name of Kent or McWilliams. He'd never been the relationship type—not that he was offering anything permanent to her. Granted, he'd made it clear that he'd be there for his child. She'd never doubted him for a second on that front. And there were so many other reasons rolling around inside her head that made her fear they would end up disliking each other if she stuck around long enough. For one, the two of them were from different worlds, different sides of the track and different backgrounds. Those differences were bound to cause arguments and drive a wedge between them. It was only a matter of time before he realized it, too.

But this wasn't the right time to bring any of that up.

"I think it's the case dredging up stress. That and the pregnancy," she admitted.

He nodded and stared intently at a patch of wall across the room.

"Thanks for coming in and checking on me," she said, trying to soften her reaction.

He must've taken it as a dismissal, because he pushed

off the bed and crossed the room. She was speechless as she watched him prepare to walk out. She struggled to string together a sentence. Her heart pounded against her ribs, and all her warning flares fired at the same time. "Stay with me. Please. I don't really want to be alone right now."

"Have you spoken to anyone about the night terrors?" He stopped but didn't turn around.

"No. But I planned to," she said a little too quickly. It sounded desperate even to her. "I know what you said before in the cabin, and I heard you—"

"Save it." The disappointment in his voice was a knife to the chest.

She expected him to walk right out the door. Instead, he turned around and came back to bed. He sat on the edge with his back to her, silent.

A torrent of words came to mind, but Courtney knew better than to open the floodgates. So she sat there, too. Quiet. Waiting. Hoping?

A minute passed, maybe two. Courtney shut her eyes and massaged her temples, but her hands were still shaking too badly to manage it for long. She brought her hands down to her lap.

Jordan eased beside her and stretched out his long legs. He had on jeans and no shirt, like she'd seen him do the week in the cabin. Her body trembled, and the quake started slowly.

"Courtney, are you okay?" There was concern in his voice—a voice that was bringing her back from the brink. Fall into the abyss and she'd be no use to anyone for days. The darkness threatened to suck her under, and her insides felt like she was paddling madly to keep her head above water. It also felt like there was an anchor tied around her ankle that was tugging her toward the ocean floor.

"Yes," she managed to get out on a burst of air. She flexed and released her fingers, needing to feel something besides the sensation of drowning. Panic was building from deep in her bones. Her muscles tensed, and there was a kink in her left shoulder that no amount of yoga stretching could ease.

"Hey, you don't sound…" His lips were still moving, but a ringing noise in her ears drowned out everything else in the room.

At this point, thinking would do her no good. She needed something to ground her, to root her back in reality and crack the concrete hardening around her brain causing her to go into fight, flight or freeze mode without being provoked. There was something stirring in the pit of her stomach. Her nervous system was on autopilot, which also meant heightened alert.

She blinked, trying to slow the kaleidoscope of images—images that had haunted her for the past year like a stalker in a dark alley. The world felt like it had tipped on its axis, spinning out of control. Instinct had her trying to grab hold of something, *anything* to keep her grounded.

Without thinking, she climbed onto Jordan's lap and kissed him. She pressed her lips to his and tunneled her fingers into his dark, curly mane. At first, his body tensed, but it didn't take much cajoling to get him to kiss her back. She parted her lips for him, and he slid his

tongue in her mouth. He tasted like peppermint toothpaste and coffee, her favorite two things combined. A
wall of memories crashed down around her with his
clean, masculine scent filling her senses every time
she took a breath.

An ache from deep within sprang up, catching her
off guard. She'd missed the sex, and part of her could
admit to how badly she'd missed Jordan, even though
she tried to convince herself that she'd confused him
with the feeling of home. *He* represented home to her.
But the side to her that didn't accept nonsense called
her out on it. She missed Jordan. She missed the feel of
his arms around her. She missed the way he tasted, and
she missed their conversations that ran too late into the
night. Seeing the sunrise and laughing about being up
all night had never held so much appeal as when she'd
been with him.

For a little while, her demons receded, and she felt
normal again. The nightmares didn't stop completely,
but they were better that week. He tried to get her to
talk about them, and she'd gotten so used to dodging
the subject. When she saw the hurt in his eyes, she put
up the walls.

Jordan's hands looped around her waist as the kiss
intensified. All other thoughts drifted into background
noise in her head. Everything calmed, and she was consumed by the need to kiss him harder.

And then he picked her up and sat her next to him.

JORDAN HAD ALMOST taken another trip down the rabbit
hole with Courtney. He wasn't sure when he'd devel-

oped this strong of a conscience when it came to turning down mind-blowing consensual sex, but somewhere along the line he'd picked one up. Damned if he knew where or why. The timing couldn't have been worse, because Courtney was smart, beautiful and beyond sexy.

Both of them sat on the bed, breathing hot and heavy. He cursed himself more than once for slowing down that runaway train, but he knew that sex would only confuse the issues between them. And his bruised ego wanted her to want *him* and not just another round of casual sex.

As he sat there next to one of the most beautiful women he knew, he realized he'd be cursing that niggle of conscience for days. There it was. He'd stopped something from happening that he'd wanted ever since he left the cabin. He couldn't take his actions back now, either.

So he apologized instead.

"Why are you sorry?" She sounded offended.

"I don't want to take advantage of you while you're vulnerable," he said.

"Pregnancy hasn't made me weak—"

"I wasn't talking about that. You had one of your nightmares." She'd refused to talk about them before, and he figured this time would be no different.

He glanced over in time to see her staring at the wall. She repositioned to where her back was against the headboard again and pulled the covers up. "They started after…"

Jordan took her hand in his. Hers was shaking.

"What happened in Dallas shook me up. I lost friends

who were like family that day." This was the most she'd said so far. She'd refused to talk about the incident while at the cabin.

"That would be hard for anyone." She was strong and needed to hear confirmation.

"The department offered counseling." She blew out a breath. "*Offered* is putting it lightly. My job depended on me attending sessions."

"Did it help?" he asked.

"I said what I had to in order to get my file rubber-stamped so I could get back to work." She pulled her hand away. "I lied and said I was okay. That I'd had a few bad dreams but was getting better."

"The counselor believed you?"

"My job depended on it." She shrugged. "I was pretty convincing. Cops always joke about what we'd say if the time came, so I had a few lines rehearsed. I did a little research, and it wasn't hard to figure out what he wanted to hear. I mean, how stupid does the department think a cop is? Say the wrong thing and bye-bye pension. Everything in the session goes into our permanent work file. No one who needs a job is going to be completely honest in a situation like that. We can't afford to be. It could ruin our careers."

He understood the logic and figured it was pretty common among law enforcement officers and military personnel. The upside to this conversation was that she was opening up to him a little. This was a start toward building a bridge of trust between the two of them. Jordan would take any progress he could get. Walking away from his child would never be a consideration.

He needed to forge a relationship with Courtney for the sake of their child.

"How about private counseling?" He knew he'd made a mistake in asking the second she recoiled.

"Thanks for checking on me, Jordan. I had a moment, but I promise I'm feeling better now." Her tone left no room for doubt that she'd put up the walls between them again.

He needed to choose his next words carefully. "Believe it or not, I wasn't trying to insult you by asking the question—"

"I never said you were." She stretched and yawned, and he could tell it was fake.

"Courtney," he started, but the right words didn't come. The last thing he wanted was to make the situation worse.

She rolled onto her side, facing away from him.

His bruised ego told him to get up and walk out the door. But she hadn't asked him to leave, so he wondered if she was pushing him away because she didn't want him around or if she was too scared to talk about what had happened that sent her into this tailspin.

So he laid down beside her and pulled her against him. Her muscles stiffened just enough for him to tell before he could feel her exhale and relax against him. Neither spoke, and that was okay with him.

It didn't take long for her slow, steady breathing to tell him that she'd drifted off to sleep again. He shouldn't breathe in the floral scent of her thick red hair. He shouldn't let that fill his senses.

She was unavailable. He realized that was probably

half of the attraction he'd felt toward her early on. He'd never been one to want to stick around the morning after a round of hot sex. He certainly hadn't been looking for anything more than a few days of the best sex of his life.

There'd been something broken in her that had connected with the broken parts of him. Their connection had gone beyond physical.

But then, he didn't make a habit of bedding friends from the past. Jordan was all about moving forward, grabbing on to the next goal without time to think about settling in or settling down. And that hadn't changed just because he'd wanted more than a string of hot nights with Courtney. If anything, he realized just how fine he'd been without being tied down in a relationship when he'd gone back to Idaho and to his work on the family ranch there.

Jordan woke with the sun shining brightly through the window. He didn't realize that he'd dozed off. He'd gotten too comfortable. All he felt was Courtney's warm body flush with his. His heart stirred—and that wasn't the only thing awake and reminding him he was alive and well.

He gently peeled her off him and slid out of the covers as quietly as he could manage. Her steady breathing said she was still asleep. He couldn't help but notice how peaceful she looked lying there. It pained him to get out of bed, but he wanted to discuss the case with Zach before she woke.

Besides, he reminded himself not to get too cozy with Courtney. His heart couldn't take getting attached and watching her walk away a second time.

Damn. Where'd that come from?

Jordan freshened up, brushed his teeth and then moved into the kitchen. He located his cell, filled his mug with a fresh cup of coffee and then called Zach.

"Morning," Zach answered. His cousin sounded like he was running on a couple hours of sleep. The mounting pressure from the anniversary of Breanna's death that loomed was evident in his tone.

"I know you're busy, so I'll get right to the reason I called," Jordan said after returning the greeting.

"What's up?" Zach asked.

"I've been getting up to speed on the Jacobstown Hacker case. I'd like to pitch in to help in any way I can. I'm home now, and plan to stick around for a while." Jordan paused a beat.

"Welcome home, cousin." Zach and Jordan had been close growing up, and his cousin had asked more than once why Jordan didn't come back to Jacobstown to live.

The town didn't feel like home, even though this was where he'd been born and bred. "What can I do to help with the investigation?"

"We need as many eyes on as much of Rushing Creek as we can muster," Zach stated. "No lone wolves, though. I want everyone to buddy up. It's even better if people go out in teams and take a coordinated approach. If you see or hear anything suspicious, be smart about investigating. We're making the assumption that the suspect is armed and dangerous. Call me immediately if you think you've come across him, no matter where you are and no matter what time of day or night."

"You can count on it. But it seems less likely that he'd return to Rushing Creek with all the attention he has to know will be there," Jordan surmised.

"True," Zach agreed. "Our community presence can deter crime. This guy is opportunistic. The fewer options he has, the better, which is also a reason we're encouraging everyone to go out in groups as much as possible."

"Makes sense. Did he kill Breanna prior to bringing her to the scene on the ranch?" Jordan's suspicions about the kind of person they were dealing with were being confirmed.

"There's no sign of blood leading up to or away from the crime scene. If he killed Breanna and waited until he was at the creek to use the cutting instrument on her ankle, there wouldn't be a trail."

"All we know about the man so far is that he's moved on to human targets. We also know his left leg or foot is significant," Zach informed.

"How did you figure that out?" Jordan knew his cousin had already checked out obvious suspects and would've sifted through as much evidence as he could find.

"Impressions in the dirt. He puts more weight on his right side, based on the data Deputy Lopez collected. He was able to measure the impressions in the soil from his footprints and noticed a difference in depth." There was no doubt Zach was one of the best at his job. What if the killer knew Zach? The man could be a volunteer. Jordan had read that killers often volunteered to help in searches when victims went missing. It was a way of keeping tabs on the investigation while being arrogant. Those killers seemed to get a thrill out of being right under law enforcement's nose.

"Which has to be a large part of the reason everyone keeps circling back to Reggie Barstock. We already know he has an issue with his left foot." Jordan paused as Zach confirmed. "Is anyone aware of Barstock's current location?"

"His whereabouts are unknown, but I've been getting reports from folks who think they see him every few days and it turns out to be nothing. Courtney reported seeing a younger man with a limp in Bexford. We've been watching for his vehicle but haven't had any hits there," Zach supplied. "I asked Liesel to notify me if Reggie shows up at the diner, where I last saw him. My deputies have been spreading the word if a barista, gas station attendant or waitress sees Barstock to notify me immediately."

"What if it's not Barstock?" The idea had to be considered.

"That's the problem. If everyone's looking for a red shoe, the green one slips under the radar." Zach had just voiced Jordan's concern. "Gus Stanton is a person of interest—"

"He's the former truck driver," Jordan said.

"That's right. You must've heard about him." Zach didn't sound surprised, which made Jordan wonder if his cousin knew about the relationship with Courtney.

"He came to mind. I actually ran into Courtney the other day in Bexford," Jordan informed.

Zach perked up. "If he makes the trip once a week

like most people, the next time he's at the store, the anniversary will have passed." Zach's voice sounded like a headache was working up. "Do you have a description of this guy?"

"That I don't. Courtney said it was probably nothing, but I figure it can't hurt to talk about." He was tossing every idea out in hopes something would stick.

"She was in a bad state yesterday. The food poisoning seemed to have hit her hard. When you saw her, did she look like she was doing any better?"

"Nothing worse than getting a hold of a bad batch of food. Stomach pain is the worst." Jordan dodged the question. Guilt hit him harder than if he'd been on a motorcycle going a hundred miles an hour and slammed into a brick wall. Going along with her food poisoning story made him feel like a jerk. Jordan needed to get the conversation back on track and away from the landmine that had anything to do with his knowledge of or relationship with Courtney. "What else should I be on the lookout for? Is there a profile on this guy?"

"The only thing I know for certain is that he'll kill again…" Zach's voice trailed off at the end.

"There any chance he's already behind bars for another crime?" Jordan offered.

"It's possible but highly unlikely with this guy's skills," Zach said.

"What if he's done? What if he built up to killing a person, did it and then decided it was too much or that he'd gone too far?" Jordan tossed a few more ideas out there.

"My fear is that he's only just whetted his appetite.

I believe Breanna was his first murder, and he's gotten a taste of what it's like. He might even realize what he did was wrong. But he won't stop, because he *can't*. There's no question in my mind that he fits the profile of a serial killer. There's typically a cooling-off period in between murders, but he seems to be working faster. In this case, we don't have a lot to go on. We don't know enough to get a clear picture of the guy. You already know about as much as we do. Other than the fact that he fits the personality type to a T, I don't have much else to tell you." There was so much frustration in his voice. Zach was a great sheriff and an even better person. It was easy to realize that he'd take this personally.

"We'll get this jerk before he hurts someone else." It was a promise Jordan meant but had no idea if he could keep.

"I hope so."

"Before we hang up, I have to ask." Jordan paused for acknowledgment. Continued after it came, "How safe are the Kent women?"

"You read my mind if you're thinking one of them could be his next target." Zach issued a sharp sigh. "In fact, now that you mention it, we should have every one of them send in a list of anyone they know who might have a beef with them from the past. This goes way back."

"I'll send out a text. I was also thinking we should make sure each Kent woman is protected," Jordan added.

"The best way to ensure safety is the buddy system.

No one should be outside alone, and that even means when on the property," Zach said.

"Especially when on the ranch," Jordan concurred.

"Hell, until this jerk is caught, I don't want anyone in this county going outside alone. I think every man and woman needs to be accounted for at all times…" Zach's voice trailed off. His fear was evident in his tone. All signs pointed to the killer targeting another woman, but he could change tracks to mix things up. It was highly unlikely but everyone needed to take precautions. Jordan heard his cousin's cell make a noise. "Hold on, I'm getting a text from Ellen."

Jordan sent off a text to his family making the request for all Kents to use extra caution and stick with a group at all times. He made a special note the victim was a woman, as were the heifers. If this guy was looking for a prize, he was going to have to look further than the Kents.

Zach returned to the line. "I was hoping to avoid a widespread panic in town. It seems it's too late for that."

"What happened?" Jordan figured every woman in the county was concerned about safety.

"I've had four missing-person reports in the last twenty minutes from concerned parents and husbands. *Four.* All of whom were found either in the yard, in another part of the house or checking the mailbox when Ellen asked them to look." Zach's voice was weary.

"The next few days are going to be a challenge until this jerk is locked behind bars," Jordan agreed. He was probably being optimistic about the timing.

"Let's just keep everyone alive and calm." Zach

rarely admitted defeat, but it was obvious this case was wearing on him. "It just occurred to me that I need to have my deputies double up as much as possible"

"If you're worried about Courtney, she's tough, and she carries a weapon. She has training to back it up. This guy doesn't seem to like a fighter," Jordan said. Courtney being put on desk duty would ease Jordan's stress, but he highly doubted she would stand for it while a dangerous criminal stalked the town.

"Those are excellent points, but I take the safety of all my deputies very seriously, man or woman. I don't want her to worry that I think she's not capable of doing her job, but she worries be because she's still figuring out the lay of the land around here. Being away from town for so many years and new to the department puts her at a disadvantage. I'll have to give this situation a little more thought before I make a decision."

Jordan figured his cousin would have even more concern about her if he knew Courtney was pregnant. For one tempting moment, he thought about sharing the news. But going behind her back wouldn't create the kind of trust they needed to bring up a child together. And Jordan would never betray his word. "We'll pull together like we always do. This town is strong, and the people here are some of the best humans I know. The panic is understandable, but it will subside. In the meantime, we'll catch this jerk and lock him away where he can't hurt anyone else."

"I appreciate your willingness to pitch in and help, Jordan. I really do. I know this time of year is busy on the ranch and hard on everyone in the family. I miss my aunt and uncle more than I can put into words," he said.

"We got past another Christmas and into a New Year." Jordan felt a gut punch just thinking about how much he missed his parents. Time was supposed to make this easier. In this case, it didn't. He missed his family even more, and it probably had to do with the fact that his siblings had all moved on and started families of their own. He'd been the odd man out for most of his life, and that was certainly true again.

As he said goodbye and ended the call, he glanced up in time to see Courtney emerge from the hallway.

Seeing her standing there in her T-shirt and boxers stirred him in dangerous places—places better left for dead.

Chapter Seven

Courtney stared at Jordan. His bottom lip had jutted out for a quick second, which meant he didn't want to tell her something.

"What is it?" she demanded.

"That was Zach—"

"You didn't tell him anything about us, did you?" Dread was a heavy blanket around her shoulders, and panic was a galloping horse in her chest.

"Of course not. But that doesn't mean I like keeping secrets while talking to my family." He turned away from her. The look on his face, the honest pain in that one sentence, struck her like a physical blow. Was she being selfish?

"I'm sorry for putting you in that position, Jordan. I really am." Although she knew that announcing a pregnancy before the second trimester was considered bad luck, it was odd to be focused on superstition when she didn't want to be in this condition in the first place. She glanced down at her stomach and realized that she was touching her belly.

Did part of her—a part tucked deep down inside—

secretly wish for a family? A *real* family and not two people who couldn't get along, not a mother who cowered and took unimaginable abuse from her husband?

Jordan was right to stop things before they got out of hand last night after that kiss. She needed to remember there was more at stake than an embarrassing morning after if they gave in to passion again. And she wouldn't risk her child's emotional stability to satisfy her own desire, no matter how strong her want for Jordan Kent was.

Jordan pushed back from the kitchen table and stood. "Are you hungry? I could fry up a couple of eggs."

"My stomach is still a little queasy. Do you have any yogurt?" That much she could keep down.

"In the fridge." He motioned toward it, so she helped herself. "Zach and I talked about the fact that this creep seems focused on women. With the crimes happening on or near Rushing Creek, we're concerned about him wanting a prize. All women and especially a Kent should take extra precautions until he's behind bars."

"That's good advice. Did he mention anything else?" She took another bite of the creamy vanilla blend.

"His phone at the office is starting to blow up. If someone's wife or daughter is in the next room and doesn't answer the first time a person calls out, his office is getting a panicked phone call." Jordan knew how much that would take away from manpower that could be focused on something more important. Trained volunteers were a good thing to have, and he hoped they'd help more than get in the way.

"Maybe I should go in to work today," she said.

"It's your day off. Besides, you won't do anyone good

if you're sick," he quickly countered. He was right. She knew it. But she wished it wasn't true. Sitting on the sidelines was driving her a little crazy.

"The yogurt is helping." That part was true. She felt useless, and keeping busy was the best way to keep the darkness at bay. She crossed and then uncrossed her legs before tapping her finger on the table.

Bemused, Jordan stared at her.

"What?" She asked but she wasn't sure she wanted to know the answer to the question.

"You're not used to taking a lazy day, are you?" He was spot-on.

"Nope. I tend to pace or clean out a closet or something exciting like that."

"That why your house was spotless?" He walked to the window over the kitchen sink.

"Probably." She didn't want to admit how bad she felt when she slowed down. Keeping busy had always somehow helped her outpace the darkness she feared would consume her one day.

"Makes sense." He set his palms on the counter. "I'm not one for sticking around in one place too long, either. Especially not here in Jacobstown."

"Why is that, Jordan Kent?" She had an idea. "You love your family. They all live here. Why is it that you won't?"

He shrugged his shoulders. "Always felt hemmed in here."

The front door opened, and Courtney felt exposed. Before she could excuse herself, Deacon and Amber walked into the kitchen. Deacon was third born out of the five brothers. Jordan was the closest in age to Amber, her being the baby of the family.

"Welcome home, Jordan," Deacon and Amber said almost simultaneously.

Jordan greeted his siblings with a hug, and Courtney couldn't help but admire the closeness of the Kent siblings. Once again, she was reminded what a tight-knit and loving bunch they were. And, again, she realized her hand rested on her stomach.

"You guys remember Courtney Foster, right?" Jordan said to his sister and brother.

"How could I forget one of my own friends?" Amber said with a side glance toward her brother as she walked over and embraced Courtney in a warm hug.

Deacon smiled and cocked one eyebrow as he took in her outfit. "I'd heard you came back to town and went to work for Zach. Welcome home."

"It's good to be here." It wasn't exactly a lie. She'd wanted to return to her hometown but coming back to the Jacobstown Hacker hadn't been her ideal homecoming.

"Courtney stayed over in the guest room last night after practically freezing out on the property. I bumped into her and asked her to stay here instead of driving home." Jordan was overexplaining, but she appreciated him leaving no room for speculation as to why she was in the house with him so early in the morning wearing her pj's.

Thankfully, he'd thrown on a T-shirt at some point, which also most likely meant he hadn't slept.

"We got your message this morning and were hoping to catch you," Amber said to her brother. She must be talking about the text he'd told Courtney about sending to his siblings earlier to warn them about going out alone.

"I'm happy to see the two of you together and no one walking around by themselves. It's strange to think we have to be so careful on our own property." Jordan filled all of them in on his conversation with their cousin.

Courtney expected a few strange looks from Amber and Deacon, but their faces were impossible to read. Courtney and Amber had lost touch after high school. It struck her as odd that she was at the Kent house with Amber's brother.

A wave of nausea hit fast and hard. "I'm sorry. Please excuse me for one second."

She didn't have time to glance at any of them to judge a reaction. All she could think about was getting to the bathroom in time. She barely made it to the washroom before what little she'd had to eat came back up.

A few rounds of dry heaves later, she rinsed out her mouth and brushed her teeth. She actually felt a little better.

Her stomach gurgled and groaned, but this time for a different reason. Hunger took over.

A knock on the bathroom door startled her.

"Are you okay in there?" Jordan's deep baritone washed over her, providing more comfort than she wanted to acknowledge.

"Better." She opened the door to find him leaning against the jamb. "Thanks for checking."

"I brought a bottle of water just in case." He held out

the offering, and she took it. Their fingers grazed as a jolt of electricity shot through her.

It was probably just hormones causing her body to overreact to his presence. She needed to get a handle on this out-of-control chemistry. She'd thought about that kiss first thing this morning. Knowing it had been a bad idea and still wishing for a repeat meant she was heading down the wrong path.

"Thanks for this." She took a sip. "I'll be right out."

He disappeared, closing the bedroom door behind him.

She dressed in fresh clothes—yoga pants and a pullover sweater. This was one of her most comfortable outfits, and she'd almost forgotten about it being there after all that had gone on so far that morning.

Taking in a fortifying breath, she walked into the next room. A dozen thoughts fought for attention. She couldn't help but wonder what Amber and Deacon truly thought about her being there. Had she and Jordan given themselves away?

How long had it been since she'd been in this house?

A rogue thought struck. How was Amber going to take the pregnancy news? More panic shot through Courtney. Before Jordan could talk her out of leaving, she had to get out of there.

She moved into the kitchen, rounded up her belongings and gave an awkward wave to the trio.

"I forgot about an appointment I made for this morning. I'm going to be late if I don't leave right now."

Jordan shot a look and seemed about to say something when she darted toward the front door and closed it behind her.

THANKFULLY, HER VEHICLE had been brought to the main house for her. Jordan must've made the arrangements last night when she was sleeping. Courtney figured she could run a few errands while Jordan gathered his family together to come up with a plan for more patrols along Rushing Creek. She'd slept in this morning, and physically felt better than she had in weeks.

The idea of a pregnancy might not be growing on her, exactly, but she was a little less freaked about it. Although she was a long way from thinking it was a good idea. Seeing Jordan being protective of her and the little bean had warmed her heart.

The first spark of the two of them actually being able to co-parent was starting to ignite. She was beginning to feel like she might not be a complete disaster as a mother or totally mess up the child before he or she got a start in life. Was it weird that she didn't have becoming a mother as part of her trajectory? Was it strange that she'd never really thought of herself as parent material?

Part of the reason she figured she'd been so attracted to Decks was his aversion to ever getting married again and the fact that he already had a child from his first marriage. Courtney had thought he'd be safe. And she'd loved him, right? Granted, she and Decks had never had the same spark she'd experienced with Jordan, but there was more to a relationship than smoking-hot chemistry.

Courtney drove through her bank's ATM line, picked up a few supplies at the grocery store and then stopped by her house to check the mail. She ate more yogurt— this time it stayed down—before changing into slacks.

She kept her favorite pullover sweater on while she wrangled her hair into a ponytail.

Some of her best ideas came when she wasn't over-thinking a case. She made a mental note to follow up on what had happened with Lopez's interview with Gus Stanton. Granted, she hadn't lived in Jacobstown in years, but her sweet elderly neighbor had. Courtney made another mental note to talk to Mrs. Farmer. Over the years, someone had to have had a foot get caught in a tractor blade or lawn mower. What other incidents could there have been? She thought way back to her earliest memories. Hadn't there been a kid who got his foot stuck in playground equipment? She remembered something about him—what was his name? John Michael?—ending up with a shattered ankle. Didn't he walk with a limp afterward? And being in the country, there had to have been a kid who'd pranked another friend with fireworks, and that could've easily gotten out of control. A foot could've been lost that way. There had to have been a decent list of teen antics that could have led to problems with a left foot.

Within half an hour, she'd charged her phone, logged on to her laptop and paid her electric bill, and freshened up her face with a little makeup. Jordan had texted with an invite to dinner, and she was debating whether or not it was a good idea to go.

On the one hand, it was dinner she didn't have to cook. That was always a plus. For another, having company to eat with sounded wonderful. She'd told him that she'd text him with an answer. Her finger hovered over the cell's keypad.

Eating with Jordan wouldn't be the worst thing that could happen to her. Besides, it was good for the two of them to practice getting along. A small part of her wished for a real family for her child. But she and Jordan could be the next closest thing. A child could do worse than two parents who got along.

Thinking of her unborn child, Courtney pulled the business card of a counselor that she'd been given by one of her colleagues after the shooting. Officer Ralph Howard had been discreet when he'd slipped the worn business card into her palm during a handshake when she'd returned to work after recovering from being shot. He'd leaned in and said, "I've used her when the job got to be too much. She knows her stuff and, more importantly, she knows how to keep private conversations private. She lost her husband to the job. She knows what the pressure is like."

Maybe it was time to think about setting up a phone appointment. Talking couldn't hurt. Right? If Courtney didn't like what she heard in the first five minutes, she could always end the appointment and hang up. She almost laughed out loud. Cops were distrustful by nature. She couldn't even trust a person whose life's work was helping people exactly like Courtney. Having an exit plan, though, eased some of the anxiety that came with the thought of opening up to a complete stranger about the intimate details of her mind, of the feeling of being judged for her thoughts.

Panic climbed up her throat like a vine, squeezing, choking out her oxygen. She gasped and brought her hand to her neck as if it was real.

She paced as questions swirled in her mind with the relentless pursuit of a stalker.

Courtney would normally distract herself with an intense workout, but she was concerned that might hurt the baby. Without talking to her doctor, she figured it best to lay off pushing her body to the point of dripping-with-sweat exhaustion. Besides, her stomach was calm for the moment, and she didn't want to stir up that hornet's nest again. She had a monthly OB appointment and no reason to push it up. Nausea was the absolute worst. It was a slow drain on the system to feel sick all day long. Courtney didn't wish the feeling on her worst enemy.

Frustration nipped at just how much her life was changing and just how out of control everything seemed. Coming home to Jacobstown was supposed to provide a respite. It was supposed to nurture her tortured soul but was becoming a mental prison instead. Wow, had she just described her life and her pregnancy as a mental prison?

Deep down, she didn't feel that way at all. She picked up the business card again and ran her index finger along the embossed name, Dr. Sara Winters.

The call could wait until she ran one more errand. Blue Trunks had been bugging her, and her mind was spinning out. The guy most likely had nothing to do with Jacobstown or the jerk terrorizing its citizens.

There was only one way to try to find him and that was to return to The Mart and wait him out.

THE FRONT DOORKNOB TURNED, catching Jordan off guard. He thought Deacon and Amber had locked it when they left. On instinct, Jordan went for the shotgun tucked above the kitchen cabinet far out of reach of little hands but easy enough to access in an emergency.

Five rapid taps confirmed Lone Star Lonnie was about to walk through the door. Jordan abandoned his attempt to snatch the shotgun and started toward the door. A sheet-white-faced Lonnie stared at Jordan.

"What's wrong?" he asked.

Lone Star's face twisted and he issued a sharp sigh.

"You need to come and take a look at what's on the porch," Lone Star said.

"What is it?" Jordan's pace quickened, making double time.

"A foot."

Chapter Eight

Jordan rushed outside and stopped dead in his tracks when he saw the freezer bag on the first step leading up to the porch.

"It's human," he said to Lonnie. "Small in size with painted toenails."

He fished his cell from his pocket and called Zach.

"What's going on?" Zach asked.

"You need to get over to the ranch as soon as possible. There's either a really sick prank on my porch steps or *he's* been here," Jordan said.

"I'm on my way now. I'm not far." Zach's rapid breathing told Jordan that his cousin had started sprinting. "What is it?"

"It looks like a female's foot," Jordan supplied.

Zach muttered a string of curses. "You already know this, but don't touch anything."

"I won't." The two stayed on the line until Zach arrived fifteen minutes later.

Zach took a statement from Lone Star Lonnie. Jordan gave his, which was little more than what he'd already told his cousin. He looked from one to the other when he said, "I'd like to keep this finding quiet. This guy is taunting us, and I don't want to tip my hand just yet."

"No one outside of this property will hear any of this from me." Jordan had every intention of telling his siblings and their spouses. The security team and ranch hands deserved to know, as well. Other than that, Jordan was fine with keeping the news on the ranch.

"We interviewed and cleared the staff last year. No one new has been hired since then. Still, I'd like to interview the staff again. Someone might've seen something." Zach was following protocol, Jordan knew that. His cousin snapped photos of the bottom step where the evidence was found and the surrounding area.

"They might have questions. You're the best one to give answers," Jordan said to his cousin.

Deputy Lopez's SUV wound up the path. Zach brought the evidence over to him and sent him away with it.

"I told him to request a rush on DNA testing," Zach said to Jordan. Breanna Griswold's death stared them in the face, and there were still more theories than evidence. The jerk responsible for killing Breanna still walked the streets. And Jordan could only hope the man had made his first mistake.

"You want to come in for a cup of coffee while Lone Star rounds up the staff?" Jordan asked.

"Sounds like a good plan," Zach said.

Lone Star broke off, and Zach followed Jordan into the kitchen.

After filling coffee mugs, Jordan joined his cousin

at the granite island in the kitchen where everyone usually gathered.

"If the DNA matches Breanna's, he kept her body part preserved." Zach punched in a few letters on the keypad of his cell phone.

"Why would he do that?" Jordan had no idea how the criminal mind worked.

"Keeping a 'souvenir' is a way to relive the experience of the crime over and over again until he or she is able to satisfy the next urge." Zach leaned back in his chair and pinched the bridge of his nose. "There might be another scenario going on here."

"A threat?" All Kent women were accounted for as of this morning. Jordan had already reached out to his brothers and sister.

"It could be a twisted gift, a warning message." Zach picked up a pen and rolled it around his fingers. "Or that bastard might be taunting us."

"He got past ranch security. He knows the area, which makes me think he's been watching our every move," Jordan stated. "How? Who could be that crafty without any of us knowing it?"

"As an investigator, I'd normally look more closely at the family and staff." The pen flipped out of his grip, crashing onto the desk. "But you guys are my family. I know that a Kent would never do anything remotely like this. And the staff on the ranch boils down to Lone Star Lonnie and a handful of his devoted guys. Then there's Kimberly, Mitch's wife. Our perp is most likely male. The person who killed Breanna is either tricky or strong, most likely both. She was five feet six inches and weighed 140 pounds at the time of her death. There was no sign of struggle, which would indicate she knew her attacker, but the few people she'd been around that day have alibis. I've had no break in this case. Now citizens are scared and reporting missing people to the tune of half a dozen a day."

"What if someone has gone high-tech with their spying?" It was probably a long shot, but every idea was fair game at this point.

"As in someone put a camera on the property?" Zach asked.

"Could be on the property. Could be using a drone. Hell, the camera could be across the street zooming in on us right now for all I know," Jordan pointed out.

"Those are valid points." Zach jotted a few notes. "We haven't looked at this from the angle of someone targeting a Kent specifically."

"Our land is vast, and you said a while ago there were reports of dead animals on other ranches in the area. None of us thought this was a specific threat to us. With the clock ticking, it's time to look at this from all angles." Jordan smacked the granite with his flat palm.

"How's Courtney?" Zach didn't look up, so he wasn't trying to gauge Jordan's reaction to the question. It was probably innocent enough and not an indication that Zach had caught on to the relationship going on between the two of them.

"She seemed better the last time I saw her," Jordan said, noncommittal.

"I spoke to Deacon, and he said she stayed over at

the main house last night after checking an area near Rushing Creek," Zach said.

"That's right. She was on the property late, and I bumped into her. She was cold, so I convinced her to come inside and eat."

Zach's eyebrow shot up, but to his credit he didn't say anything.

"It was late," Jordan added by way of explanation. "She was too tired to drive home."

"Amy has been worried about Courtney. Said she's been trying to reach Courtney without any luck," Zach continued. "Did she mention anything to you?"

Jordan shook his head. He could only hope his family wouldn't put two and two together and figure him and Courtney out before he had a chance to convince her that keeping the pregnancy secret would only cause hurt feelings later. He understood that she was gun-shy when it came to spreading the news too early. She'd only just found out and, by way of luck, so had he. It would take a minute for her to digest the surprise and get comfortable talking about their situation.

"If you cross paths—"

"I doubt I'll see her before you do." Jordan's quick rebuke must've sent up a red flag, because Zach stopped what he was doing and studied Jordan. "If I do, though, I'll be sure to tell her that Amy's on the hunt."

Zach laughed. *On the hunt* was the way they used to refer to Amy when she was looking for anyone who'd frustrated her. It was good to break the tension, and, besides, Jordan needed to change the direction of the conversation. If any one of his family members caught on that there was more going on between him and Courtney than courtesy and concern, and asked outright, he already knew that he wouldn't lie about their relationship. That much was a given. But he'd made a promise not to voluntarily spill the beans, and his word could be counted on.

Before his cousin could dig any deeper, Jordan ended the conversation by asking, "Will you let me know when the forensics results come back? I'd like to know what we're dealing with as soon as the information is available."

"You know I will, Jordan. Even with a rush request, it might take time." Zach's cell buzzed. He checked the screen. It was Ellen. "I better take this."

Zach put the call on speaker.

"Excuse me, Sheriff," she started right in.

"What's going on?" Zach asked.

"I just took a call from Liesel at the diner. She had to get off the phone pronto because she came back from her lunch break to find Reggie Barstock walking out the front door. She was afraid he'd come back inside when he saw her. He had a to-go bag in his hands," Ellen said.

Zach's expression dropped, and his lips thinned. "She say which way he was headed or what kind of vehicle he was driving?"

"She said he was in an older model white sedan." Ellen issued a sharp sigh. "Do you want me to send a deputy to speak to her?"

"I'd rather have them drive the area instead," Zach instructed. "Did she say there was anything different about his appearance?"

"He was wearing a red bandana on his head is all she said," Ellen informed. "And she said he still had that limp."

"Ask Lopez to take the call. He's the closest to the diner. Recirculate the picture of Barstock with the request and let everyone know to be on the lookout for him." Zach glanced at Jordan, who was relieved for the change in subject.

"Yes, sir," Ellen said before ending the call.

The timing of Barstock being seen when a severed foot in a plastic freezer bag showed up on the Kent property was interesting. But what could Reggie Barstock have against the Kent family? They didn't know him or his mother all that well, as far as Jordan knew. He made a mental note to ask his family at dinner tonight what the possible connection could be if there was one.

He also thought about Courtney.

Jordan figured this was a good time to redirect the visit.

"Do you need me to come down to the barn with you while you speak to the men?" he asked.

"No. I'm fine on my own," Zach said.

"There's a hefty amount of work waiting for me." And he wanted to get in touch with Courtney. Too many thoughts rolled around in his mind, and he was tempted to call Courtney the minute Zach got out the door.

Jordan fished his phone out of his front pocket and thought about what he might say. He figured she wouldn't take lightly to feeling like he was checking up on her. She'd always had an independent streak wider than the Texas sky.

He tried to convince himself that he was concerned for the child and not her. He didn't want to care about Courtney so much that he missed her the second she was gone. Courtney or anyone else, for that matter.

Jordan pulled up her name in his contacts anyway. His thumb hovered over her name.

COURTNEY SAT IN her parked car at the south end of the parking lot of The Mart, where she had the best vantage point. Here, she could see vehicles coming and going. Most people repeated the same patterns, so she figured Blue Trunks would park in or near the same parking spot as the last time if he returned.

It was a long shot that he'd come back on the same day she chose to stake out the lot, but she had to do something. It never hurt to take a chance. Sometimes, rolling the dice paid off. Kids were still at school. The Mart was overrun by cars. She usually liked to avoid big-box stores because it seemed like everyone in town came out at the same time. The aisles were cramped, and the people were cranky. Courtney wasn't one for shopping anyway. Those conditions made it even less pleasant.

After an hour, she started rethinking her judgment call on staking out The Mart. It was her day off, and she was becoming obsessed with the case. An annoying little voice in the back of her head tried to tell her that she was fixated on this case because she had a chance to solve it. Because of the one she couldn't go back and fix. What justice could she bring to the families of the eight officers who were shot dead while she was spared?

Her heavy thoughts were interrupted by the sight of a pickup that fit the description of Blue Trunks'. It was probably a long shot and not the right vehicle, but she watched it circle the parking lot. It stopped in front of the double glass sliding doors of the entrance and then made another lap. No one got in the vehicle from what she could tell at this distance.

She started the engine and kicked up the heater a couple of notches. In the last hour or so, the temperature had dipped again to a chilly forty-five degrees. It was midday and the sun was out, which was her saving grace. The vehicle had stayed fairly warm inside, especially with her long coat on, but her hands were like ice. She gripped the steering wheel and tailed the older pickup as it pulled out of the parking lot.

The pickup pulled onto Riverside Lane, which was a main thoroughfare through Bexford. Courtney had to stay far enough back so as not to draw attention to herself. From her position thirty feet behind, she could see there was no passenger in the vehicle.

The driver made a left-hand turn. Courtney tried to get a look, but all she could see clearly was that the driver wore some kind of cap, maybe a baseball cap. She slowed her pace and then made the same turn.

The vehicle was gone. A moment of panic set in. She scanned the parking pads as she drove through the neighborhood of white cottage-style homes from around the 1920s. The neighborhood road was barely big enough for one lane with cars parked on both sides of the street and on parking pads. Wire fences encased the front and backyards.

Courtney rolled her window down halfway to listen. Other than dogs barking, trying to hop the fence and chase her, there was no sign of life or hint of the vehicle. People in Texas didn't do cold weather, so there were no young kids playing in the yards while older siblings attended school. In fact, there was surprisingly little activity. She sped up a little bit, checking side streets as she passed them by.

After the fourth one, she saw it. The pickup turned right. So Courtney sped up in order to catch it. She followed as it weaved through cars in the neighborhood.

If this went on much longer, she'd be made. At the time it was about get pretty obvious that she was following, the pickup pulled onto a parking pad. Courtney pulled behind a blue Mustang but kept the ignition in Drive, just in case. She picked up her cell and turned on the camera feature.

The driver came around the front of the pickup. And then Courtney got a good look at *her*. It was a woman and not Carolina Blue Trunks. Courtney waited for the woman to go inside her front door before she slipped out of her spot and headed back toward home.

Staking out The Mart while not on official duty wasn't the smartest idea. *What if* she had found Carolina Blue Trunks? Then what? She had no reason to talk to him, and she wasn't driving an official vehicle because she didn't want to scare him off in the event he saw her. She had no backup out here.

Courtney navigated her way onto the highway. Her cell rang, and she answered it over the vehicle's speaker.

"What did you decide about dinner?" Jordan's voice

came through clearly. His masculine tone sent warmth vibrating through her, warming places she knew better than to allow.

"I should probably stay home tonight," she said without much enthusiasm. The thought of going home alone and wrestling those nightmares again was about as appealing as eating a heated can of soup for dinner. Sure, it got the job done, but that was about it.

"Zach asked me about you earlier."

"What did you say?" She couldn't hide the moment of panic in her tone.

"Nothing that he didn't already know. He spoke to my family. Speaking of which, Amy is looking for you." There was no hint of judgment in those words.

"I know. I haven't had a chance to return her call yet. Besides, I'm at a loss as to what to say to anyone right now," she admitted.

"If you don't want to come to dinner, can I swing by your place? We need to talk." Those last four words she'd been half expecting and mostly dreading.

"Think we could do it another day?" She didn't want to see him while she was feeling so vulnerable and alone. This was the time to armor up, not run toward enemy lines. But was he the enemy? An annoying little voice in the back of her head questioned. Logically, she knew he wasn't the problem. It was her. Being in his arms last night had felt a little too right, and it was a foreign feeling. No man had made her feel as safe and cherished as Jordan. And their relationship had been temporary. She'd known it would be going in.

"It's important." He'd armored up, too. But he wasn't giving an inch, and that had her concerned.

"I'm not up for another round of negotiations on when we should tell people about the pregnancy, if that's what you need to discuss." She needed to be clear on that point. The topic was closed for now.

"It's not." She picked up on the hurt—and maybe frustration?—in those two words.

"Okay. I'd rather come to your place then." It would be easier to leave when she was ready to wrap up the conversation that way. It gave her the illusion of having control over how the evening went.

"What time can you be here?" he asked.

"I can head that way now, if you're home." Better face this conversation and get it over with than dread it for the rest of the day.

"Now's good."

Chapter Nine

"Come in," Jordan said to Courtney as she stood on the same step the severed foot was found on. Jordan looked across the vast yard. He'd never given much thought to security growing up at KR. As a child, he'd been able to run free without a care.

"I can't stay long." Courtney walked inside but stood in the foyer. She didn't take her coat off, and he wondered if she was embarrassed about the kiss from last night. He'd thought about it more than he wanted to during the course of the day.

"Are you sure?" he asked.

"How much do you have to tell me?" Her beautiful eyes stared at him. She had the kind of eyes that sparked and drew him in. Her thick curly hair was pulled away from her heart-shaped face and too-pink lips.

"It's not the quantity of words," he warned.

"What happened?" She took in a breath and shrugged out of her coat. He took it from her and hung it in the hall closet.

Jordan led her into the kitchen, where he offered her a bottle of water. He watched as she took a seat at the granite island and then unscrewed the cap. She set the bottle on the hard, shiny surface without taking a sip.

"First, someone left what looks like a severed and frozen female foot on the porch earlier today," he started.

"When? I was here. I didn't see anything, Jordan."

"Lone Star Lonnie found it sometime after Deacon and Amber left." He poured a cup of coffee for himself before joining her at the island. "Also, you'll find this out when you go back to work tomorrow, but Reggie Barstock was sighted at the diner by an employee."

She immediately stood. "I need to be out there looking for him."

"It's your day off, Courtney. And I didn't tell you any of this so you'd run out of here and try to solve this yourself—"

"Either way, I should be out there helping instead of in here." Her eyes searched the room, and she looked flushed. There was a desperate quality to her voice that was a gut punch.

"Zach's involved, and we're having a family meeting over dinner. Staying here might do more good than being out there where you have nothing to go on." He paused—knowing when it was time to stop and not oversell an idea was important. "I'd like to see if anyone here can think of any reason Reggie Barstock might do something like that or if anyone's connected to him or his mother in any way other than Chelsea. Living in Idaho, I'm not always aware of the day to day here in Texas. But they are, and if they've had any interaction with Barstock, we'll know it."

"Didn't one of your sisters-in-law inherit his mother's home and business?" she asked.

"As a matter of fact, my brother's wife, Chelsea, was given the family home and business downtown," he said.

"She's married to Nate, if memory serves. When did she move here?"

"It's been a couple of months now. They've been married for a few weeks. Reggie wasn't thrilled about his mother leaving her home to Chelsea, who is her great-niece, and he pulled a few stunts to try to scare her into leaving. But the animal killings started before that," Jordan said.

"That's true. I see why all roads keep leading back to Reggie, but the evidence isn't as clear cut. He would have motive if he felt slighted by his mother and wanted to get back at the people who benefited. He could see your family as part of the problem," she stated. "He was always quiet, troubled, which is most likely why his mother cut her only son out of her will in the first place. When I spoke to Mrs. Porter the other morning, she said he wasn't stupid. She wouldn't exactly classify him as the smartest kid in class, but he held his own."

"He didn't have a relationship with his mother toward the end of her life, and he's been in and out of jail for small crimes," Jordan said.

"Serial killers don't normally work up from the kinds of crimes Reggie is known for. And, also, they rarely get caught, especially one as meticulous as the one we're dealing with." Courtney picked up a pen and started clicking it.

"Those are good points. I also keep questioning, why Breanna? How does she fit into the puzzle? She wasn't exactly friends with my sister or Amy," he said.

"From what I remember, Breanna didn't have a lot of friends. She was his first human kill that we know of." The corners of Courtney's lips turned down in a frown. "She might've been an easy mark. We know she was using again, and that could have left her vulnerable if she passed out somewhere in public. An easy mark might not be as exciting, but we know that there was no sexual abuse with her. There were no signs that she fought back. My guess is that he moved quickly."

"It seems like he'd be crazy to stick around Jacobstown. He has to know everyone has been *and* will be looking for him. If he's part of the community in some way, he has to know about all the task forces that have been put together and neighborhood watches," Jordan pointed out.

"That can be part of the thrill for a sicko like him," she said. "I followed a pickup away from The Mart earlier. I was coming home when you called. *If*, and it's a big if, he's responsible, he lives close enough to access the community without actually living here day to day."

Courtney's cell phone buzzed. She fished it out of her purse and checked the screen. "Gus Stanton was just picked up after he tried to ditch his vehicle and run after a routine traffic stop. He assaulted Deputy Lopez, who was able to subdue him. Lopez then found duct tape and rope in this trunk. They're processing Stanton's vehicle to see if there's any DNA in there."

She made a move to retrieve her coat, and Jordan was right behind her. "We can ride in my car."

"You sure about that?" he asked.

"Oh. Right. It might be best if we arrive in separate vehicles." She flashed grateful brown eyes at him, and he took a hit to the center of his chest.

COURTNEY HAD ALMOST blown it by offering to show up to work in the same vehicle as Jordan. She'd have to be more careful moving forward. At least for a few weeks until they could announce the pregnancy.

She thought about her next doctor's appointment and the counseling appointment that would follow. Her child deserved to have a mother who could work through any mental blocks.

Courtney left the house and realized when she got to the car that she'd been touching her stomach again. As much as she didn't want to admit it, she was starting to accept—enjoy?—having the little bean grow inside her. It was more than the morning sickness, but she detected changes in her—and not just ones in her body.

She hadn't started gaining any weight. And, sure, there were bags underneath her eyes that she played off as from food poisoning. She was starting to notice changes in her skin, especially certain places on her face that were dry, while other spots were suddenly oily. She was starting to wish she'd paid more attention to her pregnant former coworkers. She'd tuned out all the office chatter when she'd had to be in the station.

Ready or not, a baby was coming later this year. Which made her think about the phone number on her desk at home. She'd call the counselor first thing tomorrow before her shift.

Although, with recent developments to the biggest case in Jacobstown's history, Courtney figured she'd be working overtime alongside the rest of the department until this jerk was behind bars.

She texted Zach to let him know that she was on her way in to the office. She, like many, wanted to hear firsthand what excuse Gus Stanton had for keeping duct tape and rope in his trunk.

Jordan followed her to Zach's office and parked across the lot from her. He didn't immediately get out of his vehicle, and she appreciated him giving her a little space. She walked in and waved to Ellen.

Volunteers were set up in the conference room, so talking freely was a little more challenging. She didn't want someone overhearing something they shouldn't and spreading false information. Fortunately, the door to the conference room was closed as she walked past it.

Having so many in the community willing to help out made law enforcement's job easier. Having citizens organizing neighborhood watches in order to blanket the various areas and keep watch for any suspicious activity was a big help. Sure, there were people who got in the way. Zach grew up in this community and knew who he could trust with information and was able to sort through a lot of the less helpful folks. His history in Jacobstown was a huge benefit in a situation like this. And most folks had the best of intentions.

Law enforcement personnel were trained to watch for the one who didn't. It was true what she'd told Jordan about the perp showing up in a veiled attempt to help but actually just being there in order to revel in how he or she had fooled everyone, including the people who lived right next door.

Her instincts tried to convince her that Blue Trunks was involved, but she had no evidence to go on. She'd learned a long time ago to put 10 percent stock in instincts and 90 percent in following the evidence.

The killer was getting cocky by delivering that "souvenir" to the Kent family home. Her heart bled for what Breanna's family would have to learn, for what Breanna had endured. The jerk was also showing them clearly that he could breach security on the Kent ranch any time he wanted. Courtney needed to ask Jordan if there was surveillance footage of the house. Why hadn't anyone seen him come or go? Security had been doubled at the ranch. Which brought her to another question—was the Kent family ranch safe?

Courtney joined Zach in the viewing room, standing behind the two-way mirror, studying the occupant. It was dark on her side of the mirror, and there was another off-duty deputy sandwiched inside the small space. Gus Stanton sat across the table in the next room, facing them. He was alone, handcuffed to the solid desk that was bolted to the floor. She noticed a pad of paper and a pen on the table in front of him. She realized Zach would sweat Gus out. He'd give him that pen and paper and tell him that he could leave once he wrote down what really happened to Breanna Griswold.

"How long has he been in there?" she asked in a low voice.

"Definitely not long enough," Zach responded.

Gus wasn't more than five feet nine inches, but he was stocky. Most of his former muscle had gone soft, and he had quite the stomach—the kind that looked like he was about to birth a twelve-pack of beer. His complexion was ruddy, and his bulbous nose looked like a clown's. His light-colored hair wrapped his head, the dome of which shined. He wore overalls with a flannel shirt and looked like he'd already started on that twelve-pack.

She didn't need to set eyes on Jordan to recognize the scent of his aftershave when he walked in. She turned and acknowledged him with a small nod from across the room.

He barely glanced at her, and she felt a twinge of regret. He was only honoring the agreement she'd forced him into, and yet it still felt like rejection, still stung. She wanted to blame her pregnancy for her reaction, but it went deeper than that; she couldn't deny it. Oh, sure, maybe she could cover it up in front of others, but her heart free-fell every time he looked at her.

Movement in the interview room caught her attention. Adrenaline surged when she caught sight of Gus stabbing himself with the pen that had been on the table.

She, Deputy Lopez and Zach jumped into action. Zach went in first with Courtney a close second.

"Stop it right there, Gus," Zach demanded in that authoritative voice only law enforcement seemed to possess.

"Stay away from me." Gus's attempts to stab himself in the neck left marks, but he didn't break skin. The fear was that he'd jam it in an eye or through his ear, where he could do a lot more damage.

Gus pushed back from the table and then tried to topple it. When that didn't work, he held the pen out toward them like it was a weapon.

"You don't want to threaten an officer of the law, Gus," Zach warned. "Trust me on that one."

The three of them encircled him. He shifted his head from side to side. Sweat rolled down his forehead.

"No one will believe me that I'm innocent. Not now. The judge will take my kids away. Arresting me for this is the last straw my ex needs to cut me out of my kids' lives forever," Gus shouted. "I might as well have done whatever it is you're accusing me of."

"What do you think you're in here for?" Zach took a step toward Gus, who swiped the pen through the air like it was a knife.

"I know what you think I did. That's sick. I wouldn't do that to another human being," Gus argued. A look of disgust crossed his ruddy features as he focused his attention on Zach, which gave Courtney the opportunity to tackle him from behind. She dived into the back of his knees. Deputy Lopez took a swipe at the pen at the same time she made her move and caught Gus's meaty hand.

Courtney made contact, and Gus flew backward, landing square on top of her. He felt like he weighed two hundred pounds. His elbow caught her in the back as his heft knocked her to the floor. She scrambled to make herself into a ball in order to protect her organs, but it was too late. He was too heavy. So he flattened her like a pancake. Her mind flashed to the little bean growing in her stomach, and she flinched.

Before Gus could strike her or move, he was being lifted off her. She pushed up to all fours in time to see the others, Jordan included, slam Gus facedown onto the hard flooring. Within a few seconds, his hands were pulled hard behind his back and he was in zip cuffs.

Her stomach cramped, and her gaze flew to Jordan, who was studying her. In the next second, he was beside her, righting the chair that had been turned on its side and helping her sit in it.

"I'm fine." She couldn't afford to show signs of weakness in her line of work. She stood and dusted herself off before looking at him. "It's fine."

A muscle pulsed in Jordan's jaw. He clenched his back teeth hard. He, of all people, should understand the position she was in. When it came to doing her job, she had to show that she could pull her weight. Lives of other law enforcement officers depended on her. His gaze was fierce and protective.

"Can I have a word with you in the hall, please?" he ground out, and it look liked he was using an enormous amount of self-control to hold on to what he had to say.

Courtney's gaze flew to her boss, who nodded.

Jordan, who'd witnessed the exchange, started toward the door almost immediately.

In the hallway, Jordan whirled around on her. The intensity of his gaze almost knocked her back a step.

"You have until morning to tell him," he said. "I can't go along with this any longer in good conscience."

"That's too soon," she argued. "I need more time."

Chapter Ten

"No can do." Jordan didn't to take a hard line but Courtney was forcing his hand. He'd just witnessed her in a struggle that could've ended badly for their unborn child.

"I know you're right, Jordan. Once this jerk is put away we can circle back—" Courtney had another think coming if she thought changing the subject would help her argument to keep the pregnancy a secret.

"I won't change my mind about telling Zach tomorrow." Jordan was firm on that point.

She shot him an incredulous look, opened her mouth to speak and then seemed to think better of it as she glanced around. "This isn't the time or the place. We can discuss this matter after dinner tonight when everyone goes home. We'll make a decision then. Deal?"

"No. I'll listen to whatever you have to say, but we've done this your way so far and none of it feels right." Jordan realized she had the most to lose in the equation, and that was the reason he'd agreed to her idea in the first place. But she was putting herself in jeopardy by doing her job when she wasn't at full strength, and he doubted she even realized it or would allow herself to consider the thought. She wasn't a glutton for punishment. He wondered if the cause of the nightmares was the same reason she wasn't thinking clearly now—her past.

There was plenty she could contribute inside the office rather than going out into the field every day. A desk job was better than nothing, and Zach needed plenty of help training and organizing volunteers for neighborhood watches as well as answering the tip line. There was a lot for her to do that didn't involve physical altercations with scumbags.

Zach walked into the hallway before Courtney could mount another defense. "Both of you mind stepping into my office?"

"Not at all," Jordan said with a glance toward Courtney.

Courtney nodded, but a flash of panic crossed her features. He had no intention of rolling her under the bus. He'd told her what his intention was, and he planned to stick to it. Come tomorrow morning, he'd have a conversation with his cousin in confidence. He and Courtney could come up with a plan to tell his family together if that's what she wanted.

"What's going on with you two?" Zach didn't mince words as he closed the door to his office behind the three of them.

"Not anything we want to discuss." Jordan wasn't lying.

Zach shot his cousin a look.

"It's personal. We go way back," Courtney interjected.

"We all go way back, but you can't storm into an interview room like that again, Jordan." Zach's tone left no room for argument. "Courtney's a deputy and a damn fine one. She can handle herself."

"Any chance we can delay this conversation until tomorrow, Zach?" It was an earnest question. By then Zach would understand what Jordan's reaction was about. It would all make sense.

"I've said what I have to say about it." Zach's gaze bounced from Jordan to Courtney. If Zach had figured out there was something going on between them, he didn't let on. Jordan was relieved for Courtney's sake. He wasn't trying to force her hand. He'd hoped that she'd seize the opportunity to speak up, but that seemed to be hoping for too much.

When Courtney shut down, she was a closed book. Her arms folded, she said, "I appreciate your confidence. I'm fully capable of doing my job. I think Jordan was reacting to the fact that I've been under the weather lately."

"Food poisoning?" Zach asked.

"That's right."

"And that's the story you're comfortable telling?" Damn. Zach knew something was up.

"It is," she replied. "I'd like to request a meeting with you before my shift in the morning. Just the two of us."

"Have Ellen put it on my calendar." His eyebrow arched.

"Yes, sir," she said.

Jordan figured Courtney was giving herself the night to talk him out of making the announcement to the people he cared about. There was no amount of cajoling that could turn that into reality.

"I'll see you tonight at dinner, Jordan. Okay?" she asked.

BY THE TIME Courtney woke after her long nap, it was dark outside. She freshened up before checking her phone. Amy had called again. Courtney let her thumb hover over Amy's name. One tap and Amy would be on the line.

What would Courtney say to her former friend? To any Kent relative? The thought of sitting across the dinner table from Jordan's family kicked off a whole reaction in her body.

She tucked her phone inside her purse instead.

A wave of guilt struck as Courtney strapped on her shoulder holster. The annoying voice in the back of her mind returned. What was the point of friendships when everyone she'd cared about at one time was dead now?

Was that really true? She knew she was being irrational. Instead of fighting it, she resolved to make the call to the counselor. Right now, it was time to face the music—the Kent family.

Before she made it to the door, a knock sounded. Panic heated her veins.

She reminded herself to breathe.

After checking the peephole, Courtney opened the door to a frantic-looking Mrs. Farmer. A cold gust of wind slammed into Courtney. It was five forty-five in the evening and already dark in Jacobstown.

"Sassy got out of the yard." The woman was pushing seventy-five and loved her Yorkshire terrier more than anything. "You know there've been coyotes in the neighborhood lately, and I'm scared one will get to her."

Sassy had a habit of slipping underneath the fence. Courtney was almost convinced the little pooch did it for attention. Sassy had a flair for the dramatic.

Of course, Mrs. Farmer could've left the front door open for the mental state she'd been in. She'd walked next door and introduced herself on Courtney's first morning in her newly rented bungalow-style home. Mrs. Farmer had cooked a southwest skillet breakfast and brought it over, still steaming. It was the best first morning Courtney had spent anywhere but the cabin with Jordan. No amount of eggs and vegetables could top those seven days. But the offering had been the closest thing in recent memory. She didn't even want to think about those nights.

"I'm sure we can find her." Courtney grabbed her cell phone out of her purse and put on her belt. She met Mrs. Farmer on the porch. The woman had a full head of gray hair that she wore in messy bun. She was as tall as Courtney and had the clearest green eyes. She carried herself elegantly, like she was former royalty. Mr. Farmer had passed away six months ago, and Mrs. Farmer seemed to be in the thick of the grieving process. She never would've left Sassy outside long enough for the little Yorkie to get out of the fence in her right state of mind.

Mrs. Farmer stood on the porch, twisting her hands together and shivering.

"Let's get a coat on you." Courtney grabbed an extra

warm one from the closet nearest the door and then set down her phone in order to help. "You can't go out in those slippers and help find Sassy."

"You're probably right. I didn't have my head on straight. I saw you turning off lights and worried I'd miss you," she said.

Courtney pulled out a pair of boots from her closet. "Think these will work?"

Mrs. Farmer put them on. "They're a little big, but they'll do fine. We better get out there."

"Did you lock your place up?" Courtney asked.

"Yes, ma'am." Mrs. Farmer pulled a set of keys from her pants pocket.

"Good girl." The last time Sassy got out, she'd run into the field across from the cul-de-sac. It had been daylight and much easier to find her. "Let's start looking in the last place we found her."

"Thank you, Courtney. You can't know how much your help means to me. I'm sorry to be such a bother," the older woman said.

"You're not. Besides, I have a few minutes to spare." She didn't. She was due for dinner at Jordan's house and this would make her late, but she wouldn't tell Mrs. Farmer that or deny helping the woman. As far as neighbors went, Mrs. Farmer was the sweetest. She was like the grandmother Courtney never had.

Courtney locked up her own house and walked out of the cul-de-sac and to the neighboring field with Mrs. Farmer. The elderly woman called for her dog while Courtney trained her flashlight around to various spots on the ground and made kissing noises.

The wind blew, making it difficult to hear movement. Courtney stepped along the field, keeping near the street that led out of the neighborhood. She lived on the outskirts of town and closer to the Kent property than she'd realized when she rented the place.

Of course, finding a rental property in Jacobstown wasn't exactly easy. Most people owned their homes and had lived in them for decades, unlike in Dallas, where it wasn't uncommon to move every few years.

There was also a distinct lack of apartments in Jacobstown, being a small community. There was no motel within the city limits. If someone wanted lodging, they had to find a place up on the highway. There weren't a lot of transients in the area, and most people knew each other and went way back. It was the kind of town people brought up families in.

Courtney made more kissing noises. Activity to her left, deeper into the field caught her attention. She shined her flashlight in the area until she found the culprit, a raccoon. She tried to shoo it away. "Get out of here."

The raccoon stood on its back legs and hissed at her. Courtney tried to discourage it from coming closer by shining her flashlight directly at the creature. All she managed to do was annoy it. Rather than get into a real estate debate with a furry four-legged creature, Courtney decided it was time to move on. She located the biggest stick she could find and palmed it in case the raccoon had any ideas about stalking her.

Courtney kept searching, praying she wouldn't find Sassy in the jaws of a wild animal. For someone who lived in the country, Courtney was most definitely not comfortable out in the woods with animals at night.

The sounds of Mrs. Farmer's voice echoed with the wind from a little farther away than Courtney had intended to separate.

"Come on, Sassy," Courtney pleaded twenty minutes later with no sign of the little dog. Her cell was blowing up with texts. She checked the screen and realized Jordan was worried about her. She sent a text to let him know that she was running late. She hadn't meant to make him stress, and she realized after what had happened at his cousin's office earlier that's exactly what would happen.

She was still trying to wrap her mind around making the announcement to key people in the morning. It wasn't until she saw that fierce protective look in his eyes at the sheriff's office that she realized just how difficult this whole ordeal might be for him. In the last forty-eight hours, since finding out about the pregnancy, she hadn't thought about the impact this news would have on Jordan or his world, or about the position she was putting him in by asking him to keep quiet.

Nothing in her wanted to tell her boss or the Kent family about the pregnancy yet. For safety's sake, she might have to talk about it earlier than she'd like.

It was high time she listened to his point of view and took it into consideration. It would be good practice, because this was the beginning of many joint decisions that would need to be made about their child. *Their child.* Those were two words she never thought she's be saying out loud.

"Sassy," she said quietly, making more kissing noises. It was probably futile to keep calling out the little dog's name. Sassy never came when she was called except to Mrs. Farmer.

After another bitter cold twenty minutes had passed, Courtney decided to circle back and tell Mrs. Farmer they should check at home in case Sassy had gotten spooked and returned to her yard.

A noise stopped Courtney in her tracks. The hairs on the back of her neck pricked. The feeling that someone was watching her crept over her skin. A snorting sound from deeper in the field at the tree line caught her attention. Her first thought was wolf or coyote, neither of which were good signs for Sassy.

Courtney spun around toward the noise and trained her flashlight in its direction. She drew her weapon and held it alongside the flashlight; the bullet would hit the same target if she had to shoot. Tall weeds swayed in the breeze.

She stared at the rustling weeds, waiting for a wild animal to come pouncing out of them. There was no way she was moving until she knew what the heck she was dealing with. She had no plans to become a late-night snack for a hungry black bear. Rare as they might be in this area of Texas, sightings happened.

Just as Courtney was about to give up and walk away, she heard a familiar yip-sounding bark. It was coming from the direction of the snarls that were now echoing across the field. The beast—whatever *it* was—might be after Sassy.

"Come here, girl." Courtney raced toward the sounds

of the yips while surveying the area beyond. Sassy was not getting eaten by some wild animal on Courtney's watch. No, sir.

Unexpected tears flooded her eyes as she pushed closer toward the sound while fighting back the panic that was becoming all too familiar when she was thrust into high-pressure situations.

Her hand trembled so hard she worried she wouldn't be able to get off a clean shot when the time came. Granted, most of the time the presence of a weapon was enough to deter a criminal. That wasn't the point, her mind argued.

The thought almost stopped her in her tracks. Her career was all she had left, and she'd been stubbornly hanging on to it. Pregnancy aside, she couldn't be selfish. Her coworkers' lives depended on her, and it wouldn't be fair to them if she couldn't come through in a pinch.

Damn. She was going to have to request desk duty tomorrow morning.

Sassy's head popped up, bouncing just higher than the weeds, which meant she was struggling to get through the thicket.

Courtney's nerves were being put to the test as she raced toward the little dog. Tears streamed down her cheeks at the thought of not being able to come through for Mrs. Farmer, for Sassy. Courtney didn't even own a dog, but that didn't stop her heart from beating against her rib cage.

"Come on, Sassy. Run, girl," she coaxed.

The little head with a hot-pink ribbon tied around it like a headband bobbed up and down.

And then Courtney saw the blackest eyes focused on the little dog.

Chapter Eleven

The animal chasing Sassy was the size and girth of a coyote. Based on the intensity with which it was chasing the little Yorkie, the thing was starving.

Frustrated tears slipped out and then a moment of resolve—like a flash that rocketed through her body— steeled Courtney. Her grip around her Glock steadied, and she took aim.

"Go away. Get out of here," Courtney screamed at the top of her lungs. She made herself seem bigger by flapping one of her arms, and when that didn't stop the animal's momentum, she shone her flashlight into the beast's eyes.

The coyote shunned the bright light, turning its face away. Sassy got the break she so desperately needed to get a little bit ahead of her chaser.

Courtney shouted louder this time, "Shoo!"

With the coyote gaining ground on Sassy, Courtney took aim. If Sassy's head bobbed at the wrong time or Courtney's hand trembled when she needed it to be steady, she'd kill the wrong animal.

With a final push, she caught the coyote's gaze in the beam of light. Courtney screamed like a wild banshee.

At the last second, the coyote broke right, and for a moment Courtney worried that it would stalk Mrs. Farmer. Until it made a U-turn and bolted toward the tree line from where it came.

Courtney dropped down to her knees in time to catch a trembling Sassy. She holstered her weapon and set down the flashlight. She picked up the little fur ball and cradled her against her cheek. The dog was hard-core shaking but alive.

"Sweet girl. You're okay. You're going to be fine. I got you." Courtney's heart flooded with warmth, and she burst into tears. It was probably just overwrought hormones, but she kept that little dog against her cheek as several seconds ticked by. She whispered reassurances and tried her level best to collect herself after the ordeal.

The sound of footsteps coming closer forced her out of her reverie.

"I got her. She's safe. Your girl is fine." Courtney sniffed back tears and hurried to her feet.

Mrs. Farmer's warm smile melted what was left of the ice encasing Courtney's heart. These two, Mrs. Farmer and Sassy, had broken through to Courtney, and that gave her hope that others could, too. Others like her growing child. And maybe, someday, she could let a man inside her heart, too. If she did, it would be Jordan.

Courtney handed over the little dog, doing her level best to mask her own emotions at the reunion. Mrs.

Farmer held her dog with two hands and nuzzled the little creature.

"Sweet girl. Thank heaven you're safe. What would I do if something happened to you?" The dog's tail wagged hard.

"What do you say we get the two of you back inside?" Courtney said.

"I can't thank you enough for saving my Sassy. She would've frozen to death if she'd been out all night," Mrs. Farmer said. "Let me fix you something to eat. I bet I caused you to miss your supper."

"If I didn't already have plans, I'd take you up on that offer," Courtney said. And she wasn't being polite. She really wanted to spend a little more time with the kind woman who seemed a bit lonely.

"Maybe tomorrow then," Mrs. Farmer offered as they made the trek back to her house.

"Definitely tomorrow," Courtney confirmed. "I'm working, but my dinner break is at seven o'clock. Is that too late?"

"Not at all." Mrs. Farmer practically beamed. She started prattling on about what she might decide to cook, and Courtney wondered if the woman had eaten alone every meal since her husband had passed. Sharing a meal was the least Courtney could do for the sweet old woman.

Courtney walked Mrs. Farmer to her front door.

"Your boots," Mrs. Farmer said before Courtney could say goodbye.

"Keep 'em for now. I can pick them up tomorrow," she said.

"Are you sure? I don't think my feet have ever been so warm. You might need them," she said.

"I have another pair in black," Courtney said with a smile. Seeing Mrs. Farmer and Sassy together again after fearing the worst brought another peek of light into dark places in Courtney's heart. She couldn't remember the last time she'd seen someone love anything that much.

"See you tomorrow then." Mrs. Farmer returned the smile and waved.

"Lock up," Courtney reminded before she walked down the steps of the small concrete porch.

She moved to her vehicle and locked the door once she got inside. The creepy feeling of eyes on her returned, but it was most likely the stress of the situation. She'd had the feeling before. It had stalked her for weeks after the shooting in Dallas. She'd go to the grocery store and feel like someone watched her. She'd try to escape to the movies only to feel like she was part of the show.

Time had made it easier to cope. And that was about all she'd done in the last year. When she really thought about it like that, her life sounded awful.

Courtney navigated her vehicle onto the farm road that led to the Kent ranch, which was a mere half-hour drive from her place on the outskirts of town. Her heart still beat erratically in her chest, but a sense of calm was starting to come over her the longer she was on the road.

Almost a half hour on the dot later, she pulled up to the guard shack. Isaac stepped out as she rolled down her window.

"I'm here to see Jordan," she said.

"Yes, ma'am. He called ahead. Go on through." He pushed the magic button that made the gates open. He stood watch behind her, and she was reminded of what had happened at the ranch just that morning.

Icy fingers gripped her spine thinking about it. What sort of twisted person delivered a foot to someone's doorstep? In the wake of dealing with the Sassy crisis, Courtney hadn't thought about the case. She had a few choice words for Gus Stanton later.

Before she could park, Jordan came outside and stood on the porch. Was this what it had come to on the Kent ranch? The place that had held so much carefree fun in their youth. The family whose hearts were always open to help someone in need was being stalked.

Courtney stepped out of her vehicle. Seeing Jordan standing there on the front porch wearing a button-down shirt, jeans and boots caused her heart to free-fall with no hope of recovery.

He was strikingly handsome. The kind of handsome that took her breath away and released a thousand butterflies in her stomach.

She glanced down at the first step. "This is the spot."

He confirmed with a nod.

She skipped the first step and then walked the rest. The closer she came to Jordan, the more her heart thundered in her chest. She tried to remind herself that he was just a man, the same man who'd teased her mercilessly when they were kids. He'd called her shrimp-fry for the longest time, and once got so mad at her he told her to go play dot-to-dot with her freckles.

"Thank you for showing up. I wasn't sure if you would," was all he said, and the seriousness in his tone sank her stomach to her toes.

JORDAN HAD WAITED six hours and twenty-seven minutes to say what he needed to Courtney. He'd run over every scenario he could think of in his mind at least twice. He'd thought through every possible argument she could put up. He wasn't trying to be a jerk and he could see that her life was about to be upended even more so than his. Her career would have to slow to a crawl at least for the duration of the pregnancy.

"You want to talk on the porch?" she asked.

In the porchlight, she was even more beautiful, but he refused to let the fact sway what he had to say. What they were going through was bigger than just her career. Although he regretted the impact it would have. Hell, having a baby was bigger than the two of them. Sacrifices were going to have to be made on both sides if they were going to provide the best possible upbringing for the little sprout inside her.

Jordan realized that he hadn't reacted well to the news but now that he'd had some time for it to sink in, he would not allow his child to be caught in the middle of two parents who didn't have their acts together.

The child had nothing to do with that and didn't deserve to be punished.

"Do you mind coming inside?" he asked.

"I don't see anyone's cars. Did I miss everyone?" she asked as she walked past him and through the door he held open for her. The night was cold, and the weather was going to turn even worse before it got better tomorrow.

"No one's here."

"Okay." Courtney took the same seat she had this morning at the granite island figuring he'd explain in a minute.

"Can I get you something to drink?" He'd offer water or milk, but he didn't want to come off as a jerk because she'd been a die-hard coffee drinker before.

"I'm fine." She looked him straight in the eye, those glittery browns of hers digging deep inside him. She picked up a pen and started clicking it. "What's on your mind, Jordan?"

He shouldn't like the sound of his name rolling off her tongue. He did. The difference between being a man and a hormonal teenager meant he wouldn't act on the chemistry pinging between them.

Click. Click.

"I'm not trying to tell you what to do, Courtney. And I'm not pretending to know more than you do about what's best for you or the pregnancy." He put his hands up, palms out, in the surrender position. "But what I saw today can't be good for either one of you."

"Are you finished?" she asked with patience she didn't normally own as she kept eye contact.

"Not yet. I'd appreciate it if you'd hear me out," he said.

Click. Click. Click.

"I already told you that I can't keep lying to my family. We don't keep secrets from each other, and

especially not something this big. And *this* is huge,"
he continued.

She glanced up at him. Her face was unreadable. He
signaled that he wasn't done.

Click. Click. Click. Click. Click.

"Because not telling them and tiptoeing around like
we did something wrong is worse than any reaction
they could have, and besides, what we decide isn't any
of their business anyway," he stated. "We both know
they will support us no matter what. And I understand
if you're afraid to tell anyone too early. They'll keep
the news in the family."

Click. Click. Click. Click. Click. Click. Click.

"Would you put that pen down before you break your
fingers clicking it?" He didn't mean to sound frustrated,
but he couldn't help himself.

She released her grip on the pen, and it crashed
against the granite.

"Are you done, Jordan?"

She studied him, and it felt like she could see right
through him.

"Yes," he said.

"Good. Because I'm requesting desk duty tomorrow
morning." She said the words like they were as obvious
as the nose on her face. He waited for more of a reaction
from her, more of the ire he was used to getting when
he was pretty darn certain he'd pushed her buttons.

None came.

He must've been standing there with his mouth open,
because she issued a grunt and said, "Putting the baby
in danger isn't being responsible. I know I can be stub-

born, but I see that now. It's not just about me any longer. I never intended to do anything to cause problems with the pregnancy. And I realize that I've been selfish in asking you not to tell your family about the baby. I trust them to keep the news quiet."

If his mouth wasn't agape before, then it sure as hell was now.

"What? I'm not an unreasonable person." She looked up at him, and her cheeks flamed. "Okay, fine. I can be difficult to deal with, but I see the light now. All this has been a lot to take in, and I heard what you said about talking to a counselor, too. I'm thinking about it."

"Is that everything?" he asked.

She flinched like she was preparing to be told how wrong she'd been before.

"Courtney, I'm proud of you. It takes a lot of courage to ask for help." It was all he said, all he needed to say.

The next time she looked up at him, her clear brown eyes were watery. "Thank you for saying that, Jordan. That means a lot coming from you."

"I meant every word. I only wish I'd said it sooner," he said, dropping his voice down low as an ill-timed well of need stirred deep inside him, catching him off guard.

She pushed off the counter and stood. "If that's all you wanted to talk about, I'd better go home and skip dinner. It's been a long day."

He did his level best to mask his disappointment.

"Least I can do is feed you," he offered, not wanting to admit just how much he hoped she'd stay a little while longer.

"No, thanks. I'll figure something out at home." The wall he'd chipped away at just came back up.

COURTNEY WOKE THE next morning before her alarm went off and drank a glass of water. A few table crackers went down easy enough and kept her nausea from overwhelming her. She was learning that a greasy fast-food breakfast sandwich first thing in the morning came back up almost as fast as it went down. But table crackers kept things level. She could work with that knowledge.

She'd tossed and turned last night, thinking about the meeting she was scheduled to have with Zach. Telling her boss that she was pregnant six weeks into a new job wasn't exactly high on her list of great first impressions. And she'd have to face her coworkers with the news soon enough. Anxiety caused her shoulder blades to burn with tension. This was going to be more difficult than she'd imagined—and she'd gone full out with her worst nightmares last night. It was a conversation that had to take place. She didn't have to look forward to it. The fact that Zach already suspected the truth provided some measure of comfort.

At least the weather system had moved through the area, and the temperatures were supposed to warm up to the high fifties or low sixties this afternoon.

Courtney cleaned up after her light breakfast and locked up before heading in to work. The drive felt like it took twice as long. And she saw Jordan's vehicle in the parking lot. Her gaze flew to the driver's seat, but he wasn't there, which meant he was already inside.

There were other cars and trucks, too. Volunteers were starting to show up in droves, and the parking lot was brimming over. It was looking like she'd have her work cut out for her on desk duty.

A pang of guilt nipped at her. She hadn't been completely honest with Jordan last night. A big part of the reason she'd conceded was because of the pregnancy, but she also wanted to make sure she could handle herself out there. A cop with trembling hands who couldn't remain calm anymore was a recipe for someone getting hurt. She was embarrassed that she hadn't put her fellow law enforcement officers first. It was a mistake she couldn't allow herself to make, no matter how much she wanted to stay on the job.

She thought about the card sitting on her computer table. She'd snapped a pic of it before leaving the house this morning. After she spoke to Zach, she'd make the call to the counselor. Baby steps. She could do this if she focused on one step at a time. And then she'd call her old friend Amy.

But first, Zach.

With a sigh, she unbuckled her seat belt and then threw her shoulder into the driver's side door to open it. She shivered against the cold wind. The bright sun reminded her that it would warm up at some point that day.

Courtney badged into the side entrance. She thought about Gus Stanton, who was most likely still in the jail. Now that he'd tried to harm himself, he would need a psych evaluation. He was most likely awaiting transport to a mental facility for further evaluation.

With another deep breath for fortitude, Courtney knocked on her boss's door. She expected to see Jordan sitting in one of the club chairs when she opened the door after he called out to her. Her traitorous heart skipped a beat at the disappointment when she realized her boss was alone. Maybe she'd imagined seeing Jordan's vehicle in the parking lot. It shouldn't surprise her. His cousin was sheriff and many town residents were volunteering. Maybe she was losing her mind from all the recent stress Then, there was the pregnancy. That last part was most believable. She'd definitely been off the past six weeks.

"Morning, Zach," she said to her boss when he looked up from the screen he'd been studying.

"Is it?" His eyes were bloodshot, and he looked like he was wearing the same shirt from yesterday.

"Did you go home last night?" She took the chair closest to the door.

"No."

"I should've come in." She didn't want him holding the bag.

"You're still recovering from food poisoning, remember? And it was your day off," he pointed out.

"It wasn't food poisoning, Zach. I took a test. It was positive." She put her hand on her stomach. "Jordan is the father."

Chapter Twelve

Zach studied Courtney before he responded, and she realized he was searching for a clue from her as to whether this was good news or bad news, or she expected him to be shocked.

"It wasn't planned, and the timing is awful," she started.

"Is there ever a good time for your life to change to this degree?" He winked, and she realized she'd been holding her breath. She released the oxygen from her lungs.

"I guess not. But I just started this job—"

"These things happen, Courtney. It's life, with all of its crazy twists and turns," he stated with compassion, and she was so grateful for his understanding.

"Looks like there's a lot I can do around here to support the team." She referred to riding a desk for the rest of her pregnancy.

"We need every deputy we have right now. The task force can use a seasoned officer on it. You'll be just as valuable in here as you would be out there." He bit back a yawn.

"I can start by kicking you out of here so you can grab some shut-eye," she urged.

"That's probably a good idea." The bags under his eyes were no joke.

"Where are we with Gus?" she asked.

"He'll be transported in another couple of hours. He's on suicide watch. They're making arrangements for him at Cedars Bay," an inpatient facility that had a special wing for housing suspects and the criminally insane. Zach rubbed the scruff on his chin.

"I'm guessing he didn't give us anything to work with on Breanna's case." It was worth mentioning, but she got her expected answer in the form of a head shake. "What does your gut tell you about Gus?"

"He has an enormous amount of guilt over something that he did, which says he's done something that he's not proud of. What is it? I have no idea. Do I think he's our guy? I can't be certain one way or the other. He's an emotional mess, but that could be because of his actions, in which case he's not likely to repeat the crime. He could have slowly unraveled since then." Zach bit back a yawn. "Pardon me."

"Thanks for the update. I shouldn't keep you awake," she said. "I'm sorry about my problem."

He locked gazes with her, and his expression morphed to concern. "You're going to be okay with all this, right?"

She knew he was talking about the pregnancy. "I will be in time. I mean, I *can* get there, but I'm not there yet. You know what I mean?"

"I think I do." Zach was a good friend and a great boss.

"Mind if we keep the reason I'm on desk duty between us until I get the all clear from my doctor in a few weeks?" She hoped that wouldn't be an issue.

"You say what you want when you're ready. No one will hear a word from me," he promised, and she believed him. Zach's word was as good it came.

"Thanks, Zach. You can't know how much I appreciate that." His expression said he could come close.

"People do have a way of figuring these things out no matter how quiet we're being." He was right about that. People would talk. It was normal for folks to care what happened in each other's lives in Jacobstown.

"I won't be able to hide it forever," she said with a small smile. "Right now, I'm ready to focus on my job."

"Let me get you set up with a volunteer." He stood and ushered her through the door and to the hallway. "I have an office set up next door to mine occupied by someone I trust with my life. It's Jordan, so if you'd rather now work with him this would be a good time to mention it."

"I promise I have enough on my mind right now not to worry about working with him." She stopped next to the closed door, stepping aside to let Zach take the lead. He tapped on it a couple of times before opening it.

"Jordan, you'll be working closely with Courtney," Zach said.

Courtney's body stiffened, but she forced her shoulders to relax and her heart rate to calm down from its frantic rhythm. As it was, her heart pounded her chest like an out-of-control hammer.

Jordan glanced up from the notebook he'd been

studying in time to acknowledge her with a nod. He stood up out of respect. "Come on in. We can use all the help we can get."

Normally, Zach would pick up on the undertone in his cousin's voice, but he didn't seem to this time. It was probably due to lack of sleep. Nothing usually got past the man.

"I'll be in my office with the lights out for about the next hour if anyone needs me." Zach paused a beat as his gaze shifted from Courtney to Jordan. "You two will be okay, right?"

"Of course." Courtney shooed him away. "No one's waking you up if I have anything to say about it. We can handle things around here while you catch a nap."

Zach saluted before returning to his office next door, as promised.

"I'm going to get a cup of coffee," Jordan said before shutting his notebook on the table in front of him. "You want anything from the break room?"

"No, thanks."

Courtney wished she would've asked him to brief her on what he was working on before he disappeared down the hall. She also didn't want to think about how badly she wanted a cup of coffee right then and how sick it would make her if she gave in to the craving. She wished she could have decaf, but the smell wafting down the hall from the break room was making her sick. The only time she didn't get sick around coffee was when she'd kissed Jordan. His breath had the taste of it mixed with peppermint. The kiss stirred a few other senses that she didn't need to think about.

She walked over to the round table. The space had been set up like a war room. A map of the Kent ranch and surrounding ranches was pinned on a corkboard. There were blue stick pins dotting the landscape, most of them along Rushing Creek. This must be what Jordan was working on. He seemed to be tagging all the places animals had been found. There were yellow stick pins, too. She figured the different colors represented the kind of animal found there. And then there was a lone white stick pin at the location where Breanna had been found. Courtney's heart squeezed thinking about the tragedy.

Jordan strolled into the room, looking a little too good in his jeans and button-down shirt. She realized he had on the same shirt as last night, too. Had he been here all night?

She glanced behind him to make sure no one followed him. "I'm on desk duty, and I told him about us. I know he's your family, but it slipped out. I'm sorry I didn't give you the chance to tell him yourself."

"It's not a problem, Courtney. I thought my name might come up." His low rumble of a voice was even sexier without sleep. She remembered how good it had been at seducing her. She could listen to that man talk all day and never get tired of hearing his voice. This wasn't the time to let herself get carried away by Jordan Kent or how good he sounded. "How'd he take the news?"

"He was good about it," she said. "We're keeping it under wraps around here until I get the green light from my doctor. I'm sure word will spread once you start sharing the news."

"No one I plan to tell will breathe a word of this until I give the okay," he quickly countered. There was an edge to his voice now, and she'd be damned if he didn't sound even sexier.

"I'm on desk duty, and I've been paired up with you. Fill me in on what all this is about." She folded her arms and hugged her elbows to her chest.

"It's probably obvious what's going on here." He pointed to the map.

She nodded. "I meant to ask Zach if we got anything back from forensics on the contents of the freezer bag."

"The DNA matched Breanna's." He stood in respectful silence for a long moment.

It was probably just the news turning Courtney's stomach, but she ran to the nearest garbage can and emptied what little was in there. It was strange that crime felt so much more personal in Jacobstown. In a big department like Dallas, violent crimes rarely ever hit so close to home. Maybe that was the reason the massacre a year ago hurt so badly. It had felt so personal.

More heaves racked her.

Jordan was beside her before she could tell him to stay away. His hand was on her back, making small circles, reassuring her that she'd be okay.

When she finally stopped heaving, she thanked him and then excused herself to the bathroom. In her purse, she'd tucked a toothbrush and toothpaste. She pulled them out and brushed her teeth.

And then she took a long, hard look at herself. Her

identity had been tied to being in law enforcement. What if she couldn't hack the job anymore? What was she in a different job? She'd allowed her work to consume her for the past decade. She'd even dated another cop, one who would always keep an emotional distance.

The revelation almost knocked her back a step. Decks had never comforted her when she was upset. In fact, when she'd gotten emotional during their relationship, she'd go into the bathroom to cry. Had she ever let him see the real her? The short answer to that question was a fast *no*. Dating someone in law enforcement gave a sense of comradery but not intimacy. The connection they felt was stronger than buddies but short of love.

Courtney knew on instinct her relationship with Jordan had been different. It had scared the hell out of her. And she'd done the thing she did best—pushed him out of her life.

She pulled out her cell phone and stared at the picture she'd taken of the counselor's business card. Her finger hovered over the name. Why was taking that first step so hard? She'd called dozens of new numbers every month. Why did looking at this one and thinking about pulling the trigger make it suddenly hard to breathe?

After tucking her phone in her purse, she splashed cold water on her face. The call could wait.

TEN HOURS OF staring at a map, talking theories and overseeing volunteers had Courtney needing fresh air. Her nausea had subsided hours ago, and she'd been able to get a decent meal down for lunch. It had held her until the last hour, when her stomach decided to remind her she hadn't eaten in a while. The little nugget was demanding.

She stood up and then rolled her neck around to ease the tension in her muscles.

"I'll be back in a little while," she said to Jordan.

"Are you going out to grab something to eat?" He didn't look up.

"Yes."

"You want company?" he asked.

"No, thanks. I have plans." She didn't see the need to tell him that she was dining with her neighbor. Most everything about her life was about to become public knowledge—or so it felt—so she'd hold on to what little privacy she had left.

"With who?" Jordan glanced up. A mix of emotion she couldn't quite pinpoint darkened his gaze. Jealousy? She was most likely seeing what she wanted to. It was probably normal for her to want the father of her child to be a little bit jealous even though she was eating with an almost seventy-five-year-old widow. He didn't know that, and she hadn't expected any reaction from him at all.

"Just a friend," she said quietly. Defensively? She wasn't trying to hurt his feelings.

He mumbled something about just trying to make sure she didn't have to eat alone and refocused on the map he'd been studying.

Courtney didn't want to be late to supper with Mrs. Farmer. She'd instantly liked her neighbor, and after last night Courtney felt a special bond with Sassy, too. A special connection was forged when put in a life-

or-death situation. It was the same reason cops were so close to each other. They did life or death together every workday.

It had long since gotten dark by the time Courtney made it to her car. The winds had picked up, but the forecast called for low fifties tonight, warmer than it had been in days. That was the thing about Texas weather—even when it got freezing cold, it didn't stay that way for long.

She braced against the frigid winds, which whipped her hair around. She climbed into the driver's seat and started the engine, flipped on her headlights, and navigated out of the parking lot.

The road leading to her house was quiet. There was hardly ever any traffic, and tonight was no exception. She wound along the country road, keeping her eyes focused and alert out the front windshield. An irrational part of her brain searched for the coyote. She half expected the wild animal to run from out of the brush and explode onto her car.

The field she'd found Sassy in last night ran along one side of the road for miles. The area led to the back of the Kent property. Memories crashed down around her, and her eyes suddenly got very leaky.

Courtney didn't normally do emotional. She could blame it on last year's massacre or her current hormone levels, but suddenly she'd figured out how to cry faster than she could snap her fingers. She'd become a leaky faucet.

At the bend in the twisty road, she caught sight of a pickup parked off the road. Car trouble in this weather was no treat. Her headlights skimmed left, right and back again, moving back and forth as she wound around the road.

A moment of panic struck when she realized the pickup looked familiar. Blue Trunks? With that thought, she slowed her car and dimmed her headlights. There were no streetlamps on this stretch, so she had to leave her fog lights on or risk running off the road.

The driver of the pickup may have already seen her. She slowed to a near crawl as she approached the abandoned-looking pickup. There was no sign of anyone around, and an eerie feeling crept over her. This vehicle certainly hadn't been there this morning when Courtney drove this route to work.

She passed by a couple of times, not wanting to raise the alarm for a pickup that she wasn't exactly certain belonged to a guy she'd seen favoring his left foot at The Mart yesterday. Besides, it didn't look like anyone was inside.

Courtney made a U-turn and cruised by the pickup, repeating the path a couple of times to make certain there would be no surprises. She rolled her window down as she pulled beside the vehicle.

She shone her flashlight into the cab and saw a cell phone on the bench seat. If someone was stranded, wouldn't they take their cell with them? This area got service. Sure, it could be patchy, but they had it in several places.

Courtney picked up her radio to call in a suspicious vehicle when she heard an ear-piercing shriek coming from the wooded area beyond the field. Her pulse kicked up a few notches as she relayed her location to dispatch.

She hopped out of her SUV and palmed her weapon as she raced toward the sound. Someone was in trouble, and a force inside her took over despite her logical mind telling her to play it slow. If she could save a life, she had no choice but to try, so she bolted toward the tree line.

All thoughts of the coyote came rushing back, but she had no time to hesitate. If an animal had attacked someone who'd cut through the field, Courtney had to try to respond. She faintly heard that backup was on its way, and the closest deputy was twenty minutes to the east of her location.

Whoever made that scream might not have twenty minutes to live. Courtney was on autopilot as she pushed her legs to move faster, her flashlight in her left hand and her Glock in her right. She'd shoot any jerk who tried to charge toward her.

The flashlight did a great job of lighting the path in front of her, but she instantly realized that she was vulnerable to a side or rear attack once she reached the thicket, so she intentionally slowed her pace.

Another scream, muffled this time, sent a second shot of adrenaline coursing through her. She was on the right track, because the noise was closer.

Branches slapped Courtney's face, and she had to stomp through the underbrush, but she kept pushing forward. She was making headway and would come upon the scene in seconds instead of minutes at this pace.

And then a blood-curdling scream stopped Courtney in her tracks.

Chapter Thirteen

Courtney mumbled a protection prayer she'd learned as a small child and made a beeline toward the noise. On the edge of her flashlight beam, she caught sight of a male figure. He disappeared into the trees in a matter of seconds.

Training kicked in, warning her not to run straight to the victim. In all honesty, she wanted to even if that would be a rookie mistake. The area had to be secured first and foremost, or the attacker could return and dispense with them both. Courtney couldn't afford to let her guard down. But the gurgling noises coming from fifteen feet in front of her nearly stopped her heart.

Using her flashlight, she skimmed the ground, stopping on the victim. There was blood everywhere and more pumping out of her every second. Courtney had to fight against all her instincts to render aid.

If she made a wrong move, they'd both be dead and she'd be no use to the victim, Courtney reminded herself. This was the part of the job she had a hard time stomaching. Seeing someone hurt—dying?—and not being able to run to them was the worst feeling. A flash-back to the massacre, the blood that ran down the street and into the gutter, assaulted her. The blank look in Decks's eyes when she finally got to him. She'd been shot, too, but spared death. It seemed unfair to her that she should live when everyone on her team and her boyfriend didn't.

"Help is here, so I need you to hang on," she tried to soothe the victim, knowing that her words were empty. She couldn't help, not yet, not in the way she wanted to.

A noise like a dying animal echoed, causing Courtney's heart to clench. She scanned the area for the male figure as she moved around the perimeter, but there was no sign of him.

Courtney listened for any indication he was still around or any other opportunistic creature that might be lurking in the shadows waiting to get the drop on her. When she heard none and confirmed by sight there wasn't anyone or anything around, she radioed for help.

Then, and only then, did she let herself run to the victim.

The blonde woman was splayed on the ground, her arms and legs spread out at odd angles. Courtney dropped to her knees beside her. There was blood everywhere and Courtney didn't recognize the victim. She couldn't be more than twenty-five years old. But where was all that blood coming from?

"Stay with me, sweetie," Courtney said.

The blonde tried to talk but couldn't.

"Nod your head if you knew the person who did this to you," Courtney said. The tacky smell of blood filled the air as it gushed from the side of her head.

No response came.

The woman gasped for air as she shivered, and her gaze fixed on Courtney's face.

"No. No. No. No." There was no clear passageway in order to perform CPR. Blood gushed from the victim's nose and mouth. There was nothing Courtney could do besides feel helpless and like she'd just failed in the worst way.

Where was all the blood coming from? Courtney couldn't pinpoint all the locations. She used her flashlight to scan the victim's body and saw gashes everywhere in the back and sides of her head. She bit back a curse.

"Please stay with me," Courtney said as a few tears leaked. Not again. Courtney's heart squeezed so hard she thought it might burst. This person was too young to die.

She heard static on the radio before Lopez's voice came through.

"Where are you?" she asked Lopez.

"I don't see a pickup truck, but I do see your vehicle," Lopez said.

"I'm east about ten minutes into the woods. I need an ambulance." She was doing her best to keep it together no matter how much she wanted to break down. Looking at the victim, Courtney made a vow to nail the jerk who did this.

Courtney's next clear thought was that she wanted to see Jordan. There was something comforting about his presence. She told herself it was because she was carrying his child and he was in full-on protective daddy mode. But there was more to it than she was willing to admit.

Within minutes, the scene was flooded with personnel. Queasiness took over, and she had to step away.

In the light, Courtney recognized the blonde. Her name was Rhonda Keller, and she'd been a couple of grades below Courtney in school. Rhonda had dyed her hair blond.

"Is that the Kellers' daughter?" Deputy Lopez asked.

"Yes," Courtney confirmed. "Where's Zach?"

"He was signing paperwork on Gus," Lopez informed. "Said he'd be here as soon as he could get away."

Courtney recounted the story of what happened.

She realized that she'd forgotten all about dinner with Mrs. Farmer. "Will you write this up? I need to make a call."

Lopez nodded. "Of course. Let me know if there's anything else I can do. Take a break. You look like you need a minute."

"Lingering stomach issues" was all she said. She stepped out of earshot and called Mrs. Farmer.

"Hello." Mrs. Farmer sounded worried.

"It's me. Courtney."

"Oh, I don't have on my reading glasses, and those little screens are impossible to make out," Mrs. Farmer said.

"I'm sorry about dinner. I ended up on a work call," Courtney explained.

"That's all right, dear." It made everything worse that

Mrs. Farmer made an effort to cover the disappointment in her voice. "I hope you caught him."

"No. He got away," Courtney admitted. "You'll hear about this soon enough on the news, but a woman was assaulted near our homes. He got away, so I want you to be extra careful. Stay inside tonight, okay?"

"That's terrible news, Courtney. I'm so sorry." Those last three words threatened to break her down.

Instead of giving in to the wave of emotion building, Courtney thanked Mrs. Farmer and then got off the phone. She stared down at her cell for a long time, wishing she could bring something besides disappointment to people.

She had a moment. The kind when she knew someone was making a beeline for her and not trying to hide the fact. She glanced up…and there he came. Jordan Kent stalked toward her. She expected to see frustration on his face but saw only compassion. So she moved toward it, toward him. And the next thing she knew she was being hauled against his chest as she threw her arms around his neck, buried her face and cried.

Courtney had no idea when Zach arrived at the scene. It didn't matter. She held on to Jordan like he was the only lifeboat in the middle of a raging storm.

"I got the picture of the pickup you sent," Zach said to her, and she faintly registered the sound of his voice in the background. "I'm putting it out with every law enforcement official in the area and with the volunteers. Let's get some heat on this guy and make it impossible for him to show his face or stay on the road."

Courtney took a step back to address her boss. "Yes, sir."

"Maybe someone will recognize it and turn him in," Jordan's calming voice said.

"Cases have been solved on less. We're putting out the picture with a tip line." There was a pause before he focused on Courtney. "What do you think about doing back to the ranch with Jordan? I'll stop by to talk to you later. You did a great job tonight."

Courtney didn't agree. A victim had died in Courtney's arms.

"The ranch sounds good." She needed a minute to regroup anyway. The thought of going home alone sat hard on her chest. Before Courtney could put up an argument, she was being led out of the trees and away from the field. She didn't have the energy to argue. The fight had drained from her.

Jordan deposited her in his vehicle.

"My car," she started to protest.

"You have the keys?" he asked.

She pulled them off the clip on her belt and handed them over.

"I'll have someone pick it up and bring it to the ranch. Is there anything you need from it while we're here?" He took a step back, and panic engulfed her.

She grabbed on to his arm. "Don't disappear on me. Please."

She didn't know where that had come from, but the feeling in her chest that if he walked away she'd never see him again was real.

"Okay." He seemed to be trying to assess her mental fitness.

"I know that I'm acting irrationally. But, please, don't leave me alone right now." He glanced down at her arm, and it was clear to both of them that she was trembling.

"I'm not going anywhere but here." He clicked the lock button on her key. "I won't leave your sight. Okay?"

She leaned back in the passenger seat and clicked on her seat belt while nodding.

He climbed into the cab of the truck and managed to slip over her, which was a feat considering his brawn and height.

Once he settled into the driver's seat, he touched her hand. "You're safe, Courtney."

"She's dead, Jordan. I couldn't save her."

"I know. There was nothing you could do, Courtney. It wasn't your fault," he said.

So, why did it feel like it?

JORDAN HANDED COURTNEY a second cup of chamomile. She'd showered in the guest bathroom and put on borrowed clothes from Jordan's sister-in-law Leah, who was close to the same size. Deacon and Leah lived on the property, like the other siblings, along with their son, Carter.

"You haven't eaten dinner yet, and it's late," he said to Courtney as she took the mug from him. She was curled up on the couch in the family room and looked a little too right being in his family home. He'd poured himself a cup of coffee and was half-done by the time she spoke.

"I don't think I could keep anything down." She'd sat in that spot and stared at the same wall for the past twenty minutes.

"What about the soup? And maybe some crackers?" he urged for lack of a better idea. Feeding someone was something he figured his mother would have tried to do in this situation, and his mother was usually right about these things.

"I could try." There was no emotion in those words, and he figured she was solely trying to appease him. If it kept her healthy and strong, he'd take it.

He moved into the kitchen and heated a bowl. He found a tray and set the warmed soup on it along with a handful of salty crackers. After arranging the items on the tray, he returned to the family room. He set the tray down next to her.

"Or we could eat at the table if you'd like it better," he said.

"You don't have to fuss over me, Jordan. I'll be all right in a minute." Again, there was no conviction in her words.

"You can be whatever you need to be, Courtney. I've known you a helluva long time. I know how much of a fighter you are, so I know you won't let this win. But I also know that closing up and not talking about something only makes it fester. I'm here. I'm not going anywhere. I know you—"

She put her hand up to stop him from finishing.

"No. You need to hear this. You're one of the strongest people I know. I admire your courage. But you don't have to go it alone. No one has to be that strong," he said.

"Easy for you to say, Jordan. You're literally the toughest person I've ever met. You have a family to lean on who supports each other and genuinely cares. I've had myself to depend on. I'm good at being alone." She didn't look him in the eye. Instead, she rolled the edge of the pillow in between her thumb and forefinger. "I don't know how to let anyone else in. I don't lean on other people because they'll only let you down or leave you. Maybe not at first, but at some point, they leave. I'm not going through it again. I don't care who it's with or how long I've known them. You think I'm strong. In reality, I'm not built for that kind of disappointment."

Her words were knife stabs straight through the middle of his chest. He knew better than to take them to heart. Since her mind seemed made up, he decided not to push it. She was overwrought with emotion. Still, she wasn't alone and needed to know it.

"You may not think I'm going to be there for you, and I'm not going to try to convince you otherwise. But I need you to know that I won't walk away from my child. That baby growing in you binds us, like it or not. I have every intention of being there for him or her," he stated.

She didn't argue, and he could see by her body language that she was slowly letting go of the anger she'd felt moments ago. It would be easy to defend himself to her, but she needed proof that he would be there. Words amounted to little more than empty promises to her. He could understand that when he thought about her upbringing and then what had happened last year.

Actions spoke the loudest. It would take time.

He slowly sipped his coffee in silence. Jordan was patient. Patience won battles, and this was one war he couldn't afford to lose, no matter how much her words wounded him. They were only words. Actions were better indicators of what someone was thinking. Hers had been to cling to him in her moment of distress.

A knock at the door interrupted them.

Jordan excused himself and made the trek through the kitchen and down the hallway. This home was built before open-concept living was popular. The ceilings were high and the rooms large. It had a nice flow with the main room in the front hallway, which led to the kitchen.

Zach opened the door before Jordan could get there. His cousin had a key and was used to letting himself in. He'd practically grown up at the ranch along with his sister, Amy.

"How is she?" Zach asked before Jordan could greet his cousin.

Jordan twisted his face and lowered his voice. "Not good."

"I can't believe I didn't see the signs before now," Zach started in. "She's showing symptoms of post-traumatic stress disorder, and I have to assume it's connected to what she experienced in Dallas. The department declared her mentally competent in her file, so I didn't question it."

"She's too smart for them. They didn't know." Jordan took a moment to let Zach's revelation sink in. "She has nightmares."

"Oh."

"I know she told you that I'm the father." There was no sense dancing around the topic.

"Congratulations." Zach pulled Jordan into a brotherly hug.

"Thanks, cousin. I'm still trying to wrap my mind around being a father, but none of that will matter if she's not okay." There. He'd said it. He didn't even realize that's what was eating away at him until just now.

"I understand. Let's take care of her as much as she wants us to," Zach said.

"How are we supposed to do that? Because I seem to be making it worse." Jordan didn't like saying those words, even though they were true. He feared he was making everything harder than it needed to be, saying all the wrong things.

"We'll figure it out," Zach reassured. "In the meantime, I have news about what happened tonight."

This was the first conversation he'd had about having a baby to someone other than Courtney, and he appreciated the support from Zach. "Let's go talk to her."

Chapter Fourteen

Jordan led Zach into the family room, where he was surprised to see that Courtney had finished off the bowl of soup and eaten more than half of the crackers. The tray was sitting on the coffee table and Kitty—it was the name given the feral cat who kept showing up for meals and eventually wormed its way inside the house—was curled up in Courtney's lap as she absently stroked its fur. Courtney glanced at him with a look of apology, which he acknowledged with a nod and half a smile.

One great thing about being around someone he had history with, someone like Courtney, was that words weren't always necessary to communicate. A look, a nod could say so much between two people who were tuned in to each other.

"What's going on, Zach?" She turned her attention to her boss, who took a seat on the chair next to the leather couch.

Jordan took a seat on the matching couch opposite Courtney.

"The initial evidence is pointing to this being a separate crime," Zach started. "Rhonda Keller was home for an extended stay after filing for divorce from her new husband. She'd been communicating with her boyfriend from high school, Hughey Brown."

"I remember him. Wasn't he the captain of the basketball team?" Courtney asked, and Jordan rocked his head.

"The two decided to meet up and party, which they did in the field. Hughey says they kissed, but as things started to get hot and heavy she 'freaked out' and started hitting him for breaking up with her in high school to go out with Susan Wells," Zach continued.

This was like a blast from the past. Jordan remembered hearing about it during football practice when he was in school.

"The two argued, and Hughey says he decided he didn't want to repeat the same mistakes he'd made in high school, so he left. He said she might've been on something other than the tequila shots they did," Zach continued.

"So, he just left her there?" Courtney's shock was evident in her voice.

"She drove away from their meet-up spot but ended up with a flat tire." Zach rubbed the scruff on his chin. "Hughey claims he didn't know about it. He says the field is where it ended between the two of them. He told her to grow up and then took off. He says her car was there so he didn't worry about her getting home."

"What was his reaction to hearing she was murdered?" Courtney asked.

"He broke down and started crying. His demeanor

changed almost immediately. He said he thought she'd filed assault charges or asked for a restraining order to get him back for leaving her again." Zach's brow arched. "But when we told him the news, he seemed genuinely shocked."

"He was a jerk in high school, and he still sounds like a jerk, though," Courtney said. "What kind of person gets drunk with someone and then leaves them to fend for themselves instead of seeing them home and especially with a killer on the loose?"

"Not anyone I want my sister or cousins to know," Zach stated.

"Everyone is on high alert right now. That was a jerk move." Courtney stroked Kitty a little faster.

"He left her vulnerable." Zach paused a beat. "But there are no witnesses to corroborate his story."

"Does that mean you think Hughey might be the killer?" Courtney's hands trembled.

"He's being detained while we decide on whether or not we're going to file criminal charges against him. We're looking at public intoxication for one and, of course, more serious charges if that's what the evidence dictates," Zach informed. "Rhonda had a flat tire, and the pickup you saw might've stopped to render aid. If Hughey's story holds water, Rhonda might've trusted the wrong person."

"It's happened before. Ted Bundy comes to mind, but there were plenty of others. This guy might've walked with a limp or a cane. He could've disguised himself to look older and maybe even a little feeble in order to lower her defenses. She'd had a little too much to drink, so her judgment wasn't the best," Courtney speculated.

"He could've offered her a ride into town," Zach added.

"Once she's inside his vehicle, he thinks he has it made—and he probably does." Courtney worked the corner of the pillow in between her thumb and forefinger. "Except this has to be related to the Jacobstown Hacker. We'd assumed that he's an opportunistic killer based on Breanna's murder. Maybe he cruises around looking for targets."

"That's a good point. The odds of him driving up at the exact moment she needs help are slim, though," Zach pointed out.

"And the fact that Rhonda got a flat tire in the first place bugs me. I mean, it happens, but right at the moment she gets into a fight with her ex from high school? And then an opportunistic killer happens upon her?" Courtney issued a sharp breath.

"The killer could've wandered upon the fight without either of them knowing. He might've been scouting a location. That property backs up to the Kent Ranch and we all know Rushing Creek meanders nearby," Zach said.

"It's possible that's how he's been accessing the land all along," Jordan agreed. "I don't think we have any cameras on that side of the fencing."

"If he was watching the fight and realized she'd be a good mark, maybe he put a hole in her tire or created a slow leak," Courtney said.

"All of which makes sense," Zach concluded.

"And then there's the idea that Rhonda's argument got heated with Hughey and his temper flew out of control. The words turned physical and he killed her," Courtney said.

"Mike said there were multiple blows to the head with something that resembled the blade of an ax." Zach's face twisted in disgust at the coroner's finding. The thought that any human being was sick enough to do that to another person was mind-boggling.

"The killer might not have been planning on targeting anyone tonight. Maybe he came upon the scene and figured this was the time to act," Courtney offered.

"In which case he might've made his first mistake," Zach said. "We'll check her system for ketamine."

"I interrupted him. It could be the reason for the change in MO." There was so much sadness in Courtney's voice when she spoke those words aloud.

Jordan knew the guy they were looking for was calculating. This crime didn't fit the MO of the Jacobstown Hacker. He didn't normally strike the head. In fact, there was normally no evidence he'd been at a crime scene. Zach was still trying to figure out if the victims were killed ahead of time and taken to the spot where he'd cut off their foot or if the victim was drugged and carried to the spot. Someone who'd been bludgeoned in the head with an ax multiple times as opposed to one clean whack on the left ankle right above the foot didn't fit the bill. The date-rape drug ketamine had been found in Breanna's system, which could've explained why she didn't put up a fight. And Courtney made a good point about interrupting the killer.

Then there was Hughey to consider. He'd always been known for his bad temper. In high school he'd pushed a kid down the stairs for cutting him off. Being a star on the basketball team had gotten him out of suspension. The coach had smoothed things over with the dean of students. Athletes in Texas high schools were treated too much like rock stars.

Someone angry, who'd just been in a heated argument with an ex, might whack her the minute she turned around. But why would there be an ax anywhere near them? How would that have happened, exactly? Did the two take the ax into the woods to their love nest? And where was this supposed love nest to begin with? It had to be in the field somewhere. Only an idiot went into the trees and underbrush after dark. It was cold outside, so they wouldn't be eaten by mosquitoes, but there were plenty of opportunistic animals lurking around. Animals that would no doubt pick an easy meal.

There were a lot of unanswered questions in this case that would leave the town spinning. Half the folks were out on neighborhood watches, trying to protect each other and keep each other safe. That could also explain the killer's change in MO. Maybe he was starting to act out of desperation.

"Any word on the Barstock sighting?" Courtney asked Zach.

"No one else has seen him. Just Liesel at the diner." Zach's phone started dinging.

"Any chance she confused him with someone else?" Courtney asked.

"No." Zach checked his screen and then glanced over

at Jordan. "Would you mind if I spoke to Courtney alone for a minute?"

Jordan instinctively checked with Courtney, who nodded.

"Not a problem. I'll be in the next room if you need me," Jordan said. He left the room quickly. Although he wasn't eager for the conversation to happen.

If he had to guess, Zach was telling Courtney to take leave. Not because of the pregnancy but because of what had happened earlier that night and the signs of PTSD. After what she'd seen and experienced, Zach would want a full evaluation on her mental fitness before allowing her back on the job. Being put on desk duty had been difficult. He feared this news would set her back even more.

Jordan busied himself in the kitchen.

Much to his surprise, Zach strolled in a couple of minutes later.

"Everything okay?" he asked his cousin.

"She asked for you," Zach informed. "I can see myself out."

Jordan said goodbye before excusing himself and walking into the family room. Courtney sat there, feet tucked underneath her legs, looking more at home than he'd seen her in days.

"I have to take a few days leave," she said, and she sounded resigned to the fact.

"Would it make a difference if I talked to Zach?" He wanted to do something to help.

"It's protocol, but I suspect there's more to it than that if I'm being honest." She issued a sharp breath and fixed her gaze on a spot on the wall across from her. "I can see it in his face. He's worried about me."

Jordan took a seat next to her. "I'm sorry."

"He's right. I've been trying to convince myself that I'm fine, but I'm not and the truth just keeps stalking me," she said. "It's not going away unless I face it head-on. That's been made painfully clear to me."

"Is this about what happened last year?" He didn't want to push her, but he knew she hadn't honestly spoken about the incident in Dallas with anyone.

"What do you know about it?" She didn't look at him, and that was good. His heart went out to her for everything she'd been through, and he had a feeling her pain might be present in her eyes.

"Only what was in the news," he admitted. This was the time she normally shut down on him and quit talking. Usually he could almost feel the walls going up between them. She'd been through even more tonight, and he saw her strength and bravery. But how much more could one person take? Bottle everything up, shake the bottle and eventually the cap would come shooting off in a massive explosion. Zach could handle the stress that came with the job because he didn't bottle up his emotions.

Zach also had an amazing support network. He talked about what bothered him, and Jordan knew his cousin encouraged his deputies to take good care of themselves.

Looking at Courtney and not seeing her as fragile but someone who was trying to be too strong, Jordan couldn't help wondering whom she had to lean on. She'd been honest about that earlier.

"Eight officers killed that day in Dallas were friends or associates of mine. One of them, Decks, was my boyfriend." The words, spoken slow and deliberate, reminded him of the way she used to talk in high school when she was holding in emotion. "One of the officers killed, the one who was my boyfriend, had a nine-year-old son, Joey."

Jordan didn't want to hear about Courtney's love life, but he had no claim on her and no right to be jealous.

"Were you close with Joey?" As a girlfriend and not a spouse, Courtney would have no legal right to visit the child.

"No." She shrugged. "I've never even met him."

Jordan couldn't say he understood. His brow must've shot up because she went on to explain.

"A pension isn't enough to bring up a child, let alone send him to college if he wants to go, so I give half of my salary to his mother through a blind trust fund that I set up. She doesn't deserve to have to bring her child up alone with almost no support." Courtney paused a beat. "Now that I'm pregnant, I have another little one to think about."

"If you're worried about money, don't. I can help with anything you need," he said quickly.

"I have to pay my own way through life, Jordan." Her tone left no room for argument, so he figured he'd shelve the conversation for now. There'd be plenty of time to figure out finances, and he hadn't meant to offend her.

"I keep asking one question. Why me? Why am I still alive?" It wasn't like Courtney to feel sorry for herself, and he didn't think she was looking for an answer from him, so he waited for her to finish. "Why did I get to live and not them?"

Those words spoken aloud seemed to carry the weight of the world.

"I don't know, Courtney. But I, for one, am grateful you're here," he said.

She turned to him, climbed on his lap and kissed him.

COURTNEY KNEW THIS was dangerous territory, but she couldn't care about that right now. Kissing Jordan seemed like the most natural thing to do under the circumstances. She couldn't deny that she'd missed him over the last six weeks. She had.

She expected him to pull back and set her straight again. He didn't.

Instead he looped his arms around her waist and crushed her against his muscled chest.

His tongue in her mouth, his hands roaming her back sent electric impulses flaring through her body, warming places where his fingers trailed. His hands were big, and it felt like one could cover half her back.

She tunneled her fingers in his thick hair and deepened the kiss—a kiss she'd wanted to repeat ever since the other night.

Courtney couldn't help it. Her pull to him was the strongest she'd ever felt with anyone. She'd tried to convince herself that it was shared history, but there was so much more to it than that. It's also what scared the hell out of her. This wasn't the time to get inside her head. This was the time to feel her way through her next steps.

And the most logical next step that came to mind was to really feel Jordan, to feel his bare, naked skin against hers. To feel his weight on top of her pushing her into the mattress. To feel his hands roam all over her body.

No one had ever made her feel sexier or more alive and in the moment than Jordan.

Courtney's hands flew to the buttons on his shirt on autopilot. Her fingers trembled with need, so she fumbled a little bit.

There was a moment of hesitation on his part, and she feared this was the point when he'd stop her. But Jordan covered her hands with his, paused for a beat and then helped her finish.

A few seconds later, he shrugged out of his shirt while their lips pressed together.

Courtney wanted this more than anything. Still, a nagging question tugged at the back of her mind.

Was this a mistake?

Chapter Fifteen

Courtney pulled back long enough to look into Jordan's eyes. She needed reassurance that what was happening between them was okay.

Jordan pressed his forehead to hers and closed his eyes.

"I want this to happen, Jordan."

"So do I. More than you could know. But we're making progress, and I need to know this won't confuse the issue." He was being smart. She couldn't deny it.

"I've held someone who died in my arms earlier tonight, Jordan. I've lost people that I cared about in a snap. We can think about tomorrow and the next day and the next after that, but no one knows for certain if we'll be there to make all our plans happen. All we really have is right here, right now. And all I know is that I've missed this." There. She'd said it. "I don't know what that means or how much that complicates our lives, but I want you right now, Jordan. And I need to know you want this, too."

He opened his eyes—golden-brown eyes that had darkened with need.

For a long moment, he just stared at her like he was looking right through her. And he probably was. She couldn't care about that right now. She'd opened up to him earlier. She actually liked talking to him, and it felt like part of the weight that had been sucking her under for far too long was lifting. It would take time and understanding before she could even think about healing, but for the first time in her life, she could see a peek of light in a world that had been dark for too long.

She wanted to run toward it but knew that was asking too much of herself all at once. But she could take baby steps.

"You're sure this is what you want?" His voice was low and sexy. That deep timbre washed over her and through her.

"I've never been more certain of anything in my life." It was true. With all the craziness that she'd experienced over her lifetime, she was right where she wanted to be in this moment. She needed to block out the world, if only for a little while, and remember that she was still alive even if she wasn't living fully.

The realization struck a chord with her.

"And this won't make things more confusing between us," he said.

"I can't promise that." A smirk toyed with the corners of her mouth. She should probably just lie and say that it wouldn't. Courtney couldn't be dishonest with Jordan. He deserved the truth.

"What?" There was a hint of defensiveness in his tone.

"How much worse can it make it?"

His answer came in the form of covering her mouth with his in the kind of kiss that would make her knees rubbery if she was standing. She'd have to grip the wall behind her or risk falling flat on her back.

It was Jordan's turn to unbutton her shirt. His fingers worked their magic as her nipples beaded, straining for his touch. The guttural groan he released when her shirt hit the floor and he traced her lacy bra with his fingertips made warmth pool between her thighs.

She couldn't be sure if it was because he was so hot standing there or that she hadn't had sex with Jordan for six weeks, but her stomach literally quivered at his lightest touch. Whatever they had was so much more than shared history or hot sex. Was it love?

Courtney couldn't go there with anyone, but this was the closest she could imagine being to it.

Jordan's erection throbbed against her heat. A layer of denim and a pair of cotton shorts amounted to too much material between them. With a flick, Jordan undid the snap of her bra. He was a little too skilled at that little move, but this wasn't the time to think about that. And then he cupped her full breasts in his palms as his lips crushed down on hers and her bra tumbled to the floor.

Everything disappeared except the two of them in this moment. Everything except the need pulsing through her and the tide of desire stirring, rising from deep within. Everything felt right in the world for just a moment.

Courtney dug her knees into the couch cushion and

pushed herself up as she threaded her fingers through his thick mane and kissed him back, hard.

"We need to finish this in the other room so we're not interrupted." Jordan picked her up like she weighed nothing and she was reminded he'd taken her to the main house and not his place.

For a split second, she panicked about the thought of someone walking in on them or finding her there in the main house in their current condition. The notion was fleeting. What did she care? Her pregnancy was about to be revealed, and everyone would know who the father was soon enough. Would it really shock anyone that the two of them had slept together?

Inside Jordan's bedroom, he set her down on the edge of the bed. His jeans and boxers hit the floor a few seconds later, and she made quick work of letting her shorts and panties join them. It was a little too late for a condom—not like she trusted those things anymore—so neither bothered discussing using one this time. Lot of good those conversations had done during their week of hot sex.

The miniblinds let just enough moonlight into the room for her to see Jordan clearly. His body was muscled perfection. His thick, straining erection was silky skin over steel. "You'll laugh at me for saying this, Jordan. But you're beautiful."

True enough, a laugh rumbled out of his chest.

"I'm not," he countered. "But you are."

"You don't have to—"

"Yes. I do. You're incredible, Courtney. I'm not just talking about your looks. You have those in spades.

Your sense of humor. The way you laugh. I'd be lying if I said I didn't miss you," he admitted.

She took his hands in hers and tugged him toward her. She settled on the bed, and he positioned himself in the V of her thighs. Looking into his eyes, she guided his tip inside her. He put most of his weight on his arms as he eased himself deeper.

Courtney bucked her hips as he lowered himself on top of her. His lips met hers, and she surrendered completely to everything that was happening between them. They connected physically and emotionally—in every way that counted. Who got that?

The intensity of the emotions that had happened between them had caught her off guard, and she'd balked. None of that was important now. All that mattered was this moment.

Her body was alive with impulse as she and Jordan drove faster, harder, rocketing toward the release only he could give her.

Faster. Harder. She dug her fingers into his shoulders.

He rolled her nipples in between his thumb and forefinger, causing her to shoot over the edge. Her body was a battlefield of intense electricity. All she could do was surrender to the tide and try to hang on as she catapulted toward the edge.

Just as she felt herself hit the point of no return, all his muscles tensed, and he said her name in her ear and something that sounded a lot like *I love you*.

Those three words normally gave Courtney hives, but she actually liked the sound of them coming from Jordan.

She bucked harder and reached deeper inside as she rocketed over the edge. Sensual electricity exploded inside her body as they moved in perfect rhythm.

When her body was drained of everything left inside and she tried to catch her breath, he looked at her.

"This changes things for me. I hope it does for you." He locked gazes with her. "We don't have to discuss it now, but we will when the time's right."

"I missed you, Jordan. That's all I know right now. All I care to know."

"That's enough for today." He said it so low she almost didn't hear.

Jordan rolled onto his side before pulling her in close to his body. His warm skin against hers was the best feeling. She settled into the crook of his arm and fell into a deep sleep.

JORDAN WOKE THE next morning with the sun peeking through the blinds. He glanced at the clock, which read 6:23. Days on the ranch normally started at 4:00 a.m. He'd slept in, which was uncharacteristic for him.

Waking up to Courtney lying next to him again filled his heart in ways he couldn't afford. She'd needed comfort last night. He'd been there for her. Having sex, knowing she was going to be the mother of his child, changed their relationship.

He didn't have his mind around what that meant or what he had to offer her. His life was in Idaho, running the family business there. When he'd left Jacobstown as a young man, he'd assumed it would be for good, save for holidays and special occasions.

Every time he'd visited, he felt like an outsider. And now? It was different. Granted, he was going to have a baby now. But that was the reason this place felt more like home than he'd ever remembered. What had changed inside him?

An annoying little voice in his head seemed determined to point out that Courtney had come home. But she had her own demons at work, and aside from a rare moment here and there, she was lost inside herself.

Plus, there was the simple fact that he couldn't be in a relationship with someone who would never trust him. Jordan had been spoiled. He'd seen the kind of relationship his parents had had. The bar was set high. He could admit that. But he wouldn't settle for anything less because he'd seen the best. He'd lived the kind of love that was unconditional and grew over time to be something even more beautiful.

Something unattainable?

Being with someone who loved him with their whole heart and vice versa was the only true comfort in life. Anything less would be settling, and he'd seen how that had worked out for a few of his friends.

Jordan could admit to missing Courtney after the week at the cabin. He'd tried to discuss a serious matter with her, and she'd balked. Then she'd walked out the door and hadn't looked back. If she hit the road when things got tough once, she'd do it again. Past behavior was always the best predictor of the future. People rarely changed.

A small piece of his heart wanted to protest the logical side to him. His heart wanted to believe that she could handle a real relationship. But she'd already burned him once, and he'd never been the type to ask for a second round of punishment.

Jordan slipped out of the covers and found a fresh pair of boxers and jeans. He put on his clothes and headed toward the kitchen to make something to eat and get his caffeine fix.

He scrambled up a couple of eggs and toasted a couple slices of bread. As he ate at the granite counter, he checked his phone. The battery had died. He plugged it into the charger, and it took a few seconds to get enough juice to turn on.

By the time he'd finished his meal and drained a cup of black coffee, his cell started vibrating with messages.

Lone Star Lonnie had gone in to volunteer at Zach's office, so Jordan could take the morning to catch up on ranch affairs. Thankfully, there were no calves due for another week or two. But he needed to check on the pregnant heifers.

There were also documents he needed to sign, so he moved into the office. A stack of papers stared at him from on top of the desk. This had been his father's office. To this day, being in here was strange ever since his father had passed away.

It had been years now, and yet Jordan couldn't seem. Hell, his siblings had all found their soul mates and settled down. He'd always been the odd man out, and it seemed he would remain that way. He thought about Courtney's pregnancy, about the little nugget growing inside her. He expected to feel a sense of dread for this being unplanned. Instead, he felt a twinge of something that felt an awful lot like excitement at the thought of having his own child.

Granted, an unplanned pregnancy wasn't the way he thought he'd usher in fatherhood. In his mind, he would've followed a more traditional route of marriage and honeymoon before baby. In theory, anyway. In practice, he hadn't really thought he would find the right person or have children. Jordan loved his work. He loved being out on the land. And he loved his freedom.

Having amazing sex with the right woman was about as far as he'd ever gone with a woman. Emotional attachments got messy. He searched his thoughts for the last time he'd let himself fall for someone. His mind snapped to his high school girlfriend Sophie. He'd been head over heels for her before she got sick. The terminal brain cancer diagnosis had caught everyone off guard, including him. For years, he thought he'd cursed her in some way. Teenagers always found a way to blame themselves for every tragedy.

Damn. Had Sophie truly been the last person he'd opened up to? The only one he'd let himself love?

That annoying voice said he loved Courtney. But there was no way. She pushed him away more than she opened up to him. She most definitely didn't need that kind of upheaval in her life right now. What would loving her matter?

Jordan wouldn't risk his heart for someone who couldn't love him. Good communication and a few rounds of the best sex he'd ever had might be the most he could expect from Courtney. Would it be enough? Would she be able to stick it through with their child when times got tough? And no matter what amount of privilege a person grew up with, no one was spared losing a loved one at some point.

His phone buzzed in the kitchen, so Jordan forced himself out of his thoughts and went to answer it. Zach's name popped up. He answered the call before it rolled into voice mail. "What's up, Zach?"

"I thought you should hear this first and from me," Zach started.

That didn't sound good. "Okay."

"There's a theory circulating around town that Courtney interrupted the killer and that's why he hacked Rhonda in the back of the head in order to kill her." Zach got quiet for a long moment. He seemed to understand what that would do to her if she heard the news firsthand.

"She said as much last night. Hearing it from others won't be good for her," Jordan said.

"No, it won't." Zach issued a sharp breath.

"Is there any merit to it?" Jordan needed to know what he was dealing with before he spoke to Courtney.

"It's not an unreasonable theory." So, it might be true was what Zach was saying.

"You mentioned PTSD last night. She also has survivor's guilt," Jordan said. "She's planning to talk to a counselor about that and a few other things."

"You already know I'll support her in any way that I can." Zach was more than a good cousin. He was truly a good man.

"Thank you." Jordan meant it.

"We have to look out for our own. It's nothing any

of you wouldn't do for me." Zach was right about that. Being in Idaho away from the family, Jordan was beginning to see how lonely his life had been there. He was beginning to see that it was nice to be around people who had his back and looked out for each other. All those things had felt suffocating before. What had changed in him to make him feel differently? *Fatherhood?*

He couldn't deny that he felt a pull toward being around family for his unborn nugget. The thought of him or her growing up surrounded by love wasn't the worst thing he could think of. And, besides, he was most likely going to need a ton of parenting advice. From what he could tell so far with his nieces and nephews, those kids didn't come with any sort of training manual. Once a kid came into the world, it was go time.

"Your relationships are none of my business," Zach started.

"I care what you think, even if I don't always listen to your advice, Zach."

"I appreciate that, Jordan." Zach paused a few beats. "It was bad for her growing up here with her father."

"Yes, it was. I hate that she went through all the abuse." He was already gone by that time, and his family had never been ones for gossip. So much about what Courtney had said about only being able to count on herself made even more sense as he was reminded of her traumatic upbringing. Jordan understood just how fully she meant those words, and his heart squeezed at thinking about the abuse she'd suffered.

Instead of feeling sorry for herself, she'd gone on

to work in law enforcement in order to bring justice to bastards who took advantage of or hurt others. So many things snapped in place in his mind. He wanted to do everything he could to protect her from the story making its rounds.

"Did Hughey's story check out?" Jordan asked. Maybe there was another angle to consider.

"For the most part. Yes. I asked a judge to issue a search warrant for his home, because Rhonda had ketamine in her system as well as alcohol and a prescription opioid," Zach informed.

"Same as Breanna?" Jordan asked.

"It looks like that might be how he gets them to be compliant. He gets them comfortable with him somehow and then slips some powder into their drink when they aren't watching." A picture was beginning to take shape. It wasn't one he liked, but the puzzle pieces fit together and no one could deny it. It was a theory worth considering.

"That could be how he got his victim to the site." Zach sounded like he hadn't slept since yesterday. A pang of guilt struck Jordan, because sleeping with Courtney given him his best night's rest in recent memory. Hell, he hadn't slept that well since the last time they were together.

"I'll keep Courtney at the ranch for a few days if she'll stay. It might help keep her under the radar until talk simmers down," Jordan said.

"She'll want to call in and ask about the case. Tell her I called to check on her and to order her to rest," Zach said.

"She has an independent streak as long as Route 66 and a stubborn streak even longer. I'll see what I can do," Jordan said on a chuckle.

"Do you care about her enough to go the long haul?" Zach asked.

"I haven't figured anything out yet, and especially not my next move," Jordan admitted. "But, yeah, I think so."

"She'd make a fine partner for the right person." Zach wasn't exactly being subtle.

"We're still figuring that part out," Jordan replied.

"She's worth fighting for." Zach left it at that. "One more thing, she cares about you. I saw it before last night, but it's obvious every time she looks at you."

"Thanks, Zach. You know I always appreciate your opinion," Jordan said. "And take care of yourself."

Jordan wanted to do more to pitch in and ease the burden for his cousin. But maybe the best thing he could do right now was take care of Courtney.

If she'd let him, and that was a big if.

She'd always been headstrong. She was also smart, so she wouldn't do anything to put herself or their child in harm's way. She seemed to be coming to terms with the fact that she'd been dealing with her stress in the wrong way.

And she seemed genuinely committed to turning that around for the sake of their child. He had no idea, though, if she was capable of letting him in.

Chapter Sixteen

A day of rest after yesterday seemed like a smart option to Courtney, not for her sake but for the baby's. She'd slept in fits last night. The case was eating at her. It was difficult to walk away completely when the clock was ticking, and especially after an innocent woman had died in Courtney's arms.

For all anyone knew the Jacobstown Hacker may have already made a move on his next victim. Questions swirled about Hughey and what his role truly was. Could he be the person they'd been searching for all along? Could he be the Jacobstown Hacker?

She didn't know him well enough to decide one way or another.

The case wasn't the only thing on her mind as she brushed her teeth. Last night, when she and Jordan made love, something was different between them. Granted, the sex was hotter than ever, but that wasn't what she was talking about. A tide had shifted between them. Their lovemaking had felt more intimate.

Courtney tried to chalk it up to outside factors, like the fact that she'd been through hell and back. That

Jordan hadn't gone anywhere. He'd stayed right by her side when she'd needed him the most.

But he lived in Idaho and had willingly left Jacobstown years ago. He had his own demons to deal with, considering he'd walked away from the only place he'd ever known and hadn't looked back. She saw in him what she saw in herself—someone ready to walk away.

Courtney finished brushing her teeth and washed her face. Her mind raced with other thoughts, too.

There was a person she'd been avoiding since returning to town. Amy. Courtney had been dodging Amy's attempts to reach out to her and connect. Courtney felt bad about not returning Amy's calls.

The thought of facing Amy—one of the few people who'd actually known Courtney in Jacobstown—after having a weeklong fling with Jordan didn't sit well.

In the beginning, she didn't think she could trust herself not to slip up. And she'd made a habit of avoiding people she cared about from the past. Wasn't that just an excuse? An excuse to stay miserable in some ways? Because people she cared about who had died didn't get to reconnect with old friends. Why should she?

The people she'd been closest to were gone, all in one fell swoop. A surprising well of tears leaked from her eyes, and this time she didn't rush to wipe them away. Hadn't she been doing that to herself all along? Covering her crying? Wiping away her tears the second they fell while hoping she could erase all that came with them just as easily?

Oh damn. Was that what she'd been doing?

Courtney finished freshening up in the bathroom

before making her way into the kitchen. The smell of coffee hit her square in the face as she entered the room, and she had to hold back the nauseous feeling threatening to overpower her.

She located her cell inside her purse, but the battery was low. Not being connected to her work made her chest feel tight. The air in the room thinned, and it suddenly felt hard to breathe.

Thinking about her work made her tense, too. She'd grown used to depending on cell phones and her police radio to stay constantly in touch. Was it any wonder that she usually wanted nothing to do with those things on her days off? And yet not having full access to them was making her a little stir-crazy.

It was most likely because of the gravity of the case and not because of something else, like she feared her job wouldn't be waiting for her after her forced leave.

Jordan wasn't in the kitchen. She figured he wouldn't mind if she helped herself to some yogurt in the fridge. As she walked across the room, she heard faint sounds coming from the office down the hall. It sounded like keystrokes.

It made sense that Jordan would be working. She checked the time. How could it be nine fifteen already? She normally woke up with the sun. It was a habit that came with growing up in ranch country and had stuck well into adulthood.

After talking to Jordan last night, some of the weight she felt like she'd been carrying around for far too long seemed like it had lifted. She plugged her phone into the charger on the wall with every intention of getting enough charge going to check her e-mails and call the counselor.

It was time to learn how to live with what had happened and not run away from it. It was time to deal with her feelings instead of shoving them down deep. It was time to make the fresh start she'd so badly wanted in coming home to Jacobstown.

Maybe it took a surprise pregnancy for Courtney to realize she couldn't live like this anymore. She needed to come to terms with her past. She knew that she had to let it go in order to pave the way for a bright future for her and her child.

She'd had no idea that becoming a mother would make her want to change in almost every way for the better. To take what was good about her and find a way to do more of it. To take what was broken and find a way to fix it.

That was the power of love.

Courtney finished her yogurt and checked the pantry for some table crackers. Salty crackers sounded like they'd calm her stomach, which was doing well so far. The little nugget growing inside her must be hungry. Courtney touched her belly. "I don't know how you got stuck with me, kiddo. I promise to do my best. We'll figure this out together."

She already knew that Jordan Kent was going to be an amazing father. That much was a given. Being a Kent would give their baby everything Courtney never had and everything a child really wanted—a loving family.

Jordan walked into the kitchen, and she dropped her hand.

"Good morning. I didn't realize you were awake," he said.

A moment of hesitation struck. What they'd done last night had changed the course of their relationship. They'd muddied the waters of friendship and co-parenting, and she'd probably made a mess of everything before her child was even in the world.

Jordan walked straight over to her, took her hand and then kissed her with such tenderness it robbed her of breath. She marveled at his ability to walk into a room and make everything better.

"I don't usually sleep so late." They'd kept all kinds of odd hours at the cabin for that blissful week. He wasn't familiar with her normal life routine.

"You needed it." He walked over to the fridge and pulled out a container of food. "Kimberly made a whole mess of food when she heard you were staying at the main house. Does a southwest skillet breakfast sound good to you?"

"Normally, I'd be all over it. Right now, I can make do with yogurt and crackers. I made myself at home." She pointed toward the empty container of yogurt, thinking she probably should've found him and asked first. "I hope you don't mind."

"It would be weird if you didn't make yourself comfortable." He smiled that sexy little smile that had been so good at seducing her. Of course, his tortured look had been pretty damn good at accomplishing the same feat.

"Good. I thought you might be out on the property, and I woke up starving." She picked up her cell phone, which finally had a decent charge.

"Zach says you should leave that thing alone," Jordan stated. "That came straight from your boss."

"I promise that I'm not looking at this thing for work purposes." She held her hand to her heart like she was taking an oath. "I owe Amy a text at the very least. If she still wants to talk to me."

"She'll like hearing from you." Jordan sounded distracted as he pulled out his phone. "Now that you mention it, I haven't seen her around lately. I probably have a message from her since we've been in contact every day since I've been home. Hold on while I check."

A sinking feeling hit Courtney in the pit of her stomach as he stared at his screen, scrolling through message after message.

He looked up at her and shook his head.

JORDAN CHECKED HIS phone again. There was nothing from Amy. It was most likely the fact that everyone, including him, was on high alert, but he had a bad feeling.

"I tried texting her a minute ago. She didn't respond. She could be mad at me and I'd deserve it." Courtney held out her cell.

"That's not like her." If Amy wasn't returning Courtney's text, it could mean that she was busy. Or…

His mind dived to darker places—places he couldn't allow himself to stay for long or he'd drive himself crazy. "I'm sure Zach's heard from her. We can clear this up with a phone call. There's no reason to panic."

Jordan pulled up Zach's name and made the call.

"What's up, Jordan?" Zach asked by way of answer. His voice gave away how tired he must be.

"Is Amy around? She's not answering her cell, and I have a quick question for her." He didn't want Zach to worry. Jordan told himself that he was being overly cautious.

"No. In fact, I haven't seen her. Let me ask Ellen. My sister has probably already shown up to volunteer today. Hold on." Jordan could hear his cousin shout to his secretary even though his mouth was away from the receiver.

Jordan looked at Courtney, who was fiddling with the spoon in her hand. She looked up at him with so much worry in her beautiful brown eyes.

Zach returned to the call. "No one has seen her. I'm trying to think the last time I did. It's been a full day, which has me concerned."

"I'll reach out to Amber and Isaac. We can see if they've heard anything," Jordan immediately offered.

"Let me know what they say. In the meantime, I'll give her a call and let her know we're looking for her. I'm sure everything's fine, but I'm glad you called to check." There was no conviction in those first four words.

"Okay then. Let's all get busy." Jordan figured that between Amber and Isaac, someone had seen or spoken to Amy. His first call was to his sister.

She picked up on the first ring. "Hey, Jordan. How are you?"

"I'm good. I'm calling about Amy. Do you know where she is?" He got right to the point.

"Um, hmm. Good question. Let's see. We were supposed to go to the VFW together to drop off a baked goods. And then news spread about what happened last night, so we canceled." She paused a beat. "Hold on. There was so much confusion yesterday, now that I think about it, I'm not even sure that I talked to her. *Everyone* was calling and trying to find out what was going on, and I assumed she had, too."

"So, you didn't talk to her?" Jordan looked at Courtney.

"Now that I really think about it, no. Patsy Blair was coordinating the annual baked goods event, and I must've talked to her half a dozen times. But I actually don't remember having a conversation with Amy now that you mention it. Why? What's going on?" Concern caused her voice to raise a few octaves.

"I hope nothing. She and Isaac are still dating, right?" he asked.

"You know about that?" Amber sounded shocked.

"Pretty much everyone does at this point. They've been on and off for how many years now?" he asked.

"That's fair," Amber said quickly. And then added, "Let me know what you hear from him, okay?"

"Will do, sis." Zach and Amber spoke to Amy on a daily basis, so Jordan wasn't one bit thrilled about what he was hearing. His next call was to Isaac, who answered immediately.

"How can I help you, Jordan?" They'd long ago dispensed with formalities.

"You haven't seen Amy around, have you?" Jordan held his breath waiting for the answer.

"As a matter of fact, no, I haven't. I've been working double shifts like everybody else." Isaac and the other security personnel had volunteered their time off in order to take extra shifts. Everyone had been on heightened alert since the delivery the other morning. "Why?"

Jordan figured he might as well tell Isaac. "No one has seen or heard from her in the last twenty-four hours."

"Well, then, I request permission to abandon my post and look for her," Isaac said without missing a beat. "Frederick's here and can keep watch on the gate."

"Absolutely. Brief the others on the situation. I'll call Lone Star Lonnie personally." Lonnie was like family and he needed to know what was going on.

Breanna's murder was out there somewhere. Rhonda had been murdered in the field. A coldblooded killer was out there somewhere. And Amy was MIA.

Dammit. Dammit. Dammit.

"I'll report back the minute I hear from her," Isaac said.

"Thank you." He ended the call and fired off a text to his siblings. A rush of adrenaline blasted Jordan, and all his senses heightened.

One glance at Courtney, and he saw that she was already on the phone.

"It doesn't hurt to ask around," she said.

Within a few minutes, it was clear that Amy hadn't been seen or heard from in at least the past twenty-four hours. A mix of anger and fear rushed Jordan. "We should check her house just to be certain she's not asleep."

"I'm ready when you are." Courtney wasted no time putting on her boots from work and then her coat.

Jordan was ready, and the two of them were out the door in a matter of minutes. Zach called before they left Kent property.

"I'm at Amy's place and she's not here. Her cat's food bowl is empty, and so is the water," Zach said.

She always left food for her cat. She said Mr. Nibbles liked to snack all day. But the water was the most concerning.

Amy would never allow that bowl to go dry.

So where was she?

Chapter Seventeen

The news about Amy spread like wildfire through the community within the hour. Jordan was certain his cousin had touched just about every life in Jacobstown with her generosity and kind spirit. She could also be feisty and wild, so there was a slight hope that she was off doing something fun and had lost track of time.

She knew Isaac was working extra shifts over the next few days. It would also be like Amy, on a whim, to drive to Fort Worth or a nearby town in order to deliver those cookies meant for the VFW. She wouldn't have wanted them to go to waste and might figure everyone in town was too preoccupied with criminal activity to be able to enjoy them.

"Her cell could've run out of battery," Courtney offered as they navigated the streets of town, searching for signs of Amy.

"That sounds like her," Jordan said, but there was no energy in those words.

"We'll find her," she promised, but that was one they both knew she couldn't keep.

"If I spent more time here, I'd know more about her

habits," Jordan said. "I've been thinking about moving here full-time. I want to be closer to you and the baby."

"You said you could never see yourself living here again." Her words were true enough.

"Things have changed. I don't want to be a part-time dad who sees his kid summers and holidays," he said.

"Oh." Why did she sound so deflated?

"I thought you'd be happy about this news," he admitted.

"If you come here because of a child and not for yourself, do you think you'll resent not being able to live the life you want?" It was a fair question and one that deserved an answer.

Before he could tell her that *was* the life he wanted, his cell phone interrupted them. He pulled to the side of the road and parked.

"Hey, Zach. What's going on?" he asked his cousin.

"We just picked up Reggie Barstock. I thought you should know he's in custody," Zach informed.

"What kind of vehicle was he driving?" Courtney immediately asked.

"A white sedan," Zach supplied.

Damn. It wasn't a pickup.

"And he's not talking. He lawyered up almost immediately, but we do have his vehicle and probable cause to take it apart since he tried to outrun us. We also got a tip on the pickup. Posting the picture online brought out a few folks from Bexford. They all said the same thing. A guy by the name of Jason Millipede owns a truck that matches the picture. When they were asked to describe it, they described the same pickup you saw at the murder scene last night."

"That name sounds familiar," Courtney said. "Why do I know it?"

"Good question." Zach shrugged. "Any thoughts?"

She shook her head. "It's not coming to me. I need to think some more."

"Did you get any additional information on the guy?" Jordan asked Zach. "Did you ask about any injuries?"

"Yeah. It turns out the guy injured his ankle as a kid. His neighbors haven't seen him in a few days, but that's no surprise. They said he keeps odd hours. They all said he's quiet. I got the name of his aunt and have been trying to get in contact with her. Other than that, he has no other family around. He's been living with his aunt since he was little," Zach said.

"Did anyone have any ideas on where he might be?" Courtney shot a glance at Jordan, who was taking all this information in and trying his level best to fit the puzzle pieces together.

"No. He hasn't turned up in a few days," Zach answered.

"What about his address?" Courtney snapped into full deputy mode.

Zach hesitated. "I think the best thing the two of you can do is keep searching for Amy. This is a courtesy call to let you know your tip about The Mart is panning out and could lead to something big. I want you as far away from this guy as possible."

"Zach—"

"I'm serious, Courtney." There was a finality to

Zach's tone that she seemed to know better than to argue with.

"Thanks for the information, Zach. I'm grateful to be in the loop," she finally said on a sharp sigh.

"Lopez is on his way to investigate in Bexford. He has the case." Zach softened his tone when he said, "Right now, let's go out there, find Amy and bring her home."

"I KNOW HE said we shouldn't investigate in Bexford, but I need to talk to this guy's neighbors myself and possibly the aunt if we can locate her. Please, Jordan. It might mean the difference between finding Amy in time." Courtney could only pray her plea would work.

"Putting you in jeopardy isn't going to help anyone. We know this guy likes the ranch. Maybe we should head there instead." Jordan had a point.

"I don't know. I feel like Zach is holding back, and he should. I'm not technically part of this investigation anymore." A thought kept trying to break through. "This guy's name seems familiar, but I can't for the life of me figure out why."

"Google him and see what you come up with." Jordan motioned toward the cell in her hand.

Courtney performed the search. "There's no information here."

"If he's from the area, it makes sense that he'd be familiar with the ranch." Jordan thumped the steering wheel as he navigated onto the road and performed a U-turn toward his home.

Jordan's cell buzzed. "Will you check that for me while I drive?"

Courtney picked up his phone. "It's a text from Zach. He said Robert at the corner store said he saw Amy yesterday afternoon at lunch."

"I'm guessing Zach is also telling us to go home and wait for word," Jordan said.

"No. He didn't."

This time, Jordan's cell rang.

Courtney checked the screen. "It's your sister."

"I'll answer it on speaker." He pushed a button on his steering wheel, and two notes sounded.

"Jordan?" Amber's voice came through clearly.

"I'm driving and Courtney is with me—"

"Is it true? Is Amy missing?" Amber's voice was loaded with panic.

"I'm afraid so," Jordan stated.

"I just talked to Isaac. He said the two of them were supposed to meet up at his place later tonight. I told him to give us a call if he sees her, but…"

"Right now, it's important to stay positive," Jordan said. "Amy needs us to think with a clear head."

"You're right." Amber sniffed, and it was easy to tell that she'd been crying.

"Do you remember her mentioning a guy by the name of Jason Millipede?" Courtney interjected. "His name sounds familiar, but I can't place him."

"I can," Amber said plainly. "We met him the summer after seventh grade at Camp Pine Needles."

"Oh, right. I remember you and Amy talking about that." Courtney's father had refused to let her go, even though she promised to work in order to earn the money. He'd thought camp was frivolous spending, but this place accepted every kid, even the ones who worked in order to supplement the fees.

Amber gasped. "It was so long ago. I never really thought about it before. He shattered his ankle when a barrel rolled down the hill on him. It was awful. Gruesome. He was in so much pain. I guess he'd been out in the wooded area where he wasn't supposed to go when it happened. Some older boys tied him to a tree and rolled a heavy metal barrel down the hill aimed at him. They took off and just left him there. Amy found him first and ran to get help. I ran into her when she was on her way, so I went with her. The camp counselors never figured out who rolled that barrel at him. He never would say but he sure looked at Amy like she was some kind of savior. He'd managed to scoot around the side of the tree before the metal barrel hit more of him." She grunted as though in disgust. "I can't believe anyone would do that to another human being. I know the kid was considered weird, and I'm ashamed to admit it but I thought so, too, but he didn't deserve to be treated that way."

Courtney didn't need to ask the next question, but she did anyway. "It was his left ankle, wasn't it?"

"I guess. I mean, I never really paid attention to which one until we started talking about it just now," Amber stated. "He never even crossed my mind until I heard his name again. We were kids back then. It's been more than thirteen years. I do remember him seeming kind of fixated on Amy, though"

"Call Zach and tell him everything you just told me," Courtney instructed. "And then meet us at the main house."

Jordan barely waited for the call to end before he asked, "If Amy helped this guy, wouldn't that be a good thing?"

"It could be. It's possible that he developed a fixation like Amber said. Maybe she was the only girl who'd ever been nice to him. I'd like to get more information about his aunt. There's just too much we don't know to make a determination," she said. "Anything we say right now is just guessing without concrete information to go on. It can lead us down the wrong path. It's best to keep an open mind right now and follow the evidence."

Jordan kept his gaze on the stretch of road in front of them. His phone was going off like a pinball machine. "Do you mind taking a look and letting me know if anything important comes through?"

She picked up his cell and saw the number of texts going into the double digits. She skimmed them, but they were mostly from his family, asking if there was any new information on Amy.

"Looks like Amber put out word for everyone to come to the main house," she said. She scanned a few more before the one from Zach came. "This one looks important. It's from your cousin. Amy's car was found abandoned at the mouth of Hermosa Creek."

"That's three miles from her house." He braked hard enough for Courtney to feel it. She put her hand up against the dashboard to steady herself.

"Sorry about that," he said, and she could hear the frustration for the situation in his tone.

"Zach's already there. He won't want us to show up," she said. The cell buzzed again. "In fact, he just warned against it."

"It's the last place we know she was. Maybe she's around that area," he said.

"He wouldn't keep her near her car. That's too obvious." She pounded the dash with the flat of her palm. "Zach wouldn't tell us if there'd been any pickup sightings."

"Maybe the guy's aware of the pictures of his pickup being distributed," Jordan said. "Or one of his neighbors tipped him off about law enforcement looking for him."

"I hope not. That wouldn't be good for Amy," she replied.

"Because?"

"If he truly is fixated on her, then she's his grand prize. The others might've been lead ups or he could've killed to try to impress Amy. This kind of monster isn't playing with a full deck. He could have had some interaction with her that made him feel rejected—"

"Amy has one of the best hearts of anyone I know. She helps everyone. Her path may have crossed with his while she was doing something for others. She helps serve meals to homeless people. She's the first to take food to the elderly or anyone who is sick and can't do for themselves. If this bastard harms a hair on her head…" Jordan tightened his grip on the steering wheel.

"We'll find her, Jordan." It was a promise she prayed she'd be able to keep.

Chapter Eighteen

"Let's break into search parties. There's a good chance he'll take her somewhere on the property," Courtney said to the Kent family who'd assembled in the main house. "Women with young children might want to stay in the main house together with locked doors. Jordan and I will be Team One."

Courtney divided the rest of the Kents into two-person teams.

She turned to Leah and Amber, who were standing at the granite island. "Set the alarm while we're gone. Okay?"

"I'm going," Leah stated. As a former Fort Worth detective, no one could argue she had the skillset to track a criminal.

"You can team up with Rylan," Jordan said. "He might be hiding her close to the house. Do you want to start there?"

Leah nodded as Amber texted Rylan to meet Leah.

"Do you mind keeping things stabilized here?" Jordan asked his sister.

"Not if you think this is where I'll do the most

good." Amber could keep the situation stabilized at the main house.

Courtney looked at Amber. "Every set? You're okay with this?"

"I'll hold down the fort here and keep watch around the house," she said.

"Thank you." Walking outside, Courtney was blasted with a hit of cold air. The temperature had dropped a good fifteen degrees in the last hour, and it was becoming bitterly cold.

Zach was already out with Isaac, who'd been searching the property ever since he found out his girlfriend was missing.

When she and Jordan had been walking a solid half hour, they ran into Zach.

"What the hell are you doing out here?" Zach's question was laser-focused on Courtney. "I told you to stay out of the search."

"I'm not alone," she defended. "We need all hands on deck, Zach. I want to help find your sister." Her voice was pleading now. "I care about what happens to her."

Zach blew out a sharp breath and conceded with a warning look.

"What did you find out about Barstock?" Jordan asked his cousin as Isaac and Courtney paired up on the perimeter of the area. She stayed close enough to listen.

"We know he's not involved in Amy's disappearance, but we did find incriminating evidence in his vehicle. We threatened him with murder charges, and it didn't take long for him to start naming names and asking for immunity. He's been slipping in and out of town because he's involved with a human-trafficking ring," Zach informed. "We have enough to lock him away for a very long time. He won't get out until he's too old to hurt anyone else."

At least one scumbag was going to jail. Hughey couldn't be responsible for Amy's disappearance because he'd been with Rhonda last night. Well, it didn't completely rule him out if Amy had gone missing more than twenty-four hours ago, but it made him less likely to be a suspect.

It really was down to Jason.

Unfortunately, nothing they knew about him could tip them off to where he might've taken Amy.

Her thoughts shifted to Jordan. In every instance, he'd been there for her. He never made excuses or disappeared when life got tough. Instead, he was figuring out how to move back to Jacobstown in order to be the best father to their child.

Even when she'd tried to push him away early on, he'd stood his ground and been there when she needed him. He was her true north, and she'd been too scared to let herself acknowledge it before now.

She'd been a fool. He'd been trying to tell her that he cared about her, and she'd done nothing but run the opposite way. Granted, she had some work to do when it came to trusting others. But Jordan Kent was the most trustworthy, true-to-his-word person she'd ever met.

As soon as Amy was home safe, Courtney planned to have a conversation with Jordan about her growing feelings for him.

A shiver raced down her spine being out here and

searching for someone she'd been so close to. There was no way in hell she planned to let Amy down.

A gunshot caused everyone to scatter in order to find cover behind trees. Courtney drew her weapon, and she heard Zach and Isaac do the same.

"Everyone okay?" came Zach's hushed voice.

"I'm good," Isaac responded first.

"Same," came from Jordan.

Before Courtney could speak, she took a blow to the back of the head.

JORDAN LISTENED FOR the sound of Courtney's voice. There was no way this jerk got to her while they were all together. Right? The shotgun blast had sounded from farther away. Jordan's pulse jacked up as he moved stealthily along the tree line toward Zach.

"We'll cover more ground if we split up," he said to his cousin, his gaze searching for Courtney.

"There might be more than one person involved," Zach warned, and he seemed to catch on to the panic growing inside Jordan.

"I'll keep my eyes peeled." His pulse jackhammered his ribs when he couldn't locate Courtney. "Where is she?"

Isaac was beside them in the next beat. He was easy to hear coming. Jordan had no plans to give the Hacker warning or let him know what hit him. Jordan figured the four of them had been making too much noise and that had tipped the guy off.

Both Zach and Isaac surveyed the area.

"Courtney," Jordan called her name even though a lead ball sank to the pit of his stomach.

A moment of panic struck that the shotgun blast was the result of Amy being shot. But he talked himself out of that unproductive thinking. If this guy stayed true to form, she was tucked somewhere passed out on ketamine. The idea wasn't exactly comforting, but it was better than the alternative…

Zach cursed and Isaac tried to put his fist through a tree trunk.

"I have to find her. We'll cover more ground if we split up," Jordan said.

A reluctant nod came from Zach. "Stay in constant contact."

"Will do." As Jordan broke off from the now-trio, he realized the only thing that mattered was bringing Courtney and Amy home. Amy was family, and he would do anything for her. And so was Courtney. She was going to be his family now, too. Somewhere in his heart, he'd realized it a long time ago. Letting his brain catch up was another issue. But it had. And he loved her.

What more could he offer than that? What else mattered?

Jordan knew this part of the property like the back of his hand, and he knew exactly where Rushing Creek wound through the trees. The creek was at its widest half a mile up, so he headed there figuring that would give Jason enough space to work with now that he had two victims. Had that been his plan all along?

Courtney wouldn't have gone down without a fight or making a sound, which meant she'd been surprised.

Frustration was a punch in the solar plexus. Taking in air hurt.

He couldn't allow himself to doubt that she was alive. This jerk was rubbing their noses in his ability to come and go as he pleased, taking whatever he wanted. Well, this was Kent property, and Jason Millipede didn't belong there.

It was time for Jordan to take his rightful place alongside his brothers and sister. It was time to put the past behind him and move on with his life. It was time to look to his future—a future with Courtney, if she'd have him.

For several minutes, Jordan moved through the trees toward the small clearing. He could hear his heartbeat in his ears, thrumming at a frantic clip.

PAIN SHOT THROUGH Courtney's head as she tried to open her eyes. It felt like her head might explode. What the hell had happened?

And then it all came rushing back to her. Jason Millipede had whacked her in the back of the head with a blunt object. She was on Kent property in the woods. She tried to scream but couldn't. There was something covering her mouth. Courtney forced her eyes open and was startled to find a pair of blue eyes staring back at her.

It took a second to register those frightened eyes belonged to Amy.

Relief that she was alive washed over Courtney. Her next thought was about Jordan. If something happened to Amy, he would be devastated. Courtney strained to get a better look and could see that Amy's mouth was covered with clear tape.

She tried to move, but her hands were tied behind her back. Pain registered with movement. Courtney assessed that she was lying on her side in some type of shallow grave. Creepy-crawlies ran up her back at the thought of being buried alive.

But that wasn't the death Jason Millipede wanted for them.

On closer appraisal, Amy seemed...*off.* Courtney remembered the ketamine that had been used on the other victims. Maybe he hadn't planned for Amy to be alive this long.

There was something on top of them, and from what Courtney could gather it was a branch. Someone would have to fall into the grave with them in order to realize it was there.

Was this what he did? Stored his victims in a freshly dug grave. Drugged them so they were compliant. And then once he was ready and had them in position...

Another icy chill gripped her spine.

The ground was hard and cold. Courtney thought about the little nugget growing inside her. She became more resolved to stay alive.

Trying to talk was pretty much impossible. She tried to move her legs and feet. They were bound together at her ankles.

Movement made her brain hurt.

She heard footsteps and froze. She listened. Jordan would be looking for her, as would Zach and Isaac. The four of them had been on the hunt for Amy, and the others wouldn't give up. If anything, the search would intensify.

Courtney knew for certain if Jason took them to another spot, it would be even more difficult to escape. So, when the branch moved and she saw his face, she waited until he got close enough, and then she unleashed hell.

Amy seemed to catch on and she rolled onto her back and thrust her feet toward Jason, connecting with his chest.

He made an animal-like growl before he seemed to realize he'd made a mistake. Courtney figured it was now or never, so she kicked with everything she had and knocked him back a couple of steps. Blood squirted from his nose. She rolled onto her side and scrambled to get to her feet while Amy did the same.

Jason disappeared from view, and she realized he'd come back with something to knock out her and Amy or kill them this time.

She scooted toward Amy and motioned for her to go back to back. Tape wasn't hard to tear once a small tear was made. Courtney struggled with it for a few precious seconds before she was able to dig her nail hard enough to rip the tape on Amy's wrists. Amy immediately ripped off their mouth tape and started to work on Courtney.

"No, go. Get out of there. Undo your ankles and go get help. Jordan, Zach and Isaac are out here somewhere. Find them and bring them back." Courtney used her stern law enforcement voice. It was authoritative, and people instinctively knew she meant business.

Amy hesitated.

"Go. The second you're safely away from here, I'll start screaming to draw attention," she urged.

"I can't leave you like this. We can fight him together. We're stronger together." Amy went to work on Courtney's wrists. "I'm not as fast as you are, but I'll get it."

True to her word, she worked the tape until Courtney's hands were free. She immediately removed the tape from her ankles with Amy's help.

The two locked arms and set out to run on wobbly legs.

"Not so fast." Jason's voice was shrill. They heard the snick of a bullet being engaged in a chamber.

"On three, we need to shout as loud as we can and dive for the tree," Courtney whispered. She'd only been in there a short time, and still her legs and arms hurt. She could only imagine how painful it must be for Amy right then.

"Let's do this," came the hushed response.

"One. Two. Three." Courtney held on to Amy as they ran behind a tree, screaming as loud as their voices would carry.

"I said stop," Jason's agitated voice demanded.

When they didn't, he fired a shot.

Courtney pulled Amy to the ground. The pair huddled together as they continued to shout for help.

"How could you do this to me, Amy?" Jason shouted. "I thought you were special. You're just a tramp like the others. My aunt warned me about girls like you, and she was right. You pretend to be nice, but really all you want to do is hurt me like the others did. I did everything to show you how strong I am now. Everything I accomplished was to impress you. Instead, you look at me like I'm the one who's evil. You fight me and try to run. This is how you repay me?"

"Breanna deserved to live," Amy said quietly. "Hurting someone else to prove you're somebody doesn't make you look stronger. It makes you pathetic."

There was something almost pitiful about Jason.

But he was a coldblooded killer, and her sympathy stopped right there.

Jordan heard the screams. He also heard the shot. And then there was nothing but quiet.

Pain shot through his calves and his thighs as he pushed his legs harder. All he could think about was seeing Courtney and Amy alive again. He let that thought motivate him to run when his lungs might explode from needing air.

He was too close to lose her. So he pushed harder. And then he slowed his pace to a catlike crawl. He stalked closer toward where the noise had been.

Another shot fired, and someone screamed.

It was near pitch-black outside, but his eyes had adjusted to the dark long ago. His hands were frozen, so he rubbed them together as he neared the direction of the gunfire. He could only hope it was Courtney's gun and she was in control of it.

When he happened upon the scene, he realized Jason had the gun.

Neither Courtney nor Amy was anywhere to be seen.

He neared the lone gunman with stealthy precision. And then Jordan saw Jason put the gun to his own head.

"Oh no you don't, bastard," Jordan said as he tackled Jason from behind in time to knock his hand away from his head in time. Blood squirted, but Jordan knocked Jason onto his stomach on the hard ground. He went to work stemming the flow of blood. "You don't get to take the easy way out and die. You're going to spend the rest of your long life behind bars, where you belong."

Zach and Isaac showed up at almost exactly the same time.

"We need an EMT and zip cuffs," Jordan said to Zach.

"I have a pair right here. EMT is on the way." Zach dug his knee into the perp's back as Amy and Courtney rushed over.

"Is everyone okay?" Jordan was on his feet in half a second and by Courtney's side.

Isaac and Amy embraced a second later.

"We made it," Courtney said. "We survived."

Jordan pulled her into an embrace, where she stayed. It didn't take long for the scene to bustle with activity.

Amy gave her statement—she'd stopped to help a stranded motorist and had been attacked from behind before something was shoved into her mouth.

Jordan couldn't leave Courtney's side if he'd wanted to. He'd almost lost her once, and when all this settled down, he had something to say to her.

It took a solid hour for her to be cleared from the scene. A deputy had brought over a warm blanket. Another was given to Amy as the Jacobstown Hacker was being hauled off in handcuffs.

Jordan turned to Courtney and was pretty sure he saw nothing but love in her eyes when she looked at him. "There's no rush for our relationship to magically work out. But I know what's in your heart, and I happen to love you with all of mine. I want you to know that I'm willing to wait as long as you need to be able to say the words back. I love you, Courtney."

"I don't want to wait to tell you how I feel, Jordan. Life is uncertain and can be taken away in a second. I know that I have work to do and I'm far from perfect, but I love you in a perfect way. I want to have a family with you." She touched her stomach. "And this child will be the luckiest kid on earth to be surrounded by so much love."

He kissed her. "I have a real shock for you. I want you to be my wife."

"Then all that's left for me to say is yes. I'll marry you, Jordan. I'm ready to spend the rest of my life with you. You are the only person I've ever truly trusted with my heart. The only person I can ever see myself loving. It's always been you—even before the tragedy that left me broken. With you, I feel like I've found home, a *real* home, and not just a place to lay my head at night, because up until you that's all I've ever done."

"Good. Because I'm done running away. I want to run to you and to our family. Because I can't imagine loving anyone more than I love you. I don't care where you want to settle down, because you're my home." Jordan wrapped his arms around the woman who would be his bride and pressed his lips to hers. "I almost lost you tonight. I never want to have that feeling again."

And he kissed her. His love. His Courtney. His home.

Epilogue

"Good morning, Mrs. Farmer," Courtney said to her former neighbor.

"You're glowing," Mrs. Farmer said as she put both hands on Courtney's very round, very pregnant belly after greeting her at the door while Sassy jumped and barked around Courtney's ankles. The gold band on Courtney's left hand sparkled against the sunlight.

"She'll be here in a week or two. Maybe sooner from the way I feel." Courtney handed over a basket filled with fresh fruit and a few muffins. It had become their favorite Monday morning meal.

"Where's Amy today?" Mrs. Farmer asked, ushering Courtney through the door and to the kitchen table after Courtney picked up Sassy and gave her snuggles.

"She and Isaac decided to take a trip out of the blue. Just the two of them," Courtney said with a smile. "I wouldn't be surprised if she came back married."

Mrs. Farmer burst out laughing. "Sounds like something Amy would do. Those two deserve all the happiness in the world." She shook her index finger in the air. "And so do you. You deserve that gorgeous man you married."

Courtney's cheeks flushed at the compliment.

"Amy said to tell you she'll see you next week and that I should give you a big hug for her." Courtney embraced the woman who'd become family. "Jordan sends his love."

"I'm surprised he let you out of his sight," Mrs. Farmer teased.

"He is definitely a husband on baby watch. But I think he also knows that I wouldn't miss our breakfasts for the world." A cramp struck, and her belly felt like it contracted, reminding her that she wouldn't be waiting too much longer to meet her daughter.

Her daughter. Courtney's chest filled with so much love it felt like she might burst every time she thought about her little girl. She credited her sessions with Sara Winters for helping her break down her walls and enjoy all the love that surrounded her now. She still had work to do and it would take time, but she looked to the future with hope for the first time. Hope was a beautiful thing. Happiness was even better.

"I squeezed fresh juice this morning." Mrs. Farmer beamed.

"Well, we better eat before this baby decides to come and interrupt our meal," Courtney teased.

Mrs. Farmer caught her gaze. "Did you make a decision about going back to work after the baby's born?"

Courtney glanced down and touched her stomach. "I have a feeling that I have my work cut out for me right here. I don't want to miss a minute of her day."

"You'll never regret being home with your child," Mrs. Farmer agreed. "Jenny and Hanson are bringing my Ellie bell later this fall."

Her son-in-law's job had moved the family to Europe three years ago. They'd offered to move back when Mr. Farmer passed away, but Mrs. Farmer wouldn't have it. She'd said she wanted them to live their lives. She wasn't ready to leave Jacobstown to join them because she felt closer to her husband here.

The warmth in Mrs. Farmer's voice when she spoke about her family caused a few tears to fall from Courtney's eyes.

There were no better words than love, family and home. Having all three made Courtney feel like the luckiest person in the world.

* * * * *

COMING SOON!

We really hope you enjoyed reading this book. If you're looking for more romance, be sure to head to the shops when new books are available on

Thursday 11th June

LET'S TALK

Romance

For exclusive extracts, competitions
and special offers, find us online:

f facebook.com/millsandboon

🐦 @MillsandBoon

📷 @MillsandBoonUK

Get in touch on 01413 063232

For all the latest titles coming soon, visit
millsandboon.co.uk/nextmonth

MILLS & BOON
DARE

Sexy. Passionate. Bold.

Sensual love stories featuring smart, sassy heroines you'd want as a best friend, and compelling intense heroes who are worthy of them.

MILLS & BOON

MODERN

Power and Passion

Prepare to be swept off your feet by
sophisticated, sexy and seductive heroes, in
some of the world's most glamourous and
romantic locations, where power and
passion collide.

MILLS & BOON
MEDICAL
Pulse-Racing Passion

Set your pulse racing with dedicated, delectable doctors in the high-pressure world of medicine, where emotions run high and passion, comfort and love are the best medicine.

MILLS & BOON

THE HEART OF ROMANCE

A ROMANCE FOR EVERY KIND OF READER

MODERN

Prepare to be swept off your feet by sophisticated, sexy and seductive heroes, in some of the world's most glamourous and romantic locations, where power and passion collide.
8 stories per month.

HISTORICAL

Escape with historical heroes from time gone by. Whether your passion is for wicked Regency Rakes, muscled Vikings or rugged Highlanders, awaken the romance of the past.
6 stories per month.

MEDICAL

Set your pulse racing with dedicated, delectable doctors in the high-pressure world of medicine, where emotions run high and passion, comfort and love are the best medicine.
6 stories per month.

True Love

Celebrate true love with tender stories of heartfelt romance, from the rush of falling in love to the joy a new baby can bring, and a focus on the emotional heart of a relationship.
8 stories per month.

Desire

Indulge in secrets and scandal, intense drama and plenty of sizzling hot action with powerful and passionate heroes who have it all: wealth, status, good looks…everything but the right woman.
6 stories per month.

HEROES

Experience all the excitement of a gripping thriller, with an intense romance at its heart. Resourceful, true-to-life women and strong, fearless men face danger and desire - a killer combination!
8 stories per month.

DARE

Sensual love stories featuring smart, sassy heroines you'd want as a best friend, and compelling intense heroes who are worthy of them.
4 stories per month.

To see which titles are coming soon, please visit

millsandboon.co.uk/nextmonth